A RIVAL MOST VIAL

POTIONEERING FOR LOVE AND PROFIT

SIDE QUEST ROW SERIES
BOOK 1

R.K. ASHWICK

LASKELL

THE SINKING REACH

VINE HEART

TITAN'S NAILS

HART'S FENN

SHABRON RIVER

ELWIG FOREST

THE SCAR

DEEPRIVER

KOLKEAN DESERT

THE DRIFTWOOD

DEEPRIVER DELTA

N
W E
S

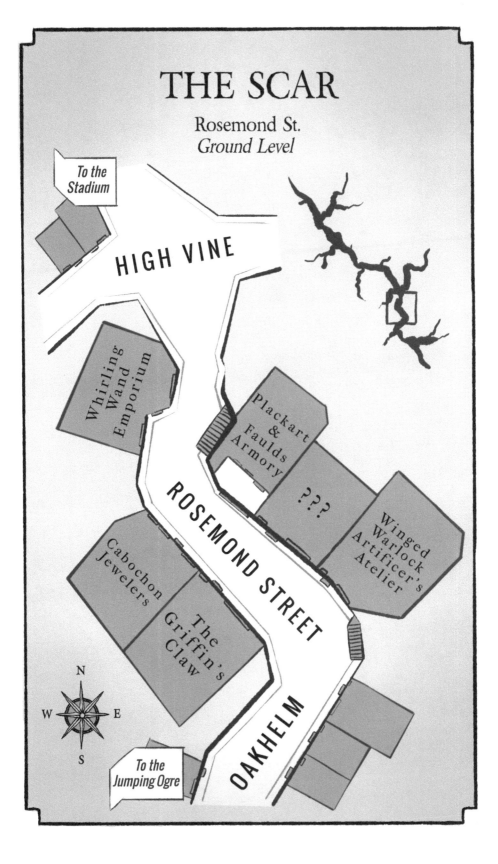

CONTENTS

STEP 1:

PREHEAT THE CAULDRON

Ambrose

BEFORE THE DOOR OPENED, everything in Ambrose Beake's life was perfect.

His potion shop stood empty and quiet, a reflection of the sleepy street outside. His footsteps echoed alone, delightfully alone, on the polished wood floor as he dusted the bottles. Glowing healing vials, smoky invisibility potions, fizzing strength serums... He swept carefully between each one, ensuring that not a speck of dust marred the glass or obscured the alphabetized labels. If adventurers sought out his shop for the best potions in the Scar—and they did—his wares had to look the part.

Once the shelves sparkled, Ambrose wandered to the door and tidied the sleeve of his navy robes. He supposed he could open early today. Flip the sign on the door, cater to the adventurers not sleeping off a hangover or a tavern brawl...

He reached for the sign. Perhaps he could close early, too, and settle into a nice evening of quiet brewing and—

"Morning, Ames!" A lanky elven figure burst through the door, knocking Ambrose backward. "You have your bet ready?"

Ambrose caught himself on the counter, inches away from a fragile display of vials. "Banneker! What are you doing here?"

Ambrose's tone had all the welcoming charm of a cactus, but Banneker shrugged it off as he loped over to the shop's bay window. His crimson hair and tilted grin gleamed in the morning light.

"Come on, we told you about the bet," he said. "For the shop across the street." As he tapped a pale finger on the windowpane, a smudge of grease from his artificer's work left behind a print. Ambrose's eye twitched.

"No, I'm afraid you didn't tell me." He stood straight, adjusted his robes, and gestured to the door. "Now, if you could come back later, I haven't quite opened yet—"

"Today's the day!" The door slammed open again, revealing an elderly human woman in a sooty leather apron. Ambrose reeled back and, this time, knocked the vials across the counter.

"Oh!" The woman clapped a gloved hand over her mouth. "Sorry, dear."

"Quite all right, Sherry," Ambrose muttered as he scrambled for the skittering glass. "But if you're here for this bet, I'd rather it not be held in my shop."

"I've got my bet!" Banneker crowed. Sherry beamed and joined the artificer.

"You finally decided?" She swept a gray curl off her forehead, suntanned after years of working in her open-air forge.

"Consulted my star chart and everything," Banneker said proudly. "It's a bakery."

Sherry snorted and tugged off her blacksmith gloves, letting trails of soot drift onto the immaculate window display. Ambrose sighed loudly, but she took no notice. "It's not a bakery," she said. "There's no room in the shop for an oven." She turned to Ambrose. "What do you think it is?"

Banneker scoffed. "Ames doesn't have a bet."

"Doesn't have a bet?" Sherry frowned, her wrinkles deepening. "But we wrote everyone about it. Hasn't he read the messages?"

The door opened one last time for two more intruders, a gray-skinned orc and a short, round elf. Ambrose braced himself against the front counter and sped through his words. "If you're here for a bet, I must insist you do it elsewhere—"

"Why?" the orcish jeweler grunted and held up a leather note-book. "Not confident in your bet, Beake?"

"He doesn't have a bet," Sherry and Banneker chorused from the window.

"Doesn't have a bet?" The orc gestured to a statue on the counter, the rings on their hand flashing. "Didn't you read the messages?"

Ambrose glanced over at the message statue, a swirl of wood and glass in the shape of a tall rose. It sat untouched at the far edge of the counter, and the tiny paper scroll at its base remained tightly furled. He pinched the bridge of his nose and waved to the door. "No, I didn't read them. If you could please just—"

"Bets close in five minutes!" the orc boomed and strode to the window. Sherry immediately tugged on their sleeve and reached for their notebook.

"Grim, what's your bet?"

The jeweler held their notebook out of reach—not a difficult task, since they towered over everyone else in the shop. "Not telling you."

As the other shopkeepers bickered, the elf who had accompanied Grim wandered not to the window, but to Ambrose. She offered up a small canvas bag, its bright purple ribbon complementing her pink tunic and flowing purple pants. "Got you some breakfast."

Finally, his one ally on Rosemond Street had arrived. Ambrose gave her a weary smile and pulled a green striped fernberry out of the bag. "Thank you, Dawn."

"Thought you might need a peace offering." Dawn hopped up and sat on the counter, then tilted her curly mohawk toward the others. "They haven't stopped talking about the new shop all week, and I made the mistake of saying The Griffin's Claw had the best view of it."

"Ah, so this is all your fault?" Ambrose gave her an exaggerated scowl. "In that case, you owe me far more than berries, Miss Kerighin. Tea and a cookie in Little Elwig, I think."

She set a warm brown hand against her forehead and leaned back dramatically. "You ask for too much," she sighed, as if they hadn't been getting tea together since they were young apprentices. "How about tomorrow?"

"Tomorrow." He nodded, and their attention settled on the traffic outside.

Rosemond Street was one of many avenues nestled at the bottom of the Scar, a deep chasm once inhabited by dragons and giant spiders. But over time, such monsters had proved to be no match for stubborn humanoids. Orcs and humans had filled the tunnels with homes, while elves and gnomes had converted the sinkholes into markets. Families soon flocked to the chasm, turning it into the four-level city that towered above Ambrose and Dawn today.

Ambrose's gaze settled on the empty shop across the street. Over the course of the past week, the former plant shop had turned into something of a mystery. A small fortress of crates now flanked its door, and a canvas cloth fluttered over the shop's sign. Its haphazard state only served to tantalize the other shopkeepers with its secrets.

"I'm telling you, man, it's a bakery." Banneker gave an exaggerated sniff. "I can almost smell the turnovers now..."

Grim twirled their pen, fangs glinting. "If you want to lose five talons this morning, that's your prerogative."

"Dawn?" Sherry twisted to face the counter. "What's your bet?"

Dawn toyed with the jewels lining her pointed ear. "I think it's another gardening shop."

Everyone else groaned.

"Please, I don't need to buy more plants," Sherry said. Next to her, Grim was already scribbling.

"Gardening shop, final bet?"

Ambrose huffed and wiped down the patch of counter next to Dawn. "Can't they just bet now and leave?" he grumbled to her.

"Come on, Ames." Dawn smiled. "This is exciting. You have a new neighbor!"

"I don't need a new neighbor." It was true—he had been enjoying the relative peace of the empty storefront. No noise, no messy deliveries of soil, no crowds at plant sales... "Besides, he who brews alone—"

"Brews fastest," Dawn finished his phrase with an eye roll. "I know."

Ambrose primly folded his cleaning cloth. Simply because Master Pearce had said it all the time didn't mean it was wrong.

But Dawn had gone to the trouble of bringing him breakfast, so he deftly changed the subject. "How are your commissions going?"

His choice in topic paid off—she turned back to him instantly, brown eyes sparkling. "Finished the lightning staff yesterday." She tapped the counter. "And I should be able to wrap up the blast wand tonight if the birthday committee doesn't go too late."

"Birthday committee?" he repeated. "You still have time for that?"

"Oh, I made time. Already got Mayor Rune obsessed with my fireworks plan." Dawn waggled her head proudly, black curls bouncing. "I can get you in on it, too, if you want. The recognition can't hurt, especially before your anniversary."

Ambrose wrinkled his nose. "No, thank you. I've got enough to prepare as it is. I have to order the new shelves, the paint, the sign..."

"The sign?" Dawn leaned forward. "Come on, show me the specs. What's it gonna say?"

Ambrose bit back a smile and pulled a notebook out from under the counter. Dawn flipped through it, her gold bangles casting bright caustics on the pages.

"Aha." Her hand stilled when she reached an orderly list. "Workshop upgrades, here we go..."

Ambrose nodded, barely masking a surge of pride. The Griffin's Claw was about to turn two hundred, and what sort of owner would he be if he didn't give it what it deserved?

"Okay, let's see." Dawn squinted at his neat, tiny handwriting. "A new silver cauldron, enchanted ingredient shelves, a larger wand rack..." She tapped a word at the bottom of the page, underlined in dark ink. "Ahem. What is this?"

"What?" Ambrose frowned at the paper. His last upgrade—and the one he was looking forward to the most—was to finally add his name to the official placard of Griffin's Claw owners. "You don't think I should add it?"

"Of course, you should add it," Dawn said. "But just *A. Beake CPM*? Come on, can't you add more flair to it? More pizzazz?"

Ambrose let slip a small laugh. "I don't think pizzazz is necessary."

"Oh, please." Dawn swept a hand through the air. "I'm thinking something like—Ambrose Beake, Certified Potion Master Extraordinaire. First of His Name, Unmatched Genius—"

"No, thank you."

"*Gods*, you're so boring."

"Ambrose!" Sherry called from the window. "Last call for a bet!"

Ambrose gave a dismissive wave, but the others latched onto the idea like leeches.

"Bet, bet, bet!" Banneker clapped. Grim tossed a look over their half-moon glasses.

"You've got one minute, Beake."

"Come on." Dawn pushed on his shoulder. "I'll get you two cookies tomorrow if you make a bet."

"Oh, how generous," Ambrose whipped back, but relented and walked over to the bay window. Banneker leaned in eagerly.

"Say it with me, dude," he stage-whispered. "Bakery, bakery..."

Sherry slapped Banneker's shoulder with her glove. "Let the boy make his own call."

Ambrose ignored them both and folded his arms. Dawn was right, as she usually was—The Griffin's Claw *did* have the best view into the old shop. From what he recalled of the space, it was a mirror reflection of his own in layout. A simple square storefront carved into the chasm wall, with a workroom, a storage room, and a second-level flat for the owner. Though the chasm kept the ground-level store mostly in shadow, the passing sun struck the windows in the afternoon, providing a welcome warmth in the current autumn temperatures.

Overall, an ideal location for any new shop owner.

"Sherry's right." Ambrose tugged on his ear—slightly pointed, but nothing like Banneker's or Dawn's. "It can't be a bakery. The work-room is too small for an oven, and given the structural integrity needed for the levels above it, the owner can't knock down the walls to make room."

Banneker groaned. "Grim, can I change my bet?"

Grim slapped their notebook shut. "No."

"Disproving Banneker's bet doesn't count as a bet of your own," Dawn singsonged from the counter. Ambrose stuck out his tongue at her, then turned back to the window and set his shoulders. The shop sign was still covered, but there was plenty to glean from the crates clustered below it.

"Look at the enchantments on the boxes," he said. The window muffled his soft voice, and the other merchants leaned in to hear him better. "Some temperature-controlled, many anti-fragile. I'm also counting at least"—he recalculated—"fifteen crates, so the owner needs a decent amount of inventory to either craft, sell, or both. And given how Rosemond is known for magical artisans..." He gave a nod. "They're a magical craftsman of some kind. Perhaps a wandmaker."

"Hey!" Dawn called. "I can't have competition!"

Sherry snorted. "Like anyone could compete with you, dear."

"Wandmaker, final answer?" Grim scribbled a line in their note-book. Ambrose stepped away from the window.

"I'm not betting. Now, will you all please vacate my shop?"

"Look!" Sherry grabbed his arm and yanked him back to the window. "There he is!"

Indeed, there he was—the root cause of Ambrose's unpleasant morning. The new shop owner had ducked out the front door, waving movers inside with a wide grin. He appeared to be a human like Sherry, with round ears and a crop of short black hair. His light golden skin almost blended in with the warm striations of the chasm wall. Though he didn't wear the typical patterns and bright colors of those living in the Scar, someone at least had the good sense to warn him not to wear white, and he had opted for neutrals instead—loose beige tunic, brown pants and boots. Much easier against the eternally dusty floor of the chasm.

"He came into town last night," Sherry said. "Oh, he's handsome. I think he's about your and Dawn's age, too." She squeezed Ambrose's arm. "Wouldn't it be nice to make a new friend?"

Ambrose grimaced. "No."

Her enthusiasm barreled on. "I should invite you all over for tea this week. Give him a few days to settle in, then I'll make some cookies—"

"Bets closed!" Grim bellowed, making them all jump. "He's revealing the sign!"

Banneker crossed his fingers. "Come on, man, I am manifesting a bakery in my mind..."

Dawn hopped off the counter to join the group, hemming Ambrose in at the window. He had no choice but to stand there as the man reached up and tugged on the cloth, letting the canvas fall away. The sign's fresh white paint made the letters stand out brightly against the stone wall.

Eli's Elixirs

Ambrose's blood flashed cold, then very, very hot.

He had been right about the craftsman—extremely wrong about the competitor.

"What is this?" he snapped. "Elixirs? Is he *joking*?"

Dawn let out a single peal of laughter. Ambrose glowered at her, and she clapped a hand over her mouth. "Sorry, sorry, I know it's not funny—"

"Of course, it's not funny!" He jabbed a finger at the sign and looked wide-eyed at all of them. "What does he—who told him he could—aren't there zoning laws against this sort of thing?"

Grim tucked their notebook under their arm. "Guess it was too hopeful to ask for a cheesemonger."

"Could've been next door to some fruit tarts," Banneker grumbled and shoved his hands in his pockets.

"Hm." Sherry seemed to be the only one reflecting Ambrose's

concern. "I think you'll be all right. If you go over there and introduce yourself—"

Ambrose recoiled, his anger flaring. "Absolutely not."

Dawn threw him a look. "Ames, he literally lives across the street from you now."

"I do not care."

"You can't ignore him forever!"

"Watch me." Ambrose spun away from the window and straightened his robes. "Now, out of my store, all of you."

This time, they obeyed him, shuffling out onto the street with groans and dashed hopes. Dawn lingered, one foot still in the shop.

"Hey." She leaned through the doorway. "Can I run some project updates by you tomorrow?"

Ah—now *there* was something familiar and reassuring.

"Of course." Ambrose swung into place behind the front counter. "But you owe me three cookies now."

"As many as you want." Her hand paused on the doorframe. "And try not to worry about the other shop. You're the Unmatched Genius, First of Your Name, remember?" She smiled. "You'll run circles around that guy."

Ambrose's gaze dropped to the counter, his cheeks tinged pink. "Thank you, Dawn."

She dashed into the street, leaving him to stew silently in his potion shop.

His clean, professional, *superior* potion shop.

He let out a breath, flexed his fingers, and carefully placed his anniversary list back under the counter. Eli's Elixirs, or whatever it was, wouldn't last more than a month on Rosemond Street. The Griffin's Claw had stood strong for almost two hundred years, and Ambrose would eat his own Guild certificate if it failed to remain so under his watch.

STEP 2:

MEASURE THE CATALYST

Ambrose

If it hadn't been for Sherry, Ambrose could have avoided his new neighbor for months.

At least, that was his estimate. Brewing enough inventory for a proper shop opening would take the newcomer at least four to five weeks, and that was if the man worked at it all day. And who would have time for new neighbors, anyway? Between all the herb drying, crystal crushing, water cleansing... In fact, he was doing the man a *favor* by not visiting. Yes, that was it. He was being generous. Conscientious, even—

Sherry set down her hammer and sighed. "Conscientious?"

"Yes." Ambrose placed a crate of bottles at the edge of her forge. "Like I said, I'm doing him a favor. Now, if these resistance potions are all you need, I'll just..."

He turned on his heel but wasn't quick enough—Sherry wrapped a firm hand around his arm and dragged him back.

"Not so fast, young man," she said, her voice carrying easily over the day's lunch rush. Her open-air forge had no visitors at the moment, but before long, she would have a small throng crowding the edges, admiring her armor and shields. Not that they could afford any of the pieces, of course—Sherry catered only to the best of adventurers, those with dragon gold and questing jewels to spare.

And today, her hard prices matched her gaze as she spun Ambrose around to face her.

"You've finished your errand and you're closed for lunch," she continued. "You have time to say hi to Eli."

"I told you, I don't want to say *hi* to him—"

She pushed Ambrose into the street, where he had very little choice but to dodge traffic and make his way to Eli's Elixirs next door. Once he successfully navigated around donkey carts and messenger dragons, he looked behind him and groaned. Sherry had slipped back into her forge, leaving him to grit his teeth through the pleasantries alone.

Then the door swung open and his new neighbor stepped out.

"Hey! Sherry mentioned you'd stop by." All smiles and fast words, the human waved him inside. "Elias Valenz, but you can call me Eli. You're Ambrose, right? Come on in."

Eli ducked back in as quickly as he'd appeared, leaving Ambrose blinking at the doorway. This was meant to be a brusque hello, not a tour of the gormless place—but he couldn't turn away now. He glanced at the forge, grumbled, and stepped into the shop.

Eli's Elixirs was a scattered mess of crates and packing straw, dappled and warmed by the afternoon sun. The empty shelves gave Ambrose some comfort—the man was nowhere close to opening— but as he took a deep breath, the scent of the place surprised him. Though the old owner had left months ago, the shop still smelled of potting soil and sunlight. Together with the whiffs of dried herbs from the crates, the shop was reminiscent of the lavender fields surrounding the top edge of the Scar.

Ambrose shook his head—the smell was almost dizzying. One more reason to get back to his shop as soon as possible.

"I know you must be busy," he said. "I don't mean to intrude—"

"No, no, it's all good." Eli rubbed his hands together and looked around. "So, you came over to talk about the shop, right?"

Incorrect—he came over to avoid Sherry's ire. But if the man wanted a straightforward conversation...

"Yes." Ambrose neatened his cuffs. "I suppose there's no use ignoring it. You are opening a potion shop, correct?"

"That's right."

"And you understand I run a potion shop across the street?"

Eli spread out his hands. "Hey, it's nothing personal. When I bought this place, I had no idea your shop existed."

Ambrose bristled—*your shop*, as if he wasn't talking to the premier potioneer in northern Laskell—but he reluctantly reeled himself in. Eli's expression was open and honest, and there was a distinct Kolkean lilt to his voice. If he wasn't from around here, he couldn't be entirely blamed for the oversight.

Though he could be a *little* blamed.

"I imagine the listing failed to mention it. Very well." He looked around at the crates. "So, when will you be moving out?"

Eli laughed. The sound grated on Ambrose's ears like metal scraping a cauldron.

"Moving?" Eli repeated. "I can't move now. You have any idea how much the seller's permit alone cost?" He turned and dragged a crate off the counter. Though packing straw speckled his hair, his smile was untarnished. "Listen, I think we can make it work. You can't tell me you've never had any competition in this city."

Ambrose swallowed his frustration once more. There was a potioneer in the northern quarter, but they focused on household brews, nothing adventure-tier. The apothecary two levels up was a specialist, and the psychic's elixirs in the south were little more than fizzy juice. "Nothing significant," he said, surreptitiously peeking into a nearby crate. Only straw peeked back at him.

"Really?" Eli frowned. "How long have you been at your shop?"

Ambrose set his shoulders back. "Twenty years."

"Twenty?" Eli gave another laugh. As he swung over to a shelf, a pair of sun-shaped earrings twirled against his neck. "What, were you born in there?"

A different, deeper anger flared in Ambrose. He shoved it down with a practiced hand. "*Apprenticed.*" He tried not to hiss the word. "I began when I was eight. My master retired and left me the shop several years ago."

"Huh." Eli shifted the crate in his sturdy arms, then set it on the shelf. "Cool."

Ambrose pressed his lips into a line. Twenty years of experience didn't exactly merit anything as lukewarm as *huh* and *cool*. "Where did you apprentice?" he asked tightly.

"Didn't apprentice anywhere." Eli shrugged. "Accredited at Driftwood College, East Kolkea campus."

"Really."

He didn't mean for the word to come out like it did—truly, he didn't—but its edges were too sharp and too venomous to be ignored. Eli straightened, his smile gone, and Ambrose scrambled to save face. "So—so you plan to join the Potion Master's Guild through work hours, then?"

Another shrug from Eli, this one more forced. "Maybe."

"Oh. Sponsorship?"

"Not that worried about joining the Guild, actually."

As Eli rolled up his sleeves and reached into the crate, Ambrose twisted the Guild signet ring on his index finger. This man clearly wasn't worth his energy. No apprenticeship, a few college credits... With his level of experience, the man wasn't going to take four weeks to brew inventory; it was going to take him four months.

"I realize you've already spent money on this place," Ambrose started, "but before you start brewing, I highly recommend you begin looking elsewhere for a—"

Then Eli began to pull out potion bottles. Filled, ready-to-go potion bottles.

Ambrose's mouth fell open.

"How did you—?" He glanced into the workroom. The cauldron there was only half-unpacked. "How did you generate the inventory so quickly?"

Eli's smile returned, twisted into an infuriating smirk. "Brewed them back home before moving here. Had to spin up enough to start selling right away, you know?" Eli placed the potions on the shelf, and Ambrose's grip on his signet ring tightened. "Have to start earning my keep as soon as I can."

"Of course." This time, Ambrose didn't care how sharp his words got. This couldn't be happening. If all of these crates contained inventory, Eli could be selling against him within the week. "Well—have you taken the time to check them for leaks?"

"Checked 'em this morning."

"And your licensing is complete?"

"Oh, don't worry." Eli's eyes narrowed. "I'm all ready to start."

They stood there for a moment, all tight-lipped smiles and cold stares, until the rose statue on the front counter flashed white. Ambrose ignored it; Eli nearly dropped the vial in his hand.

"What the...?" Eli set down the bottle and strode over to the counter, where the statue's glass petals glowed a dim white. As the glow faded, he picked up the device by its wooden base. "Sherry did something to this before she left but didn't explain what it is. Do you know...?"

He looked back at Ambrose, who weighed the pros and cons of explaining the statue to him. After considering feigning ignorance, then deciding that Sherry's judgment wasn't worth it, he sighed and took the device from Eli's hands. Briefly, his fingers brushed a smattering of scars, and his eyes immediately dropped to the white claw marks trailing across Eli's taut forearms.

"She must have..." He tore his gaze away from the scars and set the statue back on the counter. "Sherry must have written her name down here." He tapped the miniature roll of paper floating under the rose. The paper obediently unfurled, revealing Sherry's name and a written message underneath. "It's primarily an alarm system. Tap the top of the flower if you need assistance, and those who have added their name to the scroll will be alerted." He stepped back from the counter. "Every shop on Rosemond Street has one as a safety precaution."

"I see." Eli tilted his head. "So, the white flash—does that mean Sherry's in trouble?"

"Not at all," Ambrose said. "Red is for an emergency. White is simply the message function. If you want to send a message, add your name to the person's statue, then write to them on the scroll."

"Oh." Eli unraveled the scroll, and his face brightened. "That's fun."

Ambrose grimaced. *Fun* would not be the word he nor Master Pearce would have chosen for the incessant messages. Pearce had erased all the names from The Griffin's Claw scroll long ago, and Ambrose had kept the names erased upon his inheritance.

"Well, I should be going..." He started for the door. Eli held up a quill.

"Weren't you going to add your—?" He nodded to the scroll.

"No, no," Ambrose said too quickly. When Eli frowned, he searched behind him for the door handle. "Quite an unnecessary system in all honesty. I recommend you opt out before the flashing drives you mad."

"No, I get it." Eli's tone went tight again, and he tossed the quill back onto the counter. "Nice meeting you, Ambrose."

Ambrose had never heard a less sincere phrase in his life.

"Nice to meet you, Elias," he said, returning the favor. "Have a good day."

The conversation haunted Ambrose's thoughts for the rest of the day, and he closed early with a sharp flip of the door sign. Make it work? Make it *work*? What did Eli think they were going to do, skip around in circles and share profits?

"Ridiculous," he muttered aloud, then swept into the cozy stone square that was his workroom. He'd seek comfort where he always found it—in brewing a potion.

He first surveyed his robes and their gold geometric embroidery. Traditional potion master robes were never just for show—almost every stitch contained some kind of magical enchantment. Flame resistance at the hems, acid and smoke protection woven through the thread. There was even a cooling spell sewn into the collar for when he had multiple cauldrons bubbling at once. That had cost extra talons at the tailor's, of course, but it had been worth it.

Once he was satisfied that his robes and protective amulet were in good condition—no snagged threads, no dirt on the metal—he stepped in front of the cleaning table. He ran his hands over it, and the gemstones embedded into its edge flashed once. A tingling sensation rushed over his fingers as the magic cleansed them of dirt and oil. He smiled to himself—once he upgraded the table as a part of his anniversary list, the cleaning gems would work twice as fast.

The rest of his ritual reminded him of how many other anniversary upgrades he had planned. When he tugged on his gloves, he noted the empty gem slots he wanted to fill. As he selected a fire wand, he envisioned his new wand rack, with twice as many spaces and a built-in recharge function. Once the cauldron was prepared, Ambrose turned to his final pre-brewing ritual—the lucky shrine by the door.

To an outsider, this shelf of knickknacks was hardly more than a pile of silly trinkets and superstition. Tiny plants, decorative bottles, and lucky corks littered the space, a rustic defense against failed potions and misfires.

But like every potioneer before him, Ambrose didn't dare tempt fate over something so small. He reached for his personal favorite on the shelf—a bronze cat, its tiny forehead brightened from years of wear.

"Safe potioneering, eh?" He rubbed the spot between its ears and, before turning back to his cauldron, looked up at the final workroom piece to upgrade.

The wooden placard above displayed the names of all past owners of The Griffin's Claw. Some had run the place for as long as thirty years, others as little as two or three. But the store remembered them all, their names shaped by the raised whorls and vines sinking in and out of the deep, lustrous wood.

Adding a new name to this enchanted sign took more than simple woodcarver's tools, and when Ambrose had inherited the shop, he didn't have the funds to get it done right. But it had been nearly ten years since then, and with the shop's anniversary coming up...

He let out a breath. Once he had the money saved up—and he would, soon—the sign would bear his name, too. Right under Master Pearce's.

But until then, he had plenty of draughts to make. He rolled up his sleeves, pet the cat one more time, and settled in for a night of brewing.

STEP 3:

ACTIVATE THE REAGENT

Eli

"So, how's the shop?"

The voice echoed about the empty store, striking all the shelves Eli hadn't yet filled with potions. But he couldn't bring himself to begrudge the open spaces. Seeing his handiwork slowly fill the shelves was immensely satisfying, and after just a few days, he had made excellent progress. Almost all of his crates were unpacked, his cauldrons set up, his ingredients stored. His second-level flat still left something to be desired—like chairs, for example—but Eli's Elixirs would be ready to open within the week.

And Eli was counting down the minutes—the blaring amount of red in his ledger was already painful to look at.

"It'll be open real soon," he said, projecting his enthusiasm so his mother would hear it. He was leaning on the front counter and speaking toward a large, flat river stone in his palm. As his mother responded from her home in Kolkea, a faint ripple of light traveled through the striations on the rock.

"That's great, honey," June Valenz said. Snatches of footsteps and other voices faded in and out as she moved. "Now, how did the..."

But one voice kept following her—his younger sister Lily's, high and clear.

"Tell Eli I say hi!"

"I will—"

"No, tell him now!"

Eli smiled and shook his head. "Hi, Lily."

"Lily, please," June muttered, then brightened again. "How did the place look when you arrived? It was all cleaned out for you, right?"

Then her voice whipped away, replaced by a deeper one. "Eli! How's the shop?"

A tired sigh through the stone. "Marcos, we already covered this."

"I want to hear it for myself, love."

Eli grinned. "Hey, Pa. Shop's good, opening soon. The old owner left behind a couple plants, but that's it."

"Ah, any good ones?"

"Some nice basil, actually."

June gave a hum. "And how's Tom feeling about the place?"

Eli froze.

"You...did unpack her, didn't you?"

"Um." He slipped the stone into his pocket and speed-walked across the store. "Not yet."

Lily's voice sliced back in. "Come on, Eli!"

"Sorry, I had other things to do!"

He pawed through the crates until he found what he was looking for—a straw-filled box containing a wand and a smattering of tarnished objects. Forks, old daggers, a round orcish beer mug, a small broom head...

He dumped the items onto the front counter and waved the wand twice. With a shuddering jolt, the objects dragged themselves into place around the beer mug. The daggers and wheels formed legs at the base, while the forks created arms at the top. The broom head dropped itself directly into the mug with a satisfying plunk, rattling the enchanted stones at the bottom.

Miss Tomato the Automaton shook her little broom head, rubbed at her bristles with a fork hand, and turned her eyeless face to Eli.

"Good morning, Tom," he said. "Have a nice sleep?"

She reached for him wordlessly, and he scooped her into a hug. Years ago, his older brother had won her in a bet with some orcish travelers, and to his brother's dismay, the little automaton had imprinted on Eli instantly.

"How is she?" Marcos asked. Eli set Tom on the counter, where she swung her little dagger legs and looked about the store. A bubble of joy instantly filled his chest. Had she imprinted on him, or was it the other way around?

"She's perfect, as always."

"I'm glad you have her," June said. "Though I'm sure you've already made friends on the street."

The bubble of joy deflated, and he paused a second too long.

"Eli?"

"Are they being rude?" Lily's voice grew louder. "If anyone's being rude, you know I'll come over there and—"

Eli held up his hands, though they couldn't see the gesture. "No, they're all great."

"Except?"

He glanced out the window. The Griffin's Claw Potions and Tinctures shop had closed for the day, its windows dark save for one on the second floor. Through the curtains, Eli could see the silhouette of Ambrose Beake, turned away from the street, his long nose stuck in a book. Even in repose, he looked stiff and joyless.

Eli's chest tightened. Week one, and he had already bungled his new venture. "It's the shop across the street," he admitted. "There's... another potioneer."

Lily cursed on his behalf; both parents admonished her. "Another one?"

"I didn't know about him," he blurted out. "The seller never said anything, and my map didn't list out the stores—"

"What are you going to do? Is there any other place you can move to?"

"Now you sound like him." Eli scoffed. "I can't move, I don't have the money. I threw it all at this place." Stupid, stupid, stupid—

"So, you've met the potioneer?" Lily asked. "What's he like? Paint a picture so I can imagine myself punching him."

"*Lily.*"

"Pa, come on," she pouted. "He's the competition. Give me the details, give me the drama, let me live vicariously through—"

"All right, all right." Eli laughed as he moved to the workroom. Lily had all the bloodlust of a feral griffin, and he treasured the moments he could make it work in his favor. "He walks in while I'm unpacking, right? Tall, skinny, about my age. Light blue hair and eyes. Half-elf, I think."

Rustling on the other end, as if Lily was nodding. "Okay, okay, I'm thinking, like...a waify iceberg. You could take him in a fight."

"No, Lily," his father tried.

"*Yes*, Lily." Eli grinned wider. "So, he comes in and immediately judges me. Parades around his apprenticeship, asks how I'm getting into the Guild, even asks me when I'm going to close." Lily gasped. "Right? Condescending, cold, a total snob." He tensed again just thinking about it—how the half-elf had looked down his nose at Eli, his icy gaze evaluating him with a mix of annoyance and disdain.

"You should punch him," Lily said.

"Violence is not the answer—"

"Well, I'm not there to do it for him, Ma!"

While his family argued, Eli set down the stone and rifled through his college potion notes. They were stacked on the dusty workbench, reams of recipes and essays he hadn't yet filed. But if Ambrose was truly Guild-certified, Eli would have to break out the more complex recipes he knew...

He flipped over a paper from one of his higher-level courses—a piece of required reading, one he barely understood—and his fingers stilled on the name of the author.

"Just because you chased off one thief does not mean you get to..." Marcos sighed. "We'll discuss this later. Eli, you still there?"

Eli kept staring at the name.

The text underneath his fingers was clear: *A. Beake, CPM.* He looked back up to the windows. He couldn't count how many times he had seen the name in his research back at Driftwood College. He had imagined the writer to be a crotchety old armchair alchemist, or a sallow-faced academic holed up in a library.

Not the tall, young half-elf running the potion shop across the street.

"Eli?" June ventured, dragging him back to reality. "Are you all right?"

Eli threw the papers back on the bench and forced a smile onto his face. He was screwed, he was absolutely screwed. "Fine. All good, Ma. I'll be fine."

"Good." Her tone softened. "We're very proud of you, you know. It may be tough, but you can make this shop work."

Unlike everything else, Eli wanted to say. Unlike the farm, the smith, the griffin-keeping, the botanist gig...

But this would be different. The shop would be different. He swallowed his words and nodded along with his mother. "Thank you."

"So, when can I visit—?" Lily started, but her question sank under the growing tumble of other voices. His siblings—the ones still at home, at least—were tromping in for dinner, tracking in desert dust and fresh stories.

"Is that Eli?"

"Excuse you, *I* was talking to him."

"Hey, pass me the stone thing next—"

"Has he gone to a Fireball game yet?"

As they all squabbled over the device, Eli leaned against the workroom table, the splintered wood biting into his hand as much as the petty commotion bit into his heart. He was no stranger to travel nor settling into new places. But the first week away from home was always the hardest.

"Go help me set the table!" Marcos verbally swatted the others away. "Sorry, Eli, we have to go. You know how these scavengers are..."

"Ruthless." Eli picked absently at the wood. "I miss them."

"I know." His father paused. "You take care of yourself and Tom, now. She's the wisest little beer mug I've ever met."

"Yeah?"

"Well, she did pick you, after all."

Eli swallowed against the tightness in his throat. "Say hi to the others for me?"

Crackling as someone grabbed the stone on the other side.

"Hey." Lily was breathing heavily, as if she had fought someone for access. "*Hey*. Reach out next week and tell us all about how you kicked that iceberg's ass."

"*Lily!*"

Eli laughed over his father's response, and the lump in his throat dissolved a little. "Will do."

"You *got* this."

His eyes fell on The Griffin's Claw, all cold, tidy shelves and expensive wares. No advertising, no signs, no warmth. He drummed his fingers on the bench and bit his lip in thought.

"Yeah," he said. "Yeah, I got this."

STEP 4:
ADD SALT

Ambrose

THE DAY after Ambrose stepped out of Eli's Elixirs, the eponymous fool turned the new shop into an eyesore.

It started out with one banner. Just one brightly colored banner, with the words *Grand Opening* painted in heavy block letters.

That was fine, Ambrose supposed. He anticipated a less-than-grand closing in a month, anyway.

But the banners kept multiplying, all clashing colors and gaudy capitals, with messages that made Ambrose want to scratch his nails into the front counter.

Half Off All Healing Potions!
Buy One Get One Free Underwater Breathing Vials!
Twenty Percent Off Fire Resistance Tonics!

As the bold sales and nauseating colors flapped happily in the breeze, Ambrose ground his teeth and compared the prices to his own ledgers. The potions across the street were surely of lower quality than his, but they were also cheaper.

Far cheaper.

He slapped the ledger closed and shoved it under the shelf. Everything was still fine. The reputation of The Griffin's Claw couldn't be undermined by a few discounts. If adventurers wanted fire resistance potions that didn't fade on them halfway through a dragon's rampage, they'd know where to go.

Then the day of the grand opening arrived.

The door to Eli's Elixirs was wide open. Chimes above the doorframe swayed in the breeze, gentle and bright. A table of pastries sat inside the entrance, so fragrant that it made Ambrose's traitorous stomach rumble. As passersby began to stop and wander into Eli's shop, Ambrose clenched his fist around his quill.

"You, uh...all right there?" A voice dragged Ambrose out of his fuming surveillance. He quickly let go of the quill and turned to his customer, a gnome pushing a levitation potion across the counter. Behind her, two orcish adventurers milled around the window display, dual axes strapped to their backs. These two had been frequenting The Griffin's Claw for years, always tromping in with their potion belts of studded leather and fur, then filling them to the brim with healing vials.

Ambrose settled himself, gave a nod to the orcs, then took the bottle from the gnome.

"Perfectly fine, thank you," he said, then rang up the customer without further conversation. Which was quite how everything was supposed to go—Master Pearce had always instructed him not to pester the customers. They wanted potions, not small talk. Best not to bother them, or anyone else, for that matter. Ambrose found such consistency in social decorum comforting.

But as laughter spilled out of Eli's Elixirs, the orcs by the window looked up. Peeked over at the rival store. Then with a sheepish glance in Ambrose's direction, left The Griffin's Claw and walked across the street.

Ambrose froze, still holding the gnome's vial halfway over the counter.

"Mr. Beake, sir?" The gnome held out a hand. "Can I have that potion now?"

He dropped it into her palm. "Yes. And," he fumbled quietly, "thank you for your patronage."

The orcs may have been the first blow dealt, but they certainly weren't the last. As the next week rolled on, more of Ambrose's customers began to peer over at Eli's Elixirs. Peering turned into wandering, wandering into window-shopping, window-shopping into purchasing. And Eli himself was always there to welcome them, hailing Ambrose's customers with an infuriatingly sunny grin that matched the light in the store. Though it was hard to see through the sparkling window displays and hanging plants, his customers seemed to move more slowly in the shop, chatting and gossiping with Eli as they browsed.

And as Eli's crowds grew, Ambrose's ledgers shrank.

"Just terrible..." Ambrose muttered to himself. Dawn was late to their usual lunch, and he passed the time by flipping through his anniversary notebook and sighing heavily. He had been depending on sales this week to fund the new wand rack, but thanks to Eli's Elixirs, he had come up short. He grimaced, took his quill, and crossed the wand rack off the list. It was for the best, he reasoned. If he gave that up, he could save money for the—

"That bad, huh?"

Dawn's question made him jump, and he turned to find her leaning over his shoulder, scanning his maimed list.

"*No*," he retorted, then recomposed himself as she swung into the chair across from him. "I mean—no. Simply...being realistic about what I can afford for the anniversary."

"The anniversary?" Dawn tilted her head, her mohawk flopping to one side. "That's months away. You've got time."

"But most of the Guild adventurers are only in town for another few weeks." Ambrose leaned forward. "This is when I make the bulk of my profits for the quarter, and if that man cuts into it—"

"Hey, I get it." Dawn poured herself tea. "You'll be fine, Ames. You'll turn this around."

Ambrose slouched in his chair and looked about the café, their go-to spot for the last decade. The place was two levels up in the northern quarter, its stout proportions and sloped ceiling more suited to a gnome's build than an elf's. But the cinnamon cookies more than made up for the cramped atmosphere, so Ambrose and Dawn made a weekly habit of lounging in the only two human-sized seats available.

"So"—Ambrose snapped his notebook shut and tossed it onto the table— "what do you have for me today? You said it was an emergency lunch."

Dawn sipped her tea and gave an excited wiggle, her bright earrings and silks swaying with her. Today, she was drenched in fuchsia, casting a lovely pink glow on her white teacup. "Yes! Emergency lunch called to order."

"All present." Ambrose smiled. The occasion was far less urgent than the name suggested—Dawn called for them nearly every week. Emergency lunch to tell him about the new girl she had met at the tavern. Emergency lunch to describe a new commission or complain about the ever-changing needs of her customers...

The teapots rattled as Dawn dropped her own journal on the table, three times as thick as Ambrose's and spiked with extra tabs and papers. "I've got new hunting grounds for the star shine moss," she said, flipping the journal open for emphasis.

"I see." Ambrose straightened. "Where are we going next, captain?"

"I only have two more options." She set her fingers on two maps —one of a scribbling network of tunnels and one of a large, gaping hole. "Construction tunnels first, then the sinkhole, if we need to."

Ambrose swallowed at the deep, dark levels in the sinkhole drawing. "And you think you can get access to the construction tunnels?"

Dawn wiggled her fingers. "Benefits of being on the birthday committee, *thank* you. If the mayor's daughter wants legendary fireworks for her birthday parade, some strings must be pulled."

"Oh, such power. I'm overwhelmed." Ambrose pointed to her notes with a cookie. "When shall we venture?"

"You free this week?" When Ambrose raised his eyebrows, Dawn shrugged. "If I'm going to use the moss in my fireworks, I need to start working with it now."

"Provided it still exists."

"Yup." She leaned back. "The *Thirty Under 130* folks won't know what hit 'em."

Ambrose shook his head and finished his cookie. Of all of Dawn's commissions, committees, and commitments, this was her most ambitious. Rediscover a long-lost magic lichen, use it in her parade fireworks, and impress one very important group: the *Thirty Under 130* magical business journal.

"I even know where I'm gonna frame the article," Dawn continued, pointing into the air. "Right above the front counter, between the shelves."

Ambrose sipped his tea. "Didn't you hang your *Best in Scar* plaque there?"

"I can move that to the side wall."

"And oust your line of wand-making awards?"

"Whatever, I'll move those to the back shelves."

Ambrose grinned, took a flower petal from his plate, and tossed it at her. "Then how will people know you're the best?"

Dawn threw it back. "Because the article will be above the front counter!"

"Article, *please*." He scoffed. "You're going to be on the cover, and you know it."

Dawn's eyes glittered at the thought, and Ambrose gladly soaked in her excited rambling through the end of their tea.

"If I could just get my hands on the moss this month..." she continued eagerly as they walked home, navigating the chasm's network of wooden platforms and creaking rope bridges. "Do you know how much control I could add to the fireworks? I could add paths and complex movements! The *Thirty's* gonna love it—" Her enthusiastic gesture almost smacked a passing orc in the face, and she reeled back her hand. "Oh, sorry!"

Ambrose laughed. "We'll have to find that moss for you, then."

Dawn beamed. "You promise?"

"I promise."

He slowed his pace as they neared their second-favorite haunt—Widdershins' Books, a daintily carved little place north of Rosemond Street. Stained-glass flowers adorned the window, their colors casting rainbow hues over the latest books on display. Ambrose stopped to inspect the new arrivals and caught a whiff of paper and coffee from the open doorway. The scent felt overly decadent after already lounging in the café—but he tapped Dawn's arm nonetheless. "Do we have time to stop in?"

"You go ahead." She kept moving forward. "I need to pick up some iron pollen Eli borrowed."

The cinnamon cookies immediately sat heavier in Ambrose's stomach.

"Eli?" He followed her down the ramp. "Why did you let him borrow something?"

"Street policy, Ames." She laughed. "Don't be rude, let people borrow stuff. Literally, Banneker wrote those words into the rules himself."

"Fine, fine."

When they reached Rosemond Street, he tried to duck away toward his shop—but Dawn tugged on his sleeve, her grin sharp.

"Come on. Walk in with me, and you can spy on his stuff while I get the pollen back."

Ambrose glanced reluctantly at the rival store, still obscured by plants and customers, then shook his head. "He'll see right through it."

"So what? He can walk into your store at any time, and you can walk into his." She marched toward the door. "It'll only take a minute."

Eli's Elixirs still smelled of soil, sunlight, and herbs—but now that Eli had fully stocked the shelves and begun to brew, the earthy scents had softened into something more familiar. Burnt wood, metal polish, the sharp tang of healing potions. Ambrose stiffened. The idea of smelling those things here, not in his own workroom, somehow made him angry. Like Eli had stolen something of his, something he liked very much, and twisted it against him.

"Lemme know if you need help!" The thief in question was behind the front counter, smiling at a customer. When Dawn stepped in, his warm expression brightened—then dimmed when he saw Ambrose.

"Hey, Dawn!" He quickly turned the charm back on to address her. "You're here for the iron pollen, right? I'll go get it."

"No rush!" Dawn tried, but he was already half jogging to the storeroom in the back.

"No, I know you're busy!" He waved and disappeared through a door. Ambrose let out a breath and began to explore the shop, hands clasped behind his back.

It was difficult to find the right path to take. In The Griffin's Claw, the layout was a simple oval. Everything was labeled and structured in a way that allowed one to find their potions, circle back to the front, and leave.

Here, the store forced him to take a more scenic route. Tables of all shapes and sizes blocked his path to the discounts in the back, turning his route into a distracting maze. He wound his way past potions aligned in rainbow patterns, vials with bright ribbon tags, crystal bottles that glittered just so in the light...

Once he reached the back of the shop, Ambrose bit down a curse and took in the entire store. This was intentional, all of it. In his quest to reach the advertised discounts, he had unwittingly stopped several times to inspect the more expensive potions, arranged in ways that took advantage of the store's afternoon light. As he watched, an elven customer took one of the cheaper healing vials, doubled back to one of the crystal displays, and plucked a few bottles to add to his growing bundle of purchases.

Ambrose fought the urge to throw his signet ring across the room. Years of hard work and knowledge, only to be bested by—by *marketing* strategies—

"Afternoon, Beake."

Ambrose whipped around. Grim stood a shelf over, brow furrowed at a display of night vision potions. A flash of betrayal surged through Ambrose.

"You're not buying anything of his, are you?" he hissed. Grim gave him a flicker of a glance over their glasses.

"Only to test the goods," they said. "Need to make sure the man's legitimate."

"Oh." Ambrose flushed at his own outburst. "Of course, absolutely. And...what have you found?" He glanced around him. His initial inspection hadn't turned up anything subpar yet, but if Grim had discovered something...

The jeweler made a noncommittal noise and slid a bottle back on the shelf. "They're good, Beake. Not as good as yours"—another sideways glance—"but they're good."

Ambrose stifled another curse. Couldn't even pin the man for malpractice. "Very well. I'll just..."

He folded his arms and looked around, hoping the solution to his problem would materialize—but nothing came to mind. Grim copied his stance with their beefy arms. "Not sure why you're so worried."

Ambrose scoffed. "Do you see these crowds?"

"I see them." Grim's voice was quietly persistent. "Low-level adventurers taking advantage of cheap, low-level potions. But you can do better than that, can't you?" They lifted their eyebrows. "Beake, you can make potions he could never dream of making, not in a decade. You're talented. Use that."

Grim clapped him on the shoulder with a heavy hand and shuffled off. Before Ambrose could shake his surprise and form a "thank you," Eli emerged from the storeroom.

"Thanks for letting me borrow the pollen, Dawn," he said,

handing her a jar of gray dust. "I swear I put in an order a few days ago with..." He snapped his fingers. "That traveling merchant, Joss..."

"Jae?"

"Yes!" Eli brightened. "Jae, from Hart's Fenn."

"I've got an order out with her, too." Dawn pocketed the jar. "I heard the giants' migration delayed her, but she'll get here in a few days. Ames, you ready to go?"

Her words ended in a sharp point, and Ambrose realized he was glaring at Eli's back. As Eli turned around, he quickly adjusted his expression.

"Yes," he replied, his voice clipped. "Quite ready."

But as he passed by Eli, the man cleared his throat.

"Actually, I..." Eli started. Ambrose turned reluctantly. "Listen, I think we got off on the wrong foot. I'm hosting a networking night at the Jumping Ogre tomorrow. How about you join?" Then, like it was helpful, he added, "Sherry, Grim, and Banneker already said yes."

Ambrose bristled—he'd rather do literally anything else—but Dawn raised her eyebrows over Eli's shoulder, and he stifled the insult.

"Of course," he said stiffly. "I'll be there."

STEP 5:

MIX WELL

Ambrose

WHEN AMBROSE RAN out of excuses not to leave for the networking night, he formulated his plan on how to get out of the event as quickly as possible.

He'd wear his robes there, definitely. Tell the others he couldn't stay long—true—because he had to brew potions—not true—then would gracefully bow out after one drink. Just long enough to make the requisite appearance, while still leaving room for a book and a cup of tea at the end of the night.

"Took you long enough," Dawn said as he locked the shop door. She leaned against the wall outside, parrying his scowl with a bright smile.

"I shouldn't have agreed to this," Ambrose muttered.

"Oh, please." Dawn looped her arm around his elbow. "You're just going to say you have to brew a potion and leave after thirty minutes anyway. It's not going to kill you to show up."

The Jumping Ogre was close to overflowing. As a favorite of adventurers and locals alike, the tavern brimmed with boastful heroes, relaxed civilians, and, thanks to the networking event, chatty shopkeepers.

"How's everyone doing over here? Doing good?" Eli stopped by a cluster of apothecaries across the room, his voice breezing over the din. With his everlasting smile and charmingly tousled hair, he slipped easily into the role of gracious host. Offering appetizers here, making jokes there. He had dressed up for the event, too, sporting a purple vest that hugged his waist and sun earrings that clinked against his jawline whenever he laughed—which he did often. "Yes, I highly recommend the goat cheese. I think they were passing a plate back that way..."

Ambrose glanced around him—there was no direction in which someone *wasn't* passing around a plate. How was Eli paying for all this? Had he already stolen that many sales?

He glared at the name tag Sherry had slapped on him—a piece of paper with a sticky spell, sure to leave a mark on his robe—and returned his focus to a nearby booth, where an adventurer gestured with his frothy mug.

"So, the dragon's coming at me, right?" the elven hero boomed with the voice and chest of an empty barrel. "Mage was knocked out cold, ranger was out of arrows, and it's just me, my axe, and my last levitation potion. I down the vial, give the beast the middle finger, and—"

"Orange," Banneker said, breaking Ambrose's attention. In order to avoid small talk with strangers, Ambrose had found meager protection between Sherry and Banneker in the crowd. As he suffered in the combined ambience of iron and patchouli, the artificer squinted over at Eli. "Or gold. Or...something in between. Like a sunflower."

Ambrose frowned. "I'm sorry?"

"Eli's aura." Banneker folded his freckled arms. "It's orange. Orange-gold. Gorange."

Ambrose rolled his eyes. "You're just saying that because of his earrings."

"Hey, Eli!" Banneker called. "You ever work around sunflowers?"

Eli looked over. "I...worked on a farm for a bit?"

"See?" Banneker grinned at Ambrose. "Knew it, dude. In my heart."

"You were a farmer before you bought the shop?" Sherry leaned around Ambrose's shoulder. Holding a plate of honey cakes, Eli pivoted to join the Rosemond Street circle.

"For a few months," he said. "I took classes before that. Worked under a tanner after."

"Wait, I thought you worked for a griffin trainer?" Banneker asked. Eli passed the cakes to Grim, then gestured to the white scars on his arms.

"Sure did," he said. "Two years ago. Learned proper feeding techniques the hard way."

Grim frowned and stacked three cakes onto their massive palm. "Was that before or after the botany gig in the Driftwood?"

"After."

"Tell me about the Driftwood," Dawn cut in eagerly. "Does it really drift as much as people say?"

Eli's dark eyes glinted. "That's the thing—it never *stops* drifting."

Everyone except for Ambrose leaned in, but the barmaid tapped on Eli's shoulder, sparing them the insipid travel stories.

"We're starting to run out of cheese rolls," she said to Eli. "If you're up to pay for three more trays, that should cover you for the rest of the night."

Eli's smile faltered, then forcibly brightened again. "Yeah, let's do it. Thanks."

Ambrose raised his eyebrows. Perhaps Eli hadn't stolen enough customers to fund this stupid event after all.

"So, why a potion shop?" Grim asked, already halfway through their cakes. "It's a far cry from griffins and farming."

Eli shrugged. "Those other gigs were fine. I just..." He rubbed the back of his neck. "I couldn't see myself doing them for the rest of my life."

Sherry's smile was as honeyed as the cakes. "I'm glad you landed here, then," she said. "You can grow old on Rosemond Street with the rest of us."

Eli nodded firmly. "Absolutely."

Gods, Ambrose hoped not.

Then Eli's gaze swept over the rest of the circle. "What about you?" He nodded to Ambrose. "Did you always know you wanted to be a potion master?"

Ambrose smoothed out his expression. "Yes," he lied easily. "Always."

He kept the words pointed and gave no elaboration. When Dawn elbowed him, he pretended not to notice.

"Eli, have you been to a Fireball game yet?" Dawn piped up in Ambrose's stead. "My brothers and I go every weekend. You should come with if you want. You a fan of the Kolkean Bonekeepers?"

Eli's eyes lit up again. "Born and bred. You a Sussa or Stone Dragons fan?"

Dawn snorted. "Don't even bring up Sussa."

"Ah, jealous of their defense, I see?"

As the Fireball chatter continued, Ambrose assessed the level of everyone's drinks, then the pathway to the door. He could sneak away now, he reasoned. Get out before he actually had to talk to anyone...

He took one step toward the door, then Grim leaned forward and tapped on his mug. Ambrose stiffened again, expecting some sort of admonishment for his attempt to retreat—but the orc's look behind their glasses wasn't unkind. "You give any more thought to those potions we talked about?"

Ambrose blinked. "Um—yes, I did." It wasn't a lie this time. Brewing in the afternoon had given him plenty of time to think. "I was considering brewing an upgraded psychic resistance potion. The Adventurer's Guild should be releasing cairn cat licenses within the week, and that's the first thing they'll need."

"Smart." Grim gave a short nod. "Should attract the right customers."

Ambrose held back a grimace. He hoped so—the potion's main ingredient equaled the cost of another two workroom upgrades.

Grim stepped away. "Right. Well, you were looking to leave. I won't stop you."

Ambrose let out a relieved breath. "Really?"

Grim smirked. "I'm surprised you lasted this long. Go on."

Ambrose set his mug on the bar and strode off. Only a few steps now, around the huddle of bakers, past the gaggle of cobblers—but right as the path to the door opened up, the sound of his name made him freeze.

"Yeah, Ambrose is helping her," Eli said. "Hey, you're searching for the moss together, right?"

Eli, Dawn, and several local silversmiths were huddled off to the side, all staring at him. Ambrose turned on his heel—slowly, making sure to glare—but Dawn was unfazed, pulling him into the circle with her. He tried tugging out of her grasp, but her grip firmly communicated that he was *going* to be polite for once and he was *going* to like it.

"Talking about the *Thirty Under 130*," she explained sweetly, her tone not at all matching her grip. "How I'm going to use the moss in the birthday fireworks."

"Ah, yes." He tried to play along. "With your pink dragon shapes?"

"Purple," Dawn corrected. "Birthday girl's request."

One of the silversmiths nudged her. "Like the *Thirty* needs your purple dragons to know you're the best."

"Hey, you're only as good as your last award." Dawn held up a finger. Eli shook his head.

"How do you fit everything in with running the shop?"

"Magic."

The shopkeepers all laughed, and slowly, they slipped into a meandering conversation about traveling merchants and the weather. Ambrose itched to escape, but every time he slipped closer to the door, Eli would ask him questions, forcing him back into the conversation. Then Eli would smile, and laugh, and smile some more. Gods, did the man ever stop smiling?

Finally, the silversmiths wandered away, and Ambrose stretched his neck. He could almost smell the cool, fresh air out in the street...

"No, no, Lily's great." Eli toyed with his earring as he chatted with Dawn. "Wants to hop on a griffin and visit tomorrow, but she's going to train with my cousin up north. As if having one Valenz in the village wasn't enough, you know?" He nodded to Ambrose. "Probably not far from where you grew up, I'm guessing."

Ambrose's hands went cold. "I beg your pardon?"

Dawn's smile fell off her face, but Eli didn't notice.

"You grew up in the north before you started apprenticing, right?" His line of questioning lost none of its speed. "You've got a bit of the accent, and blue hair's pretty common up there. I was gonna guess Woodfall, but—"

"I have to go," Ambrose heard himself say, and he was out the door before he could process where he was going. How dare he bring that up, how *dare* he ask—

"Hey, hey, hold on." Eli followed from behind, shifting the cool air. "Ames, I'm sorry. I didn't mean to pry."

"Ambrose."

"What?"

Ambrose ground his heels into the road, anger crawling up his throat. "It's Ambrose, not Ames. You don't know me."

"Well, I'm trying to fix that." Eli gestured to the tavern. Out here, he dropped his cheery showmanship, though the tavern light still drew a warm line over his slouched shoulders. "Listen, I promise I won't ask you any more questions if you come back in. I know the Rosemond folks were looking forward to seeing you—"

"Why?" The word snapped more harshly than he intended, but it wasn't directed at them, not even at Eli. He opened his mouth, then closed it with a click. "Please just let me go. I'm not good company."

Eli folded his arms and glanced at the ground. When he spoke again, his voice was softer than Ambrose expected. "I'm sorry you think that. Have a good night."

Ambrose cursed and poured himself a third cup of tea. The warmth usually helped break the cycle in his mind, the one he had worked against for years. But it wasn't helping, not this time, and his thoughts plodded along familiar stops like a donkey in a deep rut.

He didn't care about his family. He didn't care that they had dropped him at The Griffin's Claw when he was eight, barely old enough to take on an apprenticeship. He didn't remember their accents when they spoke to Master Pearce about taking him in, and he didn't recall their hair color when they climbed back into the wagon and never returned. He didn't remember, and he didn't care.

Then the mental rut grew deeper, unearthing his more childish thoughts. Where was Woodfall, anyway? How far away was it from the Scar? Would he remember any of it if he visited? Would anyone remember him? Would he find his—

He downed the rest of the tea, tensed his jaw, and swept into the workroom. His tears blurred the ingredients and hissed in the cauldron fire, but that didn't matter. He mixed and poured on instinct, forcing his focus onto the clinking of glass and bubbling of water.

As the bitter tang of herbs filled the air, the lump in his throat lessened. He let out a long breath, wiped his cheeks, and watched the bubbles form and break. Throwing himself into one or a dozen potions always made it go away, made it feel better. It had done so for the past twenty years, and he saw no reason to stop now.

STEP 6:

INCREASE HEAT

Eli

ELI DIDN'T SEE Ambrose Beake leave his shop for several days after the networking night.

He wasn't sure what he had done wrong. Apart from Ambrose, the evening had been an unqualified success. For the low, low price of, well, another page of red in his ledger, Eli now had connections all over the Scar. Shopkeepers interested in collaborations, cross-promotions, group discounts...

He sighed as he tossed a handful of rosemary into a boiling cauldron. It wasn't that he didn't enjoy brewing healing potions—they were one of his favorites. The smell, the simplicity of the steps, the relaxing, gentle shift of the liquid from red to orange. But the routine nature of it meant there was nothing to truly distract him, nothing to block out the echoes of Ambrose's words in his head. *You don't know me*, indeed. He barely knew anything about his competitor.

He stirred the cauldron, then flipped his stained recipe sheet with more force than was necessary. *Competitor* was a stretch—the angry red in his own ledgers assured him of that much. Didn't the man realize Eli wasn't truly a threat?

Heavy footsteps approached the workroom, breaking off his thoughts.

"Still need some dried lavender?" Grim grunted from outside the door. Eli looked up and wiped his hands on his apron.

"Yes! Should only need two ounces, if you're willing..." He took the bottle from the orc and tossed a pinch of lavender on the scale. Deemed it good enough, handed the bottle back. As he moved, he caught a glimpse of The Griffin's Claw past Grim's shoulder. Quiet as ever, with no lights on in the second-level flat. "Hey, while you're here —does Ambrose usually do that?"

Grim pocketed the bottle. "Do what?"

"Hole himself up in his shop." Eli nodded to the windows. "See, I might have offended him the other night..."

Grim laughed—a heavy, barking sound that made Eli jump in surprise. "Valenz, the very idea of a networking night offends him." They waved a jeweled hand. "The man's probably just brewing something new."

Somehow, the idea of Ambrose revenge-brewing didn't inspire any relief in Eli. And when his rival emerged a day later to set up a new window display, he saw his instincts had been right.

"Hey." An elven adventurer in Eli's shop glanced across the street, then nudged her friend. "*Hey.*"

"Hm?" Her friend continued sifting through a display of speed potions. Together, the pair of them wore more swords and daggers than the entire Scarrish armory. Eli had secretly named them Stabby and McStabby. "What is it?"

"You see what the Claw's got today?"

Stabby—or was it McStabby?—shrugged off the question. "No. What?"

"Psychic resistance potions."

"What level?"

"Eight."

Eli's stomach flipped, and McStabby almost dropped the speed vial in her hand. "*No.*"

"Yes."

"But if we get that cairn cat license..."

"I know! Looks like he only has a few bottles left. You wanna head over?"

And off the Stabbys went, hurrying over to The Griffin's Claw to ogle over the turquoise potions in the window. Minutes later, they emerged with the bright blue vials on their belts, hardly giving Eli's Elixirs a second glance.

Eli could feel the red ink in his ledger burning a hole through the shelf.

"Level eight? Is he serious?"

Dawn's laughter floated in from her workroom upstairs. "It's Ambrose. He's always serious."

Eli wandered about the first level of the Whirling Wand Emporium, scowling at nothing. "Come on. My professors could make level six, max. Level eight potions are impossible."

He himself could only make level threes, most of which were now sitting on his shelf. Untouched. Expiring slowly.

And those ingredients had been expensive.

"It's not impossible for Ames," Dawn said. "Hardly anything's impossible for him."

"Except for small talk," Eli muttered. Then, more loudly: "Sorry, I'll let you finish."

"I'll be done soon!" she called. A whirring sound from the workroom muddied the rest of her words. "And you better turn that frown upside down, Valenz. I can't have you bumming out the ladies while wingmanning for me."

Eli bit back a smile and took another lap around the store.

Of all the shops on Rosemond Street, the Whirling Wand Emporium was his favorite. Not that he didn't enjoy Sherry's sunny forge, or the packed chaos that Banneker called an artificer's atelier. But Dawn's shop, seated at the northern edge of Rosemond and High Vine, was a place he could happily get lost in.

And he did so now, wandering about the first floor while Dawn finished her evening tinkering in the second-floor loft. The endless cabinets around Eli stretched upward until he could barely see the glints of crystal and wood on the top shelves. When he could no longer crane his neck up, he looked down to admire the masterpieces locked behind glass. The smallest wands on display were pocket-sized, meant for simple repairs and starting roadside cookfires. But even the smallest pieces were little delights of cedar and cherry, jewels and glass.

And the largest—*oh*, he wanted to try them out so badly. Dawn had placed the most beautiful ones on racks in the window display, where they could turn adventurers' heads every day. *These* were what heroes bought to fight dragons and beasts—massive staffs of gnarled branches, intertwined iron, crystal clusters growing like mushrooms. The most intimidating one was almost as long as Eli was tall, a thick, sturdy piece of petrified wood and pink corundum. Eli leaned down to read the label next to it: *Shield Staff. Mag Res, Phys Res, Ten Charges, Rechargeable, No Custom Work...*

He straightened. It was telling that there was no price on the card. If an adventurer had to ask, they couldn't afford it.

"Sorry, Eli!" Dawn called down from the loft. "A few more minutes, then we can go!"

Eli waved a hand. "Take your time!"

"You have Ember, right?"

He twisted to regard his shoulder, where a red-and-yellow splotched salamander met his gaze and licked its eyeball. "Yeah, we're chatting."

"Good, he loves that."

Eli patted Ember's head and climbed the stairs to the loft, passing by award plaques and shelves of wand-shaped trophies. He paused at the top of the steps, across from an open wand testing area. Years of use had pock-marked the walls and charred the floor in explosive patterns. Eli bit his lip—now he *really* wanted to take that shield staff for a spin.

"So"—he shifted Ember to his other shoulder—"how long have you had this little guy?"

Sparks shot out of the workroom door to the right. Eli deftly veered to the left.

"Hard to say." Dawn's voice was muffled. Eli peeked into the workroom—she was hidden behind a welding hood. "He belonged to my old mentor, and he's one of those phoenix salamanders, so...I think he's on his fifth life or something?"

Eli raised his eyebrows. "What a wise old buddy." He wandered past a tall, leafy potted plant, and Ember reached for it. Eli deposited him onto the leaf and scratched under his chin. A tiny flame flickered happily at the end of Ember's tail. "Could probably teach Tom a thing or two."

It was funny how Tom fit in with an apparent tradition on Rosemond Street: shop companions. Dawn had Ember, and Banneker always had at least three devices whirling around his place. Sherry claimed the onlookers to her forge were her constant companions, and Grim pretended they didn't own a cat. Everyone knew they owned a cat.

The only person who didn't have one was Ambrose—which, given his demeanor at the networking event, made sense.

Dawn pulled off her hood and rubbed her long ears. "Tell me about Eli's Elixirs. How's it doing?"

He slouched against the railing. "I thought you were trying to lift my mood, Kerighin."

"Come on, your shop looks busy every time I pass it." Dawn hung up her burn-scarred apron. "Those upfront costs still haunting you?"

Eli snorted. Haunting was a good word for it. "Maybe."

"Hey." She leaned out of the doorway. "It'll be fine."

As she puttered around her workroom, Eli took a hesitant step forward. "What got you through it?" he asked. "The first few months of running the shop by yourself?"

"Easy." She picked up the freshly minted wand, another treasure of amethyst and birch. "These got me through. Don't know what I'd do with my life if I couldn't make them."

Eli straightened. Of course—Dawn had her wands, and he had his potions. He just needed to make a little more money with them, that was all.

"You know…" Dawn bit her lip and set down the wand. "If you're up for a commission, the mayor's got some sort of potion he wants to give his daughter for her birthday."

"The mayor?" He perked up. Such a commission would pay well, for sure. "What does he want?"

She wrinkled her nose. "I don't know. Something about purple sparkles. Ambrose didn't want anything to do with the birthday stuff. I could put your name in if you'd like."

"That would be great. Thanks." Eli drummed his fingers on the railing, then shook his head. That was enough thinking about potions for one evening. "You almost ready to go?"

Dawn shuffled out of her workroom, draining a mug of coffee that Eli suspected had been made that morning. The coffee brightened her expression, and she clapped her hand against the mug with manic fervor. "Come on, let's go out!"

Eli clocked the shadows under her eyes and took the mug from her hands. It was stone cold. "Are you sure? Seems like you could do with a quiet night in, if I'm being honest."

"No." Dawn flicked a wand hanging by the door and ran her hands under the beam of light it emitted. The grime on her palms faded in a blink. "I haven't been outside in days. I've got to do something."

"See, I think that might be part of the problem."

She slapped his arm. "You gonna wingman for me or what, Valenz?"

He raised his hands, pocketing his concern for later. "Gladly, Kerighin."

"Good." She hopped down the steps and ducked behind the front counter. "Last time I had a wingman, it was Ambrose, and he just ended up arguing with the woman about the magical properties of dried scorch-flower." She straightened with a flask and coin purse in hand. "To be fair, I shouldn't have tried to pick up girls at a potion convention."

Eli laughed. "Did Ambrose pick up any girls himself?"

"Girls?" Dawn snorted. "Not his type. I tried to talk him up to some men at the after-party, but..." She took a swig from the flask. "Well, you saw him at the tavern. You can guess how that went."

The mention of Ambrose dampened Eli's mood again, and this time, he couldn't shake it. He paused at the front door, his hand on the doorknob. "What do I...do about him?"

"About Ambrose?" Dawn asked. As she spoke, the rose statue on the counter flashed white. She unfurled the scroll, scanned its contents, and scrawled down a response. "He's not going anywhere anytime soon. You're going to have to talk to him at some point."

She set down the quill. Eli's grip on the doorknob tensed. "But he won't talk to me."

"He talks plenty, just not in a crowded tavern." She looked in the direction of Ambrose's shop, and her gaze softened. "Listen, between his family and his mentor, he never quite..." She sighed. "You're just going to need to meet him on his own terms."

From what Eli could tell, Ambrose didn't have terms anyone could meet him on, except perhaps Dawn. But she was right— neither of them would be leaving the street anytime soon.

"Fine." He rubbed his forehead. "I'll sort it out, it'll be fine. Come on, let's go brag about you to some pretty ladies."

STEP 7:

STIR THE POT

Eli

A WEEK LATER, Eli had not sorted anything out, nor was anything fine.

He had ledgers and papers sprawled across the counter in a silent duel—advertising mock-ups versus his unsteady finances. Ambrose's impossible potions had dealt him a blow, pushing him back into steep discounts to attract customers. His two-for-one deal had worked well last week. If he continued that, then followed it up with something else to boost his visibility—a collaboration with another shop, or a belated launch party...

He analyzed the ads until his vision blurred, then turned wearily to another list—the potions he needed to brew that evening. With discounted goods came empty shelves, and he needed to restock. That meant churning through strength vials, basic antidotes, scarfading solutions...

Something tugged on his pant leg—Tom, scratching at his ankle with one fork and pointing to the stairs with the other. Eli gave a long sigh. It was late, and the mere thought of his comfortable bed made him slouch and close his eyes.

But if he didn't brew something tonight, he'd have very little to sell tomorrow.

"Can't go to bed yet." He rubbed his eyes and patted Tom's head. She wheeled off in a silent huff. "Sorry, love."

He fidgeted with his earring, tugging scraps of motivation out from under his exhaustion. He'd start with the scar-fading solutions first—they were fizzy and particularly satisfying to bottle up. Then he'd power through the others. After all, exhaustion was only tempo-rary. He'd shake it once he could spend less of his energy on these ads.

As he slowly gathered up his papers, the rose statue on the counter flared white. Grateful for the distraction, he unfurled the scroll under the rose and found a chicken-scratch conversation going between the other merchants.

Banneker: Does anyone have any cake?
Sherry: No, dear.
Banneker: Cookies?
Grim: She made you cookies two days ago.
Banneker: I'm hungry
Grim: Make them yourself.
Banneker: Not liking your vibes right now my dude

Eli laughed as the rose statue kept flashing, and the conversation devolved into something about sugar and stars in retrograde. Ambrose might be prickly, but the other shopkeepers were a delight. Banneker had insisted on analyzing his moon sign—or was it his star chart?—to determine if he'd have good luck that week. Grim had a tattoo on their hand that Eli knew was a banishment symbol but couldn't place where it was from. And Sherry—

"Eli?" The chimes above the door sang as Sherry poked her head in. "How are you, dear?"

Eli gave her a full grin. "Doing great. How are you?" He slipped out from behind the counter to welcome her. Her day must have ended right before his—soot still formed an abstract pattern across her arms and forehead.

"Just fine." She tugged off one of her gloves and flapped it in his direction, sending a puff of charcoal into the air. "You don't happen to have any sugar I could borrow, do you?"

"Oh." Eli deflated. He barely had lentils in his pantry. "I'm sorry, I don't. You making cookies for Banneker?"

"The man's persuasive." Sherry wandered about the window display to admire the crystal vials. "I thought I had enough sugar to get through a batch, but after I made him a pie last week—oh!"

She looked down. Tom bumped into Sherry's boot and tilted her broom head to regard the new person. After a moment of careful analysis, she whizzed in a happy circle around Sherry's feet, then reached her fork arms out to the woman. In return, Sherry beamed and scooped up the automaton.

"Who is this little one?" she cooed, bouncing Tom as if she were a toddler. The enchanted stones at the bottom of her mug rattled in time with the motion.

"That there is Miss Tomato. Or Tom, for short," Eli said. "And I think she likes you."

Sherry shook Tom's fork hand, and Eli smiled. It was just as his father said—Tom knew a good egg when she saw one.

"Well, I like her." Sherry smoothed out Tom's bristles, then frowned at the papers strewn around Eli. "I think you should take a break."

Eli waved his hand in protest, but a yawn overrode his reassurance. "I've gotta brew a few things tonight. At least some scar-fading vials..." He pulled his notes toward him, then slouched. He had forgotten he was out of wand charges for that specific brew. "You don't have any low-heat wands, do you?"

"Not for anything as delicate as potions." Sherry set Tom on the floor. "But you can always ask Ambrose for one."

Eli tensed. "I don't think that's a good idea—"

"Oh, he'll get over it. The boy is all roar, no flame when you get to know him." Sherry opened the front door. "All you have to do is go and ask."

Eli swallowed, then obeyed Sherry's expectant gaze and walked over to the shadowed windows of The Griffin's Claw. Maybe she was right. Ambrose did seem to like his own shop, if nothing else.

Perhaps these were the terms he could meet Ambrose on.

"Ambrose?" He knocked on the door; it swung open. The owner hadn't yet set up the security enchantments for the night. "You in?"

The store was empty and dark, save for a warm light spilling from an open door in the corner. The workroom, Eli guessed. His eyes followed the line of light over to the front counter, where it traveled over a scattering of papers. One of the papers had fallen to the floor, its writing obscured in shadow.

He picked up the paper and returned it to the counter. Though he tried not to read the contents, he caught a glimpse of notes for another potion, with overly complex diagrams and charts. He grimaced, then placed the paper beside an open notebook, this one littered with ink blots and cross-outs. Something about cauldrons, cleaning gems, and signs...

Glass clinked in the workroom. Eli quickly pulled away from the counter and shuffled over to the cracked door.

At first glance, the workroom was the same as the rest of the store —everything labeled and organized, and not a speck of dust or soot. The rose statue had been moved to a shadowy corner here, silent and dim. And there was Ambrose, wearing the same navy-and-gold robes he wore every day. These robes were stiffer, more jacket-like than the loose, light protection he was used to seeing in the Kolkean desert. As Ambrose navigated the room, the fabric hardly gave a ripple or a sway, a fine match for his normally unyielding demeanor.

But Ambrose himself was completely different.

This wasn't the elf-shaped chunk of ice that had stood in his store and judged him nor the one that had stormed out of the tavern. His shoulders were sloped down, his movements relaxed and fluid. He hardly looked at where he was going, and he didn't need to—his hands knew exactly where to land and what to pick up. As he reached back to pluck a vial from a neat row of ingredients, Eli caught the edge of a small smile.

Eli opened his mouth to speak but couldn't bring himself to say anything, lest he break the atmosphere of whatever had turned Ambrose into...other Ambrose.

But then his fingertips slipped on the doorway, the potion master noticed him, and everything shattered. Ambrose's shoulders stiffened; his smile vanished. Even the room itself seemed to dim as he drew himself up to his full height.

"Sorry," Eli blurted out and backed away, feeling as if he had broken a valuable vase. "Sorry, I didn't mean to intrude."

Ambrose ripped off his goggles and set them down on the cleaning table. The light of the cleansing gemstones flared in his eyes as he moved to the doorway, blocking Eli from the rest of the space.

"What are you doing in my shop?" he asked, his voice both soft and sharp.

Eli suddenly very much doubted the man was all roar and no flame.

"I, um..." Why couldn't he think of words? He could always think of words. "I just wanted to..."

Ambrose's look cooled into a sullen gray. "What do you need to borrow?"

Eli let out a breath. "How did you know?"

"Please." He neatened his cuffs. "No one comes into my store just to talk to me. What do you need?"

Eli's heart sank, and once again he found the words stuck in his throat. He didn't want to prove Ambrose's point, but...

"A low-heat fire wand," he mumbled. "If you have one to spare."

Ambrose nodded. "Level two or three?"

"Two."

Ambrose reached over to a wand rack, plucked the bottom one with long, deft fingers, and gently placed it on the cleaning table. Once the cleaning stones flashed, he held up the wand—then drew it back. His eyes narrowed, and his tone shifted to something reminiscent of Eli's old potion professors. "So, what are you brewing?"

Eli met his gaze and drew himself up as well. If this was what it took to borrow a stupid wand, he could handle it. He had handled plenty of professors like this; Ambrose was no different.

"Scar-fading solutions," he said. "Follow-up to the healing potions."

"High dose or low dose?"

"Low, meant to be taken over a few weeks."

"What's the base?" Ambrose pressed. "River or spring water?"

Eli tensed but didn't skip a beat. "Spring, specifically from the Elwig Forest. Keeps the potion stable, better for low doses."

Ambrose paused, then nodded, a silent concession. Eli felt a swell of pride, then decided to sharpen it and turn it on Ambrose. Two could play this game, after all. "What are *you* brewing?"

"Underwater shock immunity," Ambrose said coolly, as if he hadn't just listed one of the most complex potions in the book. "The mayor's about to approve hunting permits for river krakens to keep the population down. Whoever's foolish enough to take the permits will need the help. I should be able to finish it tonight."

"Tonight?" That was impossible—but Eli tried to keep his stance casual. "How are you breaking down the active ingredient, then?"

"Hm?"

"The dried silverleaf," Eli continued, gaining confidence. "It doesn't break down well. Takes days to get it to bind with any kind of base. How are you getting it all done tonight?"

He searched the man's face for any sliver of doubt, any indication he was on his back foot.

But Ambrose didn't hesitate. "Oh, I'm not binding it."

Eli's confidence cracked. "What?"

"Here." Ambrose pulled a wide bottle from the cabinet. The glass encapsulated a cage of metal mesh filled with blue-green leaves. "All I have to do tonight is brew the other elements of the potion—the anti-nausea component and the quick-release system." He pointed to the mesh. "This is coated in a specific formula to let the shock resistance of the leaf steep into the brew, rather than force a crushed version of it to bind with the liquid. Its effects are also more concentrated this way. I can brew in smaller, more effective doses, and free up space on an adventurer's belt for something else." He set down the bottle with a clink and looked back at Eli. "Ideally, something that knocks some sense into them and keeps them from hunting river krakens in the first place."

And just like that, the other Ambrose was back. The proud glint in his eye, the soft smile playing across his face. This was A. Beake, CPM, and he had just bested Eli at their little game.

He had just won, like he always did.

Before Eli could think through his irritation, his words came out like a whip, sharp and aimed to hurt. "Well, good to know there's something you can talk about after all."

He regretted the words instantly. Ambrose's smile evaporated, and his expression settled into stone. "Apologies for taking up your time." He held out the wand. "Here, you have what you came for. Don't bother bringing it back."

Eli winced. "Ambrose, I—"

"And while you're at it"—Ambrose turned back toward the cauldron—"don't come into my store again."

The apology died on Eli's tongue. If Ambrose wanted to sit alone with his impossible potions, that was fine. There was no need to apologize to this man. No need to ask him questions or get to know him.

Ambrose was right—he wasn't good company.

"Fine." Eli stalked out of the shop, the wand a heavy weight in his pocket.

STEP 8:

GOGGLES REQUIRED

Ambrose

ELI'S ADVERTISEMENTS grew more obnoxious after that night.

Ambrose supposed it could be his fault—he hadn't actually meant to kick Eli out for good. It was a foolish, thoughtless reaction to foolish, thoughtless words.

But he wasn't about to go over there and apologize. Instead, he scoffed at Eli's three-for-one ad in the paper, crumpled it up, and tossed it into the cauldron fire.

He spent the next several weeks doing nothing but brewing and running the shop. Every time Eli rolled out another discount, he'd have another potion ready. Fire-throwing, or ice-breathing, or invisibility—something he knew Eli didn't have the knowledge or the money to master.

But Ambrose hardly had the money, either. His fire-throwing brew had cost him another cauldron upgrade, while the ice-breathing vial soaked up his funds for new cleaning gems. By the time he bottled up the invisibility potion, there was only one item left standing on his upgrade list—the sign.

"Ames?" Banneker's voice bounced around the shop one day

while Ambrose was in the workroom. "You in here, my man?" The artificer laughed to himself. "I mean, when are you not, am I right? But seriously." He popped up at the door. "You good?"

Ambrose shoved the cork into the last invisibility potion. *Good* was a relative term.

"Fine, thank you, Banneker." He set the bottle down in a line with the others. "What do you need?"

"A job, actually." Banneker leaned against the doorway, hands in his pockets. "You asked me about updating that sign a few months ago, and I finally got the right tool in. You ready for me to get cracking on it?"

"Oh." Ambrose's heart lifted. "Let me check first, make sure I have enough..." He hurried out of the workroom and pulled the ledger from the shelf, flipping through it to the last page. "How much did you say it would be?"

Banneker shrugged. "The tool didn't cost much, but the real issue will be time. Working with the enchantment while getting the carving right and all. I'd say..." He looked up to the ceiling and waggled his head. "Seven hundred? Could split it into payments of three-fifty, but not smaller than that. Got some maintenance expenses coming up..."

As Banneker rambled, Ambrose's stomach dropped to the floor. The numbers on the page were quite clear—he only had two hundred talons left for upgrades.

"I see." He quietly closed the ledger. "I'm afraid I don't need it yet, but...perhaps in another month?"

The words soured as he spoke them. He wouldn't have the money in a month, nor the month after. Not as long as Eli kept up his discounts.

"You sure?" Banneker's smile faded. "You were so excited about it a few months ago."

As Banneker approached, Ambrose pushed the ledger back on the shelf.

"I'm sure," he fumbled. "It's—it's quite unnecessary."

But he didn't meet Banneker's gaze as the elf set his elbows on the counter. "I don't think it's unnecessary, Ames," he said. "I think it's important to you."

Ambrose nodded, his eyes watering at he stared hard at the counter. After a moment, Banneker tapped the wood and straightened.

"You tell me when you're ready, yeah?" He loped out to the street, then paused in the doorway. "Hey."

Ambrose looked up. Banneker grinned.

"You're my favorite dude of brew. You know that, right?"

Banneker strolled off to his shop, leaving Ambrose's response knotted in his throat.

When Ambrose next left the shop, it was to enter a different stony corner of the Scar—the rugged construction tunnels in the southern quarter where Dawn hoped to find her star shine moss.

Half-carved, half-wild, the tunnels had long since been cleared out of the Scar's more dangerous vermin. Now, they were dotted with lanterns for the workers and smelled strongly of explosive powder. According to the chatty baker one level below them, the maze would soon be converted into a mushroom farm supplying the Little Elwig market.

Given the tunnels' relative safety, it hadn't taken much convincing to get access to them without expensive adventurer accompaniment. All Dawn had to do was remind the foreman that she was on the birthday committee, and the mayor had *specifically* requested the best fireworks for his little girl, and wouldn't it be a *shame* if she wasn't able to get them done in time because the tunnels were closed off—

"All right, all right, I get it," the gnomish foreman muttered and waved them in. "You've got two hours. Just watch out for the burrowing larvae and you'll be fine."

And that was how Ambrose found himself winding through stalagmites, searching for moss and trying to convince himself he would indeed be fine in the deep, dark tunnels. It would be like his adventurer novels, he told himself. He just...didn't have a sword. Or a shield. Or a team of level-headed, mildly violent experts at his back.

Only Dawn, with nothing but a few wands and her enthusiasm bearing them deeper into the darkness.

"Now, if we find the moss here, I can dry it out in a matter of"— she hopped around a boulder—"a few days, I think. Working around the incendiary nature of it, of course."

Ambrose held his light wand higher to help her navigate. "Incendiary?"

"Yeah. I'm using it in fireworks, remember?" She flicked her own wand, and it flashed brighter. "So, when we find it, let me handle it. I've got the gloves, and it's not worth setting your hands on fire."

Ambrose swallowed. "Understood."

They ventured farther into the tunnels, straining to see any sparkling blue moss on the walls or columns. After the tenth patch of dull green moss, Dawn huffed and stopped to take a swig of water.

"You know, I think I've seen Eli's ads more than I've seen you recently." She sat on a rock and chugged from her waterskin. "How have you been?"

Ambrose folded his arms and leaned against the tunnel wall. He shouldn't bother her with his problems. This was her mission, after all. "Fine."

Dawn raised her eyebrows. He threw up his hands.

"Awful!" The word pinged about the tunnel. "Eli insulted me, his two-for-one deals ruined my plans, I can't even pay for the sign, I just..." He sighed. "I've been brewing new potions, but it's not enough. I need to make something better. Something he can't match with his stupid discounts."

Dawn hummed. "Well, I don't know about *better*..."

His hope sparked. "You have something?"

"Maybe." Dawn passed the waterskin to him. "The mayor's still looking for someone to brew a birthday gift for his daughter. Want me to put your name in?"

His spark dulled. "Would I have to attend the birthday committee meetings?"

"No, just brew the potion."

"Excellent." Ambrose relaxed and took a drink. "Yes, if you could put my name in, that would be helpful. Thank you."

Dawn held up a hand. "I should warn you, a couple folks have already applied—"

Ambrose waved it off. "Tell the mayor I'm a Guild master and have published work in several journals. I can handle whatever he's looking to make."

Once they reached a fork in the tunnel, Ambrose flicked his wand. The liquefied crystal intertwined with the wood brightened, its light casting knifelike shadows down both potential paths. "Which way, captain?"

As Dawn unfolded a map, he reached for the cuffs of his sleeves to adjust them, then remembered he wasn't wearing his robes. Cleaning the heavy fabric was already difficult—he didn't need cave dust and slime interfering with the expensive enchantments on top of everything else.

He settled for straightening his vest while Dawn squinted at both paths.

"If we assume the moss is growing deeper in the tunnel system..." She scratched at the cloth covering her hair, then pointed at the left path with a gloved hand. "That tunnel goes farther in, while the other one loops to a residential area. I say we go left."

"As you wish." Ambrose gave a small bow, then held out a hand to help her over a cluster of rubble.

As sound as Dawn's logic was, the tunnel quickly yielded them nothing but strife. Thin white crystals jutted out like daggers, catching their clothing and dripping icy water onto their necks. And as the crystals grew in size and sharpness, the path became wilder to match. Straight tunnels tilted into rocky hills, then steep slopes. Before long, they had to slalom their way down from rock to rock.

"Get to that rock," Dawn said, guiding Ambrose from the bottom of a slope. "Okay, now skid diagonally to that one there."

Ambrose pulled his hands away from the rock and grimaced—a trail of pearlescent slime followed his fingers. "Dawn..."

"I know it's gross. Just get to the next rock."

He shook out his hand and started skidding to the next spot.

"Wait, duck! *Duck!*"

His forehead smacked into a crystal, tossing stars into his vision and smearing his face with more gunk. As he staggered to the bottom of the slope, Dawn cringed at the ooze dripping into his eyebrows.

"What?" he snapped, wiping his eyes with the back of his wrists. "I can't help it if I'm tall! And what's with all this—this *ooze*, anyway? Do you think the burrowing larvae came through here?"

"I'm sure we're fine." Dawn strode forward. "Come on, I think I saw some moss farther in. If we can get that sample—"

The ground began to shake, and she latched onto his arm. Debris showered from the ceiling, clinging to the shiny goo on Ambrose's face and hands.

"You think it's the larvae?" Dawn shouted over the rumbling. Ambrose tried hard not to think about the goo close to his mouth.

"Well, it better not be a pupa. I don't have a *weapon* on me—"

Then a curtain of wriggling rock and dirt whumped to the floor in front of them, sending them staggering in opposite directions. Dawn shrieked as the detritus fell away, revealing a Scarrish burrowing larva writhing on the ground. Pearly goo formed a puddle around its pale, donkey-sized body, its tiny pincers and tinier legs clicking uselessly in the air.

"Ew ew ew!" Dawn went an odd shade of gray and ducked behind a boulder. "Ambrose, get it!"

"Me?" Ambrose yelled over the monster's squeals and sorted through the potions at his belt. Cleaning, minor healing, more cleaning... "What do you want me to do? I don't have anything!"

"Take my flare wand! It's, um..." Dawn felt around her belt, and her hands came up empty. Her eyes landed on the puddle of goo in front of the larva. "Oops."

Ambrose followed her gaze. The wand had fallen off her belt and into the puddle. As the creature moved, slime oozed thickly over the wand's handle.

"Oh, good." He slumped. "Thank you *very* much—"

The larva heaved its body toward Dawn in its panic, and she pressed herself against the craggy wall. "Just chase it off, you bastard!"

"All right!" Ambrose crouched down, suppressed a gag, and leapt forward. With a loud squish, he yanked the wand from the goo and flicked it twice. Bright, searing light burst from the tip of the wand, as white-hot as the midday sun. The larva gave a shriek of its own and thrashed away from the light.

"Go on!" Ambrose waved the wand again, encouraging it farther down the tunnel, until its round head bashed into a wall and began burrowing a new path away from the offending spell. The ground gave another brief rumble, then stilled.

"Gross," Dawn panted from the wall, then gave Ambrose a relieved smile. "Thank you. You're the bravest blue-haired potion master I know."

Ambrose dropped his wand arm with a glare. "What a compliment."

Dawn took out a cloth, wrapped it around the flare wand with a disgusted wince, then dropped it into her pack. "Let's check out the moss on the other side and head back."

They followed the larva's path to the shadowy plants ahead—and found not the brilliant blue of the star shine moss, but the flat green of normal Scarrish cave peat. Again.

Dawn groaned and slumped down on a rock. "Son of a wood-eating dragon..."

Ambrose's shoulders dropped. His skin literally itched to get out of the tunnel and take a bath—but he couldn't leave Dawn in such poor spirits. "You sure you don't want to go a little farther?" he tried. "I could walk ahead and check, if you'd like."

"No." Dawn waved a tired hand. "The path ends around that corner. We should head back." But she made no move to get up, and Ambrose sat down next to her.

"I promise we'll find the moss."

Dawn slouched even further. "I had a plan, Ames. I wanted to find the moss this month so I could get it into the wands next month. If I can't do that, my application is going to suck, and the *Thirty* journal will think *I* suck—"

"Hold on, now." Ambrose reached for her shoulder—then thought better of it, given his sticky state. "First, your fireworks never suck. You haven't needed star shine moss to make them good in the past, and you certainly don't need it now. Second, *you* never suck, either. I don't care what any business journal says." He stood up and reached for his dusty light wand. "Third, don't give up on your plan just yet. We still have the sinkhole to explore, don't we?"

His wand caught the shadows under her eyes as she smiled up at him. "You're just saying all that because you know I owe you for the goo."

"That's not why I was saying it, but..." He looked down at his clothing and immediately lost his appetite for the week. "Yes. You owe me for the goo."

Ambrose spent most of the walk back envisioning a quiet evening ahead of him, ideally with three baths, a cup of tea, and no bugs whatsoever. Dawn, however, bounced back quickly, and by the time they reached Rosemond Street, she had both a beat and an off-key tune for Ambrose's plight.

"Owe me for the goo, *mhm*."

She bumped his leg with her hip.

"Owe me for the goo—"

"Please stop."

"No, it's catchy. Owe me for the—"

The lilting sound of a different song cut her off, and they turned the corner to find music and people spilling out of Eli's Elixirs. Ambrose groaned.

"What in the gods' names is he doing now?" he muttered. All the other shops on Rosemond Street had closed for the day, but customers still milled about the other potion shop, chatting and drinking wine. A bard was folded into a corner by the window, strumming out a light, inviting song.

And of course, there was Eli, playing the host once more. Passing out glasses, shaking hands, laughing and talking. He turned toward the door, and Ambrose immediately took a step behind Dawn. "I have to go—"

"Hey, Dawn!" Eli hopped out of the doorway with a grin, which quickly fell off his face when he saw their dusty, gooey state. "What happened to you two?"

Eli's obnoxious voice was far too loud. In the street, people turned to look, and behind him, Grim, Sherry, and Banneker's heads popped through the doorway. Their eyes swept first over Dawn's state, then Ambrose's.

Ambrose wanted to sink into the ground and never return.

"She owes me for the goo," he said weakly.

But Dawn was undeterred.

"What's all this?" she asked, pointing to the festivities. "I could use a glass of wine."

"Oh, this?" Eli quickly turned to Dawn, seeming grateful for the excuse not to look at Ambrose. "Just threw a belated launch party together. I sent everyone a message through the rose, but I guess you were, um…" He gestured to the puddle of ooze dripping at their feet. "Anyway, you can come in, if you like. The Jumping Ogre tossed in some drinks, and the bard's a cousin of the cobbler on High Vine. There's snacks, too. My friend at the Elwig Market gave me a discount. Oh!" Eli twisted around. "And you should check out the new wand rack I set up. Really makes the place look more put together—"

A burst of laughter interrupted him, and he nodded and waved to someone in the store. Ambrose's embarrassment melted into anger, and he would have clenched his fists if the goo on his hands wasn't so utterly disgusting.

This was where his sign money had gone. Siphoned away by his rival to fund *his* upgrades. A horrible show-off was what this scoundrel was. With his purchases and customers and connections and *friends*—

"Well, I'm in." Dawn shrugged. "Just let me clean up first."

"Dawn!" Ambrose spluttered.

"What?" She gestured to the shop. "We fought a bug monster! I deserve some wine!"

"You fought a bug monster?" Sherry shoved past Eli. "Are you two all right?"

Ambrose barreled toward The Griffin's Claw, half out of instinct, half out of rage. He had to get behind the door before anyone could so much as look at him again. "Completely fine, ten baths to take, you understand!"

"But Ambrose—!"

He slammed the door closed and stalked upstairs.

Two baths and three cups of mint tea later, nothing had changed.

Music still seeped in through the curtains. Ambrose still smelled of rocks and larva goop. And the ball of anger was still there, seething in his ribcage.

He paced around his kitchen with his teacup. Eli had everything now. His customers, his money, his upgrades. Even Dawn was galavanting inside the rival store, eating snacks and drinking wine.

He gulped down the tea and turned on his heel, his path a straight line between the wall and his tiny kitchen table. He needed to brew something new, something that reminded everyone of his shop's superiority. Something the fool across the street could never hope to match with his elementary spring water and iron pollen...

He stopped mid-step, thoughts whipping. Iron pollen, traveling merchants...Jae. He ran over to the calendar and grinned.

That was it—Jae was coming into town tomorrow.

It was one of his favorite days of the month. Jae, the traveling merchant from Hart's Fenn, came in early in the morning, towing all manner of rare tools and ingredients. She typically set up shop in the main square, but if he caught her when she passed by at daybreak, she provided early-bird discounts. He had bought a countless number of rare goods that way—scorch-flower seeds, twisted quartz, and his favorite, bog bones. With potent enough bog bones, he could brew a corrosive resistance potion. Or an extra-strength antidote. Or a high-level acid spray—*ha*, watch Eli try to brew *that* one in his glittery, musical shop.

Ambrose tugged the curtains tighter against the wine-drunk party outside and bundled into bed, throwing two pillows over his head to block out the warbling bard and bursts of laughter. Tomorrow morning would solve things, he reassured himself. While Eli slept off a hangover, Ambrose would be getting his shop's reputation back.

STEP 9:
BRING TO BOIL

Ambrose

MINUTES BEFORE DAYBREAK, Ambrose stepped out of The Griffin's Claw, closed his eyes, and took a long, deep breath.

Fresh air—truly fresh air—was rare on Rosemond Street. Passersby, wagons, and mounts constantly kicked up dust, and no enchantment could keep it entirely out of the stores. But in the quiet emptiness of the morning, the air went undisturbed, so Ambrose drank it in and craned his neck to look upward.

It was hard to know what to admire first, from this angle—the fading stars, the velvety sky, or the earthy brushstrokes of color patterning the chasm walls. When Ambrose first descended into the Scar as a child, he had to keep his gaze on the elevator floor so the beautiful stripes didn't make him dizzy. Years later, his eyes navigated them with ease, following their waves up to the purple clouds, the constellations, then back down to the other side of the chasm. Whoever had looked upon such a sight and dubbed it something as ugly as the Scar...well, he'd certainly have words for them.

After a minute of admiration, Ambrose clasped his hands behind his back and hummed a wandering melody. He couldn't wait to buy the bog bones from Jae. He already had a scribble of thoughts in his workroom on what sorts of lovely, complex potions he could make.

He smiled. Even Master Pearce would be impressed with what he had planned.

In a rare moment of spontaneity—or as a distraction from his troubles—he had sent off a letter to Master Pearce the other day, inviting him to visit for the shop's anniversary. Though the retired potion master now lived by the Trapping Sea on a Guild pension, he had run the store for forty years, and spent the last quarter of them preparing Ambrose to do the same. Years of strict instruction on how to balance books, follow safety protocols, maintain the place...

Ambrose set a hand on the shop's doorway, gently tracing over flecks of old paint. Surely, Pearce would want to come back and visit. Surely he'd appreciate his apprentice's efforts. The new potions, the new upgrades...

Ambrose just needed a few bog bones first.

"Mr. Beake!" Jae's voice rattled through the chasm, her spiky Fenn accent jarring the morning silence. Ambrose stepped out to greet the gnome. In her swath of patchwork traveling cloaks, she looked like all the other bundles in her wagon, with only her dark face and bright smile poking out of the cloth.

"Jae." He gave the merchant, then her donkey, a polite nod. "Buttercup. Good morning."

Jae stood and smoothed out her tight black braids—but her movement was stiff, and her smile strained. "Mr. Beake," she repeated, sliding off the wagon. The dragon-warding bells on her wrists jingled as she hopped down. "What are you looking for today?"

"Bog bones, please." Ambrose glanced back at his waiting workroom. "Twelve ounces should do it."

"Twelve?" Jae's smile cracked further, erasing her irregular dimples. "Let me just, um...check in the back..."

She ducked behind the wagon and rummaged through her various bags and crates. After a few minutes, she emerged holding a tiny jar, with one skinny, bleached bone rattling inside.

Ambrose's mood sank to the floor.

"Oh." His tone deflated with him. "Not much survived the journey, I take it? I did hear of the storms out west. The bones decay so easily in humidity—"

"Oh, it's not that." She nervously stroked Buttercup's neck and pointed back down the street. "It's, um—it's just that someone already bought the rest."

It was as if his spirit had landed right into a pile of tinder; it was aflame in seconds.

"Already bought it?" he repeated loudly. "When? How?"

"He caught me right at the elevator. Bought up my whole bone stock, along with a couple other things." Jae shrugged. "Sounded real grateful for the early-bird sale, to be honest."

Then the door to Eli Elixir's chimed open, and Eli came sauntering out, yawning and rummaging through a coin purse. "Ms. Jae, I'm sorry to bother you, but if I could get one more jar of dried algae, I'm gonna need about five more ounces, I think..."

The fire in Ambrose's chest exploded.

"*You*," he spat. "You did this?"

Eli looked up from the coin purse. "Did what?"

"Bought up all the ingredients!" Ambrose gestured sharply at the cart. "Took everything so I can't buy what I need!"

"Are you serious?" Eli glared. "This isn't about you."

Ambrose matched his glare. "Oh, like this wasn't intentional."

"Intentional?" Eli pocketed the purse and strode forward. "You think I'm doing this just to spite you?"

"Well, it's certainly not to help me." Ambrose stepped forward as well. "You're taking my ingredients, stealing my customers—"

"I'm not stealing your customers—I'm trying to survive!"

"Then do it elsewhere!" Ambrose threw an arm out toward the opposing storefront. "I don't need to see your stupid banners, or go to your stupid parties, or read your stupid ads—"

"No one's making you, you self-centered prick!" Eli shouted. "Gods, do you care about anything other than yourself?" His gaze sharpened into something more venomous. "I guess I shouldn't be surprised. If I spent twenty years alone in a cauldron, I'd be a pretentious asshole, too—"

Ambrose didn't realize what he was doing until after his fingers broke.

His right hook—wild, clumsy, and far too wide—smashed into Eli's jaw, wiping the smug grin off his face. And for an instant, it felt good. Satisfying, even, taking aim right at that infuriating mouth of his.

Until a lancing pain shot up Ambrose's arm, and he staggered away, clutching his wrist to his chest.

"Shit!" He stared wide-eyed at his red knuckles, his fingers screaming. What had he *done*? He never punched people, not ever. Why did he—

Eli's response came swiftly: a fist slamming into his cheek as fast and heavy as a griffin. His feet left the ground, and he briefly floated in the air, nothing but regret keeping him aloft.

He landed hard in the dust, directly on top of his broken hand. The impact forced a strangled cry out of his lungs, and when he opened his eyes, two Griffin's Claw storefronts floated before him.

"That's *enough!*" Maroon sparks whiffed into the ground past Ambrose. With effort, he turned his head to find Jae pointing a wand between them.

"I'm not going to sell to either of you if you behave this way," she snapped. "You're scaring Buttercup!"

Buttercup flicked his ears indifferently. All the same, the anger drained out of Ambrose, leaving a heavy pool of shame as he wobbled to his feet. "I apologize, Jae. I don't know what came over me."

"Sorry, Jae." Eli shook out his fingers, looking no worse for wear. "Buttercup."

The gnome huffed and hopped back into her wagon, bells jingling. "If you two need any more ingredients, you'll come to me when I open in the square and not a moment before, you hear me?" She flicked the reins. "Come along, Buttercup."

Before Ambrose could stammer out another red-faced apology,

the cart took off, creaking its way down the chasm floor to other, more polite customers. The two men stood in the street, dust settling over their shoes.

"Boys?" Sherry's voice called sleepily from her shop. "What's going on out there?"

The question propelled them away from each other, back toward their respective shops. Eli caught Ambrose's gaze with a dark glare. "I don't want to see you in my shop again."

"Oh, like I'd want to step one foot in that hovel—"

Sherry's voice warbled out again. "Is everything all right?"

"Fine!" they both shouted, then turned on their heels. Ambrose pulled open the door to The Griffin's Claw with his good arm, slipped inside, and yanked the door closed.

STEP 10:

LET SIMMER

Ambrose

AMBROSE FILLED the shop with curses as he staggered over to the health potions. Alone in a cauldron. How dare he, how *dare* that man—

The bottles before him wavered, then doubled. He gripped the side of the cabinet to steady himself, then grabbed a vial in the back. This formula was slower to act but more effective in the long term, less prone to scarring and chronic pain. He popped the cork, drank the purple sludge, then groaned and set his forehead against the cabinet door.

As he waited for the pain to subside, his shame boiled back into anger, only this time self-directed. He didn't know where his brain had gone this morning, but it was clearly nowhere near his head. Thanks to his actions, Jae was never going to sell to him again. Eli was going to tell everyone he was a violent lunatic. Then no one would buy from him, the Guild would drop him, the shop would—

"Ambrose?" Sherry called from outside. He cursed again and hobbled toward the stairs, but it was too late to retreat—she was already through the door, with Banneker in tow. "Ambrose, please."

He sighed and glanced down at his hand. The swelling in his fingers had disappeared, and he hoped his face was showing similar signs of recovery. "What do you need, Sherry?"

"I need to talk to you." She folded her arms, the worry lines on her forehead deepening. "Eli told me what happened."

Ambrose scowled. Of course, he had. "I'd rather not discuss it." He kept a pointed edge around the words and grabbed a broom from the supply closet, if only to keep himself from having to look at their frowns.

But his tone went over their heads.

"Your aura is all over the place right now, dude," Banneker said. "You can tell us about it. We won't bite."

Ambrose stubbornly swept along the cabinets, aware of their eyes following his back. "It was nothing. Merely an argument."

"Ambrose, you punched him." Sherry tapped her gloved fingers on the counter, and he could already imagine the soot stains she was leaving. "It's just—it's so *unlike* you."

His grip on the broom tightened. "Sherry, what do you want from me?"

"I want you to go over there and apologize to Eli."

Ambrose finally whirled around, pain flaring in both his hand and his chest. "Apologize? I wasn't the one who bought everything up and started flinging insults—"

Sherry opened her mouth to argue, but Banneker set a hand on her arm. "I think he just needs some time. Why don't we come back when his aura's more settled?"

Ambrose resisted the urge to snap the broom in half. "My aura isn't..." He passed a hand over his face. "I don't have! An aura! And if you say it's blue one more time, I..." He pointed at his hair. "My hair is blue. My eyes are blue. I am literally wearing blue. Saying I have a blue aura signifies absolutely nothing—"

Banneker's gaze hardened. "It *signifies*, my dude"—he crossed his arms—"that you have some problems."

Ambrose could make the argument that there were two problems standing in his store right now—but Sherry took a hard step forward. "Go over to Eli's now and apologize."

Ambrose tossed aside the broom. "I am not apologizing to him. In fact, I'm not going to talk to him ever again. So, if you could please leave my shop—"

Something rattled the window, making all of them jump. A goat-sized dragon hovered behind the glass, bumping its dull head against the panes. As it moved, a lumpy canvas sack hung from its equally lumpy frame.

Ambrose let out an exasperated noise and yanked the front door open. This was the last thing he needed right now. "How many times have I told you, you're going to scratch the glass!"

He waved the dragon over. It bumbled forth on blurred wings and shifted to present the messenger bag to him. Ambrose wrinkled his nose at the whiff of dragon smell—stale hay and charcoal—and reached into the bag. Once his fingers touched the cloth, the bag's embroidery shivered, and a scarlet envelope slipped into his hand of its own volition.

He frowned at it and turned it over. The envelope had only his name, no seal. Was he supposed to know what the color of the paper meant? None of his Guild mail or bills were red.

Then to his surprise, the dragon swerved across the street, where Eli was sweeping his doorway. Eli stopped, reached inside the bag, and pulled out an identical scarlet envelope.

As the dragon buzzed away, Ambrose ripped open the envelope and scanned the letter inside.

Mr. Beake:
You are requested to visit the office of Mayor Rune at your earliest convenience.

Ambrose smiled, no longer feeling the bruise on his face. It was the mayor's birthday commission, it had to be. A saving grace, and at the perfect time, too—

But he wasn't the only one with a letter. He looked up at Eli.

Eli looked up at him.

Ambrose started running.

STEP 11:

BIND THE COMPOUNDS

Eli

ELI SWORE as Ambrose took off toward the mayor's office. If that son of a wood-eating dragon wanted to turn it into a race, fine. Eli wasn't going to lose this time—not to that man and his weak punches.

He sprinted forward, ducking around wagons and donkeys, until he was mere steps behind Ambrose. If he slipped left around this signpost, he'd catch up, then pass him, then...

Ambrose weaved up a ramp to the upper platforms. Good, Eli thought. Let him waste his time up there. Eli would take a more direct route, along the ground floor and through the—

Traffic.

He skidded to a dusty halt. A long line of café customers snaked across the street, forming a bleary-eyed blockade. When he tried to push through, their tired gazes went sharp.

"Hey!"

"What do you think you're—"

"Get to the back of the line!"

"Sorry, sorry!" Eli ducked around the last of them, scanning the horizon for a sign of blue hair. Up ahead, a flash of gold-embroidered robes flew down a ramp and disappeared around the bend.

"Oh, no you don't!" Eli reassessed his path and picked up his pace. The road straightened out soon, and that stick figure of a man couldn't beat him in a dead sprint.

Ambrose didn't see him until it was too late. Eli caught up and shoved his shoulder into Ambrose's, sending the man flying. The potioneer landed on his arm with a crunch.

"Ow!"

"You punched first!" Eli shouted and kept running.

A boot lashed out and caught him in the ankle, and he toppled into a line of barrels.

"You punched back!" Ambrose yelled, stumbling forward. Eli shoved the barrels away and pounded into a sprint. The government square was ahead of them now, Ambrose veering left around the fountain, Eli veering right. Then it was just a few steps to the wide staircase, the stone entrance, and the mayor inside—

They both reached for the doors, but the doors pushed out for them instead. Eli staggered back as they swung open with a groan, revealing a stout elven woman with a clipboard and a tired expression. Despite the bags under her eyes, her stance was resolute, as solid as the bas-relief carvings that swirled across the building's facade.

"Sorry, ma'am." Eli tried to move past the clerk. She pushed him back, her expression unchanged.

"Birthday business?" She nodded to the red envelopes in their hands. "Come with me."

Ambrose held up his letter, wheezing through heavy breaths. "Ma'am, I really need to see the mayor first—"

The clerk turned on her heel, green skirt spinning around her boots. "Both of you," she said, then flicked her gaze over her shoulder. "And no running."

Eli sighed and followed her, keeping to the right side of the tunnel. Ambrose did the same on the left, trying very hard not to look like he was gasping for air.

In his rush, Eli had barely glanced at the carvings on the government building—but as the woman ambled down the hall, he reluctantly took the time to admire the artwork. Like outside, the rounded bas-reliefs here portrayed farmers, merchants, and adventurers, all coming together to build the Scar. Fighting dragons, digging tunnels, growing crops. Their swords and sickles reached for the stone ceiling above, where crystal lights grew in gently pulsing clusters.

But when the clerk led them through more utilitarian offices, the stately carvings gave way to blank walls and piles of party decorations. Crates of pink candles, lavender ribbons, and deep purple streamers formed a haphazard maze, while harried assistants popped through doorways, all bearing stacks of paper and cups of coffee. Eli forced himself to slow down further—he couldn't risk getting an assistant's drink on his shirt before meeting the mayor.

Up ahead, the clerk nodded to a gilded door. "Wait here. The mayor will be with you shortly."

She disappeared back down the hall, leaving the potioneers standing as far away from each other as possible. After a minute, Eli dared one glance over at Ambrose. He was still catching his breath, his bruised face was flushed, and he cradled his arm awkwardly against his chest. He was in no state to meet a mayor.

And yet he was still here, standing between Eli and the most lucrative commission of his short career.

"What are you doing here?" Eli whispered sharply. Ambrose glared at him.

"What are you talking about? I'm here for the commission."

"Dawn said you didn't even want that commission."

Ambrose shuffled. "I didn't."

Eli's anger flared, and he gestured to the office door. "So, what, you're doing this just to spite me or something?"

"Oh, now who's being self-centered?" Ambrose snapped. "I didn't even know you had applied."

"Then why did *you* apply?"

Ambrose didn't answer; he merely set his shoulders back and

glared at the door. But the omission was a confession in itself, and it filled Eli with a cruel sort of giddiness.

Ambrose Beake of The Griffin's Claw needed the money.

But the giddiness faded quickly. It was likely Ambrose would get the money, too. With his Guild membership, and published papers, and years of living in a cauldron.

Eli folded his arms. He'd have to find some way around Ambrose, then. Undercut his bid, throw in something extra, charm the mayor. He bit back a smile at the last thought. Ambrose certainly couldn't do *that*.

The door swung open, revealing a human secretary with thick square glasses, green hair, and ink stains on their fingers.

"Mr. Beake and Mr. Valenz?" they read from a scrap of paper. "Mayor Rune would like to speak with you both."

"At the same time?" Ambrose stiffened. "As the more qualified potioneer here, I can assure you that Mayor Rune will want to speak to me first."

"Actually"—Eli thought fast—"I've got an urgent appointment later today, so if the mayor could fit me in first, I can—"

"You have no such thing," Ambrose retorted. Eli shot him a glare.

"Oh, like you know my schedule."

Two unexpected sounds beyond the door cut them off—the clopping of hooves and the wailing of a small child.

"Listen, if the little lady still wants llamas," a woman tried to shout over the wailing, "I can get you a dozen in time for the parade. But not twenty, and that's final."

A small herd of beings came around the corner behind the secretary. An elf leading a llama, and an orc in stately evergreen robes, bearing a screaming ball of thunder in his arms. As the screaming increased in pitch, the orc rubbed his forehead, his voice gravelly in its exhaustion.

"A dozen will do. If you could take your llama—"

"Miriam, sir."

"If you could take Miriam and speak with the parade officer..." He gestured wearily to the door. The elf gave a short bow.

"Thank you, Mayor."

The elf and the llama clopped off, leaving only the wailing left.

"Beatrice," the orc groaned, bouncing the squalling little girl in his arms. "We'll find Little Rabbit, I promise—"

"Little Rabbit! Little Rabbit!" Beatrice shrieked. She had the same springtime green skin as her father, but her fluffy purple dress stood out against his dark robes. As she kicked against his ribs in frustration, purple jewels on her shoes winked in the lantern light.

The mayor slouched, dug into his pocket, and pulled out a lollipop. Beatrice reached out with her sharp little teeth and chomped down on the candy. The last of her shrieks faded down the hall, and the mayor let out a breath.

"Beake, Valenz?" He nodded to them, then ran his free hand through his thinning purple hair. "Argus Rune. Thank you for coming."

Eli grinned. Rune. Rune, he *knew* that had sounded familiar. This man used to be a Fireball player.

Oh, he was going to nail this.

"Eli Valenz." He strode past the secretary and stuck out his hand. "Owner of Eli's Elixirs. Sir, I saw your final match against the Bonekeepers back in Kolkea. One of the best games I've ever seen."

As he had hoped, the orc lit up, suddenly ten years younger. Once a Fireball player, always a Fireball player.

"Thank you." He shook Eli's hand enthusiastically. "Still can't believe we played through that sandstorm."

"I still can't believe how you led that offense," Eli gushed. He didn't have to fake any of this—it *had* been an excellent game. "I mean, the Bonekeepers had the ball, they were up five to nothing, and yet you—"

Ambrose cleared his throat behind them. Eli fought the urge to shove him into the hallway and close the door.

"Right." Rune's enthusiasm dissipated, and he resumed his tired, fatherly slouch. "Apologies, you're both here to discuss the commission. Here, walk with me."

He led them down a hall crowded with boxes of pink silk flowers.

"As I'm sure you know, my daughter's sixth birthday is coming up," he said. Beatrice peered over his shoulder at them with round emerald eyes. She reminded Eli of several of his nieces back home, and he pushed aside a small pang.

"Yes, *very* exciting," Eli cooed, waving at her. She drooled on her father's robes in response.

"Indeed," Rune said flatly. "Well, I'm in need of a specific gift, and my committee says you might be able to help me."

Ambrose stepped ahead of Eli. "Certainly. What sort of potion do you need?"

The mayor turned into a side office, a tiny room filled with nothing but scrolls, boxes, and used candles. As he rummaged through stacks of parchment with his free hand, he fell silent.

After a moment, Ambrose cleared his throat again. "Sir?"

"Oh, right." Rune straightened. "Beatrice wants to be a dragon."

Eli's polite smile faltered. "A, um..." That was impossible. Wasn't it?

"Sir"—Ambrose kept his words firm—"unfortunately, animal shape-shifting brews are far too risky. The Guild strongly recommends against any such experimentation—"

"No, no, I mean..." Rune sighed and shifted Beatrice to his other hip. "She wants to fly and have wings. *Like* a dragon."

Beatrice pulled the lollipop out of her mouth with a pop. "Dragon! I wanna be a dragon!"

Eli vastly preferred the job three seconds ago, back when it was impossible.

"Dragons are great." He threw the little girl a nervous grin. "But sir, you don't mean actual flight, do you?"

"Of course not." Rune dug deeper into a stack of scrolls and uncovered a stuffed rabbit. Its fur had been reduced to patches, and half its ear was missing—but Beatrice didn't seem to care. She shrieked in delight and grabbed the doll with sticky fingers. The mayor's brow smoothed out in relief.

"Just some levitation," he said. "You know, floating, or something like that."

Eli tried to reflect his nonchalance while panic bubbled inside him. This wasn't just a potion. This was two potions in one—three, if he counted the flavoring needed to make it palatable. And for such a tiny subject? The amount of experimentation it would take, the sheer knowledge, was beyond anything Eli had ever done before.

"I can do it," Ambrose said immediately.

Eli clenched his jaw. Of course, he could.

"When do you need it by?" Ambrose continued as if Eli wasn't in the room. Rune stroked his daughter's hair.

"Well, in time for her birthday, so...four months."

The words shattered the last of Eli's hopes. Charm alone wasn't going to get him through that. Back in college, this would have been a year-long thesis, at least.

But he wasn't alone in his panic—next to him, a hairline crack ran through Ambrose's composure.

"Sir," he said, his voice wavering slightly, "I'm afraid that doesn't allow enough time to safely experiment with the components."

"Hm." Rune swung out of the office, forcing them to follow again. "What are your solutions, then?"

Eli's thoughts tumbled over each other. He had no solutions, unless he learned how to clone himself. But if Rune was willing to accept a compromise...

He stepped in front of Ambrose.

"How about just the wings?" he asked, then glanced at Beatrice's shoes. "I could do purple ones. With sparkles."

"Purple wings!" Beatrice agreed loudly, then went back to her lollipop. The mayor grunted.

"I suppose we could..."

"If you wanted only the levitation"—Ambrose took one long stride and eclipsed Eli—"I can certainly do that in four months' time." He glanced at Eli. "Two months, even. It would be perfectly calibrated for someone her size and weight."

Eli glared at him, then turned to Rune. "I could do wings and a tail in two months."

"One month," Ambrose cut in. "I can do the levitation in one month."

The mayor stopped and frowned at the air. Eli held his breath. Pick the wings, he thought, pick the wings—

Rune looked at them. "What if you brewed it together?"

The words hit Eli harder than a Fireball to the face.

"A joint commission," Rune said, brightening at his own idea. "Brew together, split the work. How does that sound?" He directed the last question at Beatrice, bouncing her up and down. As the girl giggled, Eli's stomach flipped. With another potioneer, it could be possible...but did it have to be with Ambrose Beake?

His queasiness must have shown on his face, for Rune waved a reassuring hand. "You both would be paid the same, of course."

"Ah. Of course." Eli nodded; internally, he scoffed. The pay would have to be wildly, no, *stupidly* high for him to agree—but he played along. "What is the pay, sir?"

"Five thousand talons each. A third of the pay upfront, another third in two months."

Oh.

Oh, that was wildly, stupidly high.

That amount would make up for all the red in his ledger. The crystal displays, the workroom equipment, the networking night, the launch party, the wine and the cheese rolls and the ads... Gods, he could even afford to buy more than lentils for the pantry.

Eli swallowed back a dozen curses burning his throat.

"Yes." He met Rune's gaze. "I'll do it."

Next to him, Ambrose stiffened, leaving Eli painfully suspended between hope and dread. If the pompous half-elf didn't say yes—if he squandered the offer just to sabotage him—

"I accept," Ambrose said. Eli froze.

Oh, gods. They were actually going to do this.

"Excellent." Rune gestured back to the secretary. "Tiegan will get the papers drawn up. I'll see you in four months."

He retreated into his office, both his shoulders and Little Rabbit covered in lollipop drool. As the door closed, Beatrice waved to Eli with shiny fingers.

"A joint commission, then?" Tiegan the secretary scribbled addendums on a long sheet of parchment, their hand a blur. Once the paper was covered in notes, they waved a wand, and the writing shifted to accommodate the changes. Another wand wave, and the same text appeared on a second, blank sheet of paper. Lighter, slightly blotchy, but a decent duplicate. "Here you go. Sign at the bottom."

Eli scanned the spindly writing. Temporary simulation of wings. Low-level levitation. Fernberry flavoring.

And all in four months.

He shook his head, signed at the bottom of the paper, and handed it back. Beside him, Ambrose did the same.

"Thank you." Tiegan maintained their perky tone as they took the papers and handed over another splotched copy. "The first payment will be sent to you tomorrow. Have a nice day."

A few minutes later, Eli stood on the sunbaked steps of the government building, watching the bubbling fountain and passing wagons. A shadow fell over him; Ambrose stood at his shoulder, glaring at the same view.

For a moment, they said nothing. They merely let the morning traffic go by until Eli couldn't handle the silence anymore.

"It was five thousand talons," he said. "I had to do it—"

"You think I would have agreed to it for anything less?" Ambrose snapped. "Five thousand is the *least* he could have offered for that timeframe. Four months indeed..."

As he straightened his pretentious robes, Eli pressed his lips into a line. Yeah. Four months with this man, indeed.

"So, what do we do now?" He scuffed his shoe on the step. Any plan he could think of sounded ridiculous. What, were they going to have lunch and brainstorm? Compare notes, share ideas? Stir a blasted cauldron together?

Ambrose rubbed his temple. "Give me a day," he muttered, avoiding Eli's gaze. "I'll...I'll meet you after closing tomorrow night."

The words came through gritted teeth, and Eli couldn't blame him. Just that morning, they had agreed never to talk to each other again.

If only that were still the case.

"Tomorrow night," he repeated, hands on his hips. "Fine."

STEP 12:

TEMPER THE REACTION

Ambrose

WHEN AMBROSE MARCHED into the Whirling Wand Emporium, the place was as busy as ever. Customers wandered about the first floor in fascination; up on the second floor, a rowdy huddle tested out blast wands. Judging by their ribbing jokes and easy laughter, he guessed it was an adventuring party. Normally, their hubbub didn't annoy him —but at the moment, everything annoyed him, so he crossed his arms and waited for an opening to talk to Dawn.

At the front counter, the wandmaker was packing up beautiful little boxes for her line of customers. She tried to cover a yawn with a strained smile—but when she caught sight of Ambrose, the smile dipped into a stern frown. "Hey, punchy."

Ambrose spun on his heel and reached for the door.

"No, no, don't you run away from me—we're going to talk about this!"

He slouched and dropped his hand.

"You stay right there, I'll be with you in a sec," she commanded. Ambrose reluctantly stood by as Dawn turned back to her customer, a short archer laden with leather armor and a longbow.

"You going to the Fireball match this weekend?" the archer asked, then bent to peer at Ember, the salamander napping in a dish of water on the counter. Dawn shook her head and tied a bundle of wand boxes with ribbon.

"I'm busy," she said, her bright tone faltering. Ambrose's focus on his own annoyance broke, and he leaned in to hear the conversation better.

"You tell me if Whitefall's able to beat Sussa this time, all right?" Dawn continued. The archer snorted.

"And break their cold streak?" she said, petting Ember with one finger. The salamander squeezed his eyes shut in delight. "I don't think so."

"Hey, you never know." Dawn waved her off, hiding another yawn behind her hand. "Next!"

"Excuse me," one gnome called from the back of the store. "Could I get some help with this cabinet?"

Dawn's shoulders dropped. Ambrose pocketed his swirling thoughts on the commission, strode forward, and held out his hand. "I'll help. Key?"

As Dawn dropped a small key into his palm, her eyes narrowed. "Don't think this'll get you out of—"

"Thank you." Ambrose took the key and rushed to the back of the store. "All right, sir, which one did you need?"

He met the gnome at the back cabinet of utilitarian wands—small, simple, and neatly categorized. As soon as he approached with the key, the tiny metal circle on the doorframe melted into a keyhole shape, and he unlocked it with a flick.

"Looking for a douser," the gnome grunted. "Something small, to put out campfires."

Ambrose glanced at the tinkerer's pack on his back. "How far do you typically travel?"

"As far as Elwig Forest in the warm months."

"Then you'll want this one." Ambrose plucked a wand from higher up on the display. After years of admiring—and purchasing—Dawn's handiwork, the inventory was as familiar to him as it was to the owner. "This stone can store more charges, and the wood lasts longer."

"Thanks." The gnome inspected the blue spectrolite embedded into the wand's grip. "Are you the assistant?"

Ambrose looked back at Dawn. Judging by her slumped posture, she did need one. Perhaps he should broach the topic of an apprentice with her... "No, merely helping out. Miss Kerighin will see you at the front when you're ready."

Unfortunately, the line of customers remained long, and as Ambrose waited for her, the commission papers grew heavier in his pocket. Four months? For a complex custom potion? With *that* man?

All his anger turned sharply inward. What a fool he was, so easily swayed by Rune and his money. He should have said no. He should have let Eli flounder and sought a commission elsewhere. The Adventurer's Guild, or the sparring pits, or his customers, once they returned from their reckless hunts...

But none of them would ever pay five thousand talons for a single brew.

He continued mentally pacing until the last customer stepped away from the counter. Before another could appear, he strode up and set the cabinet key in front of Dawn. "I need to invoke the power of the birthday committee."

As the key clinked on the counter, Ember looked up from his water dish and blinked. Dawn gave him an equally flat look. "What?"

"I need to speak with someone on the birthday committee," he said. "They need to get me out of the mayor's commission. Well, get Eli out of it. I can come up with a way to do it myself, I know I can—"

Dawn wrinkled her nose and held up a hand. "What are you talking about?"

"Rune turned it into a joint commission," Ambrose said. "He wants Eli and me to finish the potion together in four months." Dawn's eyes widened. "Exactly. Now, who can I speak with?"

Dawn gave a long sigh. "I don't know." She rubbed her hands over her face. "Did you sign the papers already?"

Ambrose faltered. "Yes."

She dropped her hands. "Then I can't do anything for you."

His pulse quickened, and he ran a hand through his hair. "All right. Well—what about someone else on the committee? Could they change the papers?"

"Not legally."

"Would they accept bribes in this circumstance?"

"Ames."

He set his hands on the counter in desperation. "Please, someone must be able to do *something*."

Dawn shook her head and reshuffled a stack of boxes on the counter. "Live with it. This is your punishment for punching Eli this morning."

"How did you know about the—?"

She nodded to the rose statue next to Ember's water dish. The scroll was half-open, revealing a long paragraph of Sherry's looping scrawl. "She said you punched him, then ran off for something. I can't believe you did that—"

"Excuse me, he punched me right back!" Ambrose pointed to the scroll. "Has Sherry told *everyone*?"

"Probably." Dawn pulled the scroll open further. "Grim says they'll need to teach you how to punch and..." She squinted at the writing. "They want to remind you of the street rules that *specifically* say no fisticuffs from six to seven."

Ambrose groaned and buried his face in his hands. He shouldn't have said yes to Rune. He shouldn't have punched Eli Valenz. At this point, he shouldn't have gotten out of bed this morning.

"No one needs to teach me or remind me of anything. I will..." He let his arms fall to his sides. "I will behave."

Dawn's eyebrows rose. "Will you?"

"*Yes.*"

His plan thoroughly foiled, he rested his elbows against the counter and pet Ember's tiny head in a slow, morose pattern. As the salamander squeezed his eyes shut again, the archer's conversation from earlier echoed in Ambrose's mind. "Hey." He straightened. "Why aren't you going to the Fireball game?"

"Hm?" Dawn avoided his gaze and resumed her work on the boxes. It gave Ambrose time to notice the coffee cups littering the space—on her stool, on the floor, half-hidden behind old wand awards. "No time," she said.

Ambrose frowned. Dawn always made time for the games. Snow, rain, hail—she was always there, green and gold glitter painted on her face. "I know you're busy, but I think you should still—"

"I don't have time, Ames," Dawn snapped, then closed her eyes and took a breath. "I'm sorry. After the *Thirty* application, okay? I'll get back to the games after it's submitted."

Ambrose opened his mouth to argue further—but behind him, an elf approached, wands in hand. Ambrose reluctantly stepped away. "I should get back, but...let's get lunch tomorrow." He picked up one of the coffee cups and shook it. "With real food for a change?"

"Sure." She shrugged. "The usual place?"

He didn't enjoy the flatness in her response, but the elf behind him had begun to tap their foot.

"The usual," he agreed quickly and ducked out of the shop, back into the rush of the city. The promise of a lunch had briefly brightened his mood, but it curdled once he rounded the corner. Eli's Elixirs was still there, with its hideous pennants, cheap wares, and hostile owner.

Ambrose sighed. For a brief, wonderful moment, he had been banned from ever going in there again—but, he supposed, all good things must come to an end.

STEP 13:

WIPE CLEAN

Ambrose

THROUGHOUT THE NEXT DAY, Ambrose kept two journals with him at all times. One on his right, where his commission notes puddled into an inky mess, and one on his left, where his list of anniversary upgrades stared up at him.

Just to remind him of why he was descending into this madness.

He scanned the numbers on the upgrade list one more time as a reassurance. Five thousand talons was more than enough to cover everything—the new cauldron, the wand rack, the gemstones...even the sign. Ambrose smiled. If Banneker was still free, he could start it the moment the first payment came in from Rune.

He closed both journals and repeated his mantra for the day: it was only four months. Four months of painful collaboration, and the new cauldron, the new sign, the new all of it would be his. Then Master Pearce would visit and commend him on all the work he'd done, all the ways he'd kept the shop in perfect shape. Perhaps he would even notice the update to the sign.

Ambrose kept telling himself this as he walked across the street, past the point where he had punched Eli the day before, and knocked on the door to Eli's Elixirs.

"Hello?" He peeked through the window. Inside, the only movement came from the rose statue, flashing white in a staggered pattern. He squinted past the flashing to the workroom, hesitantly pushed open the door, and took a few quiet steps inside.

He almost expected the floor to burn his feet in some form of punishment or retribution, but all it did was creak as he walked in. Everything was as he had last experienced it. Crystal displays, bright colors, discount placards. And all around, the ever-present scent of sunlight and lavender.

In the workroom, glass clinked against metal. Ambrose cleared his throat.

"Eli?" he said. "I'm...here for the commission."

The word soured on his tongue, and he gave a small grimace.

"One sec!" Eli called from the workroom, his voice spilling out alongside a plume of red-tinged smoke. After a moment, the man himself stepped out, dressed for brewing a potion at high heat. The slit at the front of his shirt was unlaced, his sleeves rolled up past sturdy, shimmering forearms. He tugged off a thick glove and wiped at his forehead, his shiny black hair sticking up at opposing angles. In all, he reflected as much light as the crystal earrings dangling at his neck.

"Just finishing up in here," he said, his voice rough, almost husky. "Can you wait a minute?"

Ambrose could suddenly feel the heat of the workroom from across the store, and his thoughts lagged in taking in Eli's question. "Fine. I'll, um, review my notes."

He quickly opened his commission notes and tugged at his collar. The cooling spell within the embroidery was supposed to activate in warm rooms such as this—why wasn't it working?

As he flipped through the pages, struggling to absorb the writing, a squealing sound reeled past Eli's legs.

"No, Tom, wait!"

Ambrose glanced at the floor. A beer mug had rolled up to his feet on two squeaky wheels. It stopped, tiny dustpan in forkish hand, then tilted its broom—its head, he realized—upward.

He found the eyeless stare both unsettling and...somewhat endearing.

"Hello?" he ventured. It made no sound in reply.

"Don't mind her." Eli waved his glove. "Takes her a while to warm up to some people."

Then the automaton set down her dustpan and raised her fork arms to Ambrose.

"I, um..." Ambrose swallowed and set his journal on the nearest table. The gesture seemed important to the little thing. "Do you... want to be picked up?"

He placed his hands around the beer mug and lifted her up, holding her at arm's length—her legs were made of knives, after all. As she began to pat his sleeves happily, he frowned over at Eli. "Does she enjoy being held like this?"

Eli was too busy gaping at him to respond. Ambrose turned back to the automaton with a ghost of a smile. It wasn't how he anticipated throwing the man off kilter today, but he would take what he could get. "Her name is Tom?" he continued.

Eli closed his mouth. "Her name is traitor," he muttered. Then more loudly: "Yes. Her name is Miss Tomato the Automaton, or Tom for short. She's been in the Valenz family for years."

Ambrose's smile dropped. To have so much family that a member tagged along, all the way to the Scar...

He set Tom on the floor and watched her roll away to Eli's ankles. "And she won't mind me being in the shop?"

"Apparently not." Eli tugged his glove back on. "I'm bottling up a speed potion. Should be done soon."

Ambrose picked up his journal and approached the workroom with caution. Something about the smoke plumes set him on edge. Speed potions were caustic, certainly, but they shouldn't release so much smoke...

"What sort of speed potion are you—?" He peeked into the doorway, then immediately staggered back, every fiber of his body gone tense. "Blasted dust, what on earth are you doing?"

Eli raised an eyebrow and held up a vial. "I told you, I'm bottling."

But it wasn't Eli's action that sent a horrified shiver up Ambrose's spine. It was the room itself. The cleaning table with missing gemstones, the ingredients stacked close to the cauldron, the smoke gathering in thick clouds at the ceiling...

"No. No, no, no." He could hardly catch his breath—everywhere he looked, the broken safety protocols multiplied. "Where are your goggles? Why are you brewing in a cauldron that large?" He pointed to the ragged cloth above the cauldron. "And how is your fume pull not working?"

Eli shrugged. "Goggles are on back order." He flicked a wand at the fire underneath the cauldron, and it snuffed itself out. "Brewing this large-scale is saving me time—"

"It could destabilize the ingredients!"

"It's got a two percent chance of destabilizing the ingredients at this scale." Eli rolled his eyes. "Fume pull, I just haven't fixed yet." He reached up and tapped the fabric draped across the wooden beams. Like the one in Ambrose's workroom, the embroidery on the sturdy canvas was meant to absorb smoke and fumes—but these stitches were clearly defunct. They refused to glow and simply let the maroon smoke bounce off into the shop.

Ambrose covered his mouth with his sleeve and took a large step back from the room. "I can't work here, I can't. We'll need to use my shop."

Eli glared at him. "Were you always this insufferable, or did that come with your Guild certificate?"

"At least the Guild taught me how not to blow my own head off when brewing a potion!" Ambrose snapped. "You're not even wearing goggles! It's a basic safety measure, Eli!"

Eli mouthed his words in a sarcastic mimic, then tossed his gloves onto the cleaning table. The gemstones clinging to its sides flickered halfheartedly.

"Fine," he said. "I'll clean up and be right over."

When Eli walked into Ambrose's shop, he had changed out of his unlaced tunic and into a fresh shirt and scarlet vest. Though his sleeves were perpetually rolled up, he had tightened the laces at his neck this time. The sight gave Ambrose an odd flicker of disappointment.

"You wanna use your workroom or your flat for brainstorming, Safety Measure?" Eli nodded to the steps. Ambrose swallowed; he wasn't about to let Eli know he only had one chair upstairs.

"My workroom. Let me just..." He grabbed the stool from the front counter and carried it into the room. "Here. That should...um, work..."

After setting the stool down, he ran through a quick safety check of his equipment, if only to ground himself. When was the last time he'd had someone else in his workroom while he brewed? It would have been years ago, with Master Pearce. He could recall his presence perfectly—watery eyes, gruff voice, hardly a break in his frown when Ambrose held up a successful potion...

And his mantra—he who brews alone brews fastest. He had said it so often, it felt almost carved into the stone of the workroom.

Ambrose wiped down his workstation and glanced over at Eli. The man stepped into the room carefully, as if the floor was going to drop out from underneath him. When the floor held, he took the stool, set it farther away from Ambrose, and sat down.

Well. So much for brewing alone.

"You said you had notes?" Eli asked, his tone surly, arms folded.

Five thousand talons, Ambrose told himself. The cauldron, the wand rack, the sign...

"I did." He opened his journal. "I believe it will be easier to split the commission between us if we break down the potion into its three components. The wing illusion, the low-level levitation, and the flavoring. I'll take the levitation, of course—"

"Why?"

"It's the most difficult component, and I'm the more experienced of the two of us."

Eli snorted. Ambrose's gaze snapped up to him. "What? Am I wrong?"

"You're judgmental, is what you are—"

"But am I wrong?" Ambrose repeated sharply. He was not going to be insulted again, not here, not in his shop. "The mind and body link for levitation potions must be precisely balanced, as the consequence of a misaligned brew is nothing short of nerve damage. One of my master potions was a level nine levitation vial, which I received full marks on. And, if I'm not mistaken, I have at least fifteen more years of experience than you." He glared at Eli. "Am I wrong, sir?"

Eli held his gaze, then looked down. "No," he said quietly. "You're not wrong."

A small moment of victory, then. Ambrose turned back to his journal. "So, if you'll let me continue—"

"Wait."

Eli stood up, and fear quickly swept away Ambrose's pride. He shouldn't have gone on that rant. If he chased Eli off, the mayor might cancel the commission. No commission meant no pay, no pay meant no sign—

Ambrose stood as well. "Eli, wait, I—"

"I think we should start over," Eli said. Ambrose stopped.

"I'm sorry?"

"We should start this over." Eli gestured between the two of them. "You know, this. We can't keep going like this if we're going to be working together."

Ambrose blinked. That was...surprisingly rational. "All right, then. How does one start over?"

Eli bit his lip—then his eyes sparked. He set aside his stool, walked out of the room, then turned and knocked on the doorframe. Ambrose frowned. "Come...in?"

Eli walked inside with his usual confident stride and stuck out his hand. "Hello. I'm Eli Valenz. I run the shop across the street."

Yes, that was the entirety of the problem, Ambrose wanted to say.

But Eli was trying, so he supposed he should try, too. He took Eli's hand and shook it, wincing at the lingering pain in his injured fingers.

"I'm Ambrose Beake, and I run The Griffin's Claw."

With a nod, Eli took the stool back and placed it near the work-table. "I hear you have some notes on the joint commission we'll be doing together?"

"Um—indeed." Ambrose sat, then paused. "If you're...willing to hear them?"

He glanced at Eli, who gave a stiff nod. The reintroduction wasn't going to fix any of the past insults nor any of the punches—but it was better than nothing. Ambrose flipped to the next page in his note-book. "So, regarding the first component..."

———

"...In my opinion, the wing illusion should tie to the same mind connection as the levitation."

"Right." Eli was up and pacing the workroom, unable to sit on the stool for more than a few minutes. "That way, you don't have two separate connections canceling each other out or amplifying each other."

Yes, he was getting to that, Ambrose wanted to say.

"Can I see your ingredient list again?" Eli asked. Ambrose handed his list over, and the man scoffed. "Alphabetized, of course..."

Ambrose bit the inside of his cheek to withhold a riposte.

"See, here's the problem." Eli tapped the paper. "Derrin vine will work great for the illusions, but it's not going to mesh with how you're structuring the levitation. You've got calendula seeds on your list, and the oil in that is just going to deactivate the magic in the vine."

Ambrose gritted his teeth—*yes*, he was *getting* to that. "Which is why I've already mapped out how to swap the seeds for dried esther, if you look at the next page."

Eli flipped the page and gave a low whistle. "You sure?" he asked. "That stuff's impossible to work with. I saw a grad student ruin five hundred talons' worth of it just by breathing on it wrong."

Ambrose stiffened. Eli wasn't wrong. Esther was difficult to work with, even for a master. And adapting it for this brew would take hours of experimentation—hours he didn't have between running the shop, generating inventory, moss exploration with Dawn...

But he wasn't about to admit any of that to Eli.

"Once I run a few tests, it will be easy," he said. Eli regarded the list once more, then shook his head and handed it back.

"All right," he said. "I can get the illusion component done in about a month if I work on it after store hours. How much time do you think you'll need for the levitation?"

Truthfully? About six months.

"Six weeks," Ambrose said. Eli's eyebrows shot up.

"You can't be serious."

"I'm very serious."

Eli's gaze went stony. "If you're trying to tank this commission—"

"Absolutely not!"

"Because that's five thousand talons on the line—"

"I know how much it is!" Ambrose snapped. "Now, if the timeline is settled, I believe we're done for the day."

Eli stubbornly held his gaze. "If you need help with the potion, you'll ask for it, right?"

Oh, absolutely not. But what was one more lie between rivals?

"Yes." Ambrose set down his notebook in a final gesture. "Have a good night, Eli."

Eli relented, holding up his hands in defeat. "Good night, Ambrose."

The parting words prodded him with guilt. Eli had been the first one to clear the air, after all. To start fresh, reintroduce himself...

As Eli turned in the direction of his shop, with his broken fume pull, half-working cleaning table, and distinct lack of goggles, Ambrose got an idea for his own way to start things over.

"Wait." He reached for a pair of goggles on the wall, and after a moment of consideration, took off his protective amulet. "Take these. For your workroom."

He dropped both into Eli's palm. Eli slid the goggle strap onto his wrist and inspected the amulet—a polished red gem encased in a network of gold vines, all hanging off a thin necklace.

"A shield spell," Ambrose explained. "Automatically generated, no charge or activation necessary." He pointed to the gem. "It's Grim's handiwork, so you can trust it. Anyway, I thought you could use it in your workroom."

Eli's grip on the necklace tightened. "Because you think I'm gonna blow my head off brewing the potion."

Ambrose backtracked. "No—no, that wasn't what I was trying to say!"

"No, I get it." Eli headed for the door. Ambrose followed, his cheeks burning.

"I realize how that sounded. Can I—can I start over, too?"

"How many of these are we gonna do?"

"What? *You* got one!"

Eli stopped at the front door, then shook his head and turned around. "Okay. You get one do-over, too."

Ambrose straightened. "All right. May I have the amulet back for a moment?"

Eli sighed and dropped it back into his palm. Ambrose rubbed his thumb over the delicate gold detail, still warm from Eli's touch, then cleared his throat. "Mr. Valenz, I am obligated to maintain your safety through the duration of the joint commission, per Guild rules. As such, I am offering you this shield amulet for you to utilize when you brew." He held out the amulet one more time. Eli's look remained flat.

"Because my workshop sucks."

"'Living nightmare' is the phrase I would use." Ambrose held it out farther. "Please, I only meant it as a peace offering."

Eli weighed the amulet in his palm once more—then slipped it over his neck. "Thank you."

"You're welcome."

Eli crossed the street and hunched back into his shop. Ambrose deflated.

This was going to be a long four months.

STEP 14:

KEEP STIRRING

Eli

ELI CAREFULLY ALIGNED his gaze with the edge of the counter.

"Fireball MVP Eli Valenz lines up the shot," he muttered, carefully setting a cork on the counter with one hand. "Thirty seconds left in the match." He set his other hand behind the cork. "He shoots..."

He flicked the cork across the counter, right between two tall potion bottles.

"He scores!" Eli threw up his hands. "Forty-four in a row! Folks, I can't believe it!" He grabbed another cork from the bucket on the floor. "He's gonna go for forty-five next, breaking the regional record. Can he do it?"

Eli closed one eye. Assessed the slight dent in this new cork, then tilted it to account for the shape. Flicked again.

The cork bounced off the bottles and careened away.

"No!" Eli tipped his head back. "His chance for a record blown. Oh, his stats will never recover from this..."

He looked around him, where forty-five corks lay scattered across the shop floor. Tom veered around them, carefully brushing them one by one into her dustpan. As she tried to scoop up the next cork, three tumbled out of her pan, and she looked at Eli with an eyeless glare.

"All right, all right." Eli trudged over to the crates sitting untouched near the workroom. "I'll unload the bottles now."

He peered into the boxes, where a line of sparkling potion bottles lay couched in straw and cloth. Infused with protective resin and painted with lovely orange swirls, these bottles were a step up from what he typically used—and it was all thanks to the mayor's commission money. He set his hands on his hips. He should unpack them now, fill them with potions, stock the window displays with his shiny new wares...

He turned on his heel and grabbed another cork instead.

"They don't call him the comeback kid for nothing!" He bent in front of the counter again. "He's making another go at the record. Will his training pay off?"

He only made it through six corks this time. When the seventh ricocheted off the bottle and plunked straight into Tom's beer mug, he groaned and set his forehead on the counter.

It would be a lie to say he didn't know how he'd gotten here. Earlier that day, he had decided to close early, as a treat for getting the mayor's commission. Then he had bought groceries—real groceries, with fruits and vegetables and everything—as another treat. After that, he had considered unpacking the bottles...and tended to his window garden instead. Then oiled Tom's wheels. Then invented this riveting new game for himself.

What he didn't understand was why he didn't want to unpack the crate. It should have been rewarding after such a victory with the mayor. It was five thousand talons, a high-profile commission, food and new bottles and black in his ledger. He should be thrilled to show it all off, to fill those vials and stack them in the window where everyone could see.

He went over to Tom and fished out the cork. Perhaps that was his problem. "Everyone" these days had shrunk down to Tom and his customers. He needed to break up the repetition—meet more people in the community, go on a date or two. Find a girl or guy to unwind with, then come back with fresh energy to brew, restock, unpack bottles...

And the Rosemond Street meeting was tonight, he told himself. That would be a decent start. Besides, he needed to get back into the street's good graces after punching one of their own.

As he cleaned up the corks with renewed determination, the speaking stone on the front counter glowed twice. He jogged over, tapped the stone, then checked the pocket watch next to it. Dammit —he was almost late for the street meeting.

So much for a decent start.

"Hey, Ma!" he shouted at the stone, then rushed back to the corks. "How's it going?"

"Good! What are you late to this time?"

Eli groaned. How was it possible for mothers to know everything, even when they were hundreds of miles away? "Street meeting at Grim's place. I gotta get there in five minutes."

"Mhm. And what else are you doing?"

He slouched. "Cleaning."

"And?"

"Unpacking bottles..."

"And?"

"...Well, I was supposed to dust tonight..."

"Love," his mother said firmly, "finish the cleaning. The dust and the bottles will be there when you get back."

"Thanks, Ma."

"I know how you get." Her voice was tinted with her smile. If he had been there in person, she would have given him a hug, for sure, one that smelled of sandalwood and the flowers she tended to every day. His heart hurt just thinking about it.

"How's the shop?" she asked. He dumped the corks back into the bucket.

"Great." He tried to keep his tone as upbeat as possible. "Really great."

Another voice jostled for attention. "Hey—*hey*, have you kicked that guy's ass yet?"

Eli grinned. Lily.

"Please tell me you've patched that up," June said. His grin faltered. He *had* kicked that guy's ass—but he couldn't tell Lily about the fight, not with their mother nearby.

He could, however, tell them about the commission.

"About that, I, uh…" He swiped the goalpost bottles off the counter. "I'm actually doing a joint commission with him. With Ambrose, I mean. We were commissioned by the mayor last week."

"By the *mayor?*" June gasped. "Honey, that's amazing! Incredible —see, you're already getting recognized for your talent."

Technically, it was Ambrose's talent that was going to get him the money. There were principles in the half-elf's levitation breakdown that he would never have thought to apply, much less bend in the ways that Ambrose did. It had been like seeing one of the man's papers being written in front of his eyes—both fascinating and utterly infuriating.

"And this commission is with Ambrose, you said?" June continued. "Is he cute?"

Both Eli and Lily groaned.

"Come on, Ma—"

"I'm just asking!"

Then Banneker passed by his shop and waved. Eli bit down a curse and waved back. "Sorry, I gotta go. Talk to you in a few days?"

But his mother was still crowing about the commission. "Just think of the commissions you could get after this one! Oh, they'll come rolling in. You could set yourself up for years on those."

A familiar, nauseous feeling crept up at the word *years.* Years of unpacking bottles, years of brewing, years of dusting, over and over…

Muffled chatter grew across the street, and he stamped down the thoughts.

"Yeah, sounds great, Ma. Gotta go."

"Love you!"

"Love you, too." He flipped the river stone twice, then rushed outside and crossed over to Grim's shop.

The enchanted jewelry store was an amalgam of heavily secured cases, chunky furniture, and deep, glittering colors. Imposing, but comfortable after a while. Grim stood behind the glass counter, a loupe in hand—but their focus was on a talkative gnome in mage's robes, who stood on her tiptoes to talk to them over the counter.

"I really can't thank you enough, Grim," she bubbled. "Those earrings you made worked just as you said they would. Saved my partner from that river kraken, and it's all thanks to you—"

"Happy to hear it." Grim's tone hardly changed from their normal grunt, but there was no mistaking the proud glint in their eyes. "Though as I said, I don't need any sort of reward." They caught sight of Eli and paused, their voice hardening. "Valenz."

Ever since the fight, Grim had regarded Eli with a certain wariness. Not worry, like Sherry, or shock, like Dawn. It was a mild suspicion, a watchfulness suggesting that if Eli had been the one to throw the first punch, he would have found his shop torched that same evening.

"Hey, Grim." Eli waved. "I'm here for the—"

"Go on up." Grim nodded to the stairs. "Sherry made cookies. We'll get started in a few minutes."

"Sounds good." Eli ducked his head and jogged up the steps.

The upstairs flat was just as dark and comfortable as the shop, leaning into the earthiness of a living space built into a chasm. Sherry and Banneker had made themselves at home on a lumpy green couch that threatened to swallow them whole. Dawn was sprawled on a neighboring armchair, tugging a thick crocheted blanket over herself. Everyone was cozy except for Ambrose, who sat upright on a wooden chair next to Dawn.

It was the first time Eli had seen him since their brainstorming session. After that night, Ambrose had taken to locking himself in his workroom again. He didn't leave his store, and the second-floor lights didn't flicker on until late at night. But in person, he appeared as stoic as ever, with only a hint of gray circles under his eyes to betray his efforts.

Ambrose briefly met his gaze, nodded, and turned back to Dawn.

"Dude of brew number two!" Banneker called with a loopy wave, then refocused his attention on Sherry. They were deep in a debate over a noodle stall, so Eli took the opportunity to admire Grim's wall decor. Most of their displays involved artwork of the mountains above Hart's Fenn—the location matching their rumbling accent—but one framed piece stood apart from the collage of pine and cloud. It was a detailed pencil sketch of the Rosemond Street merchants, carefully preserved behind glass.

Eli inspected each figure in the drawing. If he peered only at Grim and Banneker, he would have guessed this sketch was done yesterday—but one look at the others told him otherwise. Sherry had longer hair and fewer wrinkles. Dawn was shorter. And Ambrose... Yes, there he was, at the far end, standing next to a sour-faced old man.

Ah, so that confirmed it. Ambrose had always had those high cheekbones and piercing eyes. If he had bothered to smile, he would have looked better. Softer. Maybe even a little cute. But his face in the sketch was serious, like always. Eli tilted his head—a little too serious, for someone that young.

He looked over at the old man standing stiffly next to Ambrose, their poses mirror images of each other. Hadn't Dawn said something about his mentor, back in her shop?

"All right, find your seats," Grim called as they ascended the steps, flipping through a packet of papers. Eli took the spot next to Banneker and Sherry on the carnivorous green couch. Sherry immediately leaned around Banneker to inspect Eli's jaw.

"How are you, dear?" Her eyes narrowed at the spot where Ambrose had punched him. "All healed?"

Eli wanted to say that there had been hardly any bruise to heal—but he swallowed the words and nodded. "I'm fine, Sherry. Thank you."

"Good." Her lips pursed in disdain, and guilt sank into him. He didn't care what Ambrose thought of him—but he didn't want the others to think he ran around punching people. He'd have to get back in the street's good graces somehow.

"I believe we're ready." Grim stood in front of the hearth, papers in hand. "Banneker, are you taking minutes?"

"Sure am." The elf tapped his temple. "Right here."

Grim gave a long sigh and ran a finger down the page. "First, I have some housekeeping updates."

The updates were generic, as far as Eli could tell. Street cleaning was shifting days. Magical waste pick-up fees were due in a month. The city's structural check of the walkways had been delayed another week.

"And the water inspection." Everyone groaned. Grim held up a hand. "I know, I know. The city's going to do their inspection soon, but the community check of the cistern needs to happen this month. Dawn and Ambrose had agreed to it last time." Grim raised their eyebrows. "Are you both still up for it?"

Ambrose nodded silently. Dawn hummed her assent. "We'll do it," she said, her enthusiasm weak.

"Are you sure?" Sherry asked, passing her a cookie. Eli had the same question. With her lids drooping and form curled in on herself, Dawn looked far more tired than Ambrose did. "You'll need to have your wits about you in those tunnels," Sherry warned.

Dawn took the cookie. "We'll be fine."

As Sherry's lips pursed once more, a thought struck Eli. Ambrose wouldn't like the idea, but then again, Ambrose was never going to like anything he did.

"I could go with them," he offered. "Keep an eye out for things, learn the process."

"That's not necessary," Ambrose cut in first, as he predicted. "The tunnels are perfectly safe—"

But both Sherry and Grim brightened.

"Thank you, Valenz," Grim said, crossing an item off their list. "That's a good idea. It'll be safer with the three of you."

"But..." Ambrose tried. Grim glanced at him, and he clicked his jaw shut.

Once the remaining topics were complete and the floor yielded no further questions or protests, the room broke for tea.

"Grim, you got any coffee?" Banneker leapt to the kitchen. He made a beeline for the cabinets, while Grim and Sherry shuffled over more slowly, passing the plate of cookies between themselves. It was a comforting routine to witness, and Eli let himself relax on the couch. A nice end to the evening, as long as he didn't think about the bottles he had to get back to...

Over in the armchair, Dawn twisted toward Ambrose. "So, how's your joint commission going?"

Someone dropped a cup in the kitchen.

"Joint commission?" Sherry repeated. "With whom?"

Ambrose's face flushed, and he immediately tried to leap out of his chair. Dawn quickly threw her blanket over him like a net, and it trapped his arms before he could begin his sprint in earnest. Eli couldn't help but snort. Ambrose shot a glare at them both.

"What's this commission?" Sherry leaned over the back of the armchair, eyes wide. Ambrose struggled to free his arms; Eli rolled his eyes and stood up.

"Ambrose and I are doing a joint commission for the mayor," he explained. "A potion for his daughter's birthday."

Sherry lit up like a beacon. "Congratulations!"

"Wait, dude of brew one *and* two?" Banneker poked his head out of the kitchen. "For real?"

Grim stood there in disbelief, kettle in hand. "Beake is working with someone?"

Sherry turned to Ambrose. "See, I knew you could apologize. And collaborating with him, too, how wonderful—"

"It's not—*I'm* not—" Ambrose finally threw the blanket to the ground. "I have to go. Terribly busy."

He shot down the stairs. Sherry gave a resigned huff and looked at Eli. "How's the potion going?"

"Early days still. Ambrose took the hardest part, of course." He glanced at the stairs. "He hasn't said yet if he needs help."

Grim rolled their eyes. "The Deepriver will boil before that happens."

Sherry hummed in agreement. "You'll be hard-pressed to get him to admit it." She waved a hand. "What with that brewing alone thing."

Eli frowned. "I'm sorry?"

The whole room chorused in a bored monotone. "He who brews alone brews fastest."

"I'm surprised he hasn't mentioned it," Sherry said. "It was all Master Pearce ever said."

She glanced at the sketch on the wall, and as her eyes landed on the old man next to Ambrose, Eli caught the sharp edge of hate in her gaze. It was so strong, he almost flinched.

Then she turned back to him, all sunny smiles again.

"Ah, well. He'll come around in his own time," she said. "Will *you* be a dear and tell me more about the commission?"

Eli forced a smile back. "Gladly."

STEP 15:

TIPS & TRICKS

Eli

AFTER THE STREET MEETING, Eli unwrapped his new bottles and made a pact with himself to step outside the shop every day. Not just for groceries and coffee, but to breathe fresh air, see new faces. Stare at something other than his own reflection in the bubbling commission potion.

He grabbed any opportunity he could find. He tried a new pastry stall and made friends with the owner. Grabbed Banneker and Sherry to visit a new tavern and scheduled a date with the barmaid. And every time, he came back and threw his remaining energy into the shop. Into the commission, inventory, filing, cleaning...

But each time he ventured out of the shop, he found it harder to drag himself back in. Watching his potions change color no longer mesmerized or relaxed him. Every dinner, date, and dinner date ended in a low, gray haze of dread, and he tried to stay out a little longer. Just one more drink or one more dessert...

Which is how he found himself sitting with Dawn at the Jumping Ogre a month later, begging her not to leave.

"Come on, you haven't even been here a half hour," he said. A half hour was generous—she had barely been there fifteen minutes before she got up to go. He leaned over the table and poked at her mug. "And you promised to stay for a full drink with me."

Dawn already had one foot out of the booth. "I'm busy."

"You're always busy," he whined, then gave her an overly pleading look. "Please? One more round of Pick-a-Stranger with me?"

Dawn tried to stand strong against his puppylike gaze—but her lips twisted into a smile, and she slid back into the booth with a sigh.

"All right. One more." She gulped down her drink. "And then I *really* need to go."

As it turned out, Eli wasn't the only one on Rosemond Street who made up silly games now and then. Once Dawn drained her mug, she leaned back against the booth, covered her eyes with one hand, and raised the other to Eli, three fingers splayed. "Pick your poison."

He tapped the finger on the left, the one sporting a bright pink ring. She smiled.

"Okay, I pick as your *soulmate*..."

"Oh, come on."

"Your *beloved* soulmate, the one you will love forever and ever..." Eyes still covered, she raised her hand, then pointed across the tavern. "That person."

Eli looked over. Dawn peeked out from behind her fingers.

She had pointed directly to the bard at the bar: a man with long braids, a smooth smile, and a lyre tucked under his arm. As he ordered his drink, he leaned casually on his stool, flirting easily with the ladies surrounding him.

Eli rolled his eyes. "Come on, you peeked."

"Did not!" Dawn picked up her coat. "He's cute, though. I dare you to ask him out."

"Switching up games, are we?"

"Ooh, deflecting, are we?"

As Dawn pulled on her coat, Eli reluctantly pushed away his drink and stood up with her.

"Bards aren't my type," he said, helping her with her coat sleeve. Dawn tapped her chin.

"What is your type, then? Perhaps a more strapping lad or lady?" She squeezed his bicep. "You are going to be protecting us in the cistern, after all."

Eli groaned. He had forgotten all about that. "Is that this week?"

"Yup."

Eli held the door open, and they stepped into the frosty autumn air together. "What is a cistern inspection, anyway?"

"Oh, it's easy," Dawn said. "You just walk through the tunnel and make sure nothing's caught in the filtering sieves. Otherwise, the place can flood." She let out a long, slow breath, watching the air curl into a white wisp. "You sure you've got time, with the commission?"

"Like you're one to talk about time." Eli nudged her. "Yeah, I'm good. Just need to get unstuck on the potion."

The thought of it weighed down the dread already clinging to his steps, and he slowed his pace.

"Unstuck?" Dawn repeated.

"It's this—I'm having a hard time combining these components..." Eli started, then waved away his words. "It's dumb. I won't bore you with it."

"You know who wouldn't be bored by it?" Dawn nodded down the street toward The Griffin's Claw. Despite the late hour, the main floor was still lit in a warm, hazy glow. Eli groaned. When he had made a pact to see people, he had not meant for it to include Ambrose.

"What?" Dawn said. "If it's for the commission, he has to help!" She covered her eyes with one hand and pointed to The Griffin's Claw with the other. "I pick as your wise sage..."

Eli tried to point her hand away from the shop. "No—"

"Don't move it, that's cheating!"

"I don't wanna!"

"But the fates have decreed it!" She dropped her arm. "And so did those commission papers you signed."

Eli made an exasperated noise and trudged over to his own shop. "Fine. I'll get my notebook." He paused at the door. "See you at the inspection?"

"Mhm." Dawn trundled off. "And ask out that bard!"

Eli talked himself into the journey as he walked over to The Griffin's Claw, notebook in hand. This would be good, he determined. He would model asking for help. Show the man it wasn't that hard, even though he himself had just whined about it two minutes ago.

"Ambrose?" he called as he opened the door. Both Ambrose and a customer at the counter looked over at him, and he veered off toward the displays, hand raised. "Sorry, sorry. Don't mind me."

Ambrose gave him a nod, then turned back to the after-hours customer—a young orc sporting a medic's armband, bouncing impatiently on her heels.

"So, that's three bone-knitting, two bruise-mending..." Ambrose jotted the purchase down in a ledger, his voice soft and steady. His gaze flicked to her armband. "How far are you traveling?"

"The Vineheart."

Without a blink, Ambrose reached under the counter and pulled out a leather case, beautifully tooled and oiled. "Use this to keep the vials out of the sunlight. They'll last longer that way."

The orc ran her fingers over the leather strap. "How much?"

"Nothing. Guild policy for emergency workers." A card materialized in his hand. "And show this to any Guild-licensed shop along the way. They'll give you half-price refills."

The orc's eyes went wide. "Are you sure?"

"If they give you any trouble, tell them Master Beake sent you"—he pushed the card and the leather case toward her—"and that should be the end of it."

As the medic thanked him profusely and rushed off with her healing potions, Eli raised his eyebrows. Something told him Guild policy wasn't quite that generous.

Ambrose flipped his ledger closed and folded his hands. "What do you need, Eli?"

The question was stiff but not surly. Eli supposed that was a kind of progress.

"I have a question about the commission," he said. "Unless you're busy or...?"

Part of him hoped Ambrose would dismiss him, but the half-elf shook his head and came out from behind the counter. "What is it?"

Eli reluctantly opened his notebook. "I'm trying to combine scion's bane and minced reaver as the base for the illusion, but every time I do, they coagulate at the bottom of the cauldron. I've tried everything. Could you...?"

He gingerly held the notebook toward Ambrose, who crossed the store in a few strides and took it. "This page here?"

"The dog-eared one, yeah."

As Ambrose's eyes traveled down the page, Eli tensed, steeling himself for gloating or judgment. Already, he could feel a line of sharp words gathering on his tongue in defense.

But Ambrose merely gave a thoughtful hum.

"I see your problem," he murmured. "It's the derrin vine. The magic the bane releases won't react properly to the reaver if the vine is already present. But you have to add the vine first, or else...hm. Let me think about this." He strode toward his workroom; Eli hesitated, then followed.

Ambrose must have been brewing before the medic showed up—a potion still simmered in the cauldron, a ticking pocket watch floating in the air next to it. A book also lay on the workstation, with a ribbon marking his place.

"So, if you're adding the vine in step three..." Ambrose mumbled and stirred the cauldron. Now that his back was turned, Eli leaned over to peek at the book.

He had assumed it was an alchemic journal, or an encyclopedia, or whatever the man read at night to unwind. So when he caught sight of an illustration on the cover—a shining knight in intricate, embossed gold—he stifled a surprised laugh.

Sir Terrance and the Windfallen. He'd read that novel a dozen times as a kid.

This clearly wasn't Ambrose's first read-through, either. The spine was scuffed, the ribbon frayed. And this wasn't book one, but book three in the series.

Eli grinned. Ambrose Beake, icy know-it-all, read cheesy adventure novels.

He leaned farther to examine the ribbon's placement. Ambrose was about halfway through the story, which meant Sir Terrance was likely still stuck in the Wilting Woods, about to meet the forest dragon who—

Ambrose turned around, and Eli quickly drew back.

"Here's what you should do." Ambrose plucked a quill from his workstation and scribbled on a scrap of paper. "After adding the derrin vine, sift three teaspoons of cleansed sea salt into the cauldron and stir clockwise six times. No more, no less. That should keep the reaction stable." He tucked the paper into Eli's journal and handed it back to him. "Was that all you needed?"

Eli looked at the paper, expecting some sort of scholarly drivel— but it was perfectly clear. Orderly script, simple steps, even a crisp diagram explaining the method. With this addition, Ambrose may have saved him days of wasted ingredients and fruitless experimentation.

"This is great," he said. Ambrose frowned, and Eli held up the paper in reassurance. "No, really, I mean it! Thank you for this."

The sincerity caught Ambrose off guard—his frown dissipated, and he ducked back toward his cauldron. "Well, it's my responsibility to help," he mumbled.

Eli glanced back at the shop door. He knew he should leave and let Ambrose sink back into his hiding spot...but his gaze fell on the book again, and he couldn't help himself. "So, who's your favorite character?"

"What?"

He pointed. "*Sir Terrance and the Windfallen.* Who's your favorite?"

"Oh." Ambrose glanced at the book, and the tips of his ears went pink. He quickly tried to cover the novel with his papers. "I'm not— this potion takes a while to brew, you see, and this was just the reading material I had on hand—"

Eli rushed his words. "No, it's okay! I love that book!"

Ambrose paused. "You do?"

"Yeah, I read it to my sister all the time. Lady Ree was my favorite character. You know, the one with the warhammer?"

"Yes, I know." Ambrose let slip a ghost of a smile. "She does have the best fight scenes."

They stood there in silence, Ambrose twisting his signet ring, until Eli cleared his throat and jerked a thumb toward the street. "Well, I should get going. Thanks again for the help."

"Tell me if the salt doesn't work." Ambrose began to organize the papers he had thrown over the book—then his hands slowed. "And... it's Corie."

Eli turned. "What?"

"Corie's my favorite character," he said. "The farmer on the outskirts of the Wilting Woods."

"Huh." Eli tilted his head, mentally paging through the series. Corie had no magic or weapons. She just let the heroes stay at her house after their battles.

An odd choice, but he should have expected that from Ambrose.

"I can see that," he faltered. "Enjoy reading. And, um..." He paused at the doorway. "You know it's my responsibility to help, too, right? With the commission?"

Ambrose nodded. "Of course."

Then he was bent over his cauldron again, stiff and silent. Eli sighed and jogged back over to his shop. When he opened the door, he found Tom at the window, fork tines set on the glass. She looked up at him and pointed to The Griffin's Claw.

"No, he's not coming to visit, you straw-brain," he said gently, then picked her up and carried her into the workroom. Why she had attached to that man, he had no idea. "I'm gonna have to get your stones checked."

STEP 16:

STRAIN

Ambrose

AMBROSE REACHED for Dawn's teapot. "Another cup?"

"Please."

They were back in their favorite café, running the waitstaff ragged with multiple orders of cinnamon cookies and lemon cake. Their running joke was that if they were going to die in the cistern with Eli that day, they were at least going down with full stomachs.

But even as they joked, Ambrose kept a watchful eye on Dawn and her fourth cup of tea.

"How have you been this week?" he asked. She twirled a flower petal around her drink.

"Fine."

"Dawn."

"It's just..." Dawn sighed and let her spoon clatter against the side of the cup. "I was supposed to work on this fire wand last night, but...I don't know, I just stared at it. For an hour."

"Fire wand... You mean the commission for that hunting trio?"

Dawn groaned. "Yes."

Ambrose's heart sank. That had been one of her recent emergency lunches—she had been so excited about the commission, her gestures almost whacked a teapot across the room.

Dawn reached halfheartedly for the sugar. As Ambrose handed her the bowl, he parsed his words carefully. "I know you're busy, but I think you should take a break this week—"

"I can't afford to," she snapped. Ambrose drew his hand back quickly. He hadn't parsed his words carefully enough.

"I've only got a few months left," she continued, dumping sugar into her tea. "I can't afford to be lazy."

Ambrose bristled. Dawn was many things, but lazy was never one of them. In fact, he'd gladly learn how to throw a real punch if anyone ever called her such a thing. But saying so would only set her off more, so he pressed his lips into a line and let her steer the conversation.

"I think it's the moss," she muttered, nodding to the waiter for the bill. "If I can just find the moss, I'll be fine."

After they left the café, Ambrose fell in line next to Dawn on the walkway. Despite the pleasant sunbeams and lack of crowds on the third level, Dawn's pace was unusually brisk and unyielding.

"You wanted to search the sinkhole for the moss, correct?" Ambrose ventured. "Would you feel better if we put that on the calendar? Made a day of it? I could ask some of my customers if they'd be willing to accompany us."

Dawn waved a hand. "Adventurer fees are too expensive. We'll just go at night."

Ambrose stumbled on the downward ramp. "Night?"

"Too many foraging monsters during the day. And the moon'll have to be full, to chase the nocturnal ones away. But you're right, we should put it on the calendar." She bumped his arm with her shoulder. "It'll be fun."

Ambrose gave her a weak smile. He very much doubted that—but the idea had brought some light back into Dawn's face, so he nodded and followed her into Widdershins' Books.

Here, both of them settled into a more relaxed silhouette. No matter the weather outside, the air in the bookshop always remained cool and crisp, with a welcoming waft. They fell quickly into their bookstore routine: check out the new releases on the left, wander over to the romances in the back, and loop around to the scientific journals at the front.

"Nothing new from the Shieldbreaker series?" Dawn called from the romances. Ambrose shook his head.

"No." He turned away from the new releases shelf. "Don't know why I keep looking. The author's never going to finish that series, anyway."

He joined her in the romance section, where the wooden bookshelves were painted a rich maroon. Garlands of white silk flowers hung from hooks on the ceiling, and Ambrose toyed with them as Dawn read saucy sentences from books at random.

"He looked at her lustily with great lust—"

Ambrose passed a hand over his face. "No. Please, no."

Dawn's eyes glittered. "I'm gonna buy it. We *have* to read this chapter out loud over wine."

"And cheese?"

"And cheese."

As they neared the scientific journals, Ambrose reveled in the success of this outing. Dawn was feeling better, he had found a new book to buy, and there had been no mention of the—

"So, is that commission still causing you trouble?" Dawn asked. Ambrose slumped.

"Yes," he muttered. He had spent the past week cursing at dried esther petals, trying every possible method to wrestle them into his potion. But like bog bones, esther was particularly sensitive to heat, light, humidity... He had even picked up a petal the wrong way, and it had crumbled to useless dust in his hand.

And that was *after* hours of research on how to work with the blasted ingredient.

Dawn smiled. "And how's Eli doing with his part?"

Ambrose's mood snapped.

"That awful man"—he gestured with his new book—"keeps stopping by and asking me if I need help! Apparently, he's only days away

from finishing his part of the potion, so he *has time*." He put the last
two words in air quotes. The offer had made him feel something
funny, which he could only assume was something bad. "He was
probably just there to brag about it, right? Or spy on my work. Or—or
distract me from my inventory—"

Dawn's bubbling laughter bounced around the shelves.

"What?" He frowned. "What's so funny?"

"Ames, it's *okay* for someone to be nice to you."

Ambrose straightened. "He wasn't being nice! He doesn't like me!
You know, I don't think he even likes Corie!"

"Who?"

"Never mind." Ambrose held his book closer to his chest. He
knew he shouldn't have told Eli who his favorite character was. It had
been a stupid mistake, a silly slip of the tongue.

"Come on." Dawn slid her arm around his. "It's time to go meet
the mean man at the cistern."

On the way to the cistern entrance, Ambrose conceded a few things
—a *few* things—about Eli Valenz.

One: perhaps Eli wasn't actually bragging about his part of the
potion after all. Perhaps he *was* genuinely offering to help. Not that
Ambrose needed it, of course. Living in a cauldron for twenty years
had at least afforded him that advantage.

Two: it was...possible...that Eli wasn't spying on him, either. He
had no reason to; he brewed plenty on his own, and never the higher-
level potions that Ambrose excelled in.

And as for distracting him—

"Hey!" Eli called. "This is the entrance, right?"

Ambrose looked up and froze.

Eli was, in a way, distracting him.

The man stood in front of Dawn's shop, a large stone disc by his
feet. The disc was pulled out from the ground, revealing a smooth,

vertical tunnel and a wooden ladder descending into the depths beneath the chasm.

But it wasn't the tunnel that had stopped Ambrose in his tracks.

Eli appeared to be dressed for mild combat. As he folded his arms, a brown leather jerkin stretched across his shoulders, making them look broader than they already were. Leather bracers hid his strong forearms, thankfully, but the polished shield strapped to his back highlighted his silhouette. Ambrose followed the trail of glowing light from his jaw to his biceps, then down to the sword strapped at his thigh. And were Eli's pants tighter than usual? They seemed tighter than usual—

"Someone came prepared!" Dawn grinned. Eli gave a sheepish shrug and adjusted the sword at his side. Ambrose tried hard not to stare at his hips.

"Sherry caught me on the way over here and practically threw this stuff at me," Eli said. "Told me to look after you both."

"I thought she might." Dawn touched the rim of the shield. The metal flashed, and Eli's eyes sparked with gold. "I should never have told her about the larva in the construction tunnels... Ames, you have the inspection report, right?" She looked up. "Ames?"

"Hm?" Ambrose dug in his pack, grateful for the excuse to turn his burning cheeks away from both of them. "Yes, I picked it up from Grim this morning."

As he retrieved the paper and clipboard, Dawn tossed two glass baubles into the hole. Once the baubles fell into shadow, they brightened and floated around the ladder, providing her with light as she descended.

"I...um..." Ambrose fumbled with the clipboard, refusing to look at what earrings Eli had paired with today's tight leather. "I'm sorry you got dragged into this. I did try to tell them it would be fine—"

"Hey, I volunteered." Eli smiled. "I'm happy to help."

Ambrose hurried down the ladder before Eli could see his blush.

STEP 17:
TOIL & TROUBLE

Ambrose

AMBROSE QUICKLY DESCENDED into the darkness, the swirling air cooling his face. Once his heels struck the stone floor below, he adjusted the pack on his shoulder and joined Dawn at the mouth of the cistern.

Unlike the rugged construction tunnels of past adventures, this pathway was completely humanoid-made, all clean lines and stark angles. Overall, Ambrose found it comfortingly straightforward: the smooth path running straight along the canal, the rigid stone columns lining the route. The only disorderly element was the canal itself, where a barely contained river glittered wildly in the lamplight.

But the river wasn't why Sherry had thrown armor on Eli.

"Ah." Eli stopped at the base of the ladder and craned his neck upward. "Okay, I get what Sherry meant."

Ambrose followed his gaze to the ceiling. While the floor was clear to navigate, the shadowy arches above had been claimed by something else entirely. Soft, pillowy webbing blanketed the ceiling like snow, providing a downy resting place for dozens of massive cocoons. Ambrose could just make out their oval shapes broken by long, sharp spikes.

A light breeze rippled through the tunnel, and above, the cocoons swayed gently. Ambrose stiffened and grabbed Dawn's arm. They both remained frozen until the cocoons stopped moving.

"Burrowing moths," Dawn said to Eli, her gaze still fixed on the ceiling. "They'll hatch in a month or so. Blind and deaf, but if they sense something on the webbing, they'll defend themselves."

Ambrose swallowed. *Defending themselves* was a rather gentle phrase for what they did.

But behind him, Eli looked unfazed.

"I've run into these before," he said. "In the Kolkean Ridge. Those big ones"—he pointed up to the larger silhouettes, heavy and dark— "is there poison in the spikes, or acid?"

"Acid. The spikes explode on impact."

Ambrose shivered. Eli shrugged.

"How bad is the webbing?" he asked. "Anything on the path, typically?"

"Civil service clears it out every season." Dawn extricated herself from Ambrose's grip. "If it still isn't safe, they ban the community checks."

She delivered the last phrase to Ambrose, who realized he was still half reaching for Dawn's arm. He cleared his throat and pulled a pencil out of his pack.

"The sooner we begin, the sooner we can leave," he said tightly, then led the way forward.

As required by the community check, he stopped at every metal sieve in the canal, checking for blockages and ensuring each safety rune was unlit. Eli and Dawn, however, eventually tired of the routine and wandered ahead.

"Is the shop doing better?" Dawn asked. Ambrose kept his eyes on his clipboard, expecting to hear one of Eli's usual jokes or breezy comments.

"It's fine," was all he said, his tone fractured and forced. Ambrose dared a glance up—there was no smile on Eli's face. Dawn's brows knitted together in concern.

"But you got the commission." She nudged his arm in encouragement. "And those new bottles look gorgeous! You've gotta be thrilled."

"It's not that. It's..." Eli rubbed the back of his neck. "Never mind, I'm just being dumb. The shop's fine. Good, I mean. The shop's good."

Ambrose frowned. Eli's shop *was* good, wasn't it? He had constant foot traffic, consistent sales. Ambrose would know—his ledger still had to contend with them, even with the mayor's money.

He leaned in to hear more, but Eli quickly whisked the conversation away to happier things, and Ambrose returned to the inspection. Jotting down minor debris on the next sieve, noting patches of rust around the runes...

But his gaze kept drifting curiously to Eli. Despite his apparent shop troubles, the man had a certain confidence about his step here, a swagger now that he had a sword and shield in hand. And it didn't help that walking behind him allowed Ambrose an opportune view of his—

He shook his head and refocused on the clipboard's mundane checkboxes. It wasn't that he'd never seen handsome men before. Handsome adventurers and medics came into his shop all the time, and he always remained perfectly professional with them. Even when they strode in with their swords, and broad shoulders, and tight leather...

His grip tightened on the pencil. It didn't matter that Eli looked good in armor. He was a coworker, an associate. Nothing more. Besides, how could he like a man who didn't like Corie, of all people? Ambrose scoffed internally. No, Eli liked Lady *Ree*. Loud, obnoxious, brash. It made perfect sense.

"You know, I still think you should've asked out that bard," Dawn said, hip-bumping Eli. Ambrose rolled his eyes. *That* made perfect sense, too. He could picture it now. A charming woman, maybe a singer, who smiled and loved small talk and went to networking events or something—

"Nah." Eli waved a hand. "I don't think he would have worked out."

Oh.

Oh, a charming...man.

Ambrose suddenly felt lighter, then quickly batted away the feeling like a balloon. No. No, Eli was *annoying*, he was *obnoxious*, he was—he was running out of synonyms—

"Ames, did you mark off that sieve?" Dawn pointed to the silver mesh straining the canal behind him. "Looks all clear."

"Um." Ambrose blinked at the clipboard. He had missed the last three sieves.

And to make it worse, Dawn was smirking. Godsdammit, she knew. Of *course*, she knew; she could read him like a romance book from Widdershins.

"Here, I got it." She wandered back, took the clipboard from his hands, and winked. "You go on and check the next sieve with Eli."

He had no words to describe how much he did not want to walk next to Eli right now—but Dawn was already several paces behind him, and Eli waited several paces ahead.

Ambrose huffed and fell into step with Eli.

They walked silently for a while, more careful with their steps the farther they went. The cocoons' downy threads were thicker here, with patches of white swaying from arches and piling up on columns. Though most of the webbing was trimmed away from the path, a few curtains fell at eye level here and there. Ambrose took extra care in ducking around them, almost grateful for the excuse to focus on something other than Eli and the silence between them.

But he should have known the quiet wouldn't last forever.

"What potion did you bring?" Eli pointed to the green bottle at Ambrose's hip.

"A healing vial, to be safe," Ambrose said. See, he wasn't the only one who could come prepared. "Level eight."

Eli stopped and stared at him. "Level eight? For a *cistern* inspection?"

Ambrose stopped and gestured to the cocoons above. "I'm sorry I don't feel like getting my bones dissolved today!"

Eli rolled his eyes. "Oh, come on, for that kind of toxicity rate, you need a level six, max."

"That's a funny way of saying, 'Thank you for thinking of my health, Ambrose.'"

"Boys!" Dawn called. They both started walking again, staring ahead of them.

"You're right," Eli mumbled. "Better to be safe than sorry. I shouldn't have made fun of it."

Ambrose shifted his shoulders and nodded, but Eli's gaze lingered on the vial, more words clearly at the tip of his tongue.

"Can I ask a question?" he finally said.

"About the potion?"

"No, about you."

Ambrose looked at him.

"I thought I'd ask permission," Eli added hastily. "Since you didn't like questions at the mixer."

Ambrose wanted to say no, to walk the rest of the way in silence. But Eli was...trying to be civil to him, he supposed. He could try as well.

"Yes," he said. "What is it?"

"It's just—level eight brews are so..." Eli tapped his fingers on his sword as he searched for the right word. Ambrose tensed, his mind filling in the blanks for him. Showy? Unnecessary? Pretentious?

"Impressive," Eli said. "I mean, even my professors messed those up. Did your mentor really teach you all that?"

Ambrose met his gaze and found a hint of something unfamiliar —something like admiration.

He looked away quickly.

"Yes," he said. "I—I never went to any school. I learned everything from Master Pearce."

"What was he like?"

Dawn's voice crashed in, sharp and sour. "He was awful!"

Ambrose flinched at the sudden edge in her voice. Eli looked back at her, and Ambrose quickly tried to cover her words. "Don't mind her. She never really liked Master Pearce."

"There was nothing to like!" she called back. But Eli kept his gaze on Ambrose, waiting for his response, so Ambrose shoved his hands in his pockets and kept walking forward. "He...wasn't the warmest person. I'll give her that," he said quietly. "But he was smart. Incredibly so. He taught me everything I know about potions, about the store." His mind traveled back to the few, rare occasions when Pearce had shown affection. He had brought him a cake for his birthday, once. Helped him when he had a fever that one winter. Ambrose drew himself up. "I wouldn't be here if it wasn't for him, and for that, I highly respect him."

"Understood," Eli said. But his brown eyes continued to search Ambrose's face, like he was looking for more to the story. His gaze was both too soft and too piercing, and Ambrose scrambled for a way to deflect it. Get the man talking about himself, he thought. That would take his attention away.

"May I ask a question?" he asked.

"Sure." Eli's eyes didn't waver. Ambrose grabbed the first thought that came to mind.

"Tom," he said. "You said she followed you to the shop. Did your family not need her help back home?"

Eli laughed, a warm sound that bounced around the tunnels and through Ambrose's ribcage. "Don't tell Tom I said this, but her little dustpan isn't much help in the desert."

"Ah." Ambrose flushed at his own stupid question—but Eli didn't seem to mind. In fact, he relaxed as he spoke, his strides slower.

"She's just fun to have around," he said. "Though Lily wanted to keep her. Tried to hide her from me the day I left for the Scar."

"Is Lily your sister?" Ambrose ventured. Eli nodded. "Your only sibling?"

Eli snorted. "Not even close. I'm one of five."

A deep pang burrowed in Ambrose's stomach. He folded his arms against his chest to quell it. "Really?"

"Yeah. Felt like one of ten, sometimes. Our house isn't all that big." Eli smiled. "But they might come to see me soon. Lily tells me every week she wants to visit."

The pain shot deeper. What must that be like, to have family members who wanted to visit? Who spoke of it often?

"That must be nice," Ambrose said softly. "To have family."

Eli looked at him.

"To visit, I mean," he added quickly. "It's just that—Kolkea's not close by. I imagine they'd have to take a griffin, or—or a series of wagons..."

Too late—Eli was searching his face again. Very clearly putting two and two together.

Ambrose had said far too much.

"Well, I should inspect the sieve up ahead," he blurted out and strode forward. See, this is why he didn't engage in conversation. Civility simply did not pay off. "Last one, I think. Then I'll need to get the report to Grim and—"

He turned a corner too fast, unthinking, focused only on the ladder at the end of the tunnel.

His face met directly with a fluttering patch of webbing.

"Augh!" He gave an involuntary shudder and leapt back, swiping at his face and spitting out threads from his lips. "Disgusting, get it off!"

"Ambrose?" Eli called, turning the corner behind him. "You all right?"

"I'm fine." Ambrose wiped at his cheeks. "As long as the..."

His eyes followed the web upward as it swayed. It had only been a light brush, surely—the horrifying motion would stop soon.

But the vibration continued. Up the column, along the archway, into the ceiling. Then far above, where the light didn't reach, something large and round began to shiver.

He froze, his mind going blank. He only had a healing potion, and Dawn's shield wand was on her belt, yards behind him. Should he move? Would moving only make it angrier?

The cocoon rattled harder, and Ambrose's hands went cold. He should move, he *had* to move now, but fear cemented his feet to the floor, he couldn't take so much as a step—

"Ambrose!" A hand grabbed his collar and yanked him backward.

A second later, the cocoon came crashing down, a shuddering mass of spikes and acid. Ambrose flinched, his eyes screwed shut against the inevitable pain—but the acid hissed and splattered against metal instead.

"It didn't get you, did it?" Eli asked. One hand was still on Ambrose's collar, the other holding his shield in front of them. Wisps of smoke rose from the metal, and black liquid dripped onto the floor. Ambrose pressed a hand to his chest to calm its wild beating.

"No, it didn't," he breathed. Footsteps slapped against stone behind them.

"Ames?" Dawn skidded around the corner, wand at the ready. "I heard it fall—oh, gods." She took one look at the puddles of goo and turned away, her cheeks grayed. "I can't look at it, I'm gonna hurl."

"It's okay." Eli regarded the path behind them. "Listen, let's just go back the way we came and—"

The cocoon started to crawl back up the threads tethering it to the ceiling. Dawn shrieked and staggered away; Ambrose reached for her.

"No, don't—"

Too late. Dawn's foot sank into a pillow of webbing at the base of a column. She yanked her foot back, and they all held their breath.

Above, another cocoon rattled.

"Dawn!" Eli shouted and swung his shield around. Dawn raised her wand out of instinct. As the second cocoon came flying down, a filmy pink shield burst out around her, throwing the black acid in all directions. Hissing smoke rose from the magic dome, the stone floor...and the column next to her, covered in webbing.

Rattling filled the air.

"Run!" Eli pushed Ambrose toward the first cocoon, still rising toward the ceiling. They veered around it in a scramble, no longer caring about stray threads or curtains of white. Cocoons dropped all around them, black goo eating into the walls, the floor, the columns. Eli kept his shield in front, and Dawn pointed hers toward the back. Ambrose crouched shakily between them, cursing himself for not bringing something more useful.

"Almost there!" Eli said, throwing an arm out to keep Ambrose from stepping into an acid puddle. Behind them, Dawn gagged and trailed behind, a hand over her mouth. Ambrose turned to Eli.

"She needs to get out now," he said. "She's got a shield of her own. Can she run ahead?"

Eli quickly assessed the cocoons scattered between them and the ladder—some coming down, some lifting up. "It's narrow, but she'll make it if we time it right. Dawn, here." He pulled her forward and set a hand on her shoulder. "Keep the shield wand up and run through when I say so."

Her eyes went wide. "Are you crazy?"

"One...two..." When the cocoons rose above her height, he pushed her forward. "Go, go, go!"

Dawn sprinted, keeping her wand held above her head. Acid splattered every which way, and Ambrose held his breath—but she made it to the ladder unharmed.

"Can you throw the wand?" Eli shouted. Dawn reeled back and threw, but the uneven weight of the wand flung it wide. Eli leapt and caught it with one hand.

"Here." He handed the wand to Ambrose, then turned back to reassess the ever-moving cocoons. "All right. If we stick together, we can get through the rest of them. You ready?"

Ambrose looked to the smoking puddles ahead—between the liquid and the vapors, he could hardly see a free path. "*No.*"

Eli took his arm. "Come on, it'll be just like"—he gestured with the shield—"uh, dancing or something."

"I hate dancing!"

"Okay, sorry, bad comparison—"

A cocoon shuddered behind them. Eli lifted his shield and dragged Ambrose forward. "Come on!"

They wound through the cocoons and puddles, Eli with his shield on one side, Ambrose with his wand on the other. His hand shook, but Dawn's craftsmanship remained strong, not even flickering as acid hissed and spat on the magic dome.

"Almost there," Eli said at his shoulder. "You're almost—"

Ambrose's heel slipped on a puddle, and he flailed backward with a shout. He closed his eyes and braced for impact. With so much acid around him, he was going to burn as soon as his head hit the—

An arm caught his back, shoving the breath out of his lungs.

"Sorry!"

Ambrose had no time to ask what that meant. Eli hoisted him up, pulled him to his chest, and spun to catch the next cocoon with his shield. Ambrose flinched on instinct, burying his face into the oaky leather at Eli's shoulder—then they were off again, Eli half leading, half carrying him in a frazzled, dangerous waltz.

Eons—or perhaps only seconds—later, they collapsed at the end of the tunnel. Eli's arm slipped off of Ambrose's waist, and behind them, the cocoons fell still again, leaving a tang of smoke and burning metal in their wake.

"See?" Eli laughed breathlessly, a half-wild look in his eyes. "Just like dancing."

"Oh my gods." Ambrose rested his head against the stone wall, his limbs shaking. "How could you find any of that fun?"

"Oh, come on, it was a little—"

Eli tried to stand, then staggered and caught himself on the ladder, face twisted in pain. Ambrose sat up straight.

"What is it?" He guided Eli back down and knelt to inspect his lower legs. Sure enough, the cocoons' acid had eaten holes above his boots, and blood was spreading quickly across the ripped fabric.

"Shield didn't catch everything," Eli said through gritted teeth. Stomach lurching, Ambrose yanked the healing vial off his belt and shoved it into Eli's hand.

"Take it. Drink half to start."

As Eli drank, Ambrose forced himself to watch the wounds. If the potion worked right, the wounds would disappear in less than a minute.

Eli let out a string of Kolkean curses and flinched, nearly kicking Ambrose. Ambrose grabbed his shoulder and pressed him against the wall. "Please, just a bit longer."

He held his breath, counted down in his head, then gingerly released Eli's shoulder.

"Should be done. Let me see..." He bent and tried to check the wounds, but couldn't see past the blood. Swallowing, he dipped his sleeve into the canal, then held onto Eli's ankle and carefully wiped the blood off his skin.

No wounds remained—just a lingering bruise, as he had hoped.

"How do you feel?" Ambrose asked. Eli stared wide-eyed at his own legs.

"It..." He slouched against the wall. "It feels like it never happened."

"Good." Ambrose sighed in relief, running a hand through his hair. "I've never actually seen these formulas in action before. I was hoping the process would be less painful for you. I can try to tweak the recipe to add some sort of numbing effect..."

"Hey." Eli's boot nudged his knee. He looked up to find the man smiling. "Thanks for thinking of my health, Ambrose."

Ambrose's cheeks went warm, and he gave him a small smile back. "Well, I couldn't have my coworker dissolve before completing his part of the potion."

Eli tilted his head. "So kind of you."

Ambrose stared at Eli. He looked more rugged here—hair messy, a sheen of sweat over his forehead, his pants ripped. In short, he looked more handsome than when he had entered the tunnel.

Eli stood and offered Ambrose a hand up; he fought down a blush and took it.

"Come on." Eli nodded to the opening above the ladder. "Let's go see how Dawn's doing."

But when they reached the surface, four faces stared down at them.

"Oh, thank the gods—"

"Are you injured?"

Hands pulled Ambrose off the ladder and to his feet, allowing him a full view of the small crowd. Sherry stood there in full metal armor, a hammer at her side. Grim had one amulet around their neck and another in their hand. Banneker was halfway through clasping a copper hand cannon to his forearm.

Ambrose glared at Dawn, fourth in line with a healing wand in hand. "Did you call *everyone* on the street?"

"You were taking too long!" she argued. "I got scared and hit the rose alarm at my place—"

"We're all right," Eli called from the ladder. Without any trembling or fear, he hoisted himself up and casually dusted off his bracers. The only remaining evidence of their plight were the bloodstains on his legs. Sherry looked down at them and gasped.

"Did the acid get you?" She bent down to inspect his wounds.

"I'm all good." Eli patted her shoulder. "This guy's pretty good at brewing potions, if you can believe that." He smiled and handed the half-empty bottle back to Ambrose. Their fingers brushed, and Ambrose went pink.

"Yes, well..." He cleared his throat. "Speaking of that, I should probably get back to my shop."

"Sure you don't want to rest, Beake?" Grim frowned. "You don't look so good."

"Grim's right." Banneker tilted his head. "You sure you're okay, my man?"

They all stared at him. Ambrose's flush deepened. "Nothing a cup of tea can't handle, I assure you," he said, edging toward his shop.

"I'll make some tea for you," Sherry offered. "All of you, in fact. And you can stay as long as you like. I can't imagine the stress you must have been under..."

"Thanks for the offer," Eli said, then looked down at his jerkin. "I have to return all this to you, anyway."

His fingers reached for the lacing at his neck. Ambrose spun away, cheeks blazing.

"I don't need tea, I'm fine!" he blurted out and hurried off. Apart from the usual resigned sighs, no one tried to stop him. Sherry turned to Dawn, and Banneker to Grim.

But Ambrose could feel Eli's eyes on his back the entire way.

STEP 18:

MAKE A BREAKTHROUGH

Eli

SEVERAL DAYS LATER, Eli stared listlessly at the sign on his shop door. There was no getting around it—the word *Open*, painted in bright red letters, made him feel nauseous.

He had no distractions to carry him through the day, either. No upcoming dates, no Fireball games, no deliveries coming in. Just another day of brewing, opening the shop, restocking, closing the shop, then more brewing. Again, and again, and again. Forever.

He reached for the sign. He should open; he *had* to open. He had taken last night off, hoping he'd be refreshed in the morning.

And yet here he was, feeling like he wanted to throw the sign into the deepest part of the chasm.

Tom rolled up on squeaky wheels and looked at him.

"I'm gonna do it," he argued. "I just need a minute."

Or an hour. Or a day.

He shook his head and trudged into the street, the word *Closed* still facing outward. A day was what he needed. Just one more day to rest, and he'd be back at it tomorrow.

As Eli feared, his day away from the shop was his best in months.

He wandered around the upper flower market first, gladly losing himself in the colors and scents. Then two levels below, he grabbed a spot in a café and simply sat for a while, sipping coffee and letting the day pass by.

His focus eventually settled on the sculptor across the street, who was carving a new relief into the rounded corner of Redbranch Avenue and Sunrise Alley. As he watched, she applied exquisite, swirling details to a massive dragon head. Judging by the direction of its flames, it was locked in a battle against a cluster of humanoids, all atop armored griffins and dragon mounts of their own.

When the sculptor wiped dust off her brow and paused for her own cup of coffee, Eli wondered what it would be like to be such a creator. Changing the chasm with just his hands, forming art that would remain long after he had passed. But he was no artist, so his thoughts wandered to the café owner, chatting with other customers at the front counter. Then to the messenger that rushed past, a mail sack bouncing at their hip. Then to the spice merchant across the street, the wagon driver rolling by...

Eli rubbed his face and sighed. This was a familiar mental rut for him. Back when he was a tanner's assistant, he was jealous of the farmers. When he was a farmer, he was jealous of the griffin keepers. And so on and so forth until...

Well, until he found himself running a potion shop on Rosemond Street.

"Another cup?" The waiter stood in front of him, a steaming pot of coffee in his hand. Eli nodded miserably.

"Thanks."

After his second coffee, Eli wandered up to the Elwig Market on the fourth level, a crowded, open-air clutter of stalls and shouting merchants. He had intended to waste time here like he had at the flower market—but when he passed by the crystal and herb booths, his mood sank again. They reminded him of the ingredients he needed to buy, for the potions he needed to brew, for the shop he needed to run...

With the two cups of coffee now churning in his stomach, he plodded up to a booth selling seeds.

"Hi, how's it going?" He tried to smile at the merchant. "Could I get ten ounces of crushed peplum seeds—?"

Someone bumped lightly against his arm.

"Oh, apologies." The tall figure stepped away, then paused. "Eli?"

Eli looked up—Ambrose was at his shoulder, a shopping basket hanging loosely from his elbow. Here in the market, without his robes and notebooks, the half-elf looked more relaxed. His hair fell gently over his forehead, and light from the awning cast a filtered glow over his face. But his eyes were still alert, bright and piercing as they searched Eli's face.

For a brief moment, Eli's mind jolted back to their last interaction in the tunnel. Ambrose's fingers trailing his ankle, his firm hand pressing on his shoulder, looking up at him with the same piercing gaze...

He shook away the image—that coffee must have been stronger than he thought.

"Hey." He gestured halfheartedly to the pots of flowers. "Just buying some stuff for the commission."

Across the table, the seed merchant—a round-cheeked orc with a stained apron and animated eyebrows—gave Ambrose an enthusiastic smile.

"Mr. Beake! Lovely to see you, as always," she said, leaning over the flowers. "How's Dawn doing? I haven't seen her in ages."

Ambrose gave the tiniest wince. "She's been quite busy, I'm afraid. But I'll tell her you asked after her. She'll appreciate it."

The merchant reached back for a jar. "Twelve ounces of poppy seeds, like normal?"

"Yes, please."

As she waddled off to get their ingredients, Ambrose turned back to Eli, fidgeting with his basket handle. "Is...everything all right? You're usually open today." He glanced down at Eli's legs. "Are the bruises bothering you? They can last for a while. I'm sorry, I should have provided a follow-up vial to handle those—"

"No, you did great." Eli held up a hand. "Can't feel a thing."

It took no exaggeration to reassure Ambrose. He may have felt a little odd after the cistern adventure—almost bubbly, likely from the adrenaline or the potion—but the bruises had disappeared by the end of the day.

"Oh. Good." Ambrose's gaze lingered on him, then quickly shifted away to the merchant bearing two jars in hand.

"There's your twelve ounces of poppy"—another bright smile for Ambrose—"and there's your ten ounces of peplum, Mr. Valenz."

Ambrose held his jar up to the light, gave a small nod, then glanced at Eli's jar and tilted his head. "May I?" He held out a hand.

"Um—sure?" Eli frowned and handed him the jar, tensing again. What, was Ambrose going to judge him for his choice in seed? Criticize the number of ounces?

"Do you have any peplum that's brighter in color?" Ambrose held the jar out to the merchant. When she blinked at him, he quickly added lightly, "He's my associate. We're working on a commission together."

Eli stared at him.

"Oh." The merchant took the jar. "Yes, of course. Give me one moment." She shuffled off and returned with a second jar, the powder twice as bright as before.

"Color indicates the strength of the magic in the peplum," Ambrose said when Eli held the powder up to the light. "That batch should be more effective for you."

"Thank you," Eli murmured in wonder. Not at the scientific principle—he understood that, of course.

What he didn't understand was Ambrose's generosity.

"Hey, wanna come with me for the rest of my errands?" He gently elbowed Ambrose. "That leatherworker keeps giving me the stink eye every time I go over. They might like me better if you come along."

The leatherworker also might like Eli better if he stopped casually flirting with their daughter—but Eli didn't see the need to mention that.

Ambrose glanced out toward Rosemond Street. "I'm afraid I have to get back, but...tell them about the commission with me, and they should give you a better deal."

"Will do." Eli looked around at the other stalls, already mentally planning where to pepper in Ambrose's name. "Hey, how's your commission work going, by the way—?"

But Ambrose had already slipped into the crowd, basket in tow.

Eli tried not to dwell on him too much, but as he went about using Ambrose's name at every stall, it was impossible not to. Perhaps he was acting strange because he felt bad about Eli's wounds at the cistern? He *had* been concerned about the bruises, after all.

And yet even that concern seemed unusual, and as Eli walked back to his shop, he sifted through his memories of their cistern adventure. Before the cocoons, they had talked together a little. About the potion, about Tom, about his family...

An uneasy feeling rippled through him. Where was Ambrose's family? As far as Eli could tell, he received no visitors, no personal packages. He never left town. He barely left the shop.

Was he really raised by Master Pearce?

The thought unsettled him further. Sherry didn't like Pearce. Dawn didn't like Pearce. Even Ambrose had admitted he wasn't the warmest person.

Suddenly, bits and pieces of the potioneer were beginning to make sense.

Eli's gaze drifted from his shop to Banneker's next door. He had to run an errand there, anyway. Might as well settle his questions while he was at it.

"Banneker?" He opened the door. "You in?"

If Eli thought his own store was structured to trap customers, Banneker's was designed to keep them wandering for years. It was difficult to even find a path between the cabinets, crates, and scraps of metal lying everywhere. Even the beamed ceiling was cluttered with whirligigs and pieces of automatons, all floating or hanging from twine. The collection of shiny metals tinkled gently as Eli picked his way through the shop, careful not to bump his shins against an errant cannon.

"Hey!" Banneker popped up by the back wall of shelves, sliding along a wheeled ladder until he reached the sales counter. When the ladder creaked to a stop, he hopped off and leaned against the wood, brushing some screws away to make space for his elbow. "My dude of brew number two, what's new?"

Eli grinned despite his mood. "How much do I have to pay to be dude of brew number one?"

"Can't buy my heart like that, my man." Banneker dug around behind the counter. "I'm still working on your speaking stone, but you wanna pick up your goggles? Just finished them this morning. Sorry the parts took so long to come in—I heard the griffin transport workers went on strike."

He pulled out a box, flipped the latch, and opened the lid to reveal the goggles: gleaming brass and leather, anti-fogging gemstones studding the edges. Eli carefully lifted them out of their plush setting, resisting the urge to run over and show Ambrose. See? He could follow safety protocols just *fine*.

"Love them," he said. "Now I can return the ones Ambrose lent me."

As he set down the goggles, Grim shoved the front door open with their hip, a stack of crates in their arms. "Where do you want these crystals, Banneker?"

"Oh, you know, anywhere." Banneker waved. Grim shook their head, stepped over a mini-cannon, and made their way toward the back of the store. They looked over Eli's shoulder as they passed by.

"Upgrading your goggles, Valenz?" they asked.

"You could say that." Eli closed the box. "My current ones aren't really mine. Ambrose lent them to me until these came in."

"The boy lent you something?" Grim set down the box and tilted their head. "Huh."

This gave Eli an odd sense of pride, and he fished his borrowed amulet out from under his shirt. "He lent me this, too. It's a shield amulet, right? He said you made it."

Grim squinted at the jewel. "S'mine, all right. Made that for him when he got his master's certification. Check the back."

Eli turned over the amulet. On the back of the gold casing, inscribed in tiny letters on a curving vine, were the words: *For A. Beake, CPM.*

He slipped the necklace back under his shirt, his cheeks warming. This had been no small peace offering, and he had taken it as an insult.

"I'll give it back to him," he said quickly. "I didn't realize—"

"Oh, I've never worried about him actually needing it." Grim chuckled proudly. "The boy's careful as anything. He's not going to destabilize a potion anytime soon."

Banneker snorted. "It's the one good thing Pearce taught him."

Eli slipped the goggles box under his arm, then paused, tapping his fingers on the lid. "What was Master Pearce like?"

All the warmth in the shop vanished. Banneker straightened and stopped smiling. Grim folded their arms, brow furrowed.

"He gave Beake a career," they muttered. "That's the best any of us can say about him."

"You want me to cover the worst? I'll do it." Banneker hopped back up on the ladder, one arm gesturing in a sharp, wide arc. "He was awful! Had no idea how to raise a kid!"

Grim jabbed a meaty finger down on the counter. "He had no business."

"Had no right!" Banneker slid down the shelves and threw a screw into a box. "Remember that time he accidentally locked Ames in the shop?"

Eli froze. "He *what*?"

Grim grunted an affirmation. "Kid was in there for three days. We didn't realize it until I saw Dawn throwing apples at the upstairs window." A pause. "She had a good arm."

"And he couldn't even remember Ambrose's name!" Banneker slid back, ladder wheels squeaking. "Didn't deserve him, I swear..."

"Why?" The word slipped angrily out of Eli's mouth. "Why'd he stay? Why didn't he leave? Why didn't you all take him or something?"

Grim shook their head. "We tried. We tried for years. But the boy wanted to learn potions." They rubbed their stubble, their gaze growing pained and distant. "So, we looked after him as much as we could."

"But...but he was just a little kid..." Eli trailed off. Suddenly, his snipe about living in a cauldron for twenty years didn't sound so clever.

Another memory flashed through his mind, an older one this time—one of Ambrose's face, shattered in anger, in the moment leading up to his punch.

"I have to go," he said, his grip tight on the goggles box. Banneker leaned on the counter once more.

"Hey, you're still coming to dinner with us tonight, right?"

The words barely got through to Eli. "Sure, sure."

"Tell Tom I say hi!"

Eli ducked out of the shop, unlocked his own store, and went straight to the workroom.

That evening, Eli strode back out into the street, a finished vial in his pocket and two cups of coffee in his hands.

"Watch the shop while I'm out, yeah?" He turned back to Tom, who gave him a salute, then pointed over to The Griffin's Claw. Eli rolled his eyes, ducked back in, and gave her a quick head scratch. "I'll bring you over later. I gotta go help him first."

That was both the beginning and end of Eli's plan. Bring his part of the commission to Ambrose, along with coffee, and insist that he help with the esther. At this point, it was the least he could do.

"Ambrose?" He walked into the shop, making sure to clear his throat before he reached the workroom door. "Can I come in? I'm headed out soon, but I wanted to stop by..."

Ambrose's shadow made a small jump, and metal thunked against wood.

"Um..." A muffled curse and swish of robes. "Yes. You may come in."

Eli cautiously pushed the door open. This was not Ambrose at his best. His shoulders sagged, shadows weighed down his eyes, black ink was splattered all over his hand. As he ran his fingers through his hair, he left a splotch of ink on his forehead, highlighting how pale he had grown.

"Apologies," he mumbled. "I know I said I would be done with this in six weeks. I really thought my last method would work, but..."

The vial suddenly weighed heavily in Eli's pocket—he didn't want to appear like he was boasting about his accomplishment while Ambrose suffered.

"I wanted to show you the wing illusion I brewed." He placed the yellow vial on the counter, then quickly flanked it with the coffee cups. "And help you. With the levitation part, I mean."

Ambrose ignored the coffee and held the vial up to the light. A wing-shaped charm sat at the bottom of the glass, releasing orange eddies into the buttery liquid. "You were able to keep the reactions stable?"

"Finally got it to behave." Eli let a bit of excitement slip into his voice. He couldn't help it—this was his best work yet. "Grim helped me with the charm. If I keep it in there for another day or so"—he tapped the glass—"the draught should remember its shape."

Ambrose gave a small smile as the liquid tossed a bright caustic over his cheek. "Impressive. This should work well."

Pride ballooned in Eli's chest. Good, he had anticipated. Very good, he had hoped for. Impressive, he had not expected.

He gave a noncommittal shrug. "Thanks. When do you want to test it out?"

Ambrose's smile dropped, and he set down the vial. "We should wait to test the components together to ensure the mind link will work."

Eli saw his opportunity. He pressed one of the coffee cups into

Ambrose's hand, grabbed the stool from the corner, and plopped himself down on it. "Then I better start helping you out. What can I do?"

Ambrose blinked at the coffee. "But—you already made your component. To ask you to do more would be rude."

"You're not asking me, I'm offering. Drink some coffee first, then tell me what I can do to help."

Ambrose took a reluctant sip—and immediately closed his eyes and gave a soft, blissful moan.

"Where did you get this?" he asked, then took another swig. Eli stared at him, mouth open, replaying the moan over and over in his head. The sound knocked his brain askew, and his thoughts veered into strange territory. Were Ambrose's eyes always that blue? Did his hair always fall over his face in that way? Why did Eli have the urge to brush it back? What was happening to him?

Then he remembered Ambrose had asked him a question, and he waved at the street. "Um—got it at Jack and the Beanstalk, the stall one level up. It's...it's really not that good. Have you eaten anything today?"

Ambrose shook his head, drained the cup, and began to clean his workstation. Eli folded his arms and pushed aside his previous thoughts. Ambrose was handsome. Fine. That was allowed. But Eli couldn't focus on the man's face right now, not when Ambrose was finally accepting a modicum of help.

"I think it might be beneficial if you read out the steps," Ambrose said. "If you have time, that is. Grim said they had a dinner with you and Banneker?"

"I've got some time." Eli scooted closer. "There's a dumpling place they wanted to try tonight."

"Ah. What kind of dumplings?" Ambrose asked, pulling premeasured ingredients from the cabinets. A small pile of bottles quickly grew on the worktable. "Scarrish? Elwig? Kolkean?"

Eli wrinkled his nose. Scarrish dumplings were too thick and heavy, Elwig too strange in their fillings. To think that there was a stall entirely dedicated to jam and cream-filled dumplings... It turned his stomach. "Kolkean. But let's be honest, they're not gonna serve them like my ma can."

"I see." Ambrose nodded. "Have you tried the Desert Rose on the third level, near the government square? Dawn loves that place."

As he bent to add more wood under the cauldron, Eli reviewed the recipe and lined up the ingredients in the correct order. "Yeah, I've been there with her. Not enough chili paste."

"What about that stall on High Vine?"

"Too much chili paste."

"Ah." Ambrose straightened and reviewed the neat line of ingredients. "Thank you."

Eli stepped back. "Did I get the order right?"

"I believe you did." Ambrose tilted the vials up to read the labels. "I suppose you could always ask your family for the recipe."

Eli was too proud of his contribution to hear the words. "Hm?"

"Their dumpling recipe," Ambrose repeated. "You mentioned you talk to them every week. I'm sure they could share it with you."

"Oh, sure. But I can't right now, Banneker's fixing the speaking stone. Damn thing cut out five minutes into our conversation a few days ago, and I can't get it to work." A pang of homesickness struck him, and he absently rubbed his collarbone. "Family's probably wondering what happened."

"Oh. I'm sorry." Ambrose shifted over to his journal. "I'm sure they'll be happy to hear from you once Banneker's done."

For a moment, he stared at his notes, looking at them without reading them. Then he shook his head and tapped the paper. "This next experiment shouldn't take long, if you're able to stay for it."

"You mentioned your last method didn't work." Eli read the notes over his shoulder. This close, he could smell the rain-like scent of esther on Ambrose's robes. "What are you trying tonight?"

Ambrose flipped back and forth between several pages. Eli caught brief glimpses of lists, notated lists, notations on notated lists... "Well, you see, my last experiment broke down at step fifty-seven—"

"Fifty-*seven*?"

"So, I made a tweak to that step. If my calculations are correct..."

He flipped back to the clean list at the end of the notes. "This should work."

Eli gaped. "How long will this take you? Three days?"

"Fifteen minutes, if I time it right."

Eli searched Ambrose's face for any hint of a joke. There was none.

"Across all accounts, the key to using esther is speed," Ambrose continued. "Give it a spare moment at any point in the process, and it will fall apart. Every successful brew utilizing esther is brewed in ten minutes or less."

Eli was almost afraid to ask his next question. "And...how many tests of this have you done so far?"

Ambrose glanced up at the ceiling. "This will be...one hundred forty-seven."

"One hundred—?" Eli grabbed his shoulder. "Gods, man, I've left you here to—to *torture* yourself—"

"Not if I get this right." Ambrose tapped the notes and gave Eli an unhinged smile. "Then it's publishable torture."

Eli let go of him in awe.

"Now"—the madman folded up the sleeves of his robe—"if you could put on a pair of goggles and read out the steps, that will allow me to move faster."

Eli started to sweat. "Oh, I think I'd just slow you down here. I don't want to mess up test one hundred forty-eight—"

"I'm afraid it's too late now." Ambrose took a wand and lit the fire under the cauldron. "First step is to pet the cat."

Eli let out a calming breath and read through the notes. "No, it says the first step is to preheat the—"

Ambrose walked past him and rubbed a small bronze cat on a shelf. It took Eli a moment to realize what the cluttered pile of knick-knacks really was. "Is that a lucky shelf?"

"It is." Ambrose straightened. "You know it?"

"'Course I do. My aunt has one in her shop." Eli smiled. Seeing Ambrose stand resolutely next to the bronze cat was an unexpected delight. He reached forward to rub the bright spot between the cat's ears. "Okay, first step done."

If only the other steps were easier. Ten seconds in, Eli could hardly keep up with Ambrose's pace. His hands moved too quickly; ingredients were chopped, poured, and sifted in a blink. Both their voices grew louder as the energy in the room spiraled.

"Now pick up the esther." Eli pointed at the table.

"Done."

"Drop in the spring water. Wait ten and a half seconds."

Ambrose stared at his watch. Neither of them breathed. "Time."

"Remove from heat. Slice the derrin vi—"

Ambrose's hands were a blur. "Done."

"Drop it in and mix three and a quarter times."

Ambrose wiped sweat off his brow, the previous splotch of ink now covering half his forehead. "Clockwise or counter?"

"Counter. Then five clockwise." Eli's grip tightened on the journal. They were past step fifty-seven, far past fifty-seven, and going strong. "Now lower the heat. Five seconds, increase the heat—"

Soon, he was yelling the instructions, with Ambrose yelling back, moving around each other in frantic circles as the cauldron bubbled and spat and turned a deep, deep purple—

They were on the last step.

"Funnel it, go go go!" Eli clutched his hair as Ambrose funneled the steaming potion into the vial. Once the liquid was in, he staggered back and held up his hands.

They both froze, waiting for the solution to split, or crystallize, or explode.

Nothing happened. The potion held.

"You did it," Eli breathed, then grabbed Ambrose's arm and shook it. "Ambrose, you did it!"

"I did it!" Ambrose shouted. Eli looked up at his face, and his breath caught in his throat.

Ambrose was *smiling*.

This wasn't one of his smug smirks or shy half smiles. This was a full, shining, beaming grin, one that crinkled his eyes and wiped away any trace of his exhaustion.

Eli had never seen anything like it.

"Hello?" Banneker's voice floated in from the entrance. "All good in here?"

Ambrose's smile faltered. Eli gave a silent curse and ducked out of the workroom—Banneker and Grim had wandered into the shop, both of them frowning.

"We heard yelling," Grim said, their voice taut. "Everyone all right?"

"We're fine!" Ambrose called back and turned toward the work-table—but Eli dragged him out onto the shop floor. If Ambrose wasn't going to brag about his accomplishment, someone had to do it for him.

"*More* than fine," he said, giving Ambrose an encouraging grin. "This man just had a breakthrough on the commission. It was incredible, you should've seen him work—"

"Eli..." Ambrose mumbled. "I'm sure they're not interested."

But both Grim and Banneker brightened.

"Sure we are!" Banneker said. "Wanna come to dinner with us, tell us all about it?"

Eli bit his lip. There was no way Ambrose was going to go for it.

But the half-elf nodded, eyes on the floor, cheeks pink. "If it's not an intrusion. But..." He paused, glancing at Eli. "I actually have a different place in mind."

STEP 19:

SNACK BREAK

Eli

THE DINNER GAGGLE picked up Sherry, then followed Ambrose in a chatty line toward the southern end of the Scar.

"What's all this about a commission breakthrough?" Sherry asked Eli. But Eli had his eyes on Ambrose—robes shed, ink cleared off his face, a tiny bounce in his step. The bounce was hardly visible, except for when he passed the glowing crystals lining the walkway. But after Eli noticed it, he couldn't *not* stare at him. At his perked ears, then his tapered waist, his long legs...

Eli determined that Ambrose should have scientific breakthroughs more often.

"I'll make him tell you all about it when we get there," he reassured Sherry. Banneker jogged past them to join Ambrose.

"Food quest, food quest!" Banneker cheered and slapped Ambrose on the shoulder. Ambrose gave a halfhearted scowl.

"Shush, I'm trying to find it. It should be somewhere over..." He slowed, then pointed to a dimly lit restaurant across the chasm. "Yes. This one." As he crossed the rope bridge, he turned back to his followers. "Now, Dawn said she didn't like this place—"

"Good start," Banneker said. Ambrose ignored him.

"Because she said it was too spicy. But..." He looked to Eli. "I think *you* might like it."

He stopped and gestured to the door, its stone frame indicating the restaurant's age. Unlike the sleeker, more recently carved structures, this doorway was all rugged stone, haphazardly chipped to form a misshapen entryway. Eli stopped in front of it and took a deep breath. Garlic, sesame oil, chili...

A lump formed in his throat. It smelled like home.

"Will this place work?" Ambrose asked quietly. Though the others had walked on in, Ambrose hung back by the door, fidgeting with his signet ring. Eli smiled.

"It'll work great. Thanks for thinking of it, Ambrose."

"Ames."

Eli paused mid-step. Ambrose looked as surprised as he did, as if the word had slipped out of its own accord.

"You can call me Ames," he said, suddenly focusing hard on his ring. "If you'd like."

Eli wasn't sure what the greater victory for the evening was— helping Ambrose or this.

"Sure," he said, the warmth of the restaurant seeping into him. "Thanks, Ames."

The five of them stuffed themselves into a booth: Sherry, Banneker, and Grim on one side, and Eli and Ambrose on the other. Eli nestled into the corner and looked around the place in admiration. The restaurant's dim light only added to the cozy, homespun atmosphere woven by its occupants. The gruff shouting of chefs in the back, the huddles of old friends in every corner...

"They got a menu?" He turned to Ambrose, who shook his head.

"No menu," he said. "They just shout the daily specials at you. And it doesn't matter what you pick, they give you whatever they want anyway."

Eli grinned and sat back. Lily would love it. "Sounds perfect."

"Good." Ambrose's voice hardly carried in the noisy restaurant, and given his slouch, he likely assumed he had successfully slid out of the spotlight for the evening.

So, when Sherry, Grim, and Banneker leaned in from the other side of the table, Eli happily leaned in with them.

"Tell us about this potion," Sherry said eagerly. Banneker propped his chin up on his palm.

"This is the esther one, right?" He grimaced. "I never work with that stuff. You, Grim?"

"Hell, no."

"Ambrose got it to work, though." Eli pounded the table. "One hundred forty-eight tests, seventy-three steps—"

"It was only seventy," Ambrose murmured. Eli saw his way in.

"Seventy steps, *twenty* minutes—"

Ambrose took the bait.

"Actually, it wasn't twenty, it was fifteen," he corrected. "And that's only because the active ingredient requires at least a two-minute boiling stage—"

There it was. Eli imitated Banneker's propped-up pose and let Ambrose take it from there. Halfway through his increasingly breathless explanation, a human waddled up, shouted some specials at them, and waved away their order. By the time the food arrived, Ambrose was smiling again, cheeks flushed, eyes sparkling.

Between the food and the view, Eli could have easily sat there all night.

"Always knew you'd be better than Pearce one day." Grim sat back. Banneker scoffed and reached for a dumpling.

"Please," he said. "He's always been better than Pearce."

Ambrose's ears went pink. Self-conscious once more, he nudged Eli. "How are the dumplings? Are they all right?"

Eli smiled at him. Banneker was right—wherever Ambrose had learned his thoughtfulness, it certainly hadn't been from Pearce.

"They're perfect," he said. "Just like back home."

"High praise, I'm sure." Grim vied with Banneker for the next dumpling. "You getting homesick, Valenz?"

"Homesick?" Banneker won out and popped the dumpling into his mouth. "Haven't you traveled a bunch?"

While Grim mourned the loss of their dumpling, Eli grabbed the next one and savored it. It truly was perfect. Juicy, crisp, the perfect amount of chili paste. He wanted to order a hundred more. "Of course, I have. Doesn't mean I don't miss home now and then."

Banneker tilted his head. "What's the farthest you've traveled?"

The dinner fell into a comfortable, if indulgent, rhythm after that. Eli would tell a story about one of his past failed careers, they'd order more dumplings. Eli would recount an adventuring tale he had heard up north, they'd order more dumplings. Eli would recall another natural wonder he had come across, they...tried to order more dumplings, but the woman waved them off so the place could close.

"Tell me more about the Driftwood," Banneker goaded as they all wandered back to Rosemond Street, full and sleepy. But the memories of past travels kept Eli wide-awake.

"Oh, it's just as weird as you'd think it would be," he said. "It never happens when you're looking at it, you know? But you blink once, and boom—the tree in front of you is three feet to the left. The spring you walked past? Not there anymore, there's a rock over it. And forget about trying to navigate out of there without one of their wisp guides because—"

"Eli?" Ambrose called out. They had reached their shops, and Ambrose had one hand on the door to The Griffin's Claw. "Did you still want to borrow the red quartz you were talking about?"

"Oh, that's right." Eli waved to Banneker. "Tell you more later!"

"Come on by tomorrow! And bring Tom!" Banneker waved back and disappeared along with Grim and Sherry. Eli jogged into the shop, his steps as light as Ambrose's. He didn't often get a chance to talk about his old escapades.

"Sorry," he said, rubbing the back of his head. "Didn't mean to take over the dinner with my stupid stories."

"They're not stupid," Ambrose said. "Certainly more exciting than anything I can tell them about potions. I'll get that quartz for you."

As Ambrose ducked into the supply closet, Eli glanced at a notebook on the counter. He expected it to be another ingredient list or a ledger—but then he recognized the list from months ago, with all the crossed-out cleaning gems and signs. "You renovating, Ames?"

"What?" Ambrose reappeared, glass jar in hand. "Oh, that. It's nothing."

Eli raised his eyebrows. Ambrose shifted.

"It's...I have some workroom upgrades in mind for the store's anniversary," he said, his pointed ears perking up again. "I was finally able to afford them with the commission money. I've got Banneker going on a sign right now." His words picked up their pace. "I also ordered a new cauldron the other day. And if the carpenter up on High Vine can finish the wand rack in time for Master Pearce to visit..."

A warmth came over Ambrose as he spoke, his eyes trailing across the shop. The sight was familiar—something Eli had not only seen in Ambrose, but in Dawn, in Grim...

Ambrose was home. The shop was his home, and Eli was standing on the cool wood floors of Ambrose's heart.

"Anyway..." The potion master shook his head and handed Eli the jar. "It's late, and that's quite enough talk about upgrades for one evening."

Eli deflated as he took the jar and rubbed his thumb along the lid. "That's really exciting, Ames," he said softly. "Congrats."

He shuffled back to his shop, all the joy from the dinner whisked away. The chimes above the door grated his ears; the sight of bottles weighed him down. When Tom rolled up to greet him, he set the jar of quartz on the counter, knelt, and bundled her up in his arms.

Eli's Elixirs wasn't his home, nor was it his heart.

"Tom," he murmured, tears pricking at his eyes. "What am I gonna do?"

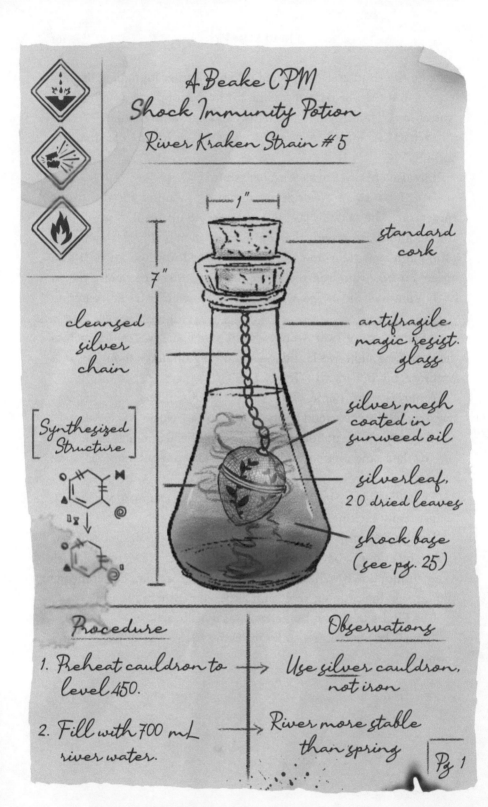

A Beake CPM
Shock Immunity Potion
River Kraken Strain #5

1"

7"

standard cork

cleansed silver chain

antifragile magic resist. glass

silver mesh coated in sunweed oil

silverleaf, 20 dried leaves

shock base (see pg. 25)

[Synthesized Structure]

Procedure

1. Preheat cauldron to level 450.

2. Fill with 700 mL river water.

Observations

→ Use silver cauldron, not iron

→ River more stable than spring

Pg. 1

E. Valenz

Lvl 4 Healing Potion

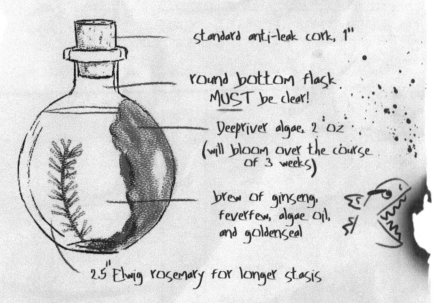

standard anti-leak cork, 1"

round bottom flask.
MUST be clear!

Deepriver algae, 2 oz
(will bloom over the course
of 3 weeks)

brew of ginseng,
feverfew, algae oil,
and goldenseal

2.5" Elwig rosemary for longer stasis

NOTES:

← it can handle a size B

- Should be brewed in a ~~Size A~~ cauldron.
- Needs to remain in sunlight.
- Expires in 8 months.
- Cannot mix with levitation potions.

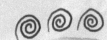

INGREDIENTS:

- 2 oz. Deepriver algae ✓
- 2.5" Elwig rosemary ✓
- 15 oz. spring water
- 5 oz. goldenseal seeds
- 1 spoon algae oil ✓

to buy!!

continued ————→ Pg 1

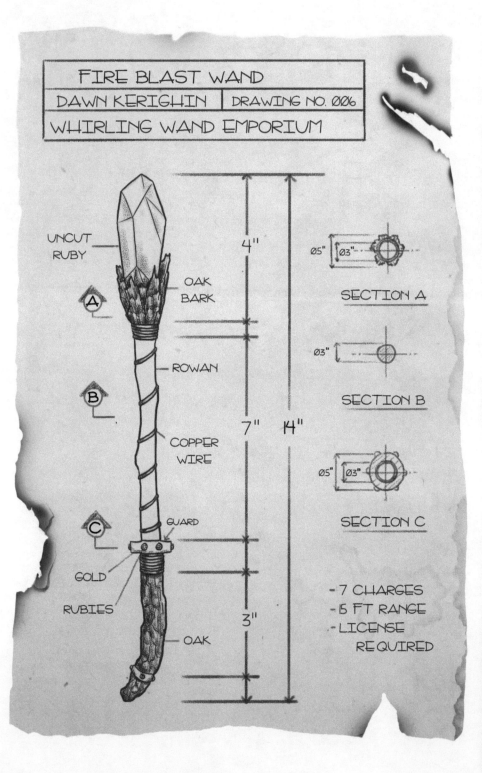

FIRE BLAST WAND

DAWN KERIGHIN	DRAWING NO. 006

WHIRLING WAND EMPORIUM

UNCUT RUBY

OAK BARK

A

ROWAN

B

COPPER WIRE

C

GUARD

GOLD

RUBIES

OAK

4"

7"

14"

3"

Ø5" Ø3"

SECTION A

Ø3"

SECTION B

Ø5" Ø3"

SECTION C

- 7 CHARGES
- 15 FT RANGE
- LICENSE REQUIRED

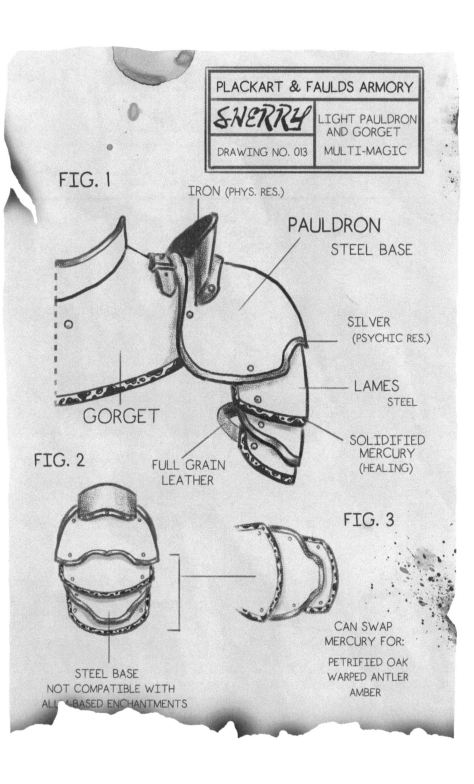

PLACKART & FAULDS ARMORY

SNERRY

LIGHT PAULDRON AND GORGET

DRAWING NO. 013

MULTI-MAGIC

FIG. 1

IRON (PHYS. RES.)

PAULDRON

STEEL BASE

SILVER (PSYCHIC RES.)

LAMES
STEEL

SOLIDIFIED MERCURY (HEALING)

GORGET

FIG. 2

FULL GRAIN LEATHER

FIG. 3

STEEL BASE
NOT COMPATIBLE WITH ALLOY-BASED ENCHANTMENTS

CAN SWAP MERCURY FOR:

PETRIFIED OAK
WARPED ANTLER
AMBER

CABOCHON JEWELERS
SHIELD AMULET

FIG. 1

40 mm

30 mm

- 14K GOLD
- RED JASPER
  OVAL CABOCHON
- GOLD CHAIN

FIG. 2

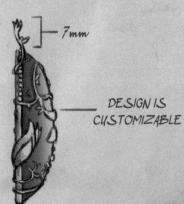

7mm

DESIGN IS
CUSTOMIZABLE

PROPERTIES:

- PHYS. RESISTANCE
- MAG. RESISTANCE

- 6 CHARGES
  → REQ. 3 DAYS TO CHARGE

- DO NOT COMBINE WITH
  PSYCHIC RES. OILS

Grim

PLATE 1

TITLE: ICE CANNON (WRIST)

WINGED WARLOCK ARTIFICER'S ATELIER

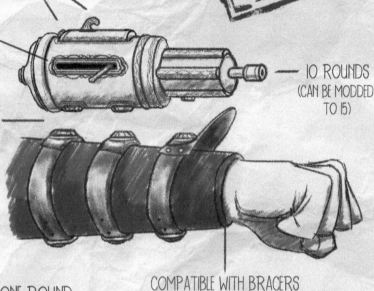

TWO–STEP FIRING SYSTEM

20 SEC. CHARGE

10 ROUNDS
(CAN BE MODDED TO 15)

ABSORBS RECOIL

COMPATIBLE WITH BRACERS
UP TO 10MM IN THICKNESS

ONE ROUND:
80 FEET
SUB–ZERO
TEMPERATURE RAY

STABILIZING SYSTEM

20MM
BONDED
SAPPHIRES

CHAMBER A REFILL:
100G ICEFALL CRYSTAL,
CRUSHED

Banneker

STEP 20:

TASTE TEST

Ambrose

As AMBROSE TOOK his customary stroll over to Dawn's place, he tried to rationalize his excitement about the coming evening. Now that two commission steps were complete, Eli was going to come over to his workshop and test out the potions. Testing new brews was a rare opportunity, if a little outside Guild protocol. And he'd be testing them with his associate Eli. His friendly associate Eli. Fine, his *friend* Eli. It was perfectly reasonable to be excited.

"Apologies for being late," Ambrose called as he stepped into the wand shop. Now that it was after closing, the first floor was empty, the front counter littered with wand boxes and hand-scribbled receipts. "My last customer wanted to talk through all my healing options, and only ended up buying one of them..." He stopped on the stairs and frowned. He was accustomed to hearing sparks, sawing, or whirring from Dawn's workshop in his after-hours visits. Today, the loft was silent. "Dawn?"

After confirming no sparks were going to pelt him, he hesitantly poked his head into the workroom. Dawn was folded into an armchair in the corner, the leather of the chair scorched and torn after spending years in such chaotic surroundings. He briefly brightened—perhaps Dawn was taking a break, after all—but then he noticed the whirlwind of notes spread around her and the miserable expression on her face. "Ah. Fireworks planning?"

"I wish." Dawn slouched lower in the chair, her dark eyes focusing somewhere in the middle distance. "I'm trying to sort out our sinkhole expedition, but I can't...I just can't..." She waved a hand at the mess. "I can't even look at it anymore. I'm never going to get it done, I'm usele—"

"Don't finish that sentence," Ambrose said sharply. "You know it's not true." He knelt to gather up the papers. "You're the opposite of useless, you always have been."

But as he collected the papers, she didn't move. Her eyes remained dull and lifeless, fixed on the space somewhere above his head. His heart sank—he had seen her tired before. Exhausted from her apprenticeship, or half-asleep after a big sale.

But he had never seen her quite like this.

"What if..." He flipped through a few of the pages. "What if I took on the rest of the sinkhole research? Freed you up to work on the fireworks?"

Dawn finally stirred, some life coming back to her face. "Are you sure? Don't you have the commission?"

Of course, he did. He had the commission, the shop, the upgrades...but all of that felt so far away when his friend was miserable in front of him. He dragged a blanket from the back of the armchair and tucked it around her.

"I can do it," he said firmly. "Just give me some time."

————————————

Later that night, all of Ambrose's enthusiasm for the taste test had sunk, hidden under the weight of Dawn's partially planned papers.

He understood potions, not sinkholes. He had no idea which level of the subterranean maze would yield the star shine moss, nor did he know how to map a safe path down. And her list of potential predators—the snub-nosed dragon, the lesser phoenix, the burrowing moth—was only half-filled. Ambrose's fears completed the list easily. Giant bats, skittering spiders, criminal hideouts...

He sighed and rested his elbows on the front counter. Was he going to have to hire an adventurer to escort them? To find some *moss*?

"You ready?"

Eli stood at the front door, a small cloth bundle in his arms. Ambrose's sinkhole worries immediately muddied with a bubbly feeling in his chest.

"What did you bring?" He pushed the bubbles aside and focused on the bundle in Eli's arms. "I hope you know you only had to make one vial."

"Brought that." Eli set the vial down on the counter and held up the cloth. "I also brought some gifts."

More bubbles fizzed in Ambrose's ribcage—he shoved them aside again. "Gifts? Why?"

"For tackling the esther part of all this." Eli shot him a sunny smile. "Gods know I wouldn't have been able to do it myself." He began to pluck jars out of the bundle, and the scent of herbs filled the air. "Here, I clipped you some Elwig mint this morning. And some rosemary, some lavender..."

Ambrose held up the jars. "Did you grow these yourself?"

"Yeah, on the windowsill. Last owner of the place left some plants behind, figured I'd make use of them." Eli handed him a sprig of rosemary. "Here, smell that."

Ambrose rubbed one of the silver-green blades under his thumb, then gave the stem a sniff. It was delightful in a way only fresh herbs could be.

"It's lovely," he said, keeping his tone even. "Thank you."

"That's not everything." Eli held up a tiny potted plant—a mottled green-and-purple succulent boasting an orange flower in the middle. "I trimmed a pup from one of the succulents left behind. Thought it might look nice next to the cat."

"The cat?"

"The cat on your lucky shelf."

Ambrose accepted the tiny succulent. Perfect in its symmetry, wonderfully imperfect in its coloration. He fought down a blush—he couldn't recall receiving something this nice in years. "Thank you. This is...incredibly thoughtful of you."

Eli lightly bumped his arm. "S'just a couple plants, Ames. Here, I'll put the herbs in your supply room."

Ambrose went over to the workroom, gently slotted the plant right next to the bronze cat, then wandered back to the supply closet. "Do you need any assistance finding—?"

Eli gave a short laugh. "Do I need any...? Come on, you've labeled literally everything in here. No, I don't need any assistance." As he stored the mint next to the milkweed, his shin bumped against a stack of crates, knocking them out of alignment. "Oh, sorry." He straightened the crates, then paused. "Hold on, why do you have a cot down here?"

"Hm?" Ambrose leaned to look at the folded cot. "Oh. I never managed to get rid of that. I'm aiming to build another shelf there soon."

Eli's eyebrows rose. "So...you used to have guests sleep in here?"

"No, I used to sleep in here."

"I'm sorry, what?"

Ambrose took a step back. "I...used to sleep here. When I was an apprentice."

"But..." Eli shot another confused glance at the cot. "But only when you were little or something, right?"

"No." Ambrose twisted his signet ring. It hadn't occurred to him that he was supposed to be embarrassed by it. "I slept here until I inherited the shop."

"*What?*"

Ambrose took another step back. Eli's face was a harsh mix of confusion and anger. "Well," he tried, "there's only one room upstairs, you see—"

"So, where did Dawn sleep?" Eli gestured toward the street. "When she was an apprentice?"

"At the boarding house with the other apprentices."

"And why weren't you there?"

Ambrose got the distinct feeling Eli wasn't going to like what he was about to say. "Master Pearce said it was too expensive."

Eli set his elbow on a shelf and pinched the bridge of his nose, letting out a single controlled exhale.

"I see what they mean," he muttered. He didn't need to elaborate on who. The other shopkeepers had made their opinions on Pearce known ever since his retirement. Embarrassment and an odd sort of fear rose in Ambrose's throat.

"Are you angry with me?" he asked. "I'm not sure what I've done wrong."

"No. No, I..." Eli looked at him with such an unfamiliar softness that Ambrose couldn't hold his gaze. "You haven't done anything wrong, and I'm not angry with you. Hey." Eli's fingers brushed Ambrose's arm, forcing him to look up. "I'm not angry with you," he repeated, his tone impossibly gentle. "I'm upset you were treated like that. That's all."

Ambrose swallowed. It was unnecessary, he wanted to say. Unnecessary to care so much about something that didn't affect him.

"Are you ready to try the potions?" he deflected, though the unevenness in his voice gave himself away. Eli held the door open for him.

"Very ready."

They set their vials on the table—Ambrose's amethyst bottle next to Eli's yellow one—and spent a good few seconds staring at them.

"So...we just drink them together?" Eli ventured.

"It's not quite up to Guild standards, but I'm afraid we don't have time for control groups and the like." Ambrose flipped to the part of his journal that was set aside for notes—duration, effectiveness, side effects—and pointed to the purple vial. "That's six ounces there.

Given the strength of the esther, three should be enough for an adult, and one enough for Beatrice."

"All right." Eli grabbed two measuring glasses and portioned out the purple liquid. "Your brew first? Age before beauty?"

"I'm only a year older than you." Ambrose glared, then accepted the glass. "Now, the vine will likely give this a bitter flavor—"

"Bottoms up!" Eli clinked his glass against Ambrose's and knocked it back. Ambrose sighed, gulped the potion in one go, and waited for the magic to take effect.

At first, he could only describe it as sparkles. Sparkles that trickled down his throat, traveled through his veins, and lifted his feet off the floor. Then the essence of the derrin vine took hold, connecting his mind to the fact that his toes now hovered several inches off the floor. That he was swimming in nothing but warm air.

He carefully lifted his legs and leaned back, testing his level of control. If the connection was too weak, he'd tumble easily. Too strong, and the air would feel paralyzing. So far, the connection seemed to—

Across from him, Eli burst into laughter.

"This is"—he twisted around, his momentum sending him through another spin and a half—"this is incredible!"

He tilted backward and flipped himself over. Ambrose fought back a laugh himself.

"How's your range of motion?" he asked, trying to remain professional. "Can you go any higher?"

Eli straightened out and lifted a few more inches—then shook his head. "This is about as high as I can go."

"Good." Ambrose's nod made him sway in the air. "Can't have Beatrice floating off into the sky."

Eli did another slow-motion spin, his sun earrings floating with him. "This is so *cool*—here, we need to try the dragon wings while we're still levitating."

Ambrose floated over and placed their cups on the cleaning table. The cleaning gemstones flashed, whisking away the last drops at the bottom of the glasses. As he poured the second potion and turned, he bumped into the sharp edge of the worktable. "Ow—"

"Watch out." Eli grabbed Ambrose's waist and gently reeled him back. A flush immediately crept up Ambrose's neck, and despite the clothing between them, he felt every inch of Eli's fingers as they slipped away.

"This one might taste sharp," Eli said, knocking back his glass. Ambrose imitated him once more, scrunching his nose when the predicted sharpness hit the back of his tongue.

"You weren't wrong," he started, then paused. His shoulders suddenly felt heavy, and he twisted around to see what it was. Two dragon wings, wispy, ephemeral, and most of all purple, glimmered behind him. A moment later, the potion linked with his mind, like a shadow of a presence between his eyes. He stretched out a thought, and the wings gave a single flap, trailing a river of pink and purple sparkles.

"How did you do that?" Ambrose breathed. It was difficult to see his own wings, so he turned to admire Eli's instead. "It feels so realistic."

Eli's eyes glittered along with his wings. "Used some iron pollen at the end to get the sense of weight. You like it?"

"It's a nice touch. A very nice touch." Ambrose floated forward to get a better look at the wings, then grabbed Eli's shoulder to stop himself. "Apologies," he mumbled. "Not used to this."

"Oh, you mean you don't float around your workshop on the regular?" Eli reached for Ambrose's waist to stabilize him. Ambrose tried to ignore the touch—the thumb under his ribcage, how easily Eli held him in place—and instead ran a hand through one of the wings. As expected, his fingers went right through it, casting off bright sparkles that swirled back to reform the illusion.

"Impressive." He floated out of Eli's grasp. "Now all that's left is to combine them and apply the flavoring."

Eli spun until he was upside down. "Ambrose, only you can say something so boring when you're floating with purple dragon wings." He crossed his arms, and his wings gave an indignant snap. Then one of his earrings fell out, and his glare lost its strength. Ambrose bit back a laugh.

"I'm trying to be professional here." He tilted forward to pick up the earring, but wound up in a front tumble, and his feet bumped into Eli's chest in slow motion. "Sorry, sorry!"

Eli gave a mock gasp and grabbed Ambrose's ankles. "Oh, *I* see what this is." His eyes narrowed. "You're trying to injure me. Corporate sabotage, I say! Off with you!"

"No, no!"

Eli spun himself upright, sending Ambrose into a sideways spin. The movement and the sparkles dizzied him into laughter, and he bumped into the workroom table once more, sending the rose statue wobbling. He reached out to steady it and threw an accusatory finger at Eli.

"Property damage!" he spluttered between laughs. "You're attempting property damage! I'll have you for this, Valenz—"

"Oh, you wanna go?" Eli grabbed a cauldron brush and wielded it like a sword. Ambrose reached for a broom and mimicked him. "It's to the death, Beake. Loser gets Rosemond Street forever—"

Ambrose poked his stomach with the broom handle. Eli tossed aside the brush, set a dramatic hand to his forehead, and floated downward.

"He got me!" he mock-wailed. "Oh gods, he got me. Tell my parents I love them. Take care of Tom. Spread my ashes in a Fireball stadium..."

His words echoed as he slowly sank into a large cauldron, descending until only his feet stuck out.

"Excuse me." Ambrose grinned and tugged on his shoe. "Could you not perish in there? That's going to be very inconvenient for me."

"I'm your rival. I'm inconvenient even in death."

Ambrose peered over the edge of the cauldron. Eli smiled up at him, hands folded over his chest, ankles crossed. His purple wings filled the cauldron, settling in a cloud of sparkles around him. "What was the last thing you brewed in here?" he asked.

"A strength potion, I believe. Had to restock yesterday."

Eli shimmied around in the cauldron. "So, if I stay in here, I'll get really strong?"

Ambrose set his chin on his hand. "Unlike you, I actually clean my cauldrons, so no."

Eli's offended noise bounced around the metal. "Rude."

"Rude or accurate?"

"I refuse to incriminate myself."

"I believe you already have."

Eli smiled briefly—but then it faded, and he turned away, running a finger aimlessly down the wall of the cauldron. "Could just stay in here forever," he tried to joke, but his tone faltered. "Wouldn't have to go back and tackle my brewing list for the week."

The response held an echo of his fractured tone in the cistern. Ambrose bit his lip and approached his next question with caution. "How are you...liking the shop?"

He expected some sort of shrug or false smile. Instead, Eli's hand paused, and he remained silent for a moment.

"I'm not like you," he said quietly.

Ambrose deflated, his thoughts drifting back to Dawn. He had seen what this type of work could do to someone, even someone who loved it. The exhaustion, the stress...

Months ago, he would have rejoiced at this. Now, he only found another friend suffering.

"Are you going to stay there?" he asked gently. More silence from the cauldron as sparkles slowly winked out around Eli.

"I don't know." Eli didn't look at him—just the blank metal in front of him. Ambrose's shoulders dropped. Potion advice, he could give for days. Career advice? He didn't even know where to start.

"You should...you should talk to someone about it," he said. "It doesn't have to be me—I mean, it could, if you'd like—but someone. It's just..." He let out a breath. "I'd prefer not to see you miserable."

"I'd prefer not to see me miserable, too," Eli mumbled, then held up a hand. "I'll talk to someone after this commission. Now, help me out of here before the potion wears off?"

A false smile was back on his face, one that put a firm end to

Ambrose's line of questioning. He nodded, took Eli's hand, and pulled.

The levitation made it easy to extricate him. Eli floated up out of the cauldron, then settled down gracefully. Ambrose's heels struck the floor with less finesse, and he stumbled forward. Without thinking, he reached for Eli's arms.

"Sorry—" he blurted out, but Eli caught him, wrapping his fingers around Ambrose's arms with a gentle laugh.

"You all good?" he asked, his voice low and soft. For a moment, Ambrose stared at him wordlessly, the warmth of Eli's palms setting his skin on fire.

"I'm fine." He pulled away and turned back to his journal on the worktable. Commission, focus on the commission. "So, due to my delay with the esther, we have a little over two months left. That gives me about—"

"What do you mean, me?" Eli brushed shoulders with him. "Come on, I'm not letting you do the combination alone."

"Well, it'll take several rounds of mixing to get them to work right..."

"That's what I signed up for." Eli shrugged. "Just tell me when you're testing and I'll come over."

Ambrose cleared his throat. The sparkles from the first potion seemed to be lingering. "How about we start tomorrow once I restock?"

Eli smiled at him and—was that a wink? Or merely the light glinting off his earring? "See you then."

STEP 21:

COMMON ERRORS

Ambrose

AT FIRST, Ambrose made the trip to inform Eli every time he was about to start his commission work. He'd wave through the window, catching Eli either cleaning, talking to his family, or both, and wait for him to free up.

"Ames." Eli leaned out of the doorway after the third such summoning. "Why don't you just use the rose statue? Would save you the walk."

"Oh. Um..." Ambrose glanced back at his shop, where his statue sat with its empty scroll. "Sherry said I could use the fresh air."

Eli tossed his feather duster between his hands. "Sounds like Sherry. I'll be over in a minute."

Eventually, Eli needed no such visit. He simply began coming over by himself, whenever his evenings weren't occupied with inventory, friends, or dates. Occasionally, he would chop ingredients, heat the cauldron, or debate the finer points of the combination process—but more often than not, he would simply keep Ambrose company as he stirred.

And every now and then, Tom accompanied him, rolling about their legs and begging to be picked up.

"So, these bonekeepers—okay, Tom, okay!" Eli picked up the automaton and placed her on his knee. Tonight, he sat in the workroom next to the cauldron, spinning a tale as Ambrose skimmed foam off the potion. "These bonekeepers are migrating straight through the farm. I mean, *right* through the fields, scaring the pygmy dragons, smashing crops. This one farmhand grabs a staff from the barn, ready to blast them, but I stop him and go—hey. Bet you twenty talons I can get these guys off the farm without wasting a charge."

Ambrose raised his eyebrows. "But they're bonekeepers. Aren't they massive?"

"Oh, yeah. About the size of the barn." Eli waved a hand as if giant crabs covered in tar and bones were normal. "Anyway, I pick up a zucchini. I walk right up to the one in front—"

"You *what?*"

"*Right* up to it. I pat its leg, and go, hey bud. Fetch. I take the zucchini, throw it out of the field..." Eli paused. Ambrose leaned forward. "And there they went. Followed it right back into the hills."

Ambrose set down the ladle and shook his head in disbelief. "You could have been killed."

Eli shrugged. "Bonekeepers love veggies. Everyone always forgets that."

As Ambrose doused the flames underneath the cauldron, Eli checked his pocket watch and stood up. "I need to head out, if that's all right. I've got a date meeting me in a few minutes."

"Oh?" Ambrose mumbled. When Eli glanced out the window, discomfort rose in his chest—but he quickly tamped it down. Eli was allowed to go on dates. That was perfectly fine.

"Mm-hm." Eli began to help Ambrose clean the workstation. "Just a casual date. Sherry introduced me to her last week." He pointed an empty test tube at Ambrose. "If this works out, maybe Sherry can start a matchmaking side hustle. Get you and Dawn some dates, too."

Their shoulders brushed, but Eli didn't pull away immediately. Ambrose gave a weak laugh as he lined up his freshly brewed bottles, all still warm from the cauldron. "Oh, please. Who in the Scar would want to date me?"

He turned to place his potions in the cabinet, and Eli leaned against the workstation. "Ah, you're right. Who in this city would ever want to date a handsome, successful business owner? A published scientist with the bluest eyes in the Scar?"

Ambrose almost dropped one of the bottles. "I'm—um—that's not—"

But Eli ignored his attempted protest, bending over to talk to Tom in a high-pitched voice. "Tom agrees with me, don't you? Of course, you do—you're in love with him, you silly little broomstick. I think you just like the color blue, that's what I think..."

As Eli babbled, Ambrose kept his face toward the cabinet, his cheeks burning. Handsome didn't mean anything. Sherry called him handsome sometimes, but in a cheek-pinching sort of way. Dawn called him handsome, but she was his friend, she was contractually obligated.

And Eli—well, he was just being polite, wasn't he?

"Eli?" a voice called from the street. The man in question looked over his shoulder.

"All right." He patted Tom on the head. "Come on, time to—"

But Tom wheeled over to Ambrose and hid behind his legs. Eli sighed.

"Looks like she wants to stay with you. Is that all right?"

"As long as she doesn't plan to commit corporate espionage." Ambrose looked down at her. "You wouldn't do that, would you?"

But Eli was already halfway out the door. "Thanks, Ames! Have a good night!"

The front door shut behind him. Ambrose swallowed. "You too."

It wasn't that he didn't enjoy his quiet nights, he thought as he hung his robes by the counter and carried Tom upstairs. There was always something to be said for the simplicity of a book, a blanket, and a cup of tea.

It was just that... Well, he had to begun to miss Eli's presence when he wasn't around. And something about his laughter in the street made it difficult to focus on the sinkhole research in front of him.

He reorganized the papers strewn across his kitchen table as a kind of mental reset. What he was experiencing was...merely professional. That was all. Having Eli assist with the potion every night was common practice for a joint commission. It didn't matter if he thought the man was handsome or if the man called *him* handsome. They were friends and professional partners, and that was perfectly fine.

As Tom wheeled around his chair, he set aside his normal, professional thoughts and focused on the sinkhole research.

"Now"—he looked to Tom and pointed at the papers—"if we enter the sinkhole from the northern side and take the stairwell down..."

He passed another hour like that, talking through his plan with Tom. Thanks to Dawn's initial notes, he had extracted what equipment to bring, and what levels of the cave system were likely growing spots, but... He tapped the sketches. The natural bridges crisscrossing the sinkhole were the only way to properly get to those levels, and he still hadn't figured out how to safely cross them. If he knew how wide they were, or how sturdy, or how sloped...

He squeezed his eyes shut against his growing headache. He had told Dawn he would get this done, but he had never actually gone near a sinkhole. In truth, he still had no idea how to get her down to the moss.

"That's enough of this for today," he muttered and pushed aside the papers. "Tom, would you like to keep me company while I read?"

He settled into the armchair with a book—the one he had bought on his last trip with Dawn. He opened the cover to the woodcut artwork on the inside. The familiarity of the hero—sword aloft, allies beside him—gave him comfort in the same way it had when he was a boy. Sitting alone in a supply closet for hours with nothing but a few novels Pearce had tossed his way one winter. Wondering what it would be like to leave the Scar and fight dragons.

Tom clambered up and sat on his knee. As she rested her broom head against his tunic, he smiled, scratched the top of her bristles, and turned to the first page.

The story began as it usually did: adventurers sitting in a tavern, ready to receive their next quest. The leader of the adventurers, the sword-swinging hero, did a lot of smiling and winking. Ambrose prodded Tom. "Sounds like someone we know, doesn't it?"

Ambrose's eyes grew heavy as the hero continued smiling, and winking, and generally being kind and open. A few chapters later, he drifted off to sleep, thinking half-coherent thoughts about Eli in gleaming armor.

"Come on, Tom, time to go... No, you can't stay here with him, you lovesick bundle of straw..."

Though sleep still pressed him into the armchair, Ambrose cracked his eyes open to find Eli delicately extracting Tom from his arms. No gleaming armor, no sword—just Eli.

"What time is it?" Ambrose mumbled. It had to be late—the fire in the hearth had dimmed to embers, their weak glow the only source of light in the room.

"Time for you to get to bed, I think," Eli said. "Thanks for looking after Tom. You really spoil her, you know that?"

Ambrose couldn't help it—in his tired fog, he could only stare at Eli, taking him in through a half-lidded gaze. Eli leaned over him, his shirt fallen open at the collar. His eyes caught the last of the firelight, soft and warm and deep. And of course, there was that smile. That kind, gentle smile of his.

Gods, he could stare at it all night.

Then Eli reached for the book in Ambrose's hand. "What were you two reading?" He flipped to the cover, and his smile widened. "The Lightbringer series?" he said. "I loved that one, too. You know, I've got the prequel, if you'd like to borrow it." He placed the book on the side table, then rubbed his thumb over the binding's gold detail. "It's nice seeing you like this."

Ambrose's voice was sleep-addled and raspy. "Like what?"

"Relaxing." Eli set a hand on his shoulder. "I think you should do more of it."

The touch sent a shock down Ambrose's chest and through his thoughts. Eli's hand was delightfully warm and heavy. What if it moved to his neck, his cheek? What if Eli placed both hands on his face, stepped closer, bent down, brought his smile to where Ambrose could taste it...

Heat washed over him, and his breath caught in his throat. Oh, no. There was nothing professional about these thoughts, nothing at all—

"I, um..." He slid out of the chair, turned away from Eli. "You're right, it's late, I should get to bed."

His half-asleep legs tingled and stung, and he stumbled. Without hesitation, Eli caught his elbow. "You okay?"

Ambrose's arm seared under his fingers. "Fine. Just feelings— feeling a headache, I mean. You know, from..." He scrambled for a distraction, and his eyes landed on the abandoned sinkhole research. "From this project. I don't have any experience with sinkholes, and I need to plan a route down to the moss in two days."

"Oh." Eli set Tom down, then picked up a paper and squinted at it in the dying firelight. "I've been down a few sinkholes. North of the Driftwood, with the botany team." He shrugged. "I could help, if you like. You have tomorrow off, right? We could go through your research together. Nail down a plan for you and Dawn."

Ambrose held his breath, an acceptance lingering on his tongue, almost tipping into words. He needed the help, he truly did. But to spend more time with Eli, alone, in close quarters... He would make a fool of himself.

He gathered up the papers, furious at the blush warming his cheeks. Master Pearce would say he had gone soft. Collaborating, asking for help, *pining* of all things...

"No," he said quickly, focusing hard on the papers. "No, I'll sort it out. Thank you for the offer."

"Suit yourself." Eli paused. "But you'll tell me when you're back, yeah?"

"Hm?" Ambrose looked up.

"When you've returned from the sinkhole. Those bridges can be dangerous, and I'd like to know you both made it back safe."

Ambrose nodded, and as Eli left with Tom, he held the sinkhole papers to his chest as if to hide his heartbeat.

To Ambrose's dismay, Eli was not the only one invested in his and Dawn's moss adventure. When it came time to depart, all of Rosemond Street hovered around them.

"You have healing potions, right?" Sherry checked Ambrose's pack for the third time, stopping him in the middle of the street. Ambrose groaned.

"Yes, several different levels."

By his other shoulder, Grim spoke to Dawn in a low voice.

"Are you sure you don't want to take an adventurer with you?" they asked. "I know a couple folks who are down at the Jumping Ogre right now. I can throw a few coins their way—"

"Don't worry. Ames has this all planned out." Dawn hoisted up her own backpack, the clink of empty jars filling the night air. "We'll be back in a few hours, tops."

She shot Grim a smile and a thumbs-up, and for once, neither looked forced. Banneker came up and clapped both her and Ambrose on the shoulder. "Remember, the first rule of science is to have fun."

Ambrose sighed. "I don't think that's the first, nor the second, but we'll try."

The last person to see them off was Eli, his head poking out of his shop door.

"Stop by when you're back, all right?" He grinned. "I wanna see this legendary moss for myself."

"You got it!" Dawn said, then skipped off toward the elevator. Eli's gaze lingered on Ambrose.

"Come back in one piece?" he asked, his voice softer. Ambrose gave him a weak thumbs-up and followed Dawn, his heart stumbling —though whether due to Eli or the looming sinkhole, he wasn't sure.

Dawn was nearly at the elevator, and he had to run to catch up with her. Not that he minded—he hadn't seen her this excited since the Stone Dragons made it to the finals.

"How many jars do you think we can carry back?" she asked. "I really only need one to start, but if the *Thirty* wants a demonstration, I should try to get at least five..."

"We'll get as many as we can," he reassured her, letting her step into the elevator first.

The rickety latticed box, operated by a tired gnome and an enchanted rope, jostled Ambrose's nerves as it bumped and shuddered its way topside. He checked his pack once, then twice. When the grate opened to reveal the plains above the Scar, he took a deep breath and led the way to the sinkholes.

He was grateful Dawn had picked a night with a full moon. Out here, it was the only light guiding their path through the natural lavender fields, tinging the purple flowers with silver. But not even the moonlight could brighten the sinkholes ahead—dark, unblinking eyes in the earth, staring up at the stars with their vast gaze.

"The stairs on the north end of the sinkhole should be easy to manage," he said as they walked toward the largest sinkhole—Titan's Eye, the maps had called it. "After that, we'll need to follow three land bridges into the cave system below."

"System E, right?"

"D to E is the quickest way, actually." He stopped at the edge of the sinkhole and held out a potion. "And you'll want to take this."

They made a quick trade—a light wand for a potion bottle. Ambrose flicked the wand; Dawn drank the brew. As soon as it passed her lips, she puckered and recoiled.

"Ugh, I hate the sour stuff!"

"Sorry, I didn't have time to add any flavoring." Ambrose held the wand out toward the stairs. It was a narrow stairway, uneven and cracked as it spiraled down the sheer cliff face. Below, the land bridges that crossed the hole were little more than silver shards in the moonlight.

Ambrose stiffened and drank his own potion. Once the sour taste dissipated, the brew's effects settled in his hands and feet like iron weights.

"An anchoring potion," he explained, pocketing the empty bottle. "It should keep your feet on the stairs and the land bridges, and make the climbs easier."

"The climbs?"

Here was the part Ambrose hated the most. "We'll have to climb down to each land bridge. There are footholds from past expeditions, of course, but..." He started down the stairs and tentatively rested a hand on the stone wall. The magic drew his fingers to the stone, giving some resistance when he pulled his hand back. "It'll be safer this way."

"And we only have to get down." Dawn pulled a device out of her pocket. Ambrose recognized Banneker's handiwork immediately—a tight series of polished, interwoven copper rings, all inset with sliding runes. "Got Banneker to whip it up for me. It's nothing fancy, but it'll teleport us back to my shop once we have the moss."

Ambrose could've kissed the device. The less time he spent in this sinkhole, the better.

They made their way down the stairs slowly and carefully, each step made heavier by the potion. But to Ambrose, it was worth it when they reached the first land bridge without incident.

"I can see the caves!" Dawn tugged on his sleeve and pointed to the dark holes in the wall below them. "That's where the moss is, I know it."

"You're almost there." Ambrose squeezed her shoulder. "Now I just need to get you there in one piece. Let me climb down first, for safety?"

"Fine." Dawn waved him forward, and he carefully set his hands and feet on the wall. "Come on, the bridge is only, like, three feet down. Be like a spider."

Ambrose set one trembling foot on the next foothold. "No."

"Speedy spider—"

"I refuse."

He eventually dropped onto the land bridge, and once Dawn was behind him, he slowly crossed the strip of rusty stone.

The bridge was as narrow as the staircase, but with the added danger of vines, moss, and puddles of slimy rainwater. Hardly breathing, Ambrose focused only on where his feet went next, waiting for the potion to anchor every step. Every now and then, he looked back at Dawn to make sure she was right behind him, taking the same steps he was.

They continued on for what felt like an hour, one foot in front of the other, until the land bridge didn't feel so frightening. This was good, he told himself. He could go back to Eli and tell him the bridges weren't so bad after all—

His foot touched springy moss. Then, with a crumbling groan, the rock gave way.

"Dawn!" he yelled as he pitched through the hole, nothing to catch him but the endless abyss below.

A hand pulled on his arm and yanked him back onto the bridge. He stumbled into Dawn, who dug her heels into the rock and held him up.

"I've got you," she said, keeping a vise grip on his sleeve.

"Thank you," he breathed, voice shaking. Once he steadied himself, he carefully leaned over and assessed the new gap with his light wand. The bridge resumed not far beyond the hole, but deep cracks webbed through the rock beyond. Against the darkness and curtains of moss, it was far too difficult to tell what was safe—and what would send them into the abyss again.

Ambrose ran a hand through his hair. Gods dammit, Eli had been right.

"Think we can jump it?" Dawn asked, leaning around his shoulder. Ambrose began to sweat.

"I don't think so." He looked around him. "The anchoring potion won't give us the right momentum, and I can't tell what part of the bridge is stable."

Dawn's expression fell. "So...how do we get down there?"

"Let me, um..." He analyzed the walls next. There were no footholds down on this side, and not even the anchoring magic could make up for the inverted angles below the bridge. "I don't know."

Dawn paced in a narrow oval on the walkway. "Don't you have another potion? Some kind of jump vial, or levitation, or anything?"

Ambrose rummaged through his bag. "I have a floating vial, but we just took the anchoring potion. For no side effects, we'd have to wait at least an hour, maybe more."

They both looked up at the sky, where clouds gathered steadily over the moon. The silver light was already tenuous—another hour could plunge them into total darkness.

Dawn covered her face and made an exasperated noise. The sound vibrated painfully in Ambrose's ribcage, and he grasped for some way to keep her hopes up.

"I'm sorry. Perhaps—perhaps we could come back tomorrow night," he offered, gesturing with the floating vial. "The moon will still be bright, and we can—"

"I don't have time!" Dawn's hands dropped from her face, her eyes shining. "I have a committee meeting tomorrow and a commission due the next morning. I don't have time, I *never* have time, I..." Tears cut off her words, but she gulped them back. "And now I'm never going to get it done, because we can't get to the tunnel!"

Ambrose recoiled and tried again. "Listen, I know you're upset, but—"

"You said you would help me with this!" Her words went sharp, cutting deep into his chest.

"I'm—I'm trying to!"

"Well, clearly it's not enough!"

His pain snapped into anger.

"Will anything ever be enough for you?" he shouted. "Dawn, you're the best wandmaker this side of the Deepriver. You don't need that journal to prove anything, and yet you're destroying yourself over this stupid moss!"

He regretted the word as soon as he said it—but there was no breathing it back into his lungs. Dawn glared at him, eyes still welling.

"Oh, so it's *stupid* now?"

He suddenly felt very small. "No, that's—that's not what I meant."

"You know what? I don't need to hear this." Dawn jutted out a hand. "Give me the floating vial and I'll go myself."

Ambrose's grip tightened on the potion. "What? No. It's too dangerous."

"If I don't get down there now, I'll never get the moss."

"Then..." He looked down at the shadowy caves below, then swallowed and pressed the bottle to his chest. "Then you won't."

The light in Dawn's eyes vanished. "Give it to me."

"I said no!"

"Ambrose—"

She reached for it, and he did the only thing he could think to do. He threw it into the sinkhole.

The bottle fell silently, the glass catching one last spark of moonlight as it tumbled. Ambrose didn't exhale until it winked out of sight.

Then words flooded out of his mouth, unsteady and pleading.

"You're already hurting yourself over this, I won't let you go and hurt yourself any further. It's not worth it, I promise it isn't." He took a ragged breath. "Please, for once in your life, just give something up!"

Dawn didn't respond at first; she stared at him, tears spilling silently.

Then she pulled the teleport rings out of her pocket. "Fine."

She took a step back. Ambrose's breath caught in his throat. "Wait. Wait, Dawn, please don't—"

She disappeared.

Ambrose's hands trembled on the climb back up, his steps faltering on the narrow stairs. He knew the potion would hold him, he knew that. But alone, he could hardly look down without stopping and pressing himself closer to the wall.

And all along the walk, as his legs burned and the stone scraped his hands, his thoughts kept swimming in the same painful circle. He had failed Dawn, and she had left him there.

Apparently, he was very easy to leave behind.

He had to get back to the shop, back to any scrap of warmth or safety. When he slouched into the elevator, ignoring the gnomish operator's concerned glances, he willed the rickety thing to go faster. And when it finally landed on the chasm floor, he picked up his pace toward Rosemond Street, the cold night air stinging his raw palms.

But the other merchants were in his way.

They had gathered back in the road, their frantic figures lit only by the crystal lamps at the storefronts. Grim, Banneker, Sherry, Eli— all of them scurried back and forth.

And Dawn was in the center of them.

"I'm sorry," she sobbed into Sherry's shoulder. "I wasn't thinking, I was just so angry at him—"

"I can't believe you left him." Eli whipped past her, stuffing vials into a pack. "He could be *hurt* down there—Grim, I'll take the bracers."

Grim tossed him a pair of leather bracers, then checked the axe strapped to their back. "We'll go get him, and we'll discuss your actions later. Banneker, you got another one of those teleport rings?"

"I'll check." Banneker turned back toward his shop and froze. "Ames!"

The entire street whipped around. Dawn started crying again.

"Oh, thank the gods," Sherry said. "Are you all right?"

They all approached him at once, and without thinking, he ran for the door to his shop.

"Ambrose, wait!" Dawn slid away from Sherry. "Wait, I'm sorry, I'm so sorry—"

"Go away." He fumbled with the key, his hands shaking again. "Please."

Eli started forward. "Don't do this—"

Ambrose slammed the door closed behind him.

STEP 22:

ALTERNATE SOLUTIONS

Eli

THE ROSEMOND STREET meeting that night was impromptu, haphazard, and down two members. Eli fidgeted between Sherry and Banneker on the couch, staring at the empty chairs where Dawn and Ambrose usually sat. No matter how hard he tried, he couldn't get Dawn's sobs or Ambrose's broken expression out of his head.

When Grim took their usual place in front of the hearth, they looked as haunted as Eli felt. Gaze unfocused, shoulders stiff. They had no clipboard or pencil today, merely their furrowed expression.

"Spoke with Dawn," they said. "She's going to take a break and spend the next few days with her family."

Sherry leaned forward. "And Ambrose?"

"Can't get him to leave his workroom."

The others nodded, unsurprised.

"I don't get it." Banneker gestured to the street. "They never fight like this."

"I should've done something," Sherry mumbled. "I should've stepped in earlier, encouraged her to take on less."

Grim shook their head. "She wouldn't have listened."

A weary silence settled around them. The clock on the wall struck midnight, but no one made a motion to leave. Eli toyed with his earrings, pressing his thumb against the dull points of the sun pendant. Dawn was with her family, but Ambrose had no one. He couldn't just leave him like that.

"What do we do?" he asked the room. Grim leaned back against the mantelpiece, arms folded.

"This is their fight," they said. "They're adults. Let them work it out."

"But Ames isn't going to leave the shop—"

"He will, in his own time," Sherry said. She stirred her tea absently, her eyes distant. "Doesn't do any good to force him out."

Grim gave a slow nod. Banneker sighed and flopped back on the couch. Eli did the same, wondering how many times the street had done this. Watched Ambrose from afar, through his Master Pearce years and beyond, waiting patiently for him to come around on his own. He supposed he would have to be patient, too.

But patience was never his strong suit.

While waiting for Ambrose to emerge from his potion-filled hole, Eli spent his days trapped in miserable circles of his own. The sight of the shelves, the register, the cauldron—he could barely stomach any of it.

If he couldn't run the shop for the rest of his life, what could he do? Could he turn the shop into something else? He wasn't a cook or a craftsman. And any new shop would pose the same problem—the endless repetition, the threat of the same day in, day out, for years on end.

But if he sold the place, where would he go? Back to Kolkea to mope? His parents would love to have him there. Lily would love to have him there. But one by one, his siblings would find callings outside of home. Lily would go off to start her training, and eventually it would be just...Eli and Tom. Doing nothing with their lives.

He grumbled as he scraped himself together for his evening plans —a date with a baker from the Elwig Market. He was hardly in the mood for it, but he needed the distraction. To get out of the cobwebs of his shop, if not the ones in his own head.

"Great conversation starter, huh?" Eli said to Tom, who spun in place while he pulled on his red jacket. "What do you do for a living? Oh, you know. Run a potion shop I hate. Fail at everything. Dream of running into the Driftwood and never coming back."

Tom stopped spinning and stared at him.

"I'm not actually going to do that, Tom."

He trudged downstairs, avoiding looking too hard at the shop around him. His eyes landed instead on The Griffin's Claw, as they often did. Though veiled by the rainfall outside, he could barely make out a sliver of orange light from the workroom within.

Eli watched the light for a moment, hoping he'd catch a glimpse of the potioneer. He didn't want to talk to a date about his problems. He wanted to talk to Ambrose. Take him up on his offer to talk, step through his options. Maybe Ambrose could just write the solution in his notebook like before, with his clear steps and diagrams. He laughed to himself—he could imagine the list now. *Step one: I told you so.*

His laughter faded as he buttoned up his jacket. He didn't even have to talk to Ambrose about the shop. At this point, talking to him about anything would be nice. Even just telling a story and hearing Ambrose's laugh would help.

But the half-elf in question wouldn't even open the door to talk about the commission. Eli would know—he had already tried twice.

Across the street, the light flickered, and Eli narrowed his eyes. His own problems could wait—but Ambrose was currently on a one-way path to turning into a cauldron.

He straightened his jacket and strode out the door. He could get through to Ambrose, nudge him back into his friendships. He just had to force open the door a little.

STEP 23:

SEPARATE THE LAYERS

Ambrose

WHEN AMBROSE CRAWLED into bed the night of the sinkhole expedition, he told himself he would visit Dawn in the morning. He'd go straight to her shop before opening and sort everything out.

But when morning broke, he couldn't do it.

The pull to hide in his workroom was too strong. It was too easy to convince himself he was busy. That he had so much to brew. And by nightfall, he had convinced himself of even more. That Dawn didn't want to see him right now anyway, that it was best to let her reach out on her own terms.

And in the meantime, he locked the door and remained on *his* own terms.

It was simple—at first. There were no lunches with Dawn to avoid, and he could afford a day or two of a closed shop. But after spotting Eli, then Sherry, then Grim peering through the window, he resorted to shutting himself in his workroom. Brewing both potions and tea would ease the knot in his stomach, he reasoned. It always did.

Then after a few days, even the comfort of brewing abandoned him, and his mood sank along with the bubbles in the cauldron. He couldn't deny that this was the longest he had ever gone without talking to Dawn—but she hadn't reached out yet. Not a visit, not even a note slipped under the door.

He stirred the potion clockwise. She would come around eventually. After all, she was still his friend, wasn't she?

He stirred the potion counterclockwise, feeling both the push of the liquid's momentum against the ladle and the words of his old mentor in his ears. Pearce had warned him about involving himself with others. If they didn't need him, he didn't need them. His mentor's logic was straightforward.

But as he doused the flames, the shameful knot in his stomach tightened painfully, and he winced. There used to be a simplicity in keeping to himself, a comfort in the isolation that eased this sort of pain. Why wasn't it working now?

A pounding on the shop door jolted him out of his thoughts.

"Ambrose?" Eli's voice butted up against the window, mixing with the rain outside. "I know you're in there. I'm just here to return a wand, all right?"

As Ambrose lined up his ingredients for the next warming potion —crushed crystal, red thyme, icefall vine, in that order—he considered staying inside the workroom. Pretending he couldn't hear Eli over the rain.

But he found himself walking to the door and turning the lock anyway.

"Apologies," he mumbled, looking everywhere except for Eli's face. "I've been busy."

"Mm-hm." Eli held out the wand. "What happened between you and Dawn?"

"Oh, gods—" Ambrose grabbed the wand and made to slam the door shut, but Eli's palm shot out and held it open. Ambrose tried to force it closed—Eli's arm held strong.

"Come on, you can't stay in there forever."

Still determined not to look at him, Ambrose strode back to the workroom. "I don't want to talk about it."

Eli's footsteps echoed behind him. "Yeah, I noticed."

Ambrose stubbornly relit the fire and poured in the water. Drops sputtered and hissed on the warm metal as he worked. But behind him, Eli kept talking.

"Sherry's worried, Grim's worried," he said. "Banneker keeps talking about negative auras and constellation retrograde—"

Ambrose glared at him. "I *said* I don't want to talk about"—his eyes finally landed on Eli—"...it."

Eli had traded his usual clothing—loose beige shirt, occasionally a vest—for a fitted maroon jacket. The short, stiff collar drew attention first to his neck, then to the splash of gold embroidery trailing like vines down his chest. Ambrose worked hard not to follow the crisp lines of the outfit all the way down to his perfectly polished boots.

He gritted his teeth. He didn't need this; he didn't need any of it.

He had to get Eli to leave.

"I tried to help her, and I failed," he snapped as he gathered his ingredients. "That's all. Now, you clearly have"—he gestured to the jacket, then cleared his throat—"um, somewhere to be."

"I've got a minute." Eli folded his arms and leaned against the doorway, his gaze softening. An infuriating warmth began a duel with the pain in Ambrose's chest. "Whatever happened, I'm sure you both can fix it if you talk to her."

"Oh, has she made an effort to talk to me?" He poured the ingredients into the cauldron, his grip too tight on the bottles—crystal, vine, thyme. Behind him, Eli sighed.

"Listen, she made a bad call. A really bad call. But you can't avoid each other forever. The sooner you both talk, the sooner this will be over."

Ambrose slammed down the bottle. "Are you truly here just to lecture me? Because, if you are, I'd rather you leave."

The sharpness in his voice had the opposite effect; Eli approached him instead. "I'm here because I got worried."

A cold laugh escaped Ambrose's lips. "Why?"

"Why?" Eli stopped and looked at him in disbelief. "Sherry said you'd do this. Told me you'd only come out in your own time."

Eli still wasn't leaving. Ambrose stirred the cauldron, then ladled out the brew, sharp spikes growing in his voice. "Then why didn't you listen?" he asked. Drops of the potion spattered clumsily across the worktable.

Eli scoffed. "I couldn't just stand by."

"Well, you should've."

"And let you push me away?" Eli stepped even closer. "Like you do with everyone else?"

"Yes!" Ambrose spat the word and whirled around to face him, potion in hand. He expected anger on Eli's face, or pity.

He found only concern, and all the spikes in his voice broke.

"Now, if—if you'll excuse me." Ambrose faltered as he brought the potion to his lips. "I need to test this, and then I'll be—"

The liquid slid like ice down his throat, and the end of his words cut off in a choke. He staggered back into the worktable, an involuntary shudder ripping through him. "Gods, that's awful. What did I...?"

He held up the bottle. Thought back to his last few steps. Froze.

He had gotten the order wrong. One swapped vial, which neutralized the active ingredient and turned it into—

He looked wordlessly to Eli.

He dropped, his knees striking the stone floor. Pain flashed up through his legs, then numbed, countered by the ice rushing through his veins. A pair of hands grabbed his arms and held him upright, but Ambrose's vision swayed somewhere over Eli's shoulder, starry and blurred.

"Stay with me!" Eli let him go and dashed off to the right. Without his support, Ambrose slumped to the floor, trying desperately to fight off the cold. But between the poison in his blood and the stone tiles freezing his cheek, there was little he could do. Coils of white air trailed off his lips, and an invisible grip tightened around his throat. He could do nothing but watch as Eli slammed his palm down on the rose statue and stepped back, his blurry form waiting for the red emergency light to appear.

Nothing happened.

"What—?" Eli repeated the motion. Still nothing. A new wave of cold rushed over Ambrose.

"There are..." he forced through chattering teeth. "There are no names."

Eli whipped around to the door. "*Help!*"

The scream echoed through the store, but no one answered. Eli leapt for the empty ingredient vials on the table. "What did you...?" He read through the labels. Closed his eyes, moved his lips silently. Nodded to Ambrose. "Hold on for me."

As Eli stumbled out into the shop, Ambrose clutched at his own closing throat with frostbitten fingers. Every breath was shorter than the last, and his thoughts came in shattered and jagged. If Eli didn't find the antidote in time or picked the wrong one—

Black clouds narrowed his vision, and he barely saw the man skid back into the room with a bottle in hand.

"I got it, I got it." He knelt, flicked off the cork with his thumb, and set the bottle to Ambrose's lips. "All in one go, all right?"

Ambrose screwed his eyes shut as the antidote passed his lips. The taste of mint was overpowering, but it couldn't mask the acrid, bubbling tang that hit right after. He fought the urge to cough, leaking hot tears from the effort.

"I know, I know." Eli set down the bottle, one hand on Ambrose's shoulder. "Try to keep it down."

Ambrose forced out a nod, swallowed, then gasped as the bubbles burned his throat. Fire quickly melted the ice in his veins, shooting jolts of confused pain through his body.

Without thinking, he reached for Eli.

"It's all right." Eli took his hand, then shifted and pulled him closer, until he was half-draped across Eli's lap. As Ambrose closed his eyes against another wave of pain, Eli placed a palm on his cheek. "It'll be over soon. I'm here, I've got you."

Ambrose grabbed the hand at his cheek and curled inward, closer to Eli, until the cool silk of Eli's jacket pressed against his burning forehead. Eli didn't move or shy away; he stayed perfectly still, rubbing his thumb across Ambrose's cheekbone until shuddering pain faded into limp exhaustion.

"Can you sit up?" Eli gently pulled away. Ambrose let out a long, slow breath and opened his eyes. Eli's worried face swam above him.

"I think so." Hands still trembling, he pushed off Eli's lap and dragged himself over to lean against the workroom table. A hundred new emotions tangled themselves inside him—embarrassment, shame, relief, echoing fear...

He rested his head against the wood and focused on breathing. "Thank you, Eli."

But the words went unanswered. Eli stood up, wiped off his knees, and stared at the rose statue, dull and still. "How long has this been like that?" he asked. His tone was soft, but the undercurrent of anger ran deep.

"It's..." Ambrose's voice came out raspy, as if he had been smoking a pipe all day. "It's always been like that. Pearce removed them—"

"*Pearce*, that son of a wood-eating dragon—!" Eli burst out, then ran his hands through his hair and started to pace. "What if I hadn't been here? What if I had walked away when you told me to? You would—you would've..."

Shame overtook the rest of Ambrose's emotions, and he pulled himself to his feet, still wobbly and wavering. "It won't happen again."

"You're right," Eli snapped. "It won't."

He grabbed the scroll under the rose statue, scribbled something down, and threw it back. With one last, hard look at Ambrose, he turned and stalked out of the room.

"I'm sorry!" Ambrose tried to follow, but a wave of dizziness kept him clinging to the table. "Eli, I'm sorry—"

The bell above the front door clanged.

Ambrose slumped and reached for the rose statue. That was it, he had lost another friend, and it was all his fault—

He tugged open the scroll with stiff fingers. There, below the crossed-out names of years past, was *Eli*, in heavy, clear letters.

STEP 24:

PICK YOUR POISON

Eli

ELI CURSED AND STARTED RUNNING, using the motion to shake out his nerves. When he had told Ambrose he had a minute to spare, he hadn't been *lying*, exactly.

He'd simply failed to mention he was late to his date with the baker.

"Hey!" He skidded to a halt in front of a tavern, where a black-haired man leaned against the wall, checking his pocket watch. "So sorry I'm late, Zander, had a bit of an emergency back at the shop."

"It's all right." Zander straightened. Unlike everyone on the ground floor, the baker wore white, breezy clothing that contrasted strongly with his bronze skin. Eli supposed he had no need to worry about chasm dust, being a merchant high up in Little Elwig. "If you need to go back and take care of anything—"

"No, no." Eli waved a hand, forcing it not to shake. Ambrose had taken the antidote. Ambrose was fine. "It's handled. Let's go in."

The tavern here was a far cry from the Jumping Ogre. It was nestled in one of the northern cracks of the Scar, farther from the main thoroughfare, and had an air of peace about it. The room was quieter, the tables less crowded, the lighting warm and soft. As they settled into a table in the corner, Eli couldn't help but think that Ambrose would like this place.

"How was the market today?" he asked, pushing the potioneer out of his thoughts.

"Just fine. Sold everything by noon." Zander smiled. A whiff of cinnamon still wafted around him, a remnant of the fluffy rolls he baked every morning. His coastal inflection made his words just as airy and light as he picked up the menu. "What do they recommend here?"

"Sherry says the mushroom stew is good," Eli said, then gave a small wince. Stew reminded him too much of cauldrons.

"Oh, my mum makes a great mushroom stew," Zander said, eyes bright. "The secret is to add a little miso paste..."

Eli gladly let Zander's cooking advice distract him until the waiter arrived.

"Which bread would you like?" the waiter asked. "Olive or rosemary?"

Ambrose loved rosemary bread.

"Olive," Eli said quickly.

As the waiter nodded and swayed off, Zander fiddled with the corner of his menu. "The emergency you mentioned—what was it? Must have been something awful. You've been frowning this whole time."

"Oh." Eli glanced down at his hands, where ink stains bloomed from writing his name on the scroll. His arms felt heavy and warm, as if he were still holding Ambrose, still feeling him clutching his hand. "Just a small alarm. But he'll be fine now."

Zander looked at him, waiting for him to elaborate. Eli deflected instead. "So, how long have you owned the bakery?"

He tried to sink fully into the evening after that, to focus entirely on his date. After all, the place was lovely, the food was delicious, and Zander had plenty of entertaining market stories.

But thoughts of that infuriating blue-haired man kept coming back.

Ambrose would have liked that joke, he thought. Ambrose would have enjoyed this soup. Ambrose would have gotten that reference.

He diluted his thoughts with a swig of beer.

"What do you like to do for fun?" he asked. Zander chewed on a bread crust and gave a pensive hum.

"I've gotten into reading again," he said, leaning back in the booth. "It can be nice, picking up a book while waiting for the dough to proof. I'm going through a few books from home, ones I read as a kid. Like that series about Sir, um..." He snapped his fingers when the name didn't come to him. "Sir Derrick? Sir..."

Eli brightened. "Sir Terrance?"

"Yes!"

"I loved that series." Eli leaned in. "Who's your favorite character?"

Zander glanced up at the ceiling in thought, and Eli cycled through guesses. Lady Ree was the fan favorite, of course, but he could see Zander liking strong-hearted Sir Terrance. Or perhaps Eban the Bold, with his love of pastries.

Zander met his gaze. "Corie."

Eli deflated.

"Oh, not you, too," he said. "Corie? Really?"

"What's wrong with her?"

"She's just a..." Eli gestured at nothing, frustration tinging his words. "She's a stupid farmer in the woods. She doesn't do anything."

"Doesn't do anything?" Zander scoffed and set down his bread. "You're right, she's not one of the heroes. She doesn't go out and kill dragons. But she's always there for the party. She heals them when they're injured, feeds them when they're sick. Encourages them, keeps them on the right path." He began to grab items on the table— the candle, the dish of butter, the spoon and fork. "You read the end of book four, right?"

"Of course."

Zander pushed the candle forward. "Lady Ree kills the dragon, saves the world, and retires her sword."

"I remember."

"But who does she go to after?" Zander asked, nudging the candle to the right. "Who's the first person she goes to for peace and rest?"

Eli paged through the scenes in his head. Lady Ree hung up her armor, rode into the forest, and went straight to... "She goes to Corie."

Zander nodded, eyes bright. "She could have gone anywhere, to anyone. The whole country loves her. Sir Terrance builds a castle next to hers. Eban the Bold gives her the key to his keep." He moved aside the spoon and fork. "But at the end of the day, she doesn't want them. She wants her friend, the person she trusts and cares about the most." He pushed the candle until it touched the butter dish. "She wants the stupid farmer in the woods."

Eli swallowed. The person he trusted and cared about was shivering alone in his workroom right now.

His thoughts flooded in unbidden. He shouldn't have left Ambrose in the shop. He should have called off the date, brought *him* here, fed *him* soup and bread. It should be Ambrose sitting across from him, talking eagerly. It should be Ambrose's hand resting on the table, close enough for Eli to touch. Ambrose's eyes flickering in the candlelight, Ambrose's lips tilted into a soft smile...

Eli stared at the candle flame. He wanted the stupid farmer in the woods, too.

"Eli?" Zander's voice dragged him back. "Are you...still worried about that emergency?"

Eli nodded, biting down a foolish grin.

"Yeah, I have to go take care of him—it. The emergency, I mean." He stood, reaching for his coin purse. "I'm so sorry, I don't mean to run out on you like this—"

Zander touched his arm. "Don't worry about the bill. Go take care of your friend."

"Are you sure?"

"I've got it handled." He nodded. "Best of luck."

Eli strode out into the drizzling rain, slipped past the windows, then started sprinting back toward Rosemond Street.

STEP 25:

BREAK IT DOWN

Ambrose

AFTER ELI LEFT, the shop was dark and silent. No fire under the cauldron, no wagons creaking in the street. Just Ambrose and a scattering of empty glass bottles, one of which had tried to kill him, and one of which had saved him.

But he couldn't bring himself to clean any of it up. Pain frayed his movements; coughs wracked his chest. He slowly reached for the largest staff he owned—an old fire starter, long since out of charges—and leaned heavily on it, catching his breath, looking around him.

He didn't know what to do next, but he knew he couldn't stay here. Couldn't continue breathing the stale air of the shop.

He limped into the street, taking in the last of the evening drizzle. Farther up the road, High Vine still bustled, and farther down, the Jumping Ogre welcomed its late dinner patrons. But here, he could simply stand and breathe.

He caught his reflection in the windows of Eli's Elixirs, his form blurred and crooked as he leaned on the fire starter. How much like Master Pearce he must look right now. Gnarled staff, potion master robes, Guild signet ring. Standing alone with no one to call on.

Master Pearce would have been proud of him.

He didn't want to be like Master Pearce.

A sound shattered the quiet air—the precise zing of metal against stone, then the crackling of flames in a forge. Ambrose responded to it with a cough, and before he realized what he was doing, he hobbled over, drawn by the distant warmth of the flame and the one who fanned it.

Sherry hummed away in her forge, finishing her work for the day. The place was a burnt umber mess of soot, smoke, metal, and tools. Ambrose had pointed out the disarray once, years ago, and she had waved him off. As long as she could navigate it blindfolded, it didn't matter what anyone else thought of it. And as he watched her now, hunched over his staff, he saw she was right. Sherry moved through her work gracefully, the practice and experience of her years lending an ease of motion that hardly anyone else on the street could claim, him included.

She didn't notice him until another cough shuddered through his lungs.

"Who's—" Her sunny smile dropped as soon as she saw him. "Ambrose?"

The attention made him move backward on instinct.

"I'm sorry, I don't mean to bother you." He tried stepping away, but it turned into more of a stagger. She rushed out and caught him in a strong grip.

"You aren't a bother," she said firmly, gray eyes searching his face. "You are never a bother. Dear, will you please tell me what happened?"

He met her gaze, and despite the pain in his throat, his words spilled out in a jumble.

"I can't talk to Dawn," he rasped, "and I accidentally drank a failed potion, but—but Eli was there, and he saved me, and he tried the alarm, but it didn't work, and now he's angry at me too, and I just..." He touched his throat and winced. "Do you...do you have any tea?"

"Yes." She flicked a wand, and the forge went out. "Yes, of course."

Ambrose had been in Sherry's flat countless times. Early on, she had dragged him over for playdates with her own children, all taller and older and overwhelming in their enthusiasm. Later, he'd come by for street meetings and teatimes he couldn't slip out of. He was used to the earthy feel of the place, the warm air and lingering scent of vanilla. But as he hobbled behind Sherry at a turtle's pace, he took the time to admire how much adventurer pride seeped into her decor.

In distinct conflict with the woman's love of tea, cookies, and gossip, the place wasn't covered in needlework and doilies, but in weapons and trophies. Intricately carved spears and magnificent axes littered the walls. Gruidenna feathers hung above one mantel, alcedon antlers on another. Every cushion and blanket smelled of leather and metal polish. As Sherry lumbered around the place, shedding her thick gloves and reaching for the tea in the cabinet, it wasn't hard to imagine that she had swung these weapons and collected these trophies herself.

"Do you like them?" she asked when Ambrose stepped closer to a string of serrated teeth. "River kraken teeth. My third son reeled it in himself. You should see his scars."

She pointed to a family portrait on the wall—no more than a rough charcoal sketch hung behind glass. There were too many people crammed in the drawing to count, all of them smiling. Sherry stood in the back of the gaggle, beaming brightest.

"Are they all out adventuring?" Ambrose asked, wondering which brawny, curly-haired man was the kraken hunter.

"Oh, yes. Out with my first son and second daughter. I imagine they're in the Driftwood by now with their cairn cat licenses." Sherry set a pot and a plate of cookies on the table. "Tea's ready, dear."

He half collapsed into the chair, his breath still rattling against his ribs. She spooned a generous amount of honey into his cup. "Do you need a healing potion?"

"I should wait an hour," he mumbled, letting the steam from the tea calm his throat. "To make sure it doesn't interact with the antidote."

"What did you take on accident?" All the color drained out of her face. "It was on accident, right?"

"Yes—yes, it was an accident, I'd never..." Ambrose went pink and sipped his tea. "It was a stupid mistake. I added the ingredients in the wrong order, and it reversed the effects of the potion."

"And Eli was there to help you?"

Ambrose couldn't bring himself to meet her gaze. "He was," he said quietly. "He saved my life."

He went on to explain about the antidote, the alarm, and Eli storming out. Then before that, the sinkhole, the land bridge, and Dawn storming out. He waited for her to berate or criticize him, but she held silent until the end.

"Later today"—she filled his teacup—"I'll come by and add myself back to the scroll. And I'll tell Grim and Banneker as well."

A protest rose in Ambrose's throat. "I promise I won't do it again—"

"You can't promise you'll never make a mistake, Ambrose." Her eyes flashed. "You know that."

He opened his mouth, then nodded and sipped his tea. She took a cookie and chewed on it thoughtfully. "I'll need to do something for Eli in thanks. Maybe I'll make him a cake." Her eyes brightened at the thought. "I haven't made a layer cake in years, you know. Not since— oh, which birthday was that?"

Ambrose frowned. "Whose birthday?"

"Yours, of course." She added another cookie to his plate. "Must have been, what, your thirteenth birthday? Pearce wasn't going to do anything for it, but Grim reminded me it was coming, so I had to whip something up." She gave a small, happy sigh. "Pearce said you loved it. Ate it right up. Not like he ever fed you any sweets to begin with."

Ambrose almost dropped his teacup.

He'd thought Pearce had given him that cake for his birthday.

Across from him, Sherry drifted further into her memories,

unaware of how still he had gone. "Grim was so good about checking in on you, too. They were the first to discover you had caught fever that one winter, you know. You might not remember it, but they even covered several shifts for you so you could sleep. And they always made sure you got your medicine on time."

A different sort of pain tightened Ambrose's throat. He *did* remember, though the memories were hazy and faded. He recalled someone sitting by his cot in the supply closet, pressing little bottles of fernberry-flavored medicine into his sweaty palm. Applying cool cloths to his forehead when he thought the fever was too much to bear.

Hot, stinging tears pricked at his eyes. He had again assumed it was Pearce.

"Oh!" Sherry munched blissfully on another cookie. "Do you recall that one winter Banneker gave everyone books? He wasn't sure if you'd like those old adventurer tales, but you were asking Pearce for more the very next day—"

Ambrose burst into tears, hiding his face in his hands.

They had been there; they had always been there. How long had they looked out for him? How much more had they done for him over the years, while all he did was push them away, swallow some stupid platitude about self-sufficiency from a man who almost let him die the first winter he was here? Whose mantra almost got him killed again not hours ago?

They had fed him, saved him, were willing to climb into sinkholes for him, and what had he done in return but run and hide?

"Oh, dear." A chair scraped against the floor, and Sherry's hand rested on his shoulder. "Was it something I said?"

It took him a while to get the words out in between sobs.

"I'm so sorry," he said, wiping the tears from his face, his throat stinging at the salt. "I can't ever pay you back. How can I ever—how can I—"

"No, no," she murmured, dragging over her chair to sit by him. "This isn't about paying us back. Not for any of it, you understand me? That's not how family works."

He blinked at her, then reached out. She gathered him up into a hug like it was perfectly normal. Stroking his hair like he was one of her own. All he could do was try to channel twenty years of withheld gratitude into the smoky scent of her leather apron.

She pulled back and wiped away one of his tears with her thumb. It would leave a soot stain, but he didn't care.

"What do I do?" he asked, his throat scratchier than before. She pressed his teacup into his hand.

"First, you drink up." Her wrinkles deepened as she smiled. "Then you see who you can support in your own way. That's all you can ever do."

STEP 26:

COLLABORATION

Eli

WHEN ELI REACHED ROSEMOND STREET, the rain had stopped, leaving him skidding on the puddles in front of The Griffin's Claw.

"Ambrose?" He tugged on the door—locked. He rushed to the window and pressed his forehead to the glass, hands cupped around his face. "You in there?"

The workroom was dark, the door ajar. Panic crept into his chest. If Ambrose had a reaction to the antidote, or if the vial hadn't been enough...

He cursed and backed away from the window, bouncing on his heels. "Okay, Ames, I'm coming in, and I promise I'm going to pay for the window after—"

"What on earth are you doing?" Ambrose demanded. Eli jumped and clutched his heart.

"Ambrose!" He whipped around to find the man standing in the street, leaning against a staff and holding a cloth bundle in his arms. "Sorry, I thought you were—I thought you might still be..." He rushed forward, reaching for Ambrose's face. He still looked pale, but his eyes were bright and his lips no longer blue. "How are you feeling? Any side effects from the antidote?" He laid two fingers on Ambrose's pulse and pressed his other hand to his forehead. "Fever? Dizziness? Brain fog?"

Ambrose stared at him wide-eyed. "I—I thought you had gone out?" he mumbled, gaze dipping down to Eli's jacket.

"I had, but I..." Eli realized his hands had dropped to cradle Ambrose's jawline. He quickly stepped away, his cheeks warming. "I'm sorry I got angry and walked away. I was scared. But that was no excuse to leave you alone." He cleared his throat and nodded to the shop. "Can I make you some tea? Get you a healing potion?"

"Sherry already gave me some, but..." Ambrose lifted the bundle in his arms. "I would like your help with something, please."

Eli stared at him. Ambrose, asking for help? Perhaps he was experiencing brain fog after all.

"Yes," Eli blurted out. "Yes, anything."

Ambrose pulled back the cloth to reveal a metal bracer. "I need to make things up to Dawn."

"Wow." Eli set his hands on his hips as Ambrose stuffed vials into a pack. "You'll really do anything not to talk to people, huh?"

"I'm *going* to talk to her," Ambrose argued. "I'm just going to talk to her *after* I hand her the moss."

Ambrose tucked away a healing potion and a light wand, then continued moving through his shop. The plan he had outlined to Eli was ostensibly simple. Win Dawn over with a jar of her long-lost moss, then take her on a relaxing day out. A Fireball game, a picnic topside, some wine and cheese in the lavender...and not a customer or half-made wand in sight.

Easy, if it wasn't for the very first step.

"Ames, are you sure about this?" Eli searched through Ambrose's cabinets and plucked a few more vials for the bag, stuffing them in alongside empty jars. He chose his next words just as carefully, hoping not to bump up against Ambrose's determination. "You weren't wrong to keep Dawn safe, you know. You don't owe her anything."

"I know that." Ambrose went to secure the pack, but his fingers slowed. "But it was my fault we failed that night. I told her I would get her the moss, and I'm keeping my word."

He looked up at Eli, his voice quiet, wide eyes pleading.

"Will you help me do it?"

When asked like that, Eli would have agreed to anything. He gave a reassuring smile and grabbed one of the bracers next to the bag. It was clearly Sherry's make—polished steel, delicately engraved with a leaf pattern.

"Of course." He held up the piece. "But you're not quite ready yet. Hold out your arm?"

"Oh. Um...let me just..." Ambrose half turned and undid the frog clasps on his robes. Eli swallowed; the sight of his fingers moving so deftly down the fabric reminded him of why he had sprinted out of his date. For a burning instant, he wanted to replace Ambrose's hands with his own, continue the path downward—then slowly push the robes off his shoulder, wrap his arms around his waist...

Oh, no. He was in deeper than he thought.

Ambrose carefully set aside his robes and held out his arm. "Bracer?"

Eli blinked at his outstretched hand, then reeled himself back. "Yup. Bracer, you got it. Hold still for a sec..."

As Eli secured the bracer straps, he regretted not having this revelation about Ambrose earlier. He could have gone to Dawn for advice. She knew Ambrose better than anyone—she'd know his signs, give advice on how to court him. Or tell him off and keep him from ruining their friendship.

But Dawn wasn't here, so Eli used the tools he had on hand.

"Other arm, please." He picked up the second bracer—but before Ambrose could raise his arm, Eli lifted it himself, gently touching his elbow, then dragging his fingers to his wrist. Ambrose blushed—but that was hardly anything new. The pale half-elf blushed easily.

"Not used to wearing this sort of thing," he mumbled as Eli worked on the straps. "Feels silly."

"Sherry's just trying to keep you safe."

"Not just me." Ambrose nodded to the table. "She packed you some armor as well."

A familiar set lay on the wood—the same jerkin, bracers, and belt she had shoved at him for the cistern inspection.

"Very thoughtful of her." He edged closer to Ambrose, turning his arm around to inspect the bracer's fit. "She didn't give you a jerkin?"

"She gave me this." Ambrose tapped the collar of his vest. Unlike his usual wardrobe, this piece was green, with looping silver embroidery at the edges. "It belonged to one of her sons."

"Hm." Eli ran a finger along the embroidery at the shoulder. Sure enough, a dull magical aura buzzed under his touch. "A defensive spell?"

"I believe so—"

Taking a risk, Eli touched the embroidery at the collar, his fingers skirting Ambrose's neck. Ambrose's breath hitched at the touch, and his words died on his tongue.

"You all right?" Eli murmured, watching carefully for any sign of Ambrose pulling away or flinching at the touch. No such rejection— he simply nodded.

"Fine," he croaked, his eyes darting down to Eli's lips.

Sparks filled Eli's chest.

"Guess I'll get dressed, then," he said smoothly and dropped his hand. "Can't disappoint Sherry."

He stepped away, giving Ambrose space to finish checking the bags—but he didn't stray far as he unbuttoned his jacket, then laced up the jerkin. For a moment, he considered asking Ambrose for help in lacing the piece. But when he caught sight of the man's furtive glances and increasingly clumsy movements, he couldn't bring himself to escalate the torture and break him entirely.

Once his armor was on, he secured the belt around his waist. Sherry had provided a dagger rather than a sword this time, an easier weapon to wield in narrow caves. He found the weight reassuring against his hip, and the pressure of the armor relaxed him.

"Ready to go?" He leaned casually against the table, making sure to show off the full outfit. Just as he hoped, Ambrose's gaze lingered, dragging over his armor and down to the dagger. Though the poor man clearly worked hard to keep his expression steady, his ears gave him away. They perked up in a tiny, adorable gesture, going pink at the tips.

Eli bit back a delirious grin, sparks escaping his chest and rushing through his limbs. Gods, this was delightful. Could he ask Ambrose on a date? Would he say yes? He'd keep the outing simple, of course. A nice, calm date, something both easy and romantic. He needed to brainstorm this—

Ambrose turned and picked up his pack. "Ready to go if you are."

Eli deflated. Oh, right. They had a quest.

Fine—quest first, then a date.

"Come on." He took the second pack and gestured to the door. "Lead the way, moss man."

STEP 27:

BLEND

Ambrose

THEY SET out as the last of the dinner rush died down, taking a relatively empty elevator topside. Once they reached the familiar darkness of the Titan's Eye sinkhole, Ambrose set his pack down at his feet. Eli had thrown an assortment of potions into it before they left, obscuring the ones he had prepared himself.

"Did you see the anchoring vials I packed?" He sifted through the bottles. "Dawn and I used them on the stairs and the bridges..."

"Oh, we won't need all that." Eli shrugged. "Take this and let's get to the first bridge." He pressed a triangular bottle into Ambrose's hand.

"One of my floating potions?" Ambrose frowned at the label. "But why—?"

"You asked for my help, right?" Eli drained his own bottle and headed for the stairs. "Take it and you'll see."

Ambrose sighed, drank the fizzy orange liquid, and followed him.

Under the effect of the potion, Eli bounced down the stairs, the magic untethering him from gravity enough to make his descent look like a floating jaunt. Ambrose followed more cautiously, fighting the magic's buoyant effects as he tugged a crystal lamp out of his pack.

"I can take that." Eli turned around and held out a hand, continuing to bounce down the stairs backward.

"Fine." Ambrose quickly handed off the lamp and resumed his useless grip on the wall. Eli took the device and moved forward, shadows swinging across the stairs with every bounce.

"No need to fear, Ames. Your potion's working great."

"I can see that," Ambrose muttered. In front of him, Eli's feet barely grazed the steps. "Could you *please* watch where you're going?"

"Concerned, are we?" Eli started bouncing higher. "Isn't this the ideal way to get rid of your competition? Oh no, Mayor Rune, he just —*fell* down a sinkhole right before we merged the components. Guess you'll have to give me his share of the money and sell his shop to literally anyone else."

"You know I don't—" Ambrose briefly slid on a slimy patch of stone, then regained his balance with a glare. "You know I don't think that. Now, if we could both get to the bridge without dying, I might live long enough to see Dawn talk to me again."

But Ambrose's problems didn't end when they reached the land bridge. The crumbling hole still remained, partially hidden by moss, vines, and puddles from the previous rain. Ambrose kept close to the wall as he pointed the danger out to Eli.

"Do you think we should jump across?" he asked. Eli snorted.

"No."

"No?"

"I mean, we *could* jump across." He peered down at the black hole of the tunnel entrance below. "Or...I jump from there, to there, to there, and boom, you're done."

Eli strode out onto the bridge. Ambrose scrambled to follow, fear tightening his chest.

"What, and—and leave me here?"

"Of course not." Eli shot him a grin. "I'll carry you. Here, hold this for me."

He handed back the lamp and scooped Ambrose up—one arm at

his shoulders, the other under his knees. The floating potion buoyed Ambrose along, lifting him up, then settling him back down into Eli's arms.

"What are you doing?" He clutched the lamp to his chest, heart hammering against it. "This is far riskier than simply jumping across—"

"But it's so much more fun." Eli's grin widened. "Don't you trust me?"

"Of course, I trust you—"

Eli leapt off the bridge.

Ambrose shrieked and buried his face in the man's neck. Wind rushed past his cheeks and cut through his clothing, and he couldn't take in a breath until Eli's feet bounced gently against the next bridge.

"I'll walk!" Ambrose shouted, eyes closed. "I'll walk, I'll walk—"

"Just two more!" Eli sounded far too gleeful as he jumped again. Ambrose grabbed a fistful of his jerkin and held his breath against his flipping stomach.

Eli's feet struck stone once, twice. When the sharp wind settled around them for the last time, the chilly air of the tunnel felt warm in comparison.

"We're here!" Eli crowed. "How are you doing?"

Ambrose kept his face buried in the crook of his neck. Between his shaking hands and the scent of herbs and sunlight coming from Eli's collar, he wasn't at all prepared to move. "I suppose I'm not dead," he muttered into the fabric.

"Come on." Eli started walking, making no move to set him on the ground. "I just saved you a few hours ago. Why would I throw all that effort away?"

Guilt forced Ambrose to extricate himself, finding the ground with his unsteady feet. Eli had already gone above and beyond that night. Why he was in a musty sinkhole with him now, he had no idea.

"Thank you again for that, by the way," he mumbled, brushing invisible dust off his vest. "I'm not even sure how to repay you for—"

"Hey." Eli touched his arm. "None of that. Seeing you alive is its own reward." He nodded into the cave. "Now, where to?"

Ambrose gazed into the misty depths of the cave and gulped.

They ventured into the dark pathways with the lantern in hand. Unlike the cisterns, these caves had been carved only by time and the occasional burrowing creature. But Ambrose still spotted something familiar—the same thin white crystals that had plagued his construction tunnel adventure. Though these didn't appear to be covered in larva slime, he grimaced and stepped carefully around their sharp points anyway.

As Eli pulled ahead into the haze, Ambrose took out Dawn's research and held his lamp over the papers. According to her, the moss grew close to the sinkhole, the precise environment it needed to thrive. If they turned left, then went down the slope, then veered right at the fork...

He squinted at the papers, blinked, and squinted again. Was his eyesight failing him, or were the notes suddenly blurry?

He rubbed his eyes and dug for a healing potion in his pack. It was time for a follow-up anyway, after the one he took at Sherry's. He took a sip from a milky green vial, then looked around him and froze.

His vision, it turned out, was fine. The air was not.

The mist had thickened into a soupy fog, surrounding Ambrose in white until he couldn't even see the walls around him. He reached out next to him, then ahead, grasping for Eli's arm. Nothing.

"Eli?" he called, his voice wavering. "Where are you?"

"Up ahead," Eli called back. "Can you not—?" A pause. "Oh. Huh."

The mist swirled around his feet, and Ambrose held his breath. He had heard of bad air in caves before. All it took was one contaminated chamber, one waft of odorless, tasteless poison...

His hand traveled to his throat unconsciously. "Have you seen this before?"

"No, but I've heard about it," Eli said. "Given what's in this region, it's likely from a snub-nosed dragon. It likes to shroud itself in mist while hunting."

"*What?*"

"Don't worry, there's no dragon here!" Eli said quickly. "It's cold where you are, right?"

Ambrose shivered. "Yes."

"Good. If the dragon was around, the mist would be warm. It probably left hours ago."

Hardly reassured, Ambrose shoved his papers back into his bag with trembling hands. His panic was quickly turning his thoughts to mush, urging him to both run blindly and not move an inch from his spot.

But neither action was going to help him actually get to Eli, so he took a breath, focused on the lamp, and swung it upward.

"How do I find you?" he shouted, trying to catch any details around him—but the light merely bounced back into his eyes.

"Turn off the light!" Eli said.

Ambrose's heart blocked his throat. "Are you sure?"

"The mist will only reflect it back. It's not going to help you."

Ambrose doused the light. Darkness immediately pressed in, and his whole body began to shake. "Eli?"

"Follow my voice!"

Ambrose slowly moved forward, fighting his instincts to run and scream. Each time his shin met with a stalagmite, or his shoulder bumped into a wall, Eli helped him navigate it.

"Your left!" he called.

"Ow—"

"Your other left!"

"I know what my other left is!" Ambrose snapped, his fear dulling the edge of his words. The mist was still thick, and there was still no Eli in front of him. "How far away are you?"

"Not far. Keep following my voice!"

Ambrose plodded forward, fingers trailing along the stone wall. It helped to envision Eli waiting at the end of the path with his dagger and broad-shouldered armor. Hand outstretched so Ambrose could take it, ensuring he didn't lose him again...

Despite his fear—or perhaps because of it—his thoughts about Eli's hand spiraled. Was Eli touching him more than usual? The bracers, the collar, the carrying. It didn't mean anything...did it?

"Ames?" Eli's voice floated ahead of him, louder this time.

"Here!" Ambrose called back and quickened his pace. No, of course it didn't mean anything. Eli had just gone on a date that evening, after all. He probably had a lovely time. His date likely knew how to smile, and flirt, and maybe kiss, and oh gods, why was he thinking about this when he was about to die in these blasted tunnels—

He barreled straight into Eli's sturdy frame, almost bowling him over.

"There you are!" Eli staggered, then grabbed Ambrose's shoulder and steadied him. "See? I told you, no dragons. You're safe."

It may have been the deep relief Ambrose felt upon seeing Eli, or the last of his panic loosening his tongue. But instead of saying anything rational, like *Thank you* or *Safe is a relative term in these caves*, he said:

"How was your date?"

The words came out breathless and strung together. Eli blinked at him, still holding onto his shoulder with a warm hand. "What?"

"Your date," Ambrose repeated. "You said you were going on one before I—you know, before you... How was it?"

He tensed in preparation for the answer—but to his surprise, Eli faltered. "I left early," he said. "Wanted to, um...check on you."

"Oh." A flash of guilt replaced Ambrose's fear. "I'm so sorry, I didn't mean to—"

"No, it's okay. Really." Eli looked at the tunnel beyond, then took Ambrose's hand and smiled. "So I don't lose you again?"

As Eli gently intertwined their fingers, Ambrose desperately hoped that wasn't the only reason.

"Come on." Eli pulled him forward. "I think you're going to like what's up ahead."

A few paces beyond them, the tunnel opened up into a large chamber. As the mist filtered away on the craggy floor, it revealed all manner of jagged shapes—stalactites, pillars, curtains of spikes frilling the walls.

And all around them, patches of deep blue moss glowed as if the night sky had been thrown in paint splatters across the chamber. The pulse was so soothing, so reminiscent of fireflies in the lavender fields, that Ambrose half expected to hear cricket song filling the air, or feel an evening breeze sweep through the space.

"This is it, right? The moss Dawn wanted?" Eli asked. Ambrose nodded, smiling as he drank in the room. If only he could capture it somehow, show Dawn what it all looked like—

Then Eli reached toward a flickering patch of moss.

"Don't!" Ambrose grabbed his wrist. "It's extremely volatile. She's using it in fireworks, remember?"

Eli quickly drew his hand back. "What do we do?"

"Quite simple. I dig up a sample and we leave." Ambrose set his pack on the ground and pulled out his gloves, jar, and trowel. He couldn't deliver Dawn the whole room, but he could at least deliver her a jar or two.

His heart swelled as he tugged on the gloves. Dawn was going to be thrilled when he handed over the jar. All that was left was for her to create her masterpiece fireworks, and her article in the *Thirty* would be all but written—

His jar and trowel clinked together, and sharp, angry chittering floated down from above. Ambrose and Eli slowly looked up.

Clinging to the largest stalactite was a massive burrowing moth, its compound eyes twin moons in the night sky of the cave. It flicked its wings once, twice; the griffin-eye pattern on its back stared down at the men, daring them to take one step farther. But its left wing was ripped, and one of its legs dangled uselessly underneath it.

"Well," Eli whispered, "I think I know what the dragon was hunting."

The chittering grew louder. Ambrose's grip on the trowel tightened.

"What do we do?" he whispered back. Eli slowly reached into his own pack and pulled out a wand.

"Easy." He took one step forward, keeping his voice low. "I light up that stalactite. Once it's entranced by the giant glowing spike in the sky, we get our moss and leave. Here, get behind me."

Ambrose ducked behind him. Eli held up the wand, aimed carefully, then flicked.

The wand sputtered to life, a bright white light flaring at the tip. Ambrose waited for it to shoot toward the stalactite and imbue it with a white glow.

The light guttered out. The moth stared straight at them.

Eli froze. "So...maybe I forgot to charge the wand before we left."

Clicking furiously, the moth launched off the stalactite and swooped down.

Eli jumped left; Ambrose ducked right. Spikes rained down by their heels, sticking into the dirt with a vibrating shiver. Ambrose stared at them in horror. They were silver needles the length of his arm, black acid sloshing in the transparent, hollow interior.

As the moth swooped back up, more needles gleamed within the gray fur on its abdomen.

"You fill the jar!" Eli called. "I'll distract the big guy!"

"Don't step on the moss!" Ambrose said, but Eli was already off, the floating potion buoying him between open spaces on the floor.

Once the moth soared away toward Eli, Ambrose knelt and frantically dug around a cluster of moss. With each touch, the sparkles within the plant flared, brighter and brighter—until the light burst, and a spark leapt out. It landed with a hiss on the skin between his gloves and bracer; he cursed and slapped it out.

"Tell me when you have enough!" Eli shouted from across the chamber, ducking left, swerving right. Sparks jumped near his feet, landing dangerously close to a large cluster of moss. Ambrose's heart leapt into his throat.

"Stay away from the—"

"I know!"

"It could set the whole room off!"

"I *know* that, just keep digging!"

Ambrose huffed and resumed his work, his pulse hammering in his ears. Sparks landed every which way now, no matter how many he caught with his glove or his arm. He winced and kept going. If he could just get this moss into the jar, in one piece, without exploding...

The clump fell with a soft plop into the glass, and he slammed the metal lid on the last escaping spark. "Got it!"

"Great!" Eli sprinted toward Ambrose. A line of acid needles ripped into the wall above him. "Now set off the moss!"

Ambrose stopped. "What?"

"Set it off!"

"But it'll explode—"

"Yes, that's the point!" The moth swooped close to Eli. He swung at it with his dagger. "*Now*, Ames!"

Ambrose gave a loud curse, then yanked up a large clump of fizzling moss, shook it fiercely, and threw it deep into the chamber.

A blinding light burst across the room, and Eli pulled him behind a pillar.

"Close your eyes!" he shouted and shoved him up against the rock. Ambrose screwed his eyes shut, huddled into Eli, and held his breath.

A wall of searing heat whipped past him. The enchantment on his vest flared to life instantly, and a cool green shield enveloped his head and torso, fighting off the blaze. He wrapped his arms around Eli and pressed harder, desperately hoping the shield would encompass him, too.

In his effort, he almost missed the shrieking mass of fur and wings barreling its way down the tunnel. He opened one eye in time to see the moth veer away, trailing smoke from its singed antennae.

"Quick." Eli pulled away. "Out of the smoke, this way!"

They followed the moth into the open air of the sinkhole, then scrambled up the nearest footholds. Eli ducked into a shallow cave— little more than a divot in the cliff face—and helped Ambrose inside.

As the smoke faded away into the moonlight, Ambrose gulped in the fresh air and checked his pack. The jar of moss was still there, the blue puff within pulsing steadily.

"We did it," he breathed and leaned back against the stone. "Thank you."

"Don't mention it." Eli coughed out the last of the smoke, then leaned out to watch the moth's lingering trail. His clothes were spotted and charred now, from his jerkin down to his boots. A vision of his bloody injuries in the cistern flashed through Ambrose's mind, and he reached for Eli.

"The spikes didn't touch you, right?" he asked, searching for any sign of blood or torn clothing. In turn, Eli's hands skimmed over his arms.

"I'm fine. Did the explosion get you?" He tugged on Ambrose's sleeves, inspecting the smoky charcoal marks.

Neither found what they feared—but while their respective searches slowed, they didn't quite stop. Hands lingered, then settled on arms and waists. As sunlight filtered into the cave, Eli met his gaze, and a flustered heat rose in Ambrose's cheeks.

Perhaps...perhaps he could concede this meant something.

He looked down at his hand and bit back a nervous smile.

"I'm afraid I'm horribly injured." He tried to deflect, lifting his wrist and tugging off his glove. "You see, a moss spark got me right there."

Eli smiled, but his gaze didn't waver. "Oh, really?"

"Mm-hm." Ambrose pretended to frown. "I'll never be able to write a recipe again."

Eli gently wrapped his fingers around Ambrose's wrist. "You poor man."

"Yes, it's tragic." Ambrose nodded solemnly. "I think I'll have to retire and—"

Eli kissed the inside of his palm. Ambrose lost all semblance of thought.

"And...and, um..."

"Better?" Eli murmured, his lips brushing Ambrose's skin as he spoke. Ambrose's knees almost gave way, and he managed a nod.

Then, as Eli cupped his cheek, a joyous sort of panic took over. He had never actually done this before. Did Eli know that? Did he need to know? Should he say something now while he was leaning in, his gaze on Ambrose's lips? Or would that scare him off? He couldn't scare him off, not now, not when Eli was so close and his hand was so warm and he just wanted that kiss—

"Can I ki—" Eli started.

"Yes," Ambrose breathed. Eli took his face with both hands and softly pressed his lips to his.

Ambrose thought his panic would spiral. He didn't know what he was doing, after all—and while it didn't *seem* complex, he figured there must be some sort of trick to it. Something that set good kissers apart from bad kissers, something that merited all the jokes and drama and gossip he had ever heard on the subject.

But Eli's kiss was simple. Soft and warm, like the hands hovering at his cheeks. Ambrose let the panic melt out of him, dropping his shoulders, unwinding the tightness in his chest. He didn't have to focus on anything except for the faint scent of herbs and soil and sunlight. Didn't have to do anything but let Eli lean into him. He could simply be at rest.

When Eli pulled away, he forgot to open his eyes for a few seconds. And when he did, when he caught sight of Eli's delighted smile, he regretted not opening them sooner.

They walked back to the Scar close together, sparks jolting through Ambrose's fingers every time their hands brushed. Exhaustion and excitement coursed through him in equal measure. He had expected to come away with the moss that night.

He had not expected to come away with his first kiss.

"What are you going to do now?" Eli asked once they entered The Griffin's Claw. Ambrose flushed deeply, excitement twisting into panic.

He had no idea what to do next.

"Well, you see, I..." He fumbled with the supply closet handle. "I've never really, um, done that with anyone, and I don't actually know what comes next. Or even if I did well enough to warrant any, you know, next steps—?"

Eli touched his arm. "I meant with the moss."

"Oh, that." Ambrose let out a deep breath. "I'll take it to Dawn tomorrow morning." He slipped into the closet and carefully placed the jar on the middle shelf, by the scorch-flower. "Give her the moss, pitch her the day out. Hope she agrees to it."

"She'll agree to it." Eli hovered in the doorway with a tilted smile. "And as for the other next steps..."

Ambrose swallowed and turned. He didn't know what came next, but there was no use denying what he wanted, not anymore.

He looked at Eli, then at his lips in a silent plea.

And Eli generously closed the gap, cradling Ambrose's face and gifting him another soft kiss. Ambrose couldn't help it—he smiled through the gesture, a tingling spreading from his face through his chest. When Eli pulled away, he had to lean against the shelf for support.

"May I take you out on a date?" Eli whispered. Ambrose lost his breath.

"Yes. Yes, I'd like that very much."

STEP 28:

LET SETTLE

Eli

THE NEXT MORNING, Eli accompanied Ambrose to Dawn's shop, working their way upstream as shutters and doors opened for the day. Part of him wanted to run to every bleary-eyed shopkeeper and inform them of what had happened last night—he had kissed Ambrose Beake, yes, that man right there—but he forced himself to remain calm and keep walking.

"I checked in with Sherry," he said, swerving around a grumpy messenger dragon. "She insisted she pack the picnic basket for tomorrow."

"Of course, she did," Ambrose said. He was nearly jogging, and Eli had to speed-walk to keep up. "And Banneker and Grim?"

"Agreed to cover her shop. She's got no excuse to back out of the fun." He took Ambrose's hand and squeezed it. "And you're sure you don't want to tell her about us yet?"

Ambrose slowed down here, a shy smile dancing across his face. "I want to, I do. But..." He squeezed Eli's hand back. "I also want this to be about her. Can we tell her after the picnic?"

The thought of not being able to tell Dawn physically pained Eli

—but he forced out a smile instead. "I mean, I guess I can hold off on hanging a banner in my window."

"A banner?"

"Yeah. It'll say, 'I kissed Ambrose Beake,' with arrows pointing to your shop."

Ambrose passed a hand over his face. "Please don't."

"Oh, yeah. It's gonna be bright yellow and everything." Eli brushed up against Ambrose's arm, if only to hear the giggles the man was trying to stifle. "Big, bold letters, maybe some glitter..."

But when they reached the door of the Whirling Wand Emporium, Ambrose's laughter evaporated. He released Eli's hand and took a breath at the stoop. "Would you mind waiting here?"

"Sure."

Ambrose walked in, and Eli hung back in front of the bay window. Given the thickness of the glass and the morning traffic, he could barely hear what was going on inside. But when Dawn emerged from the storeroom, saw Ambrose, and burst into tears, he didn't need to strain to hear her.

"I'm so sorry!" she cried and swept Ambrose into a hug. "I was going to visit you this morning, I got cookies and everything—"

Indeed, Eli spied a box of cinnamon cookies on the counter, wrapped in a bow much like Dawn's wand boxes. But it went disregarded as Ambrose returned her hug, his shoulders rounding down in relief. When he pulled away and held up a finger, his ears had perked up, a smile already on his face.

Then he pulled out the moss jar, and Dawn's beaming shriek rattled the windows.

"You *found* it!" She wrapped her arms around Ambrose and picked him straight up off the floor. As she tried to dance with both Ambrose and the jar, Ambrose eagerly waved Eli inside.

"We only ask"—Ambrose tried to get a word in through Dawn's delighted wiggles—"we only ask that you do one thing with us tomorrow."

"Yes!" Dawn continued to dance. "What is it?"

Ambrose finally managed to free himself. "Come to a Fireball game and have a picnic with us."

Her face fell, and she slowly lowered the jar. "Ames, I can't. I've been gone for days, and I've got the shop—"

Eli wandered over to them. "The street's got you covered there. Grim will cover your shop in the morning, Banneker in the afternoon. Sherry's literally packing the picnic basket as we speak, and..." He pulled three slips of paper out of his pocket. "We already got the tickets. Stone Dragons versus the Bandits, central division showdown."

Dawn gasped. Ambrose stepped forward. "I know you're busy, and I know you don't think you have time to relax, but—we'd like to do this for you. Please?"

She bit her lip, then broke into a smile. "Okay, let's do it. Thank you." She hugged Ambrose one more time—then grabbed Eli's waist and pulled him in. "Come on, Eli, you too."

As she buried her face into Ambrose's shoulder, Eli snuck a kiss on his cheek. Ambrose shook his head and hid his blush behind the top of Dawn's mohawk.

To Eli's utter delight, he found he'd severely underestimated how much Dawn loved Fireball.

"I know the Stone Dragons totally botched the second half of last week's game," she babbled as she dipped a brush into a jar of glitter. "But if they put Marlow in front like they should, they've got a chance against the Bandits' defense."

Eli scoffed from his seat on Dawn's front counter. "The Bandits have the best defense in central right now. Marlow alone isn't going to cut it, not unless he can get over his tiff with Hennie and learn how to work together like professionals—"

"Shush. Their catfights on the field give me joy." Dawn held up the brush. "Now sit still, I need to get you ready for the game."

Eli sighed at the green and gold glitter paint—the Stone Dragons' colors. He'd never live it down if his family found out he was cheering for them. "How much of that are you going to use on me?"

Dawn grinned wide, making the green spirals on her own cheeks sparkle. "As much as it takes to make you a real Dragons fan." When Eli groaned, she rolled her eyes. "All right, all right—just a swipe under your eyes, you big baby."

As the cool brush glided over his cheek, he had a thought. "Are you gonna put any of this stuff on Ambrose?"

"What kind of friend would I be if I didn't?" Dawn's brush slowed. "How is all of that going, by the way? I'm sorry, with all this work"— she gestured toward the store with her brush—"I feel like I've missed out on the whole commission."

Oh, she had certainly missed more than that. The news bubbled on Eli's tongue, but he swallowed it back.

"Fine," he said. "Commission's going well."

"Great." She pulled back to evaluate her work. "You still going on dates? Sherry said you met a baker or something."

"Eh, it didn't work out."

Her eyes lingered, evaluating more than the glitter. A smirk slowly spread across her face. "You know..."

Eli would've bet a hundred talons that he did already know. He tilted his head in innocence anyway. "What?"

Dawn dipped her brush back in the glitter and began touching up her work. "What about Ambrose?"

Ah, yes. What about Ambrose.

"What, you mean like dating Ambrose?" Laughter bounced around his teeth, but he couldn't let it out.

"Yeah." Dawn's eyes glinted. "He's cute, he's smart. I could, you know, wingman for you." She wiggled her shoulders, allowing Eli to let loose some of the laughter. Gods, he wanted to tell her so badly.

"I don't think you need to."

"Why not—?"

Then the subject himself stumbled into the shop, lugging a picnic basket twice the width of his torso.

"So, Sherry packed snacks for the game," Ambrose panted, *"and* the picnic, which means this thing is—*really* heavy—"

"I got it!" Eli hopped off the counter and took the basket from his hand. Ambrose wasn't wrong—Sherry must have packed enough for a weeklong trip. As Eli set the basket on the counter, Ambrose straightened and ran a hand through his hair.

"Thanks." He pointed to Eli's cheeks. "Ah. She got to you, I see."

Eli didn't respond. He was too busy staring at Ambrose's outfit.

He supposed he had Dawn to blame for this. She had, after all, directed Ambrose to wear something casual, as this was a game, not a business event.

But did the bastard man have to wear *those* slim pants and *that* loose, billowy shirt with the slit at the neck unlaced? On the *one* day where he couldn't openly grab him by the waist and drag him into a supply closet and—

"What?" Ambrose's hand flew up to his exposed collarbone. "Is this not casual enough?"

"No, no, it's fine." Eli immediately distracted himself with the picnic basket. "Oh look, Sherry made us cookies."

As Eli focused very hard on the tin, Dawn grabbed Ambrose's hand. "Don't think you're getting away without any paint before the game."

Ambrose groaned. "Please, not a lot."

"Okay, okay." Dawn sifted through her little pots of makeup while Ambrose slouched on the counter. "Here, how about this shimmery stuff?"

She turned Ambrose toward her, leaving Eli to munch on a cookie in frustration. Devious, evil half-elf. Who gave him the right to look so good...

"See, that wasn't so bad." Dawn winked at Ambrose and gathered her makeup with a grin. "Now just let me find my Dragons banner, and we can go!"

As she rushed up the stairs to the loft, Ambrose faced Eli, giving him a full view of her handiwork. She had indeed applied a lighter hand to Ambrose, barely dusting his cheekbones and eyelids with a light gold that reflected the morning sunlight. When combined with his icy hair and sharp jawline, the man looked like an ethereal painting.

Eli dropped his half-eaten cookie. Dawn had done this on purpose, hadn't she?

"Be honest." Ambrose scrunched his nose. "How silly do I look?"

Now, Eli knew Dawn couldn't see them...together just yet.

But Dawn wasn't in the room at the moment.

"You want me to be honest?" Eli sidled over and placed both hands on the counter, flanking Ambrose's legs. He let his voice drop low, under the pretense that Dawn couldn't overhear. "Between the shirt and the makeup, I think you look gorgeous."

A blush brightened the gold shimmer on Ambrose's cheeks. Eli immediately made a resolution to compliment him more often.

"Thank you," Ambrose mumbled, then hesitantly wrapped his fingers around Eli's wrists. "I must try to keep up with you if I'm to be worthy of another kiss."

Eli desperately wanted to carry him into the supply closet and show him how worthy he was.

Dawn's voice echoed from the loft. "My banner isn't down there, is it?"

"No," they both answered, eyes still locked on each other. Eli leaned forward. He couldn't steal Ambrose away, but he could sneak one more kiss, couldn't he—?

"Found it!" Dawn's voice was louder this time, and Ambrose let go of Eli's wrists. Eli scrambled back to the picnic basket and stuffed another cookie into his mouth right before Dawn descended, an obnoxious green banner fluttering behind her. She took one look at the crumbs falling from his mouth and sighed. "Eli, come on, we're not even at the stadium yet."

Eli shook the tin. "I had to taste test. Make sure they weren't poisoned."

"All right, gimme the snacks." Dawn grabbed the basket like it weighed nothing. "Ames, will you please keep an eye on this man?"

Ambrose slid off the counter and opened the door for them. Eli passed him with a wink, and he bit down a smile. "If I must."

The Scar's western stadium was a massive stone amphitheater carved directly into a sinkhole. Its striped stone seats, already half full, buzzed with anticipation as Eli led the way to their spot.

"So..." Ambrose followed close behind, his eyes on the sand pit that stretched at the base of the amphitheater. "I should admit, I've only been to a few of these games with Dawn, and I don't..." He paused to squeeze past a group of gnomes drenched in green and gold. "I don't entirely have a grasp on the rules."

Eli sat and cracked his knuckles. His time had come. "First things first," he said. "The ball is on fire."

Ambrose shot him a look. "Yes, I'm aware."

Dawn joined in on the crash course, and they tossed about rules, counter-rules, and regional rules as they unpacked the picnic basket. One by one, they pulled out cookies, fernberries, and so many bottles of fizzy juice that Eli had to check and make sure there wasn't an expanded storage spell on the basket.

"Wait." Ambrose held up a hand. "If they hold the ball for more than three seconds, they get a penalty?"

"Yes, one point docked." Eli gestured with a bag of berries. "Unless you're in overtime."

"But not double-overtime sudden death," Dawn added, popping open a fizzy bottle. "It's anything goes then, just to be done with the game."

Ambrose grimaced. "Let's hope it doesn't get to that."

Eli quietly made another resolution not to make a Fireball game their first date.

As the players jogged onto the field, kicking up sand and waving at the stands, he found himself getting sucked into the game, as he always did. Though he didn't have any of his siblings to help cheer, heckle, and argue over the snacks, Dawn filled in admirably. She squabbled over the last of the cookies, cheered louder than he did, and shook his arm in victory when the Stone Dragons finally took the lead in the third quarter.

And when Marlow and Hennie finally got into one of their famous fistfights, the fire-ensconced ball rolling away forgotten, both Eli and Dawn were on their feet together, cheering on the fight.

Ambrose leaned forward and squinted at the tussle. "Is this part of the game?"

"Yes!" they answered at once.

Like always, the game was over far too fast, and Eli joined the flow of outward traffic in a haze of excitement.

"I still can't believe those last two minutes." He had one arm looped around Dawn's elbow, the other swinging the picnic basket. "Marlow jumped—he *jumped*—over the defense with the ball in one hand. I mean, who does that?"

"Told you." Dawn bumped him with her hip. "Now, can I check on my shop before we have our picnic?"

"No." Ambrose took Dawn's free arm. "I promise you Grim didn't burn the shop down."

"I know they didn't, but—"

"Dawn, it'll be fine," Eli reassured her. "No work today."

As they stuffed themselves into an elevator, Eli took advantage of the pressing crowd to stand close to Ambrose. "How are you doing?" he asked, squeezing his hand.

Ambrose winced and shifted closer to him. "My ears are ringing."

"Yeah, the stadium will do that to you." Eli released his hand but kept their pinky fingers linked. "It'll be quiet topside."

Once they reached the swaying lavender fields, they let Dawn lead the way, following her down deer paths until she found a soft clearing under a tree. After that, there was little else to do but toast the cool breeze and picnic until they all turned sleepy and slow-tongued.

"I should've brought a book or something," Dawn mumbled, lying down and using her Stone Dragons banner as a blanket. "To make use of the time..."

"Come on, we said this was a should-free day, right?" Eli said. "You don't *have* to do anything."

"Right, right, I know." She adjusted her shoulders and settled in further. Within minutes, she was fast asleep.

"I'm going to take that as a sign she's relaxed," Eli whispered to Ambrose, then carefully stepped around the picnic blanket to sit next to him. "How about you?"

"Mm." Ambrose covered a yawn and nodded. "I'm considering using the basket as a pillow. Dawn had the right idea, with the banner and all."

They sat together in silence for a while, watching travelers leave the Scar. Most were Fireball fans, hustling home to the nearby villages before dark. Those in green and gold were singing and drinking; those in Bandit blue were quiet.

But in between the painted faces and wagons of families arguing over who got to hold the souvenir pennant, there were other, more interesting sorts of travelers.

"Where do you think they're going?" Ambrose asked quietly, nodding to one such pack headed north. It only took a glance to identify them—adventurers, headed out on some sort of quest. Their axes, bows, and staffs glinted in the late afternoon light, reflecting sparks of orange and pink that foretold a beautiful dusk.

Eli tilted his head. "Well, they're headed northwest, so...I say they'll make it as far as Woodfall, then rest and stock up there. There's too few of them for a field hunt or a caravan escort. Maybe something in Elwig Forest is their final stop?"

He couldn't keep the jealousy out of his voice. He missed the excitement of travel, the promise of beautiful places and new people. Not that the Scar didn't have its own nooks and crannies to explore, but...there was something different about setting out to meet the horizon itself. Something he hadn't felt since he had last left home for the Scar.

"Eli," Ambrose started, then paused, carefully weighing his words. "We are...reaching the end of the commission, you know."

"If I remember from your list, we have about thirty steps left," Eli said lightly, then glanced at Ambrose and saw he was serious. "But—yes. Reaching the end."

"And you said you wanted to figure things out after the commission."

Eli let out a long breath and toyed with the edge of the blanket. The sinking weight of defeat was familiar to him now, after so many career changes. It was a hard rock in his gut, unmoving. "I just...I really didn't want this store to be another failure."

"It's not a failure." Ambrose's voice was soft but firm. "It's not. *You* are not a failure."

Eli managed a small smile. He sounded like Eli's parents. "My family was so excited when I found the shop listing. They thought I had finally found a career. *I* thought I had found a career. I got so caught up in their..."

As he ran out of words, Ambrose laid a hand over his, the warmth of it reassuring. "I haven't met your family, but...I think the people who care about you would rather see you try a dozen more careers than be miserable sticking with this one."

Eli nodded, trying to ease the knot in his throat. Ambrose was right. How was he always right?

He looked over at the man, but there seemed to be one more thought churning in his head, one more thing he was weighing on his tongue.

"What if..." He hesitated. "Now, I'm not one to tell you what to do with your life, but..." He pointed at the adventurers. "What if you did that?"

Okay, maybe Ambrose wasn't *always* right.

"Adventuring?" Eli snorted. "I can't do that."

"I disagree." Ambrose counted off on his fingers. "Adventurers must be well-traveled. They must have an extensive knowledge of creatures and how to handle them. Remain calm in the face of danger to them and their friends." He gave a half smile. "They must retain a certain degree of foolish recklessness, as demonstrated multiple times—"

"I was on board with you until then."

"I'm being serious." Ambrose shifted to face him, kneeling and resting back on his heels. "You'd never get bored as an adventurer. Every quest is different. You'd be able to travel again, see new places like you used to..." He paled and held up a hand. "Not that I'd ever want to see you in danger, you understand, but...it may be worth thinking about. If you want to."

Eli settled back, the scratchy knit of the blanket grounding his palms. Adventuring certainly wasn't the steady job his parents had been so thrilled about. Nor was it safe, exactly. But...something about seeing the adventurers disappear over the horizon made him long to do the same.

"I'll think about it," he said, then watched the wagons of Fireball fans trail after the adventurers. "I wish I had always known what I was going to do," he mumbled. "Like you."

Ambrose picked at the grass around the edge of the blanket. "About that, I...I'm afraid I wasn't being entirely honest. When I told you I always wanted to be a potion master."

Something flickered across his face, then vanished, as if he had to sidestep his emotions in order to get the words out.

Eli sat up to listen.

"I...wasn't born in the Scar," Ambrose said, his voice as quiet as the breeze filtering through the fields. "I don't actually remember where I was raised. I recall there was a garden. I think we had a donkey." His smile was brief. "My parents, they must not have been able to... Whatever the reasoning was, when I was eight, they took me to the Scar and dropped me in front of The Griffin's Claw. Told Master Pearce I was a hard worker and convinced him to take me on as an apprentice. Then they gave me a coin for lunch, left in a wagon, and never came back. Years later, Pearce handed me the keys to the shop, left in a wagon, and, well..."

The knot in Eli's throat grew as Ambrose continued.

"I don't know what I wanted to be before my apprenticeship. I don't think it was a potion master. But...I like it now. I enjoy my work. I'm quite proud of the shop." He picked at the blades of grass in his palm. "Perhaps too proud, if my initial reaction to you was any indication."

Eli thought back to how he had called his family a few days ago. How thrilled they had been just to talk to him, how Lily was planning a visit for the birthday festival.

How he knew, beyond a doubt, that they would visit whenever he asked them to.

"I'm sorry." He wiped a tear off his cheek, his jaw hurting from holding back more. "I just—knowing how Pearce treated you all those years, I..." He ran his thumb over Ambrose's hand. "I wish I had gotten here earlier."

Ambrose nudged Eli's shoulder with his own. "What, you would have changed Pearce's ways? Turned my life around?"

"No, I meant..." Eli shook his head. "Maybe I could have kept you from being so lonely."

"Lonely? No, I wasn't alone. I never was." Ambrose's gaze focused on the middle of the chasm, toward Rosemond Street. "But I'm glad you're here now."

He gave Eli a broken smile, a small swipe of gold still shimmering on his cheek. Eli leaned forward and kissed it.

"Oh. My. *Gods*."

They sprang apart—Dawn was awake, sitting up and grinning at them. Ambrose scrambled back. "Dawn, I'm so sorry!"

"Sorry?" Her eyebrows shot up in surprise. "When were you going to tell me?"

"Tomorrow!" He held up his hands. "Tomorrow, I swear!"

"And when did this start?"

"Um." Ambrose glanced between them. "Two days ago."

Dawn's gaze locked on Eli. "*You*."

Eli froze. "Me?"

Dawn stood, rolling up the banner and imitating herself in a high-pitched voice. "Oh, I could wingman for you, Eli—no, Dawn, I don't think that's a good idea—and you had already *kissed* him? Two days ago?" She held the banner like a club, though her wide smile betrayed her. "I can't believe you—"

"Gotta go!" Eli scrambled to his feet and jumped into the lavender, leaves scratching his skin. "Sorry, Ames, can't go on that date after all!"

"You already scheduled a *date*?"

Eli grinned and ducked farther into the wildflowers, pretending to hide from Dawn, until laughter from the picnic blanket dragged him back.

"Eli, please," Ambrose called. "We're opening another bottle of wine."

"We're celebrating!" Dawn echoed.

"Well, in that case." Eli popped out of the grass, making a show of plucking lavender petals from his shirt. Dawn giggled, pulled a leaf out of his hair, and placed it on Ambrose's head.

"I'm happy for you both," she said. "Now..." She pulled a bottle out of the picnic basket and poured a glass for each of them. "To new beginnings!"

Eli held up his glass with the others. Beyond the rim, the last of the adventurers disappeared into the horizon, their armor winking out in the sunset. "To new beginnings."

STEP 29:

DATE & LABEL

Ambrose

THE DAY of the first date arrived, and while Ambrose was reasonably certain that dates only involved the couple in question, all of Rosemond Street decided it was a collective affair.

He wasn't sure how it had started, though he had a guess. Dawn had likely told Banneker, Banneker told Sherry, Sherry told Grim.

And now all of them were in on it.

"I like this one better," Dawn said, turning Ambrose around in a circle. They stood in the middle of his shop, several vest options draped over the front counter. "What do you think?"

Ambrose glanced down at his current outfit—a soft midnight vest against a crisp white shirt. "I...suppose I like it?"

It wasn't a lie—he did like the tiny gold stars on this one. He just didn't see why he had to spend the last thirty minutes changing into vests that all looked mostly the same.

"All right, vest complete." Dawn turned to the other feature of the front counter—the rose statue, now filled with names and placed firmly next to the register. For the past hour, the statue had been flashing every other second. It blinked again as Dawn unrolled the scroll, smiled at something written there, and jotted down a note.

"Any word from Eli?" Ambrose asked. Dawn let the paper roll back up with a snap.

"Nope. Now, about your sleeves..." She narrowed her eyes, then started to roll them up.

"What—?"

"It's a date, not a business meeting!" Dawn winked. "You have to seduce him."

"Oh my gods."

She was halfway through the second sleeve when Banneker strolled in, his grin as bright as his hair. "Hey, man. You almost ready?"

Ambrose gave him a flat look. "I was ready an hour ago."

"That's a lie. You should have seen the outfit he was wearing an hour ago." Dawn stepped back. "Banneker, does he look sexy enough?"

Banneker shrugged. "How should I know? I don't like people that way."

"Well, aesthetically, how's he looking?"

"I mean"—Banneker tilted his head—"blue's never been my favorite color, but my dude makes it work."

"Hm." Dawn rubbed her chin, then reached for Ambrose's neck. "You're right. Gotta unbutton the collar."

"Dawn, please—"

But their audience wasn't done growing yet. Sherry and Grim appeared at the window, whispering fiercely.

"Should I talk to Eli?" Grim pointed to Eli's shop. "I should talk to him, right? Before the date?"

"No, you'll scare him off!"

"Oh, I won't scare him off." Grim polished their glasses on their shirt. "I'll just cover the basics. That's our boy he's stepping out with, and if he hurts Ambrose, we'll throw him into a sinkhole. You know, the usual—"

Sherry shook her head and entered the shop. As soon as her eyes landed on Ambrose, she lit up. "Look how handsome you are!"

Ambrose turned to Dawn. "I'd like to die now."

They continued in this flurry for a while—Sherry cooing, Banneker making unhelpful comments, Dawn finding more buttons to unbutton—until the door to Eli's Elixirs opened, and the merchants finally scattered.

"Lunch tomorrow!" Dawn shouted and scrambled out the door with Sherry, the rejected vests draped over her arm. "You're telling me everything!"

"You'll be fine." Banneker clapped Ambrose on the shoulder. "I consulted the star chart already. All signs point to it going great—"

"All right, all right." Grim gently pushed on Banneker's shoulder to guide him out the door—but then lingered at the doorway, their eyes soft.

"Should I be home by a certain time?" Ambrose asked, half smiling. But Grim's gaze remained sincere.

"Proud of you, Beake," they said.

Ambrose bit his lip and looked at the floor. "Thank you, Grim."

As Grim nodded and left, they held the door open for something small, round, and whizzing—Tom, zooming into the shop past the orc's legs.

"Oh, hello." Ambrose crouched to greet her. "I appreciate the visit, but I'm afraid I'll be leaving with Eli in..."

She held up something in her little fork hands—a round potion bottle, stuffed with a cloud of blue flowers. Ambrose smiled. "Is that for me?"

She jostled the bottle up and down. He laughed and took it before the flowers could fall out.

Eli's voice floated in. "It was all Tom's idea." Ambrose looked up to find him standing in the doorway, hands in his pockets. He wore the same maroon jacket from the other day, the one with the gold embroidery and thoroughly distracting fit. And it proved no less distracting now—Ambrose almost missed the counter entirely when setting down the flowers.

"And did she pick out the flowers herself?" He played along as

Tom whirled around his legs. Eli waved a hand.

"Of course. Picked them out, bought them herself, all that."

"Well, she did a lovely job." Ambrose smiled. "Thank you."

Eli opened the door. "All right, Tom, thank you for the delivery. Now off with you, I'll be back later tonight." Tom waved at Ambrose, then wheeled off, leaving Eli holding the door open. "Ready?"

Ambrose straightened his vest. "Ready."

Eli started north and reached for his hand. Ambrose brightened at the touch.

"So, where are we going?" he asked, trying to sound casual. But the farther they wandered, the more he tensed. He had asked Dawn about first dates, of course, but Dawn was—well, Dawn. First-date chatter and jokes came easily to her.

"I thought I'd keep it simple," Eli said, as calm and cool as Ambrose wished he was. "How about we go in here?"

He stopped and nodded to a shop on the right. Ambrose couldn't believe their path hadn't felt familiar until now. They were standing in front of Widdershins' Books, its warm windows a beacon in the cool evening.

"Are you sure?" he asked, unable to contain his smile.

"Absolutely."

He turned to Eli. "I mean—I could spend hours in here, you understand. But if you get bored—"

Eli shook his head. "I'm with you," he said. "I won't get bored."

Ambrose was nearly giddy as they entered, the crisp air and smell of paper enveloping them. He had been so busy, he hadn't stepped inside since his last trip with Dawn. He fell into his normal routine, navigating first to the display on the left. There, the shelves presented a new release with a dazzling cover—a strapping heroine leaping to fight a great alcedon, the predator moose of Elwig Forest.

Eli picked up a copy. "Need more books to read with Tom? She loved sitting with you that one night."

Ambrose smiled. "I do have a feeling she'll be around more often." He reached for the book, but Eli quickly tucked it under his arm.

"I got it." He nudged Ambrose forward. "Show me the way."

They wandered in a leisurely circuit, calling out interesting or ridiculous titles and slowly expanding the pile in Eli's arms. They uncovered a novel Grim had recommended in the drama section. Eli nearly cried when he discovered a beloved adventure book he had lost as a child. In the romance section, they unearthed a tome so languishing and frivolous that they *had* to have Dawn do a dramatic reading of it over wine.

"I'll bring the wine, you bring the cheese, Dawn brings her voice..." Eli added the book to Ambrose's stack. "Can't wait. Hey—hey, where you going?"

"Hm?" Ambrose stopped. Eli reached forward and turned Ambrose's hips toward the magical science section.

"Oh, that's not necessary—" Ambrose tried.

"No, no." Eli grinned. "I want to see if any of your work is here."

Indeed, it was, as Ambrose already knew. He led Eli in, pointed to the line of yellow-ribboned Guild journals, then started for the next aisle. "See, there it is, now you know—"

"Mm-mm. Can't get away that easily." Eli set their books on a shelf, then snaked his arms around Ambrose's waist and rested his chin on his shoulder. "Proud of you."

Ambrose's heart melted into a warm, soupy puddle.

"Thank you." He tried to gather himself with a scowl. "But I wish they hadn't shelved me next to *that* person." He pointed to another set of journals. Eli's head tilted to read the titles, his hair brushing against Ambrose's ear.

"Why?" he asked. "I think we read their stuff in class."

Ambrose scoffed. "I should write to those professors. The author's practices are dubious at best, unethical at worse. I had a debate with them at the last potion convention, and their grasp on metallurgy as it relates to—to..."

His rant trailed off—Eli had begun to press small kisses on the back of his neck.

"Keep going," Eli murmured.

"Are you sure?" Ambrose rested his hands on Eli's wrists, his breath unsteady. "You seem to have plans."

The shape of Eli's smile imprinted itself on his skin. "Oh, I do."

Ambrose suddenly found it difficult to recall the points of his previous argument—or to recall anything at all. "Most people don't..." He let out a sigh as Eli's kisses moved up his neck. "Don't find my silly rants attractive, you know."

Eli hummed against his hair, then dragged his lips over to his jawline. Ambrose swallowed a gasp and grabbed the bookshelf. The shop was suddenly far too warm.

"Then they're not listening," Eli whispered and pressed a kiss below his ear. "I find your intelligence attractive." Another at his cheek. "Your passion." Another at the corner of his lips. "Your—"

Ambrose broke and whirled around to kiss him, completing the path to his lips. At first, he was afraid he was pressing too hard, leaning in too much—but Eli kissed him right back, cupping his face with both hands and pushing him up against the bookshelf. This was a different kiss from the one in the supply closet—rougher, warmer, more insistent. Ambrose ran his hands over Eli's back, reveling in how cool and smooth the fabric was in comparison.

As his fingers sank into Eli's hair, the bell at the front door chimed, forcing them apart with a gasp. They waited a second, two seconds.

No one passed their aisle. They relaxed against each other.

"Should we go?" Ambrose whispered. Eli nodded.

"We should go." He dove for one last kiss at his neck, and just as Ambrose closed his eyes, he grabbed their stack of books and ran. "And I'm buying these!"

They held hands on the walk back, Ambrose tightly clutching their purchased books and trying not to giggle. Did people usually feel this...floaty? Was he supposed to kiss him like that on a first date? Eli didn't seem to mind, and he supposed that was all that mattered, but...

Once they reached the space between their respective shops, they both babbled at once.

"I'm sorry," Ambrose blurted out. "I've never done any of that before—"

Eli gestured north. "Sorry, I don't normally do that on a first date, I just really—"

They both laughed and took a step back with reddened faces.

"I should admit, I've never had a..." Ambrose cleared his throat. He didn't know the right word to use on a first date, either. *Partner* felt too professional, *lover* too formal. Boyfriend—no, no. Far too weighty. "A, um...a person...before?"

Eli smiled wide.

"I'd be honored to be your person," he said. Ambrose let out a relieved breath. Yes—person would do fine. For now, at least.

Eli glanced back at his shop and gave a long, dramatic sigh. "But... I'm going to have to break the news to Tom that you're taken, and honestly, I'm not sure she'll ever get over it."

Ambrose nodded sagely. "Ah. In that case, never mind. I couldn't possibly get between you and your automaton."

Eli pressed a hand to his heart and backed away. "Oh, thank you, that's so considerate."

"Of course." Ambrose held up his free hand and walked toward The Griffin's Claw. "Far be it from me to break homes apart."

"Absolutely."

They grinned and met back in the middle of the street, hands wrapping around waists, running through hair. This kiss was different even from the bookshop one, happy and bright and earnest.

As Eli pulled away, Ambrose looked forward to discovering all the other types of kisses that might be out there.

"See you tomorrow for the commission?" Eli let one last peck linger on his cheek. Ambrose slouched—he had nearly forgotten about all that.

"Tomorrow." He nodded. "Just the last few combination steps."

Eli squeezed his hand. "Easy."

STEP 30:

MARKET RESEARCH

Eli

"ELI, GET BEHIND THE SHIELD!"

"No, *you* get behind the shield!"

They both ducked as a cork zipped past their heads, rocketing away from a frothing potion bottle. The bottle itself recoiled and crashed to the floor, and next to it, a cauldron boiled over, spilling globs of purple ooze. Eli winced and crouched behind Ambrose's shield spell. "We were almost done! I thought this part was going to be easy—"

"Easy?" Ambrose said, his hair falling wildly in front of his face. He gestured with the shield wand as he spoke. "We're combining two potions with completely different effects and purposes. I could spend *months* documenting the highly varied and completely unpredictable interactions between the vine and the crystal and the—"

The ooze burbled and hissed. Ambrose grabbed a second wand from his pocket. "Oh, enough of this!"

He spun the wand once to charge it, then flicked. The errant cauldron flashed, and the burbling stopped. Once the light died down, Eli could see the corner was covered in ice, freezing the potion mid-bubble.

Ambrose pocketed both wands and pinched the bridge of his nose. "That's going to take hours to clean," he muttered. "I suppose we'll have to try this again tomorrow."

Eli groaned. That was the fifth failed brew this week. "Do we still have enough ingredients? This thing is due in almost a month."

"I'll have to rush order more." Ambrose set his hands on his hips. "But I'm afraid my workroom is out of commission for the night."

"We could use my place?"

"If we use your place, the potion will destroy it," Ambrose said. "No offense."

Eli gave a halfhearted shrug. The man wasn't exactly wrong. He didn't have nearly the number of protective wands or cleaning supplies Ambrose had.

And he still hadn't gotten that fume pull fixed.

"Fair enough," Eli said, then wrapped his arms around Ambrose's waist. Both of them could use a distraction at the moment. "Well, if you've got nothing left to do for the night..."

He found it delightfully easy to make Ambrose melt. Just a few well-placed kisses, and Eli had him pressed up against the ingredient cabinet, one hand threading through his hair, the other trailing along his back.

Even so, he kept a constant eye on Ambrose's reactions—any pulling away, any sort of tension. He wanted to do more with Ambrose, do more for him, of course. But he knew this was all new to him, so he held himself back.

And besides, taking it slow allowed him to appreciate everything more. Appreciate how Ambrose smiled at the end of a kiss, or moaned when Eli's lips strayed to his throat. How soft his hair was when Eli pushed it back, how warm the skin under his shirt was when it rode up...

Eli carefully pulled away before he lost himself, leaving one last kiss on his cheek. "You reading tonight?" he asked, running his thumb along Ambrose's jawline. Ambrose nodded, his eyes still closed.

"Thought I might, yes."

"Can I join you?"

Ambrose finally opened his eyes but kept them half-lidded. It took everything in Eli not to start making out with him again. "No tavern with Dawn tonight?"

Eli lifted his hand and kissed his knuckles. "Thought I'd spend some time with my person."

Now there was another reaction he loved—the pink blush that still bloomed in Ambrose's cheeks whenever Eli showed affection.

"Very well." Ambrose intertwined their fingers. "I still have a few cookies Sherry brought over, if you're interested."

Soon, they were both curled up on the sofa with books, nestled under a comforting mass of blankets, pillows, and plates of cookie crumbs. Eli wiggled his shoulders and sank further into the pile. Ambrose may not have owned a second dining chair—something he needed to rectify at some point—but at least he had a comfortable couch.

Ambrose gave a small gasp, and Eli looked up from his book with a questioning hum. Ambrose shook his head and turned the page.

"Didn't see that coming," he mumbled to himself. "I should've seen it coming..."

Eli's gaze dropped to the book cover, where adventurers leapt into danger, weapons unsheathed. Did Ambrose really think he could do something like that?

Could he?

Adventurers did travel a lot, something he wasn't a stranger to. He had seen a few monsters in his day, and considered himself reasonably fit when he needed to be. And he enjoyed having a group, a community of sorts. He had bonded easily with the other farmers and the botanists...

Eli stared at the page of his book without registering the words. He didn't have to make any decisions now, he told himself. He could start small.

He'd go visit the training grounds tomorrow on his lunch break.

The training grounds weren't far from Rosemond Street—convenient for all the adventurers who needed to stock up on items or get their armor repaired. As Eli navigated the western tunnels, the sound of clashing metal and friendly jibes bounced around the neatly carved walls. He continued forward, strolling past elves with swords and orcs with staffs, until the tunnel dropped him into the vastness of the training grounds.

Long ago, the Adventurer's Guild had commandeered an old sinkhole next to the chasm, turning it into the practice pit that now stretched before Eli—a massive, sand-filled fighting ring, encircled by a raised wooden walkway. He counted at least five adventuring parties making use of the space, their members either sparring in the pit or making helpful observations from the ramparts.

"Good one, ya turtle!" a gnome called down to their friend, leaning over the railing with a sharp smirk. "If that had been a real dragon, you would have been digested by now!"

"Oh, shut up!" A dulled practice hand ax whiffed past the gnome's shoulder, and they cackled. "You were distracting me!"

Eli wandered along the walkway, watching the adventurers spar. Back in Kolkea, he had seen smaller parties practice. Worn armor, tired weapons, fighting against wooden dummies or each other.

But in a major adventuring hub like the Scar, fighters had no time for wooden dummies. Their trainers pulled levers in the walls, and out came illusions of all kinds—giant alcedons, hissing dragons, river krakens gliding through the air. Eli stopped at the railing to admire the groups fighting in perfect sync. They barked orders in a shorthand and surrounded the monsters in a barrage of blades and spells, too fast for him to follow. They took dragons down in seconds, sliced river krakens in half. Eli couldn't tear his eyes away—these fighters were fast and strong, clear and communicative.

They were incredible.

"You looking for someone?" A gruff voice finally distracted Eli. Behind him, a beefy, grizzled elf sat on a bench, sharpening his sword.

"No," Eli said quickly. The elf's eyes narrowed, and Eli silently cursed. He should have thought of some excuse before coming here.

Then his gaze landed on the half-filled potion bottles at the adventurer's belt.

"Where'd you get those?" Eli pointed to them, leaning back against the railing as if he wandered through the training grounds all the time. Confidence was half the battle, after all.

"Griffin's Claw," the elf grunted and pushed himself to his feet. One of his legs was in a knee brace, and the keys to the illusion levers dangled at the man's hip. A trainer of some sort, then, or an adventurer waiting out a recovery. "You in the market?"

"In the market to sell, actually. I'm here for research—you know, looking to see how adventurers actually use potions." It wasn't a bad idea—he wished he had thought of it before. He nodded over to one of the groups in the pit. "How do you get to be one of those folks, anyway?"

"What, be an adventurer?" The elf limped over to the railing and watched the party work. His gaze followed their every move, quick and calculating. "None of these kids started out cutting dragons' heads off. They all started in backwaters. Places that need a few swords against a few wolves to make it through the day. You start there and work your way up."

Eli internally slumped. That's what he'd thought the man might say. Go somewhere new. Start over again.

"But..." the elf said. Eli perked up a little too fast, and the adventurer stared at him for a moment. "Sometimes the groups here take on trainees. Usually in the winter months, when all the bigger pests have gone into hibernation."

Eli tried to remain casual. "Yeah?"

The elf shrugged. "The Wildpine Seven's got a spot opening in a few months. Same with the Dragon Riders."

"Oren!" an adventurer called from the pit. The elf raised a hand in acknowledgement, then straightened and stretched his back.

"How long is the program?" Eli asked quickly. Surely there was no harm in taking a look at the application.

"About two years, if you pass the test." Oren unclipped a vial from his belt. "And no backing out once you're in. These parties wouldn't survive with a halfhearted trainee at their backs. Trainee wouldn't, either." He held out a scarred, weathered hand. "Oren."

Eli took it and tried to match his strength. "Eli."

"If you need the application, Eli, come to me. I'm here most days of the week, looking after these fools." He sauntered off, raising the potion in his hand. "All right, Hickory, which one do you need?"

As Oren slid down the ladder to the pit, Eli tapped on the railing, his enthusiasm deflating. A trainee program here in the Scar... If he passed the test, he could hardly ask for a better opportunity. He could stay near Ambrose and try something new, all at the same time.

But two years?

He toyed with the chain around his neck, Ambrose's amulet cold against his skin. He couldn't commit to something like that. The last time he'd gotten swept up in his excitement and committed to a costly endeavor, he'd ended up with a shop he didn't want to run.

A shop he still had to run, once his lunch break was over.

He sighed and turned back toward Rosemond Street. It was time he learned his lesson for once. Avoid commitments, and avoid disappointing everyone around him—himself included.

STEP 31:

DISCOVERY

Ambrose

It was late at night, and the potioneers had gone to war with their commission.

Between the shield wand, ice wand, and dousing wand, Eli's hands looked like they had long wooden claws. Ambrose caught a nervous glance from him through his own welding hood, which he adjusted with thick, sturdy gloves.

"How you feeling?" Eli straightened the hood for him, searching for his eyes through the cloudy glass.

"Quite safe, actually." Ambrose held up his hands. "The material of these gloves is impressive."

"I meant about the potion, but"—Eli bit back a smile—"you do look very handsome all dressed up."

"Really?" Ambrose shook his head, a more difficult gesture with the hood on. "Is this better than that low-cut shirt you keep asking me to wear?"

"How about a compromise—the low-cut shirt paired with those gloves?"

Ambrose rolled his eyes and gently pushed him away from the cauldron. "All right, I need to focus on this potion, thank you."

His smile faded as he faced the bubbling water. Unlike previous tests, he couldn't get this one wrong. They only had two weeks left— if he wasted all his ingredients now, rush-orders wouldn't make it in time. Besides, he still needed to properly temper the potion, secure the packaging...

And both of them desperately wanted to be done brewing the same thing over and over.

"If you get this right"—Eli readied the dousing wand, his grip tight on the handle—"I'll give you whatever you want."

"Whatever I want?"

"Whatever you want."

Ambrose caught a hint of the amulet at Eli's neck, the gold chain gleaming, then winking out of sight under his collar. His thoughts immediately wandered. He could unbutton that shirt to see what the amulet looked like against Eli's chest...

No, he had to focus. He turned back to the cauldron. "Noted, thank you."

He tapped the glass pipette above the cauldron, and it began to drip the illusion component into the levitation brew. He counted each drop. Five, four, three, two—

The cauldron sputtered, and he quickly poured in the stabilizing solution. Three stirs clockwise with the gold spoon, two counter-clockwise with the silver. Ladle in the reactant, skim off the foam. Sweat trickled down his forehead, but there was no time to stop and wipe it away. He rushed breathlessly into the last steps, with mere seconds between each move. The neutralizers, the counter-acting components, the three drops of flavoring—no, four, to be safe—

He ladled the potion into the bottle and stepped back, hands raised. Eli held up the shield wand, one arm already stretched in front of Ambrose.

But nothing happened. No oozing, no hissing, no corks shooting into the air. Just a lovely amethyst potion, slightly glittery, with bubbles clinging gently to the sides of the glass.

"Is it done?" Eli lowered the wand. "Are we...actually done with the commission?"

Ambrose tugged off the hood and pulled at the gloves, trying to balance his own excitement. "It's worth one more taste test once it's fully tempered, but..." He set the gloves on the cleaning table and grinned. "Yes. I believe it's done."

"*Yes!*" Eli picked him up and spun him around. "We did it!"

Ambrose laughed as Eli set him down. Had it really already been four months since Rune gave them that contract? And at the same time—had it only been four months? Hating Eli felt so distant. Particularly when Eli looked up at him like that, holding tightly onto his waist...

"All right, I made you a promise," Eli said, still flushed and grinning. "What do you want?"

Ambrose knew exactly what he wanted. He had just never asked for it before.

"You," he breathed, then dipped down to kiss Eli.

It took Eli a moment to respond—but he answered in full force, matching him with an energy he hadn't shown before. Ambrose quickly lost himself in a tangle of hands and lips and sighs. It wasn't until Eli started undoing the clasps on his robe that he had the wherewithal to pull away.

"Upstairs?" he murmured.

Once they were upstairs, they didn't quite make it to a proper bed. Ambrose wasn't sure how, but he was suddenly lying on the sofa, robes cast aside, Eli shifting on top of him. Almost dizzy, he closed his eyes and let his hands wander along the back of Eli's waistline, finding places to slip up under the shirt. As he eagerly dragged his fingers along the taut muscles there, Eli groaned against his collarbone and rocked into him with his hips.

Ambrose gasped on instinct, and Eli stopped.

"Sorry," he whispered, his grip on Ambrose's hair relaxing. "Are you okay with this?"

"Yes," Ambrose breathed—then as he took full stock of their position, nerves swept back in. "I do want this, I just...I don't know what I'm doing."

"It's okay," Eli said quickly. "I won't ever do anything you're uncomfortable with. But..." He paused to sweep a hair off Ambrose's forehead. "You *will* have to communicate with me. Even just a simple yes or no to start, all right?"

Ambrose let out a breath, and his nerves sank into the cushions under him. This was Eli he was with. He was going to be fine. "I can do that."

Eli was true to his word, as Ambrose knew he would be—following every yes, no, and the occasional laugh when he found a ticklish spot.

"There?" He grinned wickedly and dug his fingers under Ambrose's ribcage. Ambrose's knee jerked up as he laughed, striking Eli's arm.

"Yes, there—I mean, *no,* there—" he managed between giggles. "Please—"

Eli buried his smile into Ambrose's neck and kept exploring with his hands. They took their time, until bits of clothing dropped to the floor one by one, and yeses and nos turned into gasps and soft repetitions of Eli's name.

But before he got too far, Ambrose fought through the warm haze to turn the focus on Eli. "Eli, you...can I—?"

It wasn't his most polished or even coherent attempt at communication, but Eli understood, nodding and letting him take the lead. Ambrose quickly found both pleasure and pride in exploring how to make Eli say yes—how to make him gasp, say *his* name. Mentally filing every little reaction away to remember for later, for next time.

"I thought you..." Eli stifled a moan. "Thought you said you didn't know what you were doing."

Ambrose smiled. "I'm a fast learner. Was always hoping I could apply that to multiple fields."

"You're ridiculous." Eli pulled Ambrose toward him. "Come here."

They continued the back and forth until Ambrose completely let go, unaware of anything except for Eli and what he was doing to him, what they were doing for each other.

Afterward, there was no need to go back to the real world right away. Neither of them had anything to brew nor places to be. Ambrose grabbed a blanket and nestled back into Eli's arms, warm and sleepy and smiling to himself. He had no idea that any of this— even the simple feeling of Eli's slow breath against his skin—could make him so happy. How did he manage this sort of luck? What had he done to merit this? How did anyone like him ever deserve to be in lo—

His eyes snapped open.

Was he? No. It was too early, wasn't it? He was being silly. It was only because they had just... He should wait to see how he felt in the morning, right? Or maybe a week later. Or months from now, or a year from now. Would Eli still be with him then? Oh gods, how did Eli feel about him? What if he wasn't very good at this and Eli decided he didn't want to stay with—

"You all right?" Eli murmured. He had one eye open, his thumb rubbing Ambrose's shoulder blade. Ambrose realized he had drawn away from Eli, shoulders stiff, breath quickened.

"I'm okay," Ambrose whispered, stuffing down the mental spiral. "It's nothing."

Eli saw straight through his words. He gently pulled Ambrose back in, kissed his forehead, and tugged the blanket over his shoulder. "Everything is fine. Take a few deep breaths and stay with me."

As Ambrose curled back inward, Eli drew a hand through his hair, slow and soft. Ambrose focused on the motion and nestled into Eli's warmth until his breathing slowed and his thoughts trailed off into a sleepy murmur. After several minutes of this—or perhaps hours or days, Ambrose wasn't sure—Eli kissed his forehead once more.

"You okay if I sleep here tonight?" he whispered. "I can make you breakfast in the morning."

Ambrose sighed in relief—so Eli did want to stay after all.

"Pancakes?" he whispered back.

"Pancakes."

Eli pulled him closer, his contented hum sending a lovely vibration through Ambrose's chest. As Ambrose burrowed, his thoughts crept up like shadows behind his eyes, persistent in their truth.

He had to concede it. He loved Eli Valenz.

STEP 32:

BOTTLE IT UP

Eli

SPENDING the night quickly became a habit of Eli's—slipping in after the day's brewing was done, then scuttling back across the street at dawn. Evenings at Ambrose's required a bit more work—buying that second dining chair, for example—but seeing his smile when Eli came in for the night was more than worth it.

Even if they didn't make it past the supply closet sometimes.

"Tom, I'm back," Eli whispered one morning, gently closing his shop door behind him. "Tom?"

After a sleepy second, wheels squeaked toward him, and Tom appeared around the counter, holding something in her fork hands—the speaking stone.

"Oh." Eli blinked. "It's..." In his early morning daze, he struggled to recall what day it was. "You're right, I owe them a chat."

He took the stone and weighed it in his hands. He hadn't yet sorted out what to say to his family.

Not about Ambrose, of course. He'd already decided to tell them about him in person when they visited for the birthday festival. They wouldn't be surprised he was dating a man. They had always known his preferences, ever since he was six and couldn't decide on whom to marry—his neighbor's daughter, with the flowers in her hair, or his other neighbor's son, who picked the flowers for her.

No, it wasn't Ambrose that would worry them. It was his career.

Like always.

The shop itself was still afloat. Between the commission money and his returning customers, he had eased up on his deep discounts. And as Ambrose started stocking his complex potions more heavily, their markets had slowly begun to separate, easing the burden on both of them.

But after his run-in with Oren at the training grounds, Eli had begun to meet with other adventurers, most of them his customers. It had been easy—starting a conversation as he rang up their potions, expressing an interest in their work. Adventurers were always looking for a chance to brag about themselves, so more often than not, they were the first to offer a beer or a lunch.

Yet when it came down to it, they all spouted similar advice to Oren's—if he wasn't willing to commit to the Scarrish training program, he had to look outside the city. The Scar was for veterans, the ones bards wrote songs and plays about. *New* adventurers were better off starting in smaller villages, gaining experience with wood dragons and other common pests. And there were plenty of nearby villages that could accommodate them, of course. But if he wanted to be an adventurer, he'd have to leave the Scar. He'd have to leave Rosemond Street, leave the other merchants...

Eli glanced over at The Griffin's Claw, where the owner was dusting potion bottles.

He'd have to leave Ambrose.

The thought flipped his stomach, and he shoved the river stone onto a shelf. He couldn't talk to his parents, not right now. He'd have to tell them about the career change in person, too.

The churning in Eli's stomach only grew as the day rolled on, and a steady flow of craftsmen, not customers, occupied The Griffin's Claw. They dragged in new cauldrons, a new wand rack. Even Banneker dropped in with something rectangular wrapped in cloth. And while Eli couldn't see the actual renovations being done in the workroom, he could tell Ambrose was thrilled just by how he strode proudly about the store.

Eli grimaced and rubbed his chest. Ambrose's excitement only made this worse. He was going to have to say something to him soon, before the words vomited out of his mouth of their own accord.

He waited until the end of the day. After brewing a quick batch of night-vision potions—in the extra-large cauldron, too, Ambrose would have hated it—he jogged over to The Griffin's Claw and slipped inside.

"Saw all the deliveries today," he said. "You happy with how it all turned out?"

Ambrose didn't respond. He stood stiffly at the counter, neck bent to review a letter in front of him. Eli slowed his steps. "Ames?"

Ambrose snapped to attention, then folded the letter. "Apologies, um—yes. The workroom is looking nice, I'm happy with it."

Judging by how weak his smile was, there was clearly something in the letter he wasn't happy with. Eli pointed to it. "What's that?"

As far as Eli could tell, Ambrose didn't receive much mail other than Guild correspondence, copies of scientific journals, and the occasional request to guest lecture. Eli sometimes wondered if he would have developed a crush on Ambrose at college if he had ever accepted one of those requests.

Ambrose reluctantly unfolded the letter. "Master Pearce is... unable to make it back for the shop's anniversary."

Eli's heart sank. "Are you serious?"

Ambrose tried to laugh as he handed the paper to Eli, but the sound was broken. "I shouldn't have bothered. He didn't even spell my name right."

Eli took the letter and glared at the spindly writing, narrow and concise.

Dear Mr. Beak—

"I hate this guy," Eli muttered and kept reading.

*I regret that I cannot attend the shop's anniversary celebration, as
the westward winds bar any sort of griffin travel from—*

Eli's temper flared. "Bull*shit*, those winds don't even pick up until
spring. He's such a—"

He prepared to crumple the letter and throw it into the street—
then reluctantly recalled that this wasn't his letter to destroy. Instead,
he threw it back on the counter and wrapped Ambrose in a hug.

"I'm sorry," he murmured, holding him tight. "If he retired closer
to here, you know I'd go over there myself and punch him in the
face."

Ambrose laughed again, a more genuine sound this time. "That
would be unnecessary, but I appreciate the thought." He pulled away,
the color returning to his cheeks. "Would you like to test the commission now?"

The commission—amidst everything else, Eli had nearly
forgotten.

"You mean see you in glittery purple wings again?" Eli squeezed
his hands. "I want nothing more."

Ambrose led him over to the workroom, where he had two purple
vials waiting on the table. But Eli could hardly look at those now—
there was so much else to see in the renovated space. Ambrose had
done far more than purchase new cauldrons. The cabinets had been
refinished, the crystal lamps polished. The new wands on the wand
rack sparkled.

While checking to see if the lucky shelf had gotten any love, Eli
spotted the sign on the wall above it. It was finally back now, its deep
luster almost glittering in the crystal light—and on it was Ambrose's
name. Not burned or carved, but grown into the wood in elegant
vines and whorls. Upon closer inspection, it looked like someone had

even burnished the letters so Ambrose's name appeared brighter than the others.

"Do you like it?" Ambrose asked. Eli beamed.

"Do you?"

As the half-elf nodded, his ears perked up and went pink. "I do."

But ever the professional, he turned to the purple vials and held them up. "Now, I would like to test these, if only to ensure we're not poisoning Beatrice. If it works, I'll bottle the rest for our delivery. If not, well..."

The thought of it gave Eli flashbacks to cramming for frantic college finals—but Ambrose was unfazed as he handed over a vial. "Your purple wings, sir."

"Thank you, sir."

They both downed the potion in one go, the pleasant fizz of fernberry masking the sharper notes from the active ingredients. Just as Eli hoped, his feet slowly lifted off the ground. He tilted backward when a mild weight settled onto his shoulders, and the magic quickly linked both the floating and the wings to his mind.

"Perfect," he breathed. Ambrose floated, too, wreathed in purple sparkles from the lightly beating dragon wings behind him. The sparkles only amplified his grin.

"I knew I wouldn't have to fix anything," he said. Eli set both hands on Ambrose's hips.

"You look good in purple, potion master."

Without warning, he twisted Ambrose, sending him gently spinning in the air. As the wings spun, they released a long trail of purple sparkles until Eli could hardly see Ambrose through them. He laughed and reached in through the suspended glitter.

"You know," he said, pulling Ambrose into him—one hand on his waist, the other finding his hand. "While we're up here, you should teach me a Scarrish dance."

Ambrose wrinkled his nose. "Teach you a dance?"

"For the festival." Eli twirled him around once, the wing illusion brushing against him like a breeze. "You haven't taught me any yet.

You want me to embarrass you in front of everyone?" He drew Ambrose closer. "Or did you think you were going to escape the dancing entirely?"

Ambrose held back a smile. "I was rather hoping to run away before the dancing started."

"Well, that was never going to work." Eli gave him a look. "You know Lily will want to dance."

"Lily," Ambrose repeated. "She's your...youngest sister?"

Eli nodded. "And Althea's the—"

"Oldest, yes," Ambrose said. "I think I've got them all memorized. Oh, and if your parents end up staying at the Striped Orchid, the orc who runs it owes me a favor, so I'm certain I can get them a discount. And I've been reading that Kolkean book I bought, but I'm afraid I'm not far enough along to string a sentence together. Will they be terribly disappointed?"

Eli shook his head. "Not at all. And you don't have to do all that."

"No, I do." Ambrose smiled. "I want to."

Overwhelming happiness and uncomfortable guilt made for a terrible mix in Eli's insides.

Ambrose was making it far too easy to fall in love with him.

He had been silently testing the word *love* for a week now, rolling it around in his head, testing its weight. He had fancied himself in love before, of course, when he was younger. With his career changes came flings as strong as they were short, passing through like sandstorms.

But this time, the word rooted itself in his thoughts, heavy and stubborn. He wasn't even sure when it had started growing, but there was no use ripping it up now. Every time Ambrose smiled, the roots only dug deeper, until the truth was immovable. He loved Ambrose Beake.

Why did he have such terrible timing?

"Thank you." Eli kissed him on the cheek. "They're going to love you. I can't wait to tell them about us as soon as they're here." Then his grip tightened on Ambrose's waist. "I also need to tell them about some...career thoughts I've been having."

Ambrose brightened; Eli held back a wince. "So, you think you'll try out the adventuring? That's excellent. You were always so happy when you came back from those meetings. I mean, I didn't want to influence you by pointing it out, but..." He trailed off as he met Eli's gaze. "What's wrong?"

Slowly, the potion let them settle until their feet were back on the stone and the glitter had faded away around them. Eli took both of Ambrose's hands in his.

"All the adventurers recommended I start with smaller groups first," he said. "Smaller than what's based in the Scar, I mean. I'd...I'd have to move away."

All the brightness in Ambrose's face disappeared, and he hurried to finish the explanation.

"Not far, though!" he said quickly. "Some of the villages they recommended are only a day's ride from the Scar. I'd come back and visit whenever I can."

"Oh." Ambrose faltered. "And—and there's nothing here in the Scar?"

Oren's offer stirred in the back of Eli's mind; he pushed it aside.

"Not here, no. But I haven't accepted anything outside the Scar, either. I thought I'd talk to you first."

Though Ambrose remained in place, Eli could see him withdrawing—his posture shrinking, voice lowering, eyes dropping to the floor.

"Thank you for telling me," Ambrose murmured. "I won't get in the way of your choice. If you're able to visit, then I'd like to make this work. But if you're not able to visit..." His gaze flicked briefly to the letter on the counter outside, and Eli's heart snapped. "Then I won't hold you back."

There were a hundred things Eli wanted to say. He didn't want to lose Ambrose, he would never abandon him like Pearce, or—oh gods, like his parents—but before he could open his mouth, Ambrose let go of his hands and stepped back. "I actually have a few things to brew for the shop, if you don't mind..."

"Of course." Eli swallowed the rest of his words and backed away, hands in his pockets. He'd resume the conversation when Ambrose was ready and not a moment before. He had learned that much, at least. "See you tomorrow?"

Ambrose nodded and closed the workroom door behind him.

STEP 33:

CONSULTATION

Ambrose

Ambrose stared hard at the rose statue the next day. He reached for the scroll, then withdrew his hand. Reached for it again, then let his fingers rest on the counter.

Gods damn himself—he had gotten better about talking, hadn't he? And this was Dawn he was reaching out to. He could talk to Dawn.

His fingers twitched. He would be such a bother, reaching out like this—

No. *No*, he was not a bother. Sherry had even said so.

He set his shoulders and grabbed the quill next to the statue. The painful weight in his throat wasn't going to go away just by arguing with himself.

Emergency lunch, please? he wrote on the scroll, then tossed the quill back onto the counter.

Emergency lunches were typically Dawn's tool—Ambrose had never once called for an emergency lunch himself. So, he wasn't all that surprised to find Dawn at his doorstep five minutes later, coin purse in hand.

"Tea," she said. "Now."

It was to her credit that she didn't press him on the reason for the lunch. Not on the way there, and not even when their tea arrived. When she did raise her eyebrows in a wordless question, she let him start the conversation.

"I was wondering how your fireworks were going," he deflected, his stomach flipping against the tea. It would be nice to hear her talk first, he thought. It would give him time to gather his courage. Dawn scanned his face, then sat back.

"I told you last week about the shapes, right?"

"The dragon shapes, yes."

"Well, I finally got the wood to play nice with the moss." She stirred her tea. "You know, get the shapes' choreography to line up with the timing spell..."

She continued for a while, generously carrying the conversation until she had no more details to give. Even more generously, she let him remain silent after, until he gave a broken sigh and stopped fiddling with his spoon.

"Has Eli told you about his plans to—?"

"*Yes.*" Dawn collapsed miserably in her seat. "Ames, I don't want him to go, either."

"What do I do?" Ambrose blurted out, the knot in his throat blurring his vision. He blinked hard and focused on the flower in his tea. "Dawn, he's not going to come back."

She reached over and set another cookie on his plate. "Don't think like that. He's going to start small. He's not going to go off and get eaten by a dragon."

"No, I mean..." Ambrose took the cookie but couldn't bring himself to eat it. He held it instead, sandy crumbs gathering on his fingers. "To visit. He'll never... *They* never..."

He didn't need to specify who. Dawn took his hand.

"Eli isn't them." She added a hardness to her words to make him look up. "You *know* he isn't them. Have you talked to him about this?"

Ambrose shook his head. It was taking all his effort just to keep from crying. "I can't hold him back like that—"

"That's not what I meant," Dawn said. "Talking to him won't make him stay, but you still need to tell him how you feel. Just to get it out there."

Ambrose swallowed his tears and sniffed. "You make it sound so easy."

"I never said it would be." Dawn let go of his hand to pour herself more tea, a small smile playing across her face. "Telling someone you love them can be scary."

Ambrose stopped with the cookie halfway to his mouth. Dawn giggled.

"So, you...you don't think it's stupid?" he warbled. "That it's too early or something?"

"Stupid that you love him?" Dawn plucked the cookie out of his fingers and ate it. "Ambrose, I think it's the smartest thing you've ever done."

STEP 34:

PIVOT

Eli

THE DAY BEFORE THE FESTIVAL, Eli's Elixirs was filled with excitement and nerves.

Ambrose followed Dawn about the shop, straightening his sleeves while she chased Tom around the tables. "Dawn, do I look all right? Please, I need to make a good impression—"

"I already told you, you look handsome." Dawn bent and scooped up Tom. "Who's the cutest? *Who's* the cutest?"

Eli tugged Tom out of her arms. "Come on, her bristles can't fit her ego as it is." He tucked Tom into the crook of his elbow and kissed Ambrose's cheek. "You look great. You always do."

"Not as nice as you." Ambrose ran his fingers over the maroon fabric at Eli's shoulder, lingering at the embroidery on the collar. "Wish I owned something like this."

Eli set a hand on Ambrose's waist, imagining it wrapped in a fitting, silky jacket. Perhaps a midnight blue, with sharp, vertical patterns that emphasized his height...

"Best that you don't," Eli said, then grinned up at Ambrose. "Wouldn't be able to keep my hands off you."

"And that's my cue to leave." Dawn rolled her eyes and strolled out into the street. "Eli, don't forget—if you don't bring your family to my shop, I *will* hunt you down."

Eli waved her off. "Don't worry, they'll be visiting everyone. But don't you dare sell Lily a wand, you hear me? I don't care what it does, she'll engineer it to do something worse."

Dawn's ears perked up. "Is she looking for an apprenticeship?"

"Rosemond Street would literally explode."

The creak of wagon wheels filled the air, and Dawn jumped away from the door. "Looks like they're here. Have fun, send them over!"

As Dawn left, Ambrose made an indistinct gulping noise. Eli took his hand and kissed it in reassurance. "Don't worry. They're going to love you."

In truth, someone in this shop already did. But he held his tongue on that front.

"And you'll introduce me?" Ambrose asked. "As your, um..."

Eli cycled through the possible terms in his head. *Person* didn't feel like enough anymore—Ambrose was far more than that to him now. But he didn't want to usher Ambrose into *boyfriend* territory too quickly, no matter how deeply he felt. So, he waited patiently for Ambrose to weigh the terms on his own tongue.

"Partner?" Ambrose finally said. Eli squeezed his hand.

"Absolutely."

Ambrose nodded, and together they watched the window while Tom wheeled impatiently around their ankles.

As Eli expected, Lily was first through the door, nearly kicking it down in her excitement. "*Where* is she?" she shrieked in Kolkean. Tom zoomed right for her, kicking her little dagger legs as Lily picked her up and threw her into the air with glee. "There she is! My little broom dragon! I'm stealing you back, don't tell Eli—"

"Tom!" Marcos stepped in and caught the automaton in midair. "How's Eli been treating you? Oiling your wheels every week?"

"Hm." June reached around Marcos and carefully realigned a bristle on her head. "She's a bit dusty."

"Excuse me?" Eli spread his arms, grinning so hard he thought his jaw might break. "Listen, I get that I'm not as cute, but—"

The avalanche of hugs was swift, arms and elbows all but knocking Ambrose aside in their quest to smother Eli. Somewhere in the joyful, babbling shuffle, he managed to pick Lily up and swing her around, her dusty boots barely missing the displays. She was taller now—teenagers, always growing when he wasn't looking—and the effort was harder than he wanted it to be.

"When are we getting dumplings?" she asked, her voice rattling in his ear. Behind her, their mother June bent to examine a display, dark eyes sparkling.

"This place looks wonderful!" She picked up a potion. "You really brewed all these yourself?" She was still dressed for Kolkean weather —loose maroon linens swirling around her stout frame, black hair pulled in a thick braid. As she put the potion back, Eli spotted her nails, all painted red with yellow flowers. It had been a festival tradition of hers ever since Eli could remember, and it warmed him to see them painted now for tomorrow's festivities.

Across the room, his father Marcos scanned the shelves. "It's a lovely location," he said, his hands proudly on his hips. The family all claimed that Eli had inherited his features, including his smile— which didn't miss a beat when he finally noticed Ambrose. "Did you hire an assistant, too?"

"Oh." Ambrose looked to Eli. "I'm—"

Lily clocked his blue hair and gasped. "What's *he* doing here?"

June and Marcos looked at each other in confusion. Ambrose stiffened.

"Um." Eli rushed over to Ambrose and gently took his arm. "Everyone, this is Ambrose Beake. He runs The Griffin's Claw potion shop across the street."

Recognition flashed across his parents' faces. "Oh, I see."

Eli failed to hide a grin. "He's also my partner."

Ambrose cleared his throat. "It's lovely to meet you," he said in stilted, overly formal Kolkean.

His parents' faces brightened like lanterns. Eli could have kissed him then and there.

"Lovely to meet you, too." Marcos jumped to shake his hand. "We've heard all about the commission you two are working on."

"Can we see your place next?" June crowded Ambrose's shoulder —a feat, considering he towered over her. "Eli promised us a tour of the whole street."

As they drowned Ambrose in smiles and questions, Eli went over to Lily, who was leaning against the counter, eyes narrowed. "So, you're really dating him?" she asked.

"Yes, Lily."

"And it's not some corporate conspiracy to get rid of your competitor?"

"No, Lily."

"Okay." She pressed her lips into a line. "I had committed to some sabotage on the way here, you know. Tripping him in the street, breaking a cauldron—"

"*Lil.*"

She raised her hands. "But I guess I'll hold off for now. Just tell me if it's ever needed, okay?"

Eli leaned against the counter next to her. "I really think you'll like him if you give him the chance."

"Oh, I believe it." She toyed with her earring, the red crystals she always wore for festivals. "I mean, he changed *your* mind, didn't he?"

"He did."

Across the shop, Ambrose made a valiant effort to tread water against the tide of his parents' chatter. Eli smiled, his chest a puddle of warmth. So many people he loved, all in one place. "He really did."

———

Ambrose was far more generous than Eli expected him to be that day. He accompanied them on a tour of the other shops, answered his father's endless questions about the Scar, and carried Tom around when Lily got tired of holding her. Eli bit his lip—Ambrose always looked attractive when he was carrying Tom around.

So, when they found themselves back at Eli's shop, he snuck a kiss on Ambrose's cheek and gave him a way out. "I can take my family from here," he said, pointedly raising his eyebrows, "if you need to get some brewing done."

Ambrose gave a small sigh and nodded. "Thank you," he mumbled. "All right if I join you for dinner?"

"Please do," Eli said, and watched him slip back across the street, navigating the pre-festival crowds that choked the dusty road. June came up and set a hand on Eli's shoulder.

"He's very handsome, sweetheart."

"And he's been published." Marcos pointed to the other shop. "He's a little young to be that sort of scholar, isn't he?"

Eli ignored their remarks—he could already hear the admiration oozing out of their voices—and instead turned to Lily, who was bouncing Tom on her hip. She tilted her head, then shrugged. "He's cool."

Eli grinned. That was about as high of a compliment as Ambrose was ever going to get from her. "I'm glad you like him," he said. "I like him, too."

But now it was time to tell them something else. Something significantly less fun than who his partner was. He let out a grounding breath.

"I like him a lot," he said. "Which means I...sort of have a problem."

———

Eli led them upstairs to his carefully thought-out display of maps and ledgers and ran them through his new adventuring plan as best he could.

He'd find a village near the Scar, preferably one southwest, a little closer to Kolkea. He'd try out the work there, then if he liked it, seek out larger adventuring parties—ones that traveled more, took on larger jobs. Those could get him Adventurer's Guild hours, if he found the right group. Then it was on to Guild certification, Guild jobs, Guild money and benefits...

His family had few interjections while he spoke. They all had experience in these conversations before, from the farm, the botany team, the griffin-keeping... They knew what questions to ask, and Eli knew how to answer them.

But the conversation hadn't gotten any easier for him. The further he stepped into the plan, the more it filled him with that same self-doubt, that uncertainty that came with all his past failures. He did his best not to let it spill into his words—no stumbling, no mangled explanations.

Once he reached the end, his family remained silent for a while. June quietly turned the Scarrish map toward her, running a finger over the circled villages around its perimeter, while Marcos squinted at the ledgers. Eli looked to Lily.

She was always first to speak, and she was usually right.

"I like it." She sat back in her chair and tapped her fingers against Tom, who sat happily in her lap. "You're right. This would be good for you."

"Really?" Eli blurted out, then reined himself in. "You think so?"

Lily nodded. "It's like you said. You'd travel, see new things, meet new people. You'd never get bored, and you'd be helping others." Her mouth twisted into a smile as she gave a light curse in Kolkean. "Wish *I* had thought of it for you."

"And this was your idea?" His father looked up from the ledger.

"Yeah," Eli lied. He didn't want his parents thinking Ambrose was trying to kick him out of the business. "Just came to me as I talked to my customers, you know?"

His mother traded the map for the ledger, her gaze quickly absorbing the numbers. "And you think selling the shop will allow you to buy the armor you need?"

Now there was one thing he could feel confident in.

"I ran the numbers past Sherry," Eli said. "You met her earlier, the one with the cookies?"

His family hummed in recognition.

"Well, she looked over everything and agreed that I should have enough for both moving costs and the basic set of weaponry. Even said she'd let me take her kids' old gear if she can find it. She made some of it herself."

Lily set Tom on the floor. "And Ambrose?"

There were times when Eli didn't appreciate Lily's acuity, and this was one of them.

"He's supportive," he said, this lie coming out bumpier. "It's just... He worries."

His mother closed the ledger and smiled. "Then he sounds like someone who cares about you."

Eli looked around at all of them, their placid silence unnerving. There were usually more questions at this point, not to mention more concerns. "So...you're not...angry with me?" He gestured toward the stairs. "I know you were excited about the shop—"

His father waved a hand. "Eli, we knew the shop might not hold your interest forever. It was a good idea, and we wanted to be supportive." He grinned, betraying where Eli had gotten his own smile from. "And for what it's worth, I don't mind my son going off and becoming a hero."

Eli rolled his eyes to cover the happy bubbling in his chest. "Pa, please."

Lily leaned forward, a glint in her eye. "Can you get, like, a cool scar? Not your griffin ones. I'm thinking, like, a neat line across your cheek. And you can make up a different story every time someone asks you about it—"

"Lily," her mother warned.

"What? It'd be cool!"

As his family filled the space with conversation again, Eli gathered up his maps, his tension melting. His plans never felt real until his family got behind them.

Now there was just one more person to reassure.

STEP 35:

DELIVER THE POTION

Eli

ELI AND AMBROSE stared down at the polished mahogany box. The carpenter had done a wonderful job with her finishing touches. The diamond carvings on the box matched the pattern on the crystal vial, which was couched in a bed of soft purple velvet. A lovely, if unorthodox, birthday present for a lovely, if unorthodox, little girl.

Eli scratched his cheek. "You don't think she'll float away, do you?"

Ambrose frowned. "Highly unlikely."

"Probably wouldn't get paid if that happened." Eli tilted his head. "Would be kind of funny, though."

"It would be a little funny."

As Ambrose smoothed out the velvet, Eli trailed a hand up his back, along the gold pattern of his robes. "You know, I kind of want a replica or something."

"What do you mean?"

"I dunno." Eli set his chin on Ambrose's shoulder. The purple potion winked up at him in the morning light. "I mean, where would we be without it? Us, I mean."

He tried to picture it—months of them glaring at each other

through their shop windows. Locked in some sort of advertising war. Sitting on opposite sides in every street meeting, then going home to sulk—Eli struggling to make ends meet while Ambrose shut himself in his workroom every night...

Ambrose gently closed the box. "I never thought I'd be so glad to have voted for Mayor Rune."

Eli kissed Ambrose's shoulder, then stepped away, trying not to overanalyze how sadly Ambrose was gazing at the box. He had meant to discuss his career change with him again last night, but Ambrose had clammed up at dinner whenever anyone mentioned it. His mother had chalked it up to simple worry—adventuring was dangerous, after all—but Eli had spent enough time around Ambrose to know when he was holding back something he wanted to say. When he was fighting years of old habits just to get the words out.

He also knew better than to pry him open, especially on a festival day. Instead, he took Ambrose's hand and walked with him out of the shop.

"After we drop off the potion," he said, "promise me you'll have a little bit of fun at the festival?" He kissed the back of his hand. "Just a little?"

To his surprise, Ambrose stopped walking and kissed Eli's forehead in return—a delicate gesture that delighted him every time. "I will have the minimum amount of fun."

"There we go."

As they walked along the main parade route, Eli tried to balance his attention between the festival crowds ahead of him and the festival decorations above him. Gauzy purple banners fluttered from ramparts and rope bridges, embroidered with roaring dragons. The closer they got to the government square, the more purple assailed them—amethyst food carts by the fountain, mauve flowers perfuming the windows...

Eli glanced at their box and hoped Beatrice wouldn't be tired of purple by the time she opened it.

"Gifts?" Tiegan called from their table by the stairs. The secretary's lime-green hair clashed terribly with the purple they had been assigned to wear for the day. "Go ahead and join the queue."

Eli's shoulders sagged when he saw the long line snaking its way up the stairs and through the double doors. People bearing bags, boxes, and crates all shuffled inward at a snail's pace. Ambrose touched his arm. "If you need to go attend to your family..."

"No, no." Eli shook his head. "They're helping Sherry and Banneker stake out a parade spot. I can stay. But..." He glanced back at the food carts. "I might grab us some breakfast. Be right back—"

The moment he stepped out of line, he nearly crashed into a blurred pink shape barreling down the stairs. He staggered away and caught the person's arm before she could stumble.

"Dawn!" he said. "So sorry—are you getting the fireworks ready?"

"Trying to," she grumbled, adjusting her flowing pink dress. She looked like a firework herself today, with her wide starburst earrings and bright, round patterns down her skirt. "If I can just wrangle these mages to line up the staffs like they're supposed to..." Her gaze flitted to the box in Ambrose's hand. "Dropping off the potion?"

"Eventually." Ambrose tilted his head to the line. Dawn grimaced.

"Have fun with that. Beatrice was in a bad mood fifteen minutes ago. Heard she smashed a jar of Elwig candies on the floor because they smelled funny." She gave a huff and picked up her skirts. "Best of luck!"

She dashed off, and Ambrose's eyes went wide.

"If she smashes it"—he held the box closer to his body—"we would still get paid, wouldn't we? I need to pay the final installment for the cabinets."

"Rune'll pay us." Eli tried to sound more confident than he felt. He had already earmarked that money for a good sword. "He has to. We brought the potion just like he asked."

Ambrose looked to the doors, then shoved the box toward Eli. "You give it to her. You're better with children."

"Me?" Eli shoved the box back. "Come on, you're great with Tom."

"Tom isn't a child! She doesn't throw things!"

"Then clearly you've never seen her throw a scorpion."

They continued like this, the box trading hands with each argument, until they reached the front of the line.

"Next!" Rune called out, and they stepped carefully into the soaring reception room. Here, distant skylights dappled the tile with bright morning light, and the building's typical carvings stretched twice as tall. All the reliefs of heroes and farmers stared down at the middle of the room, focused on Mayor Rune, Beatrice, and a pile of half-opened presents.

"Next!" Beatrice echoed, bouncing her little legs on the chair until they lifted her like a lever. Her dress dripped with violet gems that tinkled as she moved.

Ambrose stared down at the box in his hands—then straightened and stepped forward. "Happy birthday, Miss Rune." He gave the little girl a half bow. "Your father requested we make this for you."

Rune took the box, and Ambrose hurried back to stand next to Eli. Eli gave him a small thumbs-up.

"Beatrice," Rune said sweetly. "What have you been asking for for months?"

Beatrice beamed. "Dragon," she said. "I wanna be a dragon!"

Rune opened the box. "Well, these two talented men have created a potion just for that. We can try it later if you—"

Beatrice grabbed the vial with her little fingers and began tugging on the stopper. "Now, now!"

"All right." Rune let out a small sigh, tossed the potioneers an apologetic smile, then helped Beatrice with the stopper. "Here you go."

Eli swallowed. This was better than throwing it on the ground, surely. But what if she *did* float away? Or worse, not float at all? His potion career was already ending, but Ambrose's wasn't. If he managed to ruin both of their livelihoods in one fell swoop—

Beatrice drank the potion in one gulp, a single lavender drop dribbling down her green chin. Nothing happened. Eli held his breath.

Then, just as they had tested, she began to float. Little dragon wings, ephemerally pink and purple, sprouted from her back. She shrieked and clapped, then reached out for her father with her tiny hands.

"I'm a dragon!" she shouted. The wings flapped once, and she lifted an inch higher, sparkles marking her path. "Daddy, fly with me!"

"Fly with you?" Rune stood up and took hold of her waist. "How high can you fly?"

He tossed her up. For a moment, she was a giggling, weightless ball of purple—then she twirled and slowly floated back down to his hands.

Both potioneers gave a sigh of relief.

"Again!" she said, spinning in a whirlwind of sunlit sparkles. In a swell of pride, Eli glanced over at Ambrose. He was beaming, his eyes reflecting back the pink and purple light. Eli resisted the urge to take his hand, for fear of breaking the spell. He wasn't sure who was happier in this moment—Beatrice or Ambrose.

As the mayor twirled his daughter, someone waved at the potioneers from the wall—Tiegan, poking their green head through a side door. Both men nodded politely to the mayor and began to step away.

"Hold on." Rune held up a hand. "Beatrice, what do you say to the potioneers?"

Beatrice pushed off from him, tumbled through the air, and latched onto Ambrose's neck.

"Thank you!" she shouted into his ear, then floated over to Eli and did the same. Eli gave her a hug. He wouldn't mind making more birthday commissions if they were all this well-received.

"Happy birthday, Beatrice," he said, then lightly tossed her back to her father and followed Ambrose out to the secretary.

"All right." Tiegan plopped down at a desk obscured with papers. Despite the mess, they expertly flipped through a stack and handed each of them a page. "Records of the last third of the payment being sent to you. Should arrive in three days."

Eli almost vibrated with excitement. Once the money was in, he'd be able to start a proper search for equipment. He couldn't buy anything at Sherry's, of course, but he could go on a spree in the upper levels, haggle for a few pieces...

"Thank you," he started, but Tiegan gestured to the door.

"Go on, the parade will start in an hour. Enjoy."

Eli hurried into the square, then pulled Ambrose into his arms, pouring his pride into the gesture. He didn't need to say congratulations—Ambrose's tight grip and long, relieved breath said more than enough.

Then he drew away, placed his hands on his knees, and released a slow breath of his own. The commission was done—and with it, the end of his shop was in sight.

He never thought he'd be so thrilled to see it.

"Okay." He straightened and stretched. "*Now* I can enjoy the festival."

Next to him, Ambrose made no such theatrics. Merely neatened his cuffs and stared out into the square. "I am a little sad to see it go."

"Yeah?"

"I won't have any distractions in my workroom anymore." Ambrose smiled at him. For a moment, his expression fractured— then it smoothed out, and he descended the stairs, his casual tone forced. "Do you think Sherry had to fight anyone from High Vine for a good parade spot?"

Guilt clogged Eli's excitement, but he followed and tried to imitate Ambrose's lightness. "If she did, she would've had Lily as back-up. High Vine never stood a chance."

STEP 36:

CELEBRATE

Ambrose

THE ROSEMOND STREET crew and the Valenz family had nabbed an excellent parade spot. They were settled firmly on the fourth-level ramparts, taking command of an open-air café that kept their stakeout well-supplied with coffee and pastries.

Sherry tugged on Ambrose's sleeve as soon as he arrived. "How did it go?"

"All right, I think." He settled down between her and Eli. Eli rolled his eyes.

"It was excellent," he corrected, for both Sherry's sake and the sake of his family across the table. "The potion worked perfectly and Beatrice loved it."

Banneker gave a snort and stuffed a cinnamon roll into his mouth.

"Knew it would," he said, his voice muffled by the roll. "Saw it in my card reading last week."

Next to Banneker, Grim sighed. "What he meant to say is that he had every confidence in your abilities."

"Well, yeah." Banneker shot them a look. "And so did the cards."

Their open-air vantage point gave them a lovely view of both the street and the sky, allowing them to drink, eat, and lounge through the entirety of the parade. As Beatrice had requested, llamas were at the forefront of the procession, followed by jugglers, fire-breathers, and, oddly enough, the entire Stone Dragons Fireball team. They looked as happy to be there as everyone else, soaking in the applause as they wound through the chasm. Soon, they would join the llamas in the government square to watch the fireworks and enjoy the rest of the festival.

When the parade finished, Ambrose and the group laid blankets out around the tables—a bold move the café had only allowed after several purchases of quiche and a few extra talons on the side.

"So, Dawn found this old moss, right?" Eli explained the fireworks to his family. "And it's got this crazy spark, and it's supposed to allow her to control the fireworks' movement—"

Lily yawned, lay back, and rolled her head toward Ambrose. "Are the fireworks cool?"

"Cool?" Ambrose smiled and lay back himself. The vivid sky, blazing orange sinking into dramatic indigo, filled his vision. "Trust me, they're far better than cool."

Once the sky faded and night fell, the fireworks surpassed both Eli's hype and Ambrose's assurances. With Dawn's new development, the fireworks didn't simply burst in the sky. They flew through the Scar, whizzing above the ramparts in whirligigs of sparks. Flocks of dragons danced together in perfect time, their colors dazzling in a rainbow of orange and pink and purple. They even breathed fire—as they opened their jaws, bursts of yellow sparks spiraled into their own miniature firework shows.

Dawn had held nothing back in her masterpiece. Just when Ambrose thought the show had ended, that it couldn't get any bigger, more fireworks burst into life. Spirals, stars, streamers—then, finally, dragons exploding into flowers at the end of their magnificent routine. As the last of the sparkles drifted down in trails of pink smoke, Ambrose took immense joy in imagining Dawn watching those same sparkles, a beaming grin on her face from a job perfectly done.

Next to him, Eli let out a low whistle.

"She's incredible," he murmured, then nudged Ambrose's arm. "All of you are."

Ambrose's proud smile faded. There was a sharp line in the compliment—Eli no longer considered himself a part of the merchants on Rosemond Street.

"Thank you," he mumbled, tamping down the pit in his stomach. He was going to do as Eli said. Enjoy the fireworks, enjoy the festival. Enjoy the warmth of Eli's arm next to him, and not worry about the future.

When they met the victorious wandmaker in the square, it became easier to forget about Eli's comment. Surrounded by a throng of family, admirers, and journalists, Dawn shone as brightly as the pink crystals around the fountain, as if she were a centerpiece amidst the food carts and fire-breathers.

"Congratulations." Ambrose gave her a tight hug once he had fought his way past Sherry and Grim. "What a triumph, truly."

"Thank you!" Dawn beamed when the rest of the group echoed him. "I just hope Beatrice saw some of it." She nodded across the square. On the other side of the chaos, Mayor Rune held his daughter as he chatted with another politician. The birthday girl was asleep, drooling on his shoulder.

"What are you going to do next?" a journalist asked Dawn, scribbling furiously in their notebook.

"Sleep," she said, and her audience laughed. "But seriously, no commissions for a few months. Then I'll be back in action."

Before long, the group split in different directions—Grim to the carts of lavender-flavored pastries, Banneker to the peddler selling flower crowns, and Eli's family to...ah.

The dancing.

The dancers circled around the central fountain, their footwork nearly as dazzling as the fireworks. But it looked far more complicated than it was—Ambrose knew it was little more than bouncing in a series of interconnected circles, switching off partners until the dancer landed back with their original.

The endless jumping made him feel as exhausted as the birthday girl, and he began to back away.

"I think I'll head out for the night," he started, already searching for the clearest path out of the square. To his dismay, the group rounded on him immediately.

"But we've been here for two seconds!" Banneker whined and tossed a flower crown onto his head.

Grim gestured to the square. "Come on, Beake. Festival's got at least another three hours left in it."

Ambrose groaned. He didn't have another three hours left in *him*.

Sherry patted Grim's arm. "Now, if he truly is tired, he doesn't have to stay with us old folks—"

"Don't say that, I'm not an old folk." Dawn grabbed Ambrose's hand. "Come on, let's go."

"Wait, is Ambrose dancing?" Eli immediately wrapped his hands around Ambrose's waist. "Did I live to see the day?"

Ambrose crossed his arms. "I thought we discussed the minimum amount of fun, Eli—"

"Just one dance?" His grip was soft, and his voice softer. "For me?"

Ambrose closed his eyes. There was no denying him anything, not when he asked like that.

"Why don't we all dance?" Sherry said, and that was that. As Sherry and Banneker dragged Grim toward the fountain, Dawn and Eli surrounded Ambrose like vultures. He held up his hands.

"This isn't necessary!"

But it was too late. They pushed him into the dance line, and Eli took his place across from him.

"After this"—Eli grinned as he circled him—"you can go home."

Ambrose gave him a flat look. "Promise?"

"Promise."

The dance then required him to hold Eli's hands and step close together. As he did, Eli smirked and snuck in a quick kiss on his cheek.

"Not following the steps, I see," Ambrose mumbled.

"I recall someone not teaching me the steps," Eli whispered into his ear, then spun away. Ambrose twisted his neck to watch him go, then reluctantly focused on his new partner—Dawn, her eyes sparkling mischievously.

"Have you talked to him yet?" she asked. Ambrose sighed.

"No."

"You know," she pressed as Ambrose went round her, "I hear festivals can be pretty great places for love confessions."

"Dawn."

"All the lanterns, the flowers, the dark alleyways..."

"*Dawn.*"

"I'm just saying!"

She twirled away and sent him to Sherry, who reached up and adjusted his flower crown.

"My dear," she said gently. "How is everything going?"

"With what?" He frowned. She nodded over to Eli, who was laughing at something Banneker had said. Heat flared across Ambrose's face. "Oh, not you, too!"

"If you have a problem, you should talk it through with him—"

The words came out as a knee-jerk response. "I'm fine, I don't have a problem!"

Ambrose looped back and found his hands in Eli's again.

"Purple looks good on you, Ames." Eli plucked a tiny flower out of Ambrose's hair, then let his hand trail down his temple. Ambrose's heart stumbled, and he quickly spun back to Sherry. Her eyes glinted, and he slouched.

"I have a problem."

"It'll be all right—"

"Sherry, he's about to *leave*." He twirled her despondently. "What do I do?"

"Just what I said," she replied. "Talk it through with him."

After another circle, Sherry deposited him with Grim. Ambrose let out a breath. Grim surely wasn't one for talking during dancing, particularly not about something so personal as love. "Hello, Grim."

"You should tell him, you know," Grim said gruffly. Ambrose fought the urge to pull his own hair out.

"I *hate* this—"

"You wait too long, you're going to miss your chance," they pressed. Ambrose groaned.

"I..." He reluctantly held out a hand as the orc moved around him. "What if I don't know what to say?"

"You're a smart man," Grim said. "You'll think of something."

Ambrose glared as he linked with the other dancers. "Helpful, thanks."

Banneker was last, dancing as if attuned to a slightly different beat.

"Dude, your aura is all over the place," he said immediately, now wearing three flower crowns where there once was one. "What's up?"

Ambrose bit his lip. "Banneker, you've never once second-guessed a word you've said."

"Nah."

"So, if you had to say something difficult, how would you do it?"

Banneker paused as he twirled, then shrugged. "I analyze my dreams first. Then I know what to say."

Ambrose dragged a hand over his face. "Why did I ask?"

Banneker released him, and he landed back in Eli's arms at the end of the song, far more exhausted than when he had started. Eli, on the other hand, was as bright-eyed as ever.

"You having fun?" he asked. Ambrose nodded miserably. Eli laughed and looped an arm around his shoulders. "Come on, I'll walk you home."

Eli waved to his family, then to the rest of the group. As the merchants watched them walk away, a mixture of hope and expectation on their faces, Ambrose's stomach flipped.

They gradually left behind the swaths of purple and reentered the normal earth tones of the chasm, muted and comforting in the evening shadows. But the closer they got to The Griffin's Claw, the more Ambrose's insides churned, love and nerves swirling in equal measure. Once they reached the shop, Eli released him with a frown. "Hey, you all right? You were pretty quiet on the walk back."

"Just tired." The words were instinctual—and far too quick to be believable. He pressed on anyway. "I'm fine."

"Okay." Eli hesitated when Ambrose opened the door. "You...you know you can talk to me about anything, right?"

Ambrose paused with his hand on the doorknob. "I know."

He could tell Eli right now. He could say he loved him, right there on the doorstep, with no preamble or pretense. He loved him, and he was afraid he'd never see him again. It would be so easy.

In theory.

In practice, he pushed open the door, already ashamed of himself. "You should get back to your family."

"Okay," Eli said. Ambrose winced—he could hear the disappointment in Eli's voice. "Have a good night."

Ambrose nodded and slipped into the shadows of the store.

STEP 37:

DETONATE

Ambrose

THE VALENZ FAMILY all piled into a wagon the next morning, destined for the griffin takeoff site at the south end of the Scar.

"I left some food in the pantry," June said as she fixed Eli's collar. "And there's money on the counter so you and Ambrose can go out for a nice dinner."

"Ma…" Eli flushed. Ambrose smiled; seeing Eli embarrassed was a rare treat. "You didn't have to do that."

"I did." His mother kissed him on the forehead, then stepped into the wagon alongside her husband. "Lily?"

Lily stood in front of Ambrose, staring him down. Or, well, up, given her diminutive stature. But the intention was crystal clear.

Ambrose straightened, met her gaze, and waited for her to speak.

"You'll look out for him?" she finally asked.

"Of course."

"And Tom?"

"With my life."

Her eyes narrowed. "And if you mess up, I'll—"

"I'll hand you Sherry's hammer myself."

She relaxed her stance and glanced back at his shop. "Hey, before I go, can I get one of those floating potions—?"

"All right, in you go." Eli grabbed Lily and plunked her into the wagon, deftly dodging her attempts to kick him. "Hugs to everyone for me, yeah?" Lily stuck out her tongue. He returned the gesture, then clapped a hand on his father's shoulder and nodded to the wagon driver. In moments, the Valenzes were off, waves of dust clouding their departure.

"Thanks again for spending time with them," Eli said, his voice tight as the wagon creaked away. "Really meant a lot."

Ambrose set a hand on his back. It meant a lot simply seeing Eli's family around him. "I'm glad I got to meet them."

Once the wagon turned the corner, Eli pulled himself together and looked back at his shop. "Guess I have to get back to brewing my own stuff, huh?"

Ambrose gave a hum; he had to do the same. "Small batches this time, please?"

Eli snorted. "Not when I've got days of brewing to fit into, uh..." He glanced at the sun. "Eight hours."

Ambrose sighed. "Eli..."

The man grinned. "Don't worry, I'll be careful." He gave Ambrose a quick kiss and jogged into his shop. Ambrose opened his mouth, then shook his head and retreated as well.

By the time night fell, Ambrose wished he could invent a cloning potion just to kick himself in the shins.

The word *should* rattled uselessly in his brain as he paced in circles around the shop. He should have said something to Eli last night, or even that morning. Or days ago, or weeks ago...

He hung up his robes and ran a hand through his hair. He couldn't change the past, but he had time now, and Eli was likely wrapping up his work for the evening. He could simply...go over there and say it.

Did he know what to say? No, of course not. But Grim was right. He would think of something. He rolled his shoulders back and turned for the door.

Then a thunderstorm struck Rosemond Street.

The light blinded him first, barreling through the windows in a molten burst of white. Ambrose threw up an arm, but could do nothing against the thunder at its heels. Its roar rattled the ground, his bones, every vial on the shelf.

When the window glass struck him, he was both blind and deaf to it.

The broken shards slit lines across his cheeks, over his arms and shoulders, into his chest. He screamed and twisted, but his feet were no longer on the floor, his body thrown backward by the wall of light and pain.

Then the floor slammed hard into his back. He lost his breath and lay there, eyes half-open, ears ringing. Dozens of blurry shards skidded past him across the wood, the last of the lightning captured in their edges.

Ambrose stared at the broken glass in a haze. His healing potions were steps away, but he couldn't bring himself to move, much less stand. If he waited for the pain to subside, if he closed his eyes for a few moments—

The glass caught the reflection of orange flames, and smoke burned his nose.

"Fire!" someone yelled outside. Ambrose clenched his jaw and forced himself up.

It wasn't a thunderstorm. Not even an errant lightning strike. It was a blast, and through the shattered grid of the bay window, Eli's shop was a wall of flames.

Ambrose scrambled to his feet, his pain gone. His bloody hand slipped on the door handle; he kicked the door open instead and staggered out into the smoke-filled street. Down the road and along the walkways, others did the same.

"What the—?"

"Call for help!"

Ambrose shut them out and sprinted toward the one moving thing in front of him—Tom, her wheeled legs pinned under a piece of burning wood.

"Tom!" He shoved away the plank, embers spiraling as it struck the ground. "You all right?"

As soon as Tom pushed herself to her wheels, she whipped back toward Eli's shop. Ambrose grabbed her with shaking hands.

"Tom, *no*." He had to give her something to do, send her elsewhere. "Go get Dawn. Go!"

He let her go, and off she flew, weaving around onlookers in the direction of Dawn's shop. As he staggered back to his feet and looked breathlessly into the flames, Sherry rushed into the road.

"Ambrose!" she yelled. "Ambrose, don't you dare—"

He ran headlong into the shop.

It was easy to get inside—the door had been blown off its hinges, the counters and tables thrown to the edges of the store. Off to his right, the rose statue lay shattered on the ground, its pieces flashing a frantic red. And flames in every color clung all around him. To the cabinets, the floating shelves, the hanging plants. Without his robes, the heat seared him, and he rushed into the middle of the room.

"Eli?" he shouted. "Where are you?"

No response.

He stumbled toward the workroom, choking on smoke, tears streaking his face. Surely there was no point to all this. He'd be dragging out a charred—a charred—

He sank to his knees when he saw him.

Eli lay at the edge of the workroom, a shimmering net of white lines forming a protective dome around his body. Though blood pooled around his head, nothing else in the room could touch him. Smoke swirled harmlessly over the dome, and flames hissed away from it. Eli's destabilized potion, still oozing from its broken, twisted cauldron, slithered away from the dome like a snake. And all the while, the white shield pulsed steadily, pulling its power from the amulet at Eli's neck.

Ambrose pressed a hand to his heart and looked back at the door. Eli was safe for now. He could run out, get someone to—

Then the shield flickered. He leaned forward and squinted at the amulet. Several of its fine gold lines were cracked, leaking wispy vapors. As he watched, the shield flickered once, twice, then disappeared.

Eli was out of time.

"Come on, Eli, let's go..." Heart bashing against his throat, Ambrose slid his arms under Eli and picked him up. Under the new weight, he immediately blundered into the charred doorway. The heat from the blackened wood bit angrily through his shirt—he cursed and staggered back into the middle of the store.

His path back was murky now, blurred by smoke and shimmering flames. As he heaved forward, the potions to his right began to rattle in the heat. He gasped and tried to spin away.

"No, *no*—"

The bottles exploded. Burning acid and glass knives leapt out, tearing holes in his shirt and skin. He bit back a scream and stumbled toward the door.

But he wasn't fast enough. All around him, bottles shattered and potions destabilized in the heat. Portals opened and closed like maws behind the front counter. Tendrils of foam whipped around the broken tables, latching onto his ankles. His legs went numb, and he stumbled backward, past puddles and flames and spheres of snapping light. He could no longer see the door nor breathe in the hazy air. Gasping, he fell to the floor, clutching Eli's body to his chest with violently shaking arms. Smoke tore at his eyes, and he screwed them shut.

"Help!" he shouted. His voice died at his lips. "*Help!*"

"Ames!" someone yelled. Bright light seared his eyelids, and he opened them to find nothing but pink. A wall of fierce, crackling pink light dragged the smoke from his throat and evaporated the puddles around him. Through it, he could barely make out Dawn's silhouette in the doorway.

"This way!" she called. Ambrose dragged himself to his feet. She was only a few steps away, just a few steps. His body shook, his knees faltered—then he collapsed into the cool air at her feet, Eli's weight pinning down his arms.

"Gods, Ames." Dawn gestured with the staff, and the pink light disappeared. "What were you thinking—?"

As soon as the shield vanished, ice water pelted his shoulder, hissing and spitting against his burns. He screamed and doubled over against the pain.

"Get the flames over there, that's it!" Sherry called. She and Grim were pointing staffs at the burning shop, dousing the flames with water and foam. Down the street, Banneker waved down a white-striped wagon with both arms.

"This way, they're over here!" he shouted, then twisted to look at Ambrose. He went pale immediately. "They need help!"

Ambrose gritted his teeth and checked Eli's pulse. It was there—weak, but there.

"Hey." Dawn knelt next to Ambrose, her staff clattering to the ground. She tried to keep her eyes on him but couldn't. "You stay still, I'll—I'll get a healer for you."

Ambrose looked at his hand. That wasn't Eli's blood on his fingers.

"I need him to wake up first." He touched Eli's cheek with his knuckles. "Eli? Eli, please wake up." Nothing. Ambrose held his breath and took hold of the man's shoulders, leaving bloody prints on his shirt. "Please—"

Then Dawn moved away, and new figures and shadows crowded around him. Voices he didn't recognize, hands he didn't recognize, dragging him away from Eli and Eli away from him.

"No," Ambrose tried to yell, but his attempt dissolved into wracking coughs. "No, don't take him away—"

"Don't worry, son, the healers have him."

Ambrose's heart stumbled as shapes and silhouettes dragged Eli up into the wagon. What if they couldn't wake him? What if he didn't come back?

What if he didn't come back—

"*Eli!*" He fought against the hands, and they slipped and slid against the blood on his skin. In his struggle, he tried to get to his feet, only to crash back to his knees, his arms pinned behind him by the stranger's grip. "Eli, don't go—please, don't leave me, I'll do anything—I'll dance with you hundreds more times, thousands, I promise, please just come back to me!"

"The boy's in shock," someone grunted behind him.

"We can't heal him like this. Knock him out."

"*No*—"

Ambrose kicked behind him, but he was too late. Someone held a cloth up to his mouth, as acrid as the smoke in the air, and the last thing he saw was his own blood blooming across the fabric.

STEP 38:

DAMAGE CONTROL

Ambrose

AMBROSE WOKE SEVERAL TIMES—THOUGH when or where, he could hardly say at first.

The first time was nothing but pain and black spots in his vision. His shoulder screamed, and he couldn't move his face or arms. A sudden, sweeping fear gripped him. He didn't recognize the walls, nor the scents, nor even the bed underneath him.

In his panic, he must have made some kind of sound, for someone spoke off to his left.

"It's all right. Keep sleeping, dear," they said—Sherry said—and despite his fear, he obliged, sinking back into the pain.

The second time he woke, he could vaguely make out his bedroom ceiling. Sherry was a shape now, hunched by his bed, smiling down at him.

"How do you feel?" she asked. Ambrose winced. The pain had dulled into a low throb, but the bandages across his arms made him feel stiff, and the paste on his cheeks was uncomfortably warm. Sherry's smile faltered.

"I think you should have some broth and rest a little more," she murmured. "Just another day or so."

"Another day?" he tried to repeat—but his throat burned, and his dry lips cracked. "How long—what about—"

"Don't worry about him," Sherry said, lifting a bowl to his mouth. "Drink this, then rest."

He got a brief taste of chicken and onion, and the salt stung his lips. Sherry took the bowl away, then sprayed a mist over his head, floral and cool. He was asleep again in an instant.

The third time he woke, he was alone.

A bowl of cold broth sat on the nightstand. His parched throat screamed for it, but he remained hesitant in his motions, testing out his pain. His shoulder still ached but could move. He had lost most of the bandages on his arm, and someone had wiped the healing paste off his face. But as his fingers wrapped around the bowl, his half-healed cuts limited his hand motion. He glanced up at the window—similar wounds streaked across his face in his reflection.

He tried the broth first. Despite the salt still pricking his lips, his stomach felt like it had shriveled in the days he was asleep. After a few clumsy mouthfuls, he set down the bowl to inspect the various bottles and salves littering the bedside.

The healers had sent him home with the kitchen sink. Healing potions, burn salves, lung-clearing mist, enchanted bandages, anti-scarring paste... He lifted a hand to his cheek. The herbal scent of the paste was what he could smell wafting around him, on his face, on his collar. He looked down at his shirt—it was a fresh one, unmarred by blood and soot. Fresh bandages, too, if he inspected the wrappings on his arms.

He set his arms down at his sides, fighting back a wave of guilt and shame. Someone—no, multiple people—had been taking care of him for days.

As he pushed himself to his feet—slowly, knees creaking—he saw a note on the side table, half-hidden in the pile of medicine. It read, in Banneker's unmistakable chicken-scratch: *Eli's ok.* Then, below it: *Breathe.*

He slumped, released a long breath, and held the note to his chest. He was alive. Eli was alive.

Voices murmured gently from somewhere downstairs, and he set the note aside.

"Hello?" he called, then coughed. "Who's there?" He fumbled through the kitchen and hobbled down the steps.

He stopped halfway down.

Sherry, Banneker, and Grim were in his shop. Banneker swept dust with Tom on his hip while Grim aimed a repair wand at the window. Sherry was cleaning the bottles that had remained intact during the blast.

"Don't you worry," she cooed at Tom as Banneker passed by. "He'll be back soon. They'll both be back soon."

Tom caught sight of Ambrose first. Once her little broom head swiveled toward him, she was nothing but a clattering whirlwind of metal limbs trying to get out of Banneker's arms.

"What the—oh!" Banneker set down Tom. "He's awake!"

While Tom latched onto Ambrose's leg, the group gathered and spoke at once, their words spilling as if they expected Ambrose to kick them out at any moment.

"I had the Guild assess the damage," Grim said, gesturing to the road. "Insurance money should be coming soon. And a get-well card from the office, if I had to guess."

Banneker pulled Tom off Ambrose's shin and set her wheeling happily around the piles of dust on the floor. "Fixed up this little one's arm. Little dudette is resilient, just like you."

"And Dawn's been checking on Eli at the healer's," Sherry added quickly. "He should be out later today. I can stop by again if you'd—"

Ambrose pulled her into a hug first. Then Banneker, then Grim, until they were a warm huddle at the base of the steps, their embrace keeping Ambrose's heart from leaping out of his chest.

"Thank you," he whispered. "You all are too kind to me, and I love you."

See, the words had been so easy. He was such an idiot.

STEP 39:

REBLEND

Eli

ELI HATED the healer's wagon.

First, it was unnecessary. He had insisted he could walk back—and in fact, had every intention of running—but the healers had given him a look, checked his head for the tenth time, and plopped him on the back of the wagon instead.

Second, it was slow. The donkeys up front stopped for everything. Pedestrians, other wagons, carrots poking out of the back of those wagons... Eli could have sworn he aged three years just getting through one intersection.

Third—he didn't have a third. This wagon just wasn't near Ambrose. That was the main problem.

"Is he okay?" were Eli's first words as soon as he could talk to someone—and that someone had been Dawn, reviewing the last part of her *Thirty* application while he slept.

"He's fine."

He tried to sit up, but she pushed on his shoulder.

"Sherry's already taken him back," she said. "They'll look after him while he recovers."

"But—but all the blood, and the glass, and..." Dawn winced, and he quickly closed his mouth. "Sorry."

When Dawn left and Grim swapped in, guilt swept away Eli's thoughts. All that blood and glass had been his fault. How much had his one destabilized potion destroyed? How much of Ambrose's *shop* had he destroyed?

"Grim..." He turned to the orc, who was reading a book with their lips pressed into a line. "How mad will he be when he wakes up?"

Grim's gaze flicked over their glasses. "I think he'll be happy you're alive." They flipped the page. "But you're lucky I'm not suffocating you with your own pillow."

Sherry and Banneker turned out to be far better company. Sherry brought cookies, Banneker brought playing cards, and neither of them threatened him with murder.

Though they did have other things to say.

"Eli," Sherry said, passing a card to Banneker. "Are you still planning to leave the shop? It'll be...well..."

"It'll be harder to sell the shop now that it's gutted," Banneker finished for her. "Not impossible, but man, that place is a wreck." He held up a card. "Anyone have a four of trolls?"

Eli sank into the blankets, his nausea growing. Not just at the thought of the shop's twisted wreckage, or Ambrose's injuries, but at the echoes of Ambrose's last words in his head. He had briefly woken toward the end, as the healers were dragging him into the wagon. He had seen Ambrose covered in blood, heard him screaming. Saw the others trying to hold him back.

Was he really going to leave the Scar now, after everything Ambrose had said? He couldn't. The idea made him sick. But was he really going to stay in his shop, brewing and dusting forever?

He couldn't. The idea made him sick.

Now he sat in the healer's wagon once more, running his hand over the new scar on the back of his head. Sitting in bed for days had brought him no closer to resolving any of his looping thoughts.

"We'll be there soon," the gnomish driver called back. The wagon moved forward an inch. "I think."

As Eli slouched, laughter spilled into the upper walkways above him. Adventurers were wandering out of the training grounds for dinner, chatting and stretching sore muscles. In the back of the shuffle, Oren waved to one of them, shook his head at one of their jokes, then wandered back into the tunnels.

Eli wanted to slap himself. He could have fixed this weeks ago.

He leapt out of the wagon.

"Hey!" the driver shouted. "Where are you—?"

Eli was already halfway up the ramp, sprinting toward Oren.

By the time the Whirling Wand Emporium came into view, Eli was thoroughly out of breath. He had filled out the trainee papers right in front of Oren, ensuring they made it to the elf's stack of applications, then booked it to Rosemond Street. Running up and down ramps, weaving across bridges to dodge traffic.

It wasn't exactly the sort of activity the healers had recommended upon his release, but he didn't care.

He skidded to a stop in front of The Griffin's Claw. The shop was still there—damaged, but there. Though someone had repaired the windows, tiny shards of glass still glittered in the road below them, and the door was slashed and scarred. Eli swallowed. Where had Ambrose been when the cauldron exploded? Was the blood from the explosion, or from saving him? Did it matter, when it was his fault either way?

"Ambrose!" Heart aching, he cupped his hands around his mouth, projecting his voice toward the darkened windows on the second floor. "*Ames*—"

"Here!" Ambrose's voice, weak and hoarse, sounded behind him. "I'm over here."

Eli whirled around. Ambrose stood in the charred doorway of Eli's shop, leaning on a staff. Bandages hung from his arms, fading scars crisscrossed his face. His skin stood ghostly white against the yawning black of the smoke damage behind him.

But he was there, alive and breathing.

"Oh, gods." Eli reached for him. "I'm sorry. I'm so, so sorry—"

They met in the middle of the street. Ambrose half collapsed into Eli's arms, and Eli sank to his knees with him in a desperate grip. Ambrose smelled like the healers' place—herbal paste, algae from the potions, the lingering scent of smoke. But he was still Ambrose underneath it all, clutching his back, pressing his cheek against Eli's hair.

And he was talking.

"I'm sorry I didn't say it before the explosion," he babbled, his sentences halting and veering. "I should have, but—and maybe you won't agree with the sentiment, and that's all right. And don't feel pressure to respond to it, either. You don't have to say anything back if you don't want to."

As Ambrose stopped to catch his breath, Eli could only stare at him. Despite what Grim said, he had expected anger upon his return. Anger, and silence, and a long road of apologies and distance and effort to make up for his reckless, ghastly mistake.

Not this.

"You'll think I'm ridiculous, but I..." Ambrose took Eli's hands in his. "Eli, I love you and I don't want you to leave. I mean, I *do* want you to pursue what you want. But, please understand, so many have left me, and if I never see you again..." He wiped his eyes and laughed bitterly at himself. "Gods, I'm such a fool."

Eli's heart filled his chest, then his throat, swelling and lifting him until he couldn't feel the road under his knees. He took Ambrose's face with both hands, careful to avoid the cuts there.

"Please," he said, gently shifting a strand of hair off Ambrose's forehead. "How could I ever leave my boyfriend behind?"

Ambrose broke into a fiercely blushing smile, and Eli leaned in to capture it with his lips, memorizing everything about it. Its curve, how it changed the shape of his face under his fingers. The tiny crinkles at the edges of his eyes, the warmth of his blush, the little sound he made when Eli pressed further.

He broke away, then pressed his forehead against Ambrose's.

"I came back," he breathed. "I came back, and I'm not leaving you. I love you, Ames, and if that makes us the two biggest fools on Rosemond Street, I don't care."

STEP 40:

ACHIEVEMENTS

Ambrose

THE NIGHT before its two hundredth anniversary, The Griffin's Claw was quiet. The workroom had been finished months ago, of course, but at Eli's gentle encouragement, Ambrose had expanded the renovations as part of his post-explosion repairs. Soon, the shop had a new door, fresh paint, and even some framed artwork along the stairway.

But Ambrose's favorite part was still the sign in his workroom.

A. Beake, CPM. The tenth person to own The Griffin's Claw, and hopefully not the last. Perhaps an apprentice of his would take it on one day—someone who loved the shop as much as he did.

"Ames? I finished hanging up the art," Eli called, then poked his head into the workroom. "There you are. Admiring the sign again?"

Ambrose stepped back from the sign. "Just making sure it's not crooked or anything."

Eli gave him a knowing grin, then wandered in and wrapped his arms around his waist, setting his chin on his shoulder. Ambrose smiled and leaned back into him.

"Still think you should've put *Extraordinaire* at the end," Eli murmured.

"Dawn told you to say that."

"She did not." Eli pressed a kiss to his neck. "I finished putting up those frames by the stairs. Not sure what to do with the middle one, though."

"Mm?" Ambrose went out to view Eli's handiwork. The once-bare stairwell looked a little homier, now bearing a sketch of the shop, an old map of Rosemond Street, and a vintage potion recipe.

"Yeah, not sure the recipe goes." Eli frowned. "Sorry, I wanted to make it look all nice for tomorrow."

Ambrose lifted Eli's hand and kissed it. "It looks wonderful. I think it'll—"

The sound of running footsteps cut him off. They moved to the door to find Dawn rushing toward them, a piece of paper fluttering in her hand.

"It came!" she shouted, her grin doing more to light up the street than all the crystals combined. "It came, it came—"

"The article?" Ambrose ran into the street. "They wrote it already? But they only interviewed you a month ago!"

"I know!" Dawn panted and shoved the paper toward him. "They sent me a mock-up and everything. Look, there I am!"

Indeed, there she was—a lovely pencil sketch of her alongside a lengthy article in thin, neat type. The sketch caught everything that made Dawn, well, Dawn: the gleam in her eye, the spark in her smile. The glint in her many, many earrings. It all had the typical faded quality of a magically copied piece of paper, but Ambrose liked it that way. It made her look like some sort of historical figure.

"It's beautiful," he said, and Eli echoed the sentiment behind him. "You must be so happy with it." He started to hand the paper back, but Dawn pushed on his wrist.

"Please, they sent me a few copies." She nodded eagerly to the writing. "Read the bottom."

Eli peered over Ambrose's shoulder as he scanned the bottom of the article.

*Ms. Kerighin's rediscovery of the star shine moss was done in
conjunction with Mr. Ambrose Beake, CPM, and Mr. Eli Valenz.
Mr. Beake runs the Guild-certified and journal-acclaimed potion
shop The Griffin's Claw, which celebrates its 200th year this winter.
She highly recommends that after you visit the Whirling Wand
Emporium, you stop by The Griffin's Claw for all your potion needs.
You will not find a better potion master—nor a better friend.*

Eli was the first to respond.

"Hey, it's me!" He hugged Dawn. "You're so sweet, you didn't have
to do that."

"Dawn, I..." Ambrose blinked. The words on the paper had
blurred all of a sudden. "I thought we had agreed there was no need
to mention me—"

Dawn snorted. "Right, like *that* was going to happen."

As Eli continued to gush over the sketch and the article's glowing
words, Ambrose held the paper to his chest, smiled, and rushed into
the shop. Took down the old potion recipe, pried open the back of
the frame. Slotted in the article and hung it back up.

"There," he said as Eli and Dawn came up behind him. "I think
that looks better, don't you?"

"Ames..." Dawn looked up at him, eyes shining. "Come on, you
sure you want my mug on your wall?"

"Yes." He nodded firmly and set an arm around her shoulders.
"How else will people know that you're the best?"

STEP 41:
CLEAR THE WORKSPACE

Ambrose

"Bets close in five minutes!"

"No, no!" Banneker waved his arms. "Gimme a minute, Grim, I need more time!"

After much cleaning and an absurd number of repair wands, Eli's Elixirs had been fixed and sold. And on this clear, crisp winter morning, someone new was moving in.

To Rosemond Street's dismay, Eli wouldn't say who.

"I've been trying to poke him about it all week," Sherry grumbled, leaning against the window display of The Griffin's Claw. "He won't say a thing."

"That would be cheating, Sherry," Eli chided from the front counter, adjusting his jerkin.

Sherry's eyes narrowed. "But you told Ambrose!"

"Of course, he did." Ambrose reached over the counter to retie Eli's bracer. "I helped him with the paperwork."

"What's the training for today?" Dawn asked, lightly kicking the sword at Eli's belt while she sat on the counter. As Ambrose had expected, Eli had passed the adventurers' initial tests with such efficiency that nearly every group in the Scar wanted him as their trainee.

Ambrose may or may not have bragged about him to all his customers for a full week after.

Eli brightened at Dawn's question. "Oren said we'll be starting on dragon stuff today. Types, and abilities, and regions—"

"Wait, dragon stuff?" Ambrose repeated, his fingers going cold. "But—but I didn't make you a resistance potion. You said that would be next week—"

Eli waved a hand. "It's all right. No fire today, I promise."

"Hey!" Banneker called from the other side of the store. "Talk later, hint now! You promised me a hint!"

Eli rested an elbow against the counter and toyed with the vials on display. "Hint, a hint. Hm...what should I tell you..."

"Three minutes," Grim called, taking clear delight in Banneker's groan.

"*Eli!*"

"Fine, fine." Eli pointed to the bag next to Ambrose. "Hey, you got our breakfast in there?"

"Indeed, I do." Ambrose gave a formal nod and passed the bag over to him. Together, as discussed, they pulled out two sweet rolls, their icing still warm.

"I heard," Eli said, "that they did some construction to the workroom. I don't know, an...oven, maybe?"

They bit down on the pastries together. A prickling ran along Ambrose's scalp, and he watched as Eli's hair turned pink. Banneker's eyes bugged wide.

"A bakery?" he breathed. "A *bakery*—" He sprinted out the door and punched the air. "Yes! I knew it! I knew it before all of you!"

As Banneker's wild laughter faded down the street, Sherry tugged Grim toward the door. "Do you think they make cakes?"

"Not as good as yours, I'm sure." Grim snapped their journal shut. "But if we need to stop by on opening day and investigate their quality..."

"Wait, hold on," Ambrose called. "Are you still coming over for dinner tonight?"

"If I can get her away from the baker." Grim sighed, then opened the door for Sherry and ushered her outside.

While the others forged ahead into the half-unpacked bakery to greet the newcomer, Ambrose handed a roll to Dawn. "Don't think I forgot you in all this."

"Knew you wouldn't." Dawn meticulously unrolled the cinnamon spiral. "So, how do you feel, no longer having a competitor?"

"Relieved." Ambrose smiled as he dusted the potions behind the counter. "My competitor was just so obnoxious."

Dawn licked a stripe of icing off her thumb and grinned at Eli. "*So* obnoxious."

"Obnoxiously handsome, obnoxiously smart..." Ambrose continued. Eli hummed and finished his pastry, his hair fading back to black.

"Sounds like you got a crush, Ames."

"Me?" Ambrose lowered the feather duster in mock offense. "Never, how dare you think so."

"All right." Dawn shook her head and slid off the counter. "I'm leaving before you start making out."

"Come on, we never—"

"You did, literally last week." Dawn waved at Eli with her deconstructed roll. "Fireball game tomorrow?"

"Stone Dragons are going down, Kerighin."

"You wish." She stuck out her tongue at them and disappeared into the morning shuffle outside. Eli did one more visual check of his equipment, then set his shoulders back. Ambrose couldn't help but smile at him. It was true, he did look handsome in his adventurer's gear—but more importantly, he looked comfortable in it. Like he had been born with a sword at his hip.

"You promise no fire today?" Ambrose asked as Eli sauntered around the front counter to join him. "I'll make you a resistance potion tonight. I have time."

Eli cupped his face and kissed him, the taste of icing still on his lips. "No need, love. I'll be fine."

"I know you will." Ambrose wrapped his fingers around Eli's wrists, his face tingling pleasantly at the touch. "Vanquish all the dragons for me?"

"I'll vanquish all of them in your name." Eli gave him a serious frown. "Every single one, in the name of my boyfriend, Ambrose Beake, Certified Potion Master Extraordinaire, First of his Name—"

"Oh, gods."

"I'm gonna yell it out before every fight, my team will love it—"

"Please go." He pretended to push Eli away, then pulled him back. "I love you."

"Love you, too." Eli kissed him one more time, then swung up over the counter and jogged out. "See you tonight!"

With a smile and a wink, Eli was off, leaving Ambrose with simply himself, his feather duster, and his shop.

WANT MORE?

Did you enjoy *A Rival Most Vial*?

Spread the word and leave a review!

Want bonus scenes?

Sign up for my newsletter to three bonus scenes:

https://rkashwick.com/newsletter/

Also written by R.K. Ashwick:

The Stray Spirit

Up Next in the Side Quest Row Series:

A Captured Cauldron

A Draught for a Dragon

ACKNOWLEDGMENTS

The Dudes of Brew have been living in my mind rent-free for years now, and in my quest to make them pay rent, I've amassed a sizable adventuring party. I may not have any gold or jewels to bestow them, but I can certainly give the party my thanks.

First, to my beta readers, sensitivity readers, and art reviewers, who helped shape this book into what it is today: Joe, Emma, Zach, Charlotte, Aelina, Hali, Jessica, Rachel, Kat, HolyAtlas, Kat Key, Natalie, Alec, Anmol, J.L. Heeren, Morrigan, and Etta. Thank you so much for your time, insight, and expertise.

Second, to my copy editor Kim Halstead and my proofreader Stephanie Slagle. You once again survived my onslaught of unnecessary commas and misplaced hyphens. You are absolute gems and I thank you for your patience.

Third, to my cover designer Andrew Davis. As always, your work is brilliant. Thank you for humoring my thoughts & ideas with the utmost grace.

Fourth, to my husband Joe, who specifically requested he go fourth: I love you. Thank you for coming up with the phrase "dudes of brew" in the first place.

Finally, to my writing group, online writing community, family, and friends, who have supported Ambrose, Eli, and Dawn ever since the phrase "rival potion shops" bounced into my head one night. I hope you know this book wouldn't be here without you.

ABOUT THE AUTHOR

By day, R.K. Ashwick herds cats in the animation industry. By night, she writes, bakes, and herds her literal cat around her living room. She lives with her husband (and said cat) in California.

A Rival Most Vial is her second novel after *The Stray Spirit*.

For more information, visit https://rkashwick.com/.

Made in United States
Troutdale, OR
11/27/2023

14994812R00206